ErJ,

We hope this book will come in handy
on one of those nights when you
or Sebastian can't decide on a
bedtime story to read.

Happy Reading !!!

Ricky ~ grace

# Disney

# 365

# Bedtime Stories

# Disney PRESS
New York • Los Angeles

# New Year's Day

It was the first day of the new year, and Pongo and Perdita were out for a walk with their pets, Roger and Anita.

Perdita sighed happily. "Oh, Pongo. What a wonderful year we've just had. We found each other, and now we have fifteen puppies to be thankful for!"

"Yes, darling, and think of all we have to look forward to this year," Pongo said.

"Can you believe the puppies stayed up until midnight last night to ring in the new year?" Perdita asked. "And still awake when we left! I do hope they don't tire out poor Nanny."

"Yes, that was quite a party we had last night," Pongo agreed. "Lucky would have spent the whole night watching television if we had allowed him to. I have never met a dog who liked to watch so much television!"

"Perhaps we should be getting home now," said Perdita.

"I suppose we should," said Pongo. "But I'm sure Nanny has been taking good care of them."

Pongo and Perdita gently pulled on their leads to let Roger and Anita know it was time to go home.

"Nanny! Puppies! We're home!" called Roger as he and Anita took off their boots and Pongo and Perdy brushed off their paws on the mat in the hall. But no one answered.

"Pongo!" exclaimed Perdita, her panic rising. "Where are the puppies?"

Pongo raced up the stairs and began searching the rooms one by one. Perdita went to check the kitchen.

Pongo hurried into the sitting room to rejoin Perdita, who was on the brink of tears. "Oh, Pongo!" she cried. "Where can—"

"Hush, darling," said Pongo, his ears pricked intently. The two dogs fell silent.

Then they both heard it: a tiny snore coming from the direction of the couch. There, nestled among the cushions, were the puppies, sound asleep!

"I found Nanny!" Roger called. "She fell asleep in her chair!"

Perdita was busy counting the sleeping puppies. ". . . twelve, thirteen, fourteen . . . Oh, Pongo! One of the puppies isn't here!"

But Pongo had trotted into the next room. "Here he is, darling!" he called. "It's Lucky, of course. He's watching the New Year's Day celebration on television."

# The Arrival of a Space Ranger

Andy was a young boy with a big imagination. He loved playing with all his toys, but his all-time favorite was Woody, a pull-string cowboy doll.

Andy took Woody everywhere. "Come on, Woody!" he called, racing around his room with the cowboy. Just then, Andy's mother called upstairs. Andy's friends were about to arrive.

"It's party time!" Andy shouted happily. He dropped Woody on his bed and headed downstairs.

The room was quiet for a moment. Then Woody sat up. "Okay, everybody, coast is clear!" he shouted.

Andy's toys had a secret. They came to life when there were no humans around to see them.

Woody gathered the toys for a special meeting. First he reminded them that Andy's family would be moving to a new house in one week. Then he blurted out the big news: "Andy's birthday party has been moved to today."

The toys started squeaking and shouting! What if Andy got a new toy and replaced them?

Hamm went to the window and peered outside. "They're here!" he shouted. Andy's guests were arriving, and they had lots of presents!

Woody sent the Green Army Men downstairs to spy on Andy's party. They set up a baby monitor inside a potted plant and watched as Andy unwrapped his gifts. As each present was revealed, the soldiers sent the news back to Andy's room.

Woody and the other toys listened to the excited gasps as Andy unwrapped his last present. Before the Green Army Men could report back, the baby monitor cut out. The toys were frantic! What had Andy been given?

Just then, Andy and his friends burst into the bedroom. They ran around happily, then rushed out again—leaving the mystery toy on the bed. In the excitement, Woody was knocked to the floor. The toys watched anxiously as he climbed back onto the bed.

The new toy turned and blinked. He was white and green and stood with his hands on his hips.

"I'm Buzz Lightyear, Space Ranger," he declared. The toy thought he was a real space hero!

Woody sighed. He knew this newcomer was going to be trouble.

# Basil Saves the Day

It was young Olivia Flaversham's birthday, and she was celebrating with her father.

Suddenly, there was a knock on the door. Mr. Flaversham told Olivia to stay in the cabinet while he investigated.

Olivia hid, but then she heard a commotion. She peeked her head out to see what was happening and saw a big, scary bat grab her father.

Olivia needed help. And so she set off to find Basil, the great mouse detective.

Basil knew who the bat was. His name was Fidget, and he worked for Basil's archenemy, Professor Ratigan!

Later that evening, as Basil paced back and forth, Olivia screamed! Fidget had appeared in the window. Basil, Olivia, and Basil's friend Dawson raced outside and followed the bat to a toy shop. Inside, Basil noticed that mechanical parts were missing from many of the toys. Suddenly, Fidget jumped out of a toy cradle. The bat stuffed Olivia into a bag and flew away!

Now Basil and Dawson had to save Olivia *and* her father!

Dawson showed Basil a piece of paper that Fidget had left behind. It had come from the riverfront. The two tracked down Fidget and followed the bat to Ratigan's secret lair.

But Basil had walked right into a trap! Ratigan tied Basil and Dawson to a mousetrap and then left.

Basil thought hard. He calculated the timing of the trap and came up with a brilliant idea that would save them.

"Ready . . . steady . . . now!" Basil yelled to Dawson.

Basil and Dawson found Olivia and raced to Buckingham Palace. There they discovered what Ratigan was up to: he had forced Olivia's father to build a robot replica of the queen. Then Ratigan had replaced Queen Moustoria with the robot.

A huge crowd was listening to the robot queen. It was announcing that Professor Ratigan was her new royal consort!

Offstage, Basil and Dawson finally took control of the robot queen.

Ratigan's plan was foiled!

Basil rushed onstage and yelled, "Arrest that fiend!"

Ratigan was defeated. But even better, Olivia and her father were reunited at last.

# Monkey See, Monkey Do

"Come on, Abu!" Aladdin called across the busy Agrabah marketplace.

From his perch atop the basket seller's cart, Abu barely heard the call. He was captivated by the monkey he had just spotted peeking out at him from behind the fruit seller's cart. Abu jumped off the basket cart and darted over to say hello.

But the other monkey scurried away and hid behind a wheel. From his new hiding place, he peeked out at Abu.

Abu looked around, trying to think of a way to draw the monkey out.

The fruit seller was distracted, so Abu hopped up onto the cart and picked up an apple. He balanced it on top of his head. Then he scurried over to the edge of the cart and peered down, hoping to attract the monkey's attention.

Abu heard monkey chatter behind him. He turned around to find the monkey standing at the other end of the fruit cart, balancing an apple on *his* head, just like Abu.

Abu picked up a pear and an orange. He began juggling them in the air, hoping to amuse the other monkey.

Not to be outdone, the monkey also picked up a pear and an orange and began to juggle them, just like Abu.

Abu grabbed hold of the cart awning, then flipped over and swung from the awning by his tail.

The other monkey did the same.

Abu thought this game was fun. But now he wanted to find a stunt that the other monkey couldn't copy. Abu looked around and saw Aladdin coming his way.

Abu had an idea. He jumped off the fruit cart, darted over to Aladdin, and scrambled up the length of his friend's body until he was lounging comfortably on top of Aladdin's head.

The other monkey stared at Abu in amazement. The closest human was the fruit seller.

Throwing caution to the wind, the other monkey scurried over to him. But he'd only climbed as high as the fruit seller's shoulder before the man chased him away.

Hiding behind the basket cart, the other monkey crossed his arms, pouted, and watched that sneaky Abu laugh and wave good-bye as he was carried away on top of Aladdin's head.

# Donald Takes Flight

"Daisy, I have a surprise for you," said Donald Duck one clear spring day. "I've been taking flying lessons."

"That *is* a surprise," said Daisy Duck.

Donald took Daisy to a nearby airport. On the runway sat an old-fashioned plane with open-air seats. Together they climbed into the small plane. Then Donald started the engine.

"Can you do any tricks?" shouted Daisy.

"Sure!" called Donald. He steered the plane into a loop-the-loop.

"You're a very good pilot, Donald!" Daisy cried, clapping her hands.

Donald was so proud of himself, he decided to fly out to sea. Before long, however, the plane's engine began to cough and choke.

"Uh-oh," Donald said as the plane began to drift toward the water.

"Is anything wrong?" asked Daisy.

Donald knew they were running out of gas, but he didn't want Daisy to find out. "Everything is fine, Daisy," Donald said nervously.

He looked down and saw something floating below them. It looked like an airport runway! But what would a runway be doing in the middle of the ocean?

As the plane drifted closer to the water, Donald realized he had no choice. He'd have to land his plane on the floating runway.

Suddenly Donald realized it wasn't a runway at all. It was the top deck of a huge ocean liner!

"Duck!" yelled one of the passengers.

Donald zoomed over their heads and carefully landed the plane on the long, wide deck.

"Hey, it really *is* a duck!" cried one of the passengers.

Just then an announcement came over the ship's speakers. "Good evening, ladies and gentlemen. Dinner is served!"

Donald helped Daisy out of the plane. He was sure she would be upset. But she wasn't.

"Dinner on a cruise ship!" she cried. "Donald, you're just full of surprises, aren't you?"

"Yes, indeed," said Donald with a huge sigh of relief.

"Oh, Donald, you're the best," said Daisy.

No, I'm not, thought Donald. What I really am is one lucky duck.

# Stranded

A new toy called Buzz Lightyear had just arrived in Andy's room. Buzz was a space ranger. He could fly . . . or so he thought. Buzz jumped off Andy's bed, bounced off a ball, and flew into the air. "To infinity and beyond!" he cried.

The other toys were impressed, but Woody rolled his eyes. "That wasn't flying. That was falling with style," he complained.

But Woody had bigger problems than the toys liking Buzz. With the space ranger in Andy's room, nothing was the same. The cowboy posters on the wall were replaced with space posters and Andy started running through the house in a space costume. But Woody got his biggest shock at bedtime. When Andy climbed under the covers, he took Buzz with him. Woody was left in the toy chest, alone and forgotten.

One evening, Andy's mom suggested a trip to Pizza Planet. Andy was only allowed to take one toy along. Woody wanted to make sure he was chosen. He planned to knock Buzz behind the desk, where Andy couldn't find him. But instead, Buzz fell out the window!

"It was an accident!" Woody told the other toys. But they didn't believe him. Before the toys could gang up on Woody too much, Andy ran into the room. He searched high and low for Buzz, but couldn't find the space ranger anywhere. Finally, he grabbed Woody.

Andy ran downstairs and hopped into the car with his mom and his sister, Molly. As the car started up, a small figure jumped onto the bumper. It was Buzz!

On the way to Pizza Planet, Andy's mom stopped at a gas station. Buzz jumped into the backseat with Woody.

"Buzz! You're alive!" Woody exclaimed.

But Buzz wasn't so pleased to see Woody. "Even though you tried to terminate me, revenge is not an idea we promote on my planet," Buzz said. Then his eyes narrowed. "But we're not on my planet, are we?"

Buzz leaped onto Woody, and the two began to fight. As they wrestled, the toys tumbled out of the car.

Suddenly, Andy's mom drove off—without them!

Woody and Buzz were stranded at the gas station. How were they ever going to get home?

# A Rookie Race Car

Rookie race car Lightning McQueen was waiting for the Piston Cup championship—the biggest race of the year—to begin.

"Speed. I am speed," Lightning told himself as he roared onto the track.

Lightning knew he was fast, but could he beat The King, the legendary race car who had won the most Piston Cups in history, or ruthless Chick Hicks, who always finished a close second?

The race was on! Lightning and Chick sped around the track side by side. Suddenly, Chick slammed into Lightning, sending him skidding off the road. Then Chick swerved across the track and caused a pileup! In seconds, wrecked cars littered the track. Lightning dodged and leaped over wrecks. To Chick's fury, the rookie race car took the lead!

But then Lightning made a huge mistake. He was so focused on winning that he refused to let his pit crew put on fresh tires.

On the last lap—*BANG!*—Lightning's old tires blew out! As he limped toward the finish line, The King and Chick Hicks caught up. It was a three-way tie!

The judges decided that there would be a tiebreaker race held in California in one week.

Lightning wanted to leave for California immediately. But his driver, Mack, reminded Lightning that he had to make an appearance for his sponsor, Rust-eze. Lightning reluctantly greeted his old, rusty fans. As soon as he was finished, he raced into Mack's trailer. Mack was tired and needed to get some sleep, but Lightning insisted.

"We're driving all night," he told his driver.

As Mack struggled to stay awake, four flashy cars pulled alongside him and shoved him back and forth across the road. Startled, Mack swerved. Inside the trailer, a trophy fell and landed on the ramp button. The back of the trailer lowered and a sleeping Lightning rolled out!

Lightning woke up on a busy highway. There were giant trucks coming right at him! Lightning was lost in the middle of nowhere, and all because he'd forced Mack to drive, even though he was too tired.

What was the rookie going to do now?

# The Firebird

Once there lived a magical bird—the Firebird! The Firebird sprinkled music from her feathers, filling the land with song and dance. But the mean ogre, Katschai, didn't like music. He trapped the Firebird to lock her in his secret palace. As he carried her away, a single magical feather blew off the Firebird. A gust of wind picked it up and carried it far away. . . .

Rocket saw the Firebird's feather and caught it in his Mini Grab Nabber. He knew that his friend was in trouble and needed help.

"To save the Firebird, we'll need to get past Katschai," June said. "And he'll use plenty of magic spells to try to stop us."

With the help of the Look-and-Listen Scope, the team made their way to the Instrument Forest. When they arrived, not a single instrument was playing its music! Rocket waved the Firebird's magical feather over the forest, and the instruments began to play. When Katschai heard the music, he became angry. He created spooky animals to scare away the Little Einsteins.

"I've got a plan," Quincy said. "Leo, play the flute to make the bats disappear. I'll play the violin to get rid of the mosquitoes. June, play the xylophone to make the spiders leave. Annie, make the bear go away with a trumpet."

It worked! The spooky animals disappeared.

Katschai wasn't done. He created a snowstorm to stop Rocket from going any farther.

"Rocket is stuck under that huge pile of snow. He can't fly!" cried Quincy.

"Don't worry, Rocket," Annie said. "I know a special song that can make the sun come out and melt the snow."

Finally, the team reached the secret palace. Rocket found the special rainbow key and unlocked the birdcage.

The Firebird was free! She soared through the sky, sprinkling her musical power everywhere.

"The Firebird's even sprinkling her musical power on Katschai," Leo giggled.

Quincy laughed. "It's time for Katschai to finally face the music. He can't escape it now!"

# A New Friend

If you lived in the twenty-ninth century, you would live off in space with all the other people from Earth.

Long ago, Earth had been evacuated because it was too polluted. No one could live there until someone cleaned up the planet. And there was someone left behind to do that work.

WALL·E was a Waste Allocation Load Lifter, Earth class. He didn't mind his lonely job of compacting trash. He looked at it as a sort of treasure hunt. He never knew what he would find each day in the trash.

But WALL·E wanted more in life. He didn't ask for much—he just wanted to hold hands with someone he loved. He had seen this while watching his favorite movie over and over. It was his dream.

One day, WALL·E was out compacting and cubing trash when he found something special. It was a plant. He had never seen anything like it before. WALL·E took it home to keep with his other treasures.

Soon afterward, another robot landed on Earth. WALL·E was very excited to have some company! He fell in love with the sleek new robot at first sight. Her name was EVE. WALL·E watched her in awe.

Over time, WALL·E figured out that EVE was looking for something. But she wouldn't tell him what it was. WALL·E took her to his home and showed her all the treasures he had collected from the trash. He was very proud of the things he had found.

But when WALL·E showed EVE the plant, she immediately grabbed it from him and stored it in a secret compartment in her chest! Then she shut down. She slept and slept. No matter how hard WALL·E tried, he could not wake her up.

Before long, EVE's ship returned to take her away. WALL·E loved EVE. He didn't want her to leave.

As the ship prepared to fly away with EVE inside, WALL·E decided he couldn't let her go. He latched on to the outside of the ship. WALL·E had finally found someone he wanted to hold hands with, and he was not going to let her leave without him. And so WALL·E followed EVE into space. . . .

# Mowgli Finds a Friend

Mowgli had grown up in the jungle. He had been raised by a wolf pack. One day, bad news arrived in the jungle. Shere Khan the tiger had returned after a long absence. The tiger was mean and hated everything. More than anything, though, Shere Khan hated Man. This meant that it was no longer safe for Mowgli to live in the jungle. The wolves held a meeting and decided that he should go to a Man-village at once.

Bagheera the panther had kept watch over Mowgli through the years and volunteered to take him. But Mowgli didn't want to leave the jungle. It was his home.

"I don't want to go to the Man-village!" he shouted. Then he added, "I can take care of myself."

Although Bagheera cared for the boy, he eventually became tired of the Man-cub's fighting. He walked off into the jungle, leaving Mowgli alone. He thought that once Mowgli was by himself, he might realize that he *couldn't* take care of himself.

Before long, a bear named Baloo walked out of the jungle and spotted Mowgli. The bear tried to be friendly, but Mowgli told Baloo to go away and leave him alone. Baloo didn't listen. He decided the little Man-cub needed to have some fun.

"Hey, kid, Baloo's gonna learn you to fight like a bear," he said, jumping around. The bear's silly behavior made Mowgli laugh, and soon he was dancing and boxing just like Baloo. When they finished, Mowgli jumped up on his new friend's stomach and tickled him. "You're all right, kid," Baloo said gently.

Just then, Bagheera walked over to them. He was worried about the boy and had returned to make sure Mowgli was okay. The panther told Baloo that he thought Mowgli should go to the Man-village so he'd be safe from Shere Khan.

Baloo didn't want his little buddy to go to a Man-village. "They'll ruin him. They'll make a man out of him," the bear said.

Bagheera sighed as the pair jumped into the river and floated lazily away. He knew it would be hard to persuade Mowgli to leave now that he had made friends with Baloo.

# Discovering Paris

Deep in the French countryside, a colony of rats was busy sifting through a pile of trash. It was one rat's job to make sure the food was safe to eat. That rat's name was Remy.

Remy had highly developed senses of taste and smell. He was the "poison checker" for the rest of the rat colony. But Remy had much bigger dreams than smelling trash. He wanted to be a great chef, like his idol, the legendary Auguste Gusteau.

Remy and his family lived in the attic of an old woman named Mabel. One day, Remy and his brother Emile snuck into her kitchen. Remy enjoyed looking for spices in her cupboards. The nervous Emile did not. Their father, Django, said that humans were dangerous, and Emile believed him.

Suddenly, Remy raced from the kitchen to the TV. He saw his idol Gusteau was on the news! Sadly, Remy learned that Gusteau had died from a broken heart when his restaurant lost its five-star status.

Remy was so shocked by the news about Gusteau that he didn't notice Mabel waking up! He and Emile scrambled to escape as Mabel chased them! In the chaos, the ceiling cracked and the entire rat colony fell to the floor!

"Evacuate!" Django shouted.

As the other rats headed out the door, Remy went back for Gusteau's cookbook. He couldn't leave it behind. But it was Remy who got left behind as all the other rats made it to the evacuation boats.

Separated from his family, Remy floated through the sewers on the cookbook. Finally he found a landing place and tried to dry out the pages of his cookbook.

Suddenly, Gusteau seemed to come to life on one of the pages! "If you are hungry, go up and look around," he said. "If you focus on what you've left behind, you will never be able to see what lies ahead."

So Remy climbed up and up until he saw . . . Paris!

"All this time I've been underneath Paris? Wow! It's beautiful!" he said.

Remy looked to his left. His jaw dropped. There was the sign for Gusteau's restaurant! Remy knew his adventures were only just beginning.

# Captured by Sid

Woody and Buzz Lightyear were stranded at a gas station. They had been on their way to Pizza Planet in Andy's mom's car when they had started to fight. The two toys had fallen out of the car and been left behind!

Woody knew it was his fault. He had wanted Andy to take *him* to Pizza Planet. He had tried to knock Buzz behind a desk, but instead, the space ranger had fallen out the window. Now Woody had to find a way back to Andy so he could bring Buzz home.

Just then, Woody spotted a Pizza Planet delivery truck. The truck could take the toys to Andy!

Woody told Buzz that the truck was a shuttle that could return him to his home planet. Buzz, who didn't know he was a toy and not a real space ranger, happily hopped aboard.

At Pizza Planet, Woody quickly spotted Andy.

"Get ready, Buzz. . . . Buzz?" Woody turned around to see Buzz striding toward the Spaceship Crane Game. The space ranger thought it was a real spaceship!

Buzz climbed into the Spaceship Crane Game. Woody followed. Suddenly, the machine started whirring. Then the claw dropped—right on Buzz.

Woody grabbed Buzz and tried to drag him back down. But it was no use. Both toys were pulled into the air and dropped into the prize slot.

"All right! Double prizes!" shouted the kid, seeing the two toys.

To Woody's horror, he saw that the boy was Sid, Andy's nasty neighbor! All the toys in Andy's room knew Sid. He lived next door and was the cruelest kid on the block. Andy's toys had often watched Sid torture toys in his backyard.

Sid looked at Buzz and Woody with evil glee. "Let's go home and play!" he said with a wicked laugh.

Sid carried Woody and Buzz home and up to his bedroom. The room was dark and eerie. Inside were lots of scary tools that Sid used for toy "operations."

Woody and Buzz heard strange rustling sounds under the bed. Sid's mutant toys were creeping out of the darkness.

Woody and Buzz clung to each other in fear. How would they ever escape . . . ?

# Out for a Spin

One day, Princess Kida was showing Milo and the rest of the explorers the wonders of Atlantis. The explorers wanted to search for treasure, but Milo preferred to go exploring with Kida.

The princess led him up the staircase of a huge pyramid. When they reached the top, they found a shark-shaped vehicle.

"It's an Aktirak," Kida told him.

"Can we take it for a spin?" Milo asked.

"If you wish," Kida said.

Kida used a crystal that hung around her neck to start the engine. Then she and Milo climbed on.

Milo pushed a button and the Aktirak blasted into the sky! He and Kida dove low over the water, skimming the waves. Suddenly, a school of flying fish burst out of the water and surrounded the flyer. One flapped in Milo's face and he nearly lost control.

"We've got to get back to land!" he exclaimed.

The Aktirak shot up into the sky.

"Beware of the cliffs ahead!" Kida warned.

Milo tried to maneuver the vehicle, but the Aktirak could not fly high enough. They were about to crash!

"The cave!" Kida cried, pointing to a hole in the side of the mountain.

Milo steered the Aktirak through the entrance. Twisting the flyer, he dodged stalactites hanging from the cavern roof. Then he saw the head of a huge stone fish in the cave wall. Its mouth was open, and daylight streamed through it. He twisted the controls, and the Aktirak flew right through the fish's gaping mouth.

Just then, the flyer's tail scraped the stone fish and the Aktirak flew out of control.

"Hang on!" Milo cried.

The flyer hit the side of the pyramid and bounced. It landed at the exact spot where Kida and Milo first found it.

The others heard the crash and rushed over. They found Milo and Kida standing next to the wrecked flyer.

"What happened?" Audrey cried.

"We went out for a spin," Milo said.

"Are you saying you actually *flew* this wreck?" Audrey demanded.

"I did!" said Milo. "But it's pretty obvious I need to sign up for Atlantean driver's ed!"

# There's No Place Like Home

"I see you guys are getting excited about the production of *The Wizard of Oz*," said Manny.

"The show is a fund-raiser to pay for a swimming pool at the community center," Rusty explained.

Just then, Mrs. Hillary arrived. "Hi, Manny! Hi, tools! I brought the props for Friday's show."

"Terrific!" said Manny. "We'll install hooks in them, attach wires, and then hang them over the stage for you before tonight's rehearsal."

Manny and the tools got to work. They had just finished hanging up the rainbow and the clouds when all the lights went off. The theater was so dark, everyone had to go outside!

Soon Mayor Rosa appeared. "I just spoke with the electric company," she said. "We had a major power outage. Sheet Rock Hills probably won't have electricity until Sunday."

Everyone was upset, particularly Mrs. Hillary. "That means we can't put on the musical tomorrow!" she said.

"I'm sure we can find a way to make this work," said Manny.

"Since it's summer, why not move the show outside?" said Stretch.

"That's a great idea!" said Mrs. Hillary. "We could do it in the park!"

Manny and the tools had work to do. They drove around town looking for items they would need for the outdoor performance. Finally they found everything.

Soon the park was ready. Before the show started, Mayor Rosa spoke.

"If it weren't for quick thinking on the part of Manny Garcia and his tools, tonight's performance would not have been possible. Please give a round of applause to the 'wizard' of Sheet Rock Hills!"

Manny blushed as the crowd cheered.

Mayor Rosa also announced that— thanks to the money from the play— work could begin on the new swimming pool very soon.

When the show was over, Turner told his friends, "I'm impressed with the townspeople. They really have a heart."

"It took a lot of courage to go on without electricity," said Rusty.

Manny smiled at the tools. "Well, as Dorothy from *The Wizard of Oz* said, 'there's no place like home!'"

# The Road to Paradise Falls

Young Carl Fredricksen dreamed of being an adventurer. His hero was the world-famous explorer Charles Muntz.

One day, Carl met a girl named Ellie. She had turned an old house in their neighborhood into a Charles Muntz clubhouse! Ellie invited Carl to be in her explorers' club. From that moment on, the two were best friends.

Ellie made Carl promise to take them to Paradise Falls one day. "Cross your heart!" she told him.

Carl crossed his heart.

When Carl and Ellie grew up, they got married and moved into their old clubhouse. Carl sold balloons from a cart, and Ellie took care of animals at the local zoo. They were happy together in their little house. They still dreamed of going to Paradise Falls, but they could never save quite enough money to go on their trip.

Many years went by, and Carl and Ellie grew older. After Ellie passed away, Carl continued to live in their house. But he was lonely. Things weren't the same without Ellie.

Then, one day, a boy named Russell knocked on Carl's door. Russell was a Junior Wilderness Explorer. He wanted to help Carl so that he could earn his Assisting the Elderly badge.

But Carl didn't want anyone's help. He told the boy to find a bird called a snipe, and Russell headed off to look for it. He did not know that there was no such thing. Carl had made it up to get rid of him.

Soon afterward, Carl learned that he was being forced to go and live in a retirement home. Carl didn't want to leave his home. All his memories of Ellie were in that house.

Remembering his old promise to Ellie, Carl came up with a plan. He tied thousands of balloons to his house and set sail for South America!

"We're on our way, Ellie," he said happily.

As the house flew over the city, someone knocked on the door. Carl was stunned. Who could be knocking?

It was Russell! He had been under Carl's porch looking for the snipe when the house lifted into the sky. Carl had no choice but to let the boy inside. It seemed he would have a companion for his adventure after all. . . .

# Just a Toy

**W**oody and Buzz had been captured by Andy's nasty neighbor, Sid! All of Andy's toys were afraid of Sid. He performed "operations" on his toys and turned them into mutants. Woody and Buzz had to escape before Sid hurt them, too!

The toys ran into the hall—and straight into Scud, Sid's vicious dog! In the confusion, they were separated. Buzz ducked through an open door. Inside, he heard a voice cry, "Calling Buzz Lightyear! This is Star Command!" Then he heard, "The world's greatest superhero, now the world's greatest toy!"

The sound was coming from a TV. As Buzz watched the commercial, he heard the voice say, "Not a flying toy."

Buzz stared at the TV. Was the ad true? He walked to the stairs and saw blue sky through the hall window. He was sure he could fly . . . couldn't he?

Gathering his courage, Buzz climbed to the top of the stair railing—and jumped. For a moment, Buzz seemed to hang in the air. Then, with a mighty *CRASH!*, he fell onto the stairs and his left arm broke off.

Buzz Lightyear finally understood the truth: he was a toy.

Upstairs, Woody was searching for Buzz. He peeked into a room and saw Sid's little sister, Hannah, playing with her dolls. Woody could hardly believe his eyes. One of the dolls was Buzz!

Hannah had found the space ranger and added him to her tea party. Woody waited until Hannah left, then ran to help Buzz. Buzz was upset because he wasn't a real space ranger. "Look at me," he moaned. "I can't even fly out of a window."

That gave Woody an idea. Sid's window was directly across from Andy's bedroom window! Woody ran into Sid's room, pushing Buzz in front of him. He climbed up onto the desk, where he could look out of the window. On the other side of the garden he saw Andy's window!

Woody opened Sid's bedroom window. "Hey, guys!" he called.

The toys turned to look, amazed.

"Son of a building block!" Mr. Potato Head said.

"He's in the psycho's bedroom!" said Hamm.

Andy's toys rushed to the window. Were Woody and Buzz saved?

# Stuck in Radiator Springs

Lightning McQueen had just raced in the Piston Cup championship. The race had ended in a three-way tie. Lightning could have won if he had listened to his pit crew, but he thought he knew better than they did. Now he had to get to California for the tiebreaker race.

Eager to get to the race in California, Lightning told his driver, Mack, to drive all night. As Mack struggled to stay awake, some flashy cars shoved him back and forth. Startled, Mack swerved. A trophy fell down, hitting the button that opened the back of the truck, and Lightning rolled right out of the trailer!

Lightning awoke on a busy road. He searched for Mack, but he couldn't find him!

Suddenly Lightning heard a siren blaring and saw flashing red lights. A sheriff cruiser was after him!

Panicked, Lightning crashed through a fence. Tangled in fencing wire, he roared through a sleepy little town, destroying its main street.

"Boy, you're in a heap of trouble," Sheriff said when he caught up to Lightning.

When Lightning woke up the next morning, he was at an impound lot. A rusty old tow truck named Mater was grinning at him.

"Where am I?" Lightning asked.

"Radiator Springs," Mater answered.

Mater hooked himself to Lightning and towed the race car to court. Doc Hudson, Radiator Springs' judge, did not like race cars. He tried to throw him out of town, but Sally, the town lawyer, asked that he be forced to fix the road he had ruined.

Soon Lightning was hooked up to Bessie, the road-paving machine. He was furious. But if he wanted to leave, he'd have to do the job.

Lightning hauled Bessie down the road as fast as he could.

"It looks awful," said Sally.

"Now it matches the rest of the town," Lightning replied grumpily. He was still only thinking of himself. He didn't care about Radiator Springs and the cars that lived there. He just wanted to get to his race.

But the cars were angry at the poor job Lightning had done on the road. If he didn't fix it, they wouldn't let him go to California!

# Peter Pan's Visit

John and Michael Darling sat on Michael's bed, listening to their sister, Wendy, tell them a story about their favorite hero, Peter Pan.

"And then," Wendy said, "with a quick slash of his sword, Peter Pan cut the evil Captain Hook's hand right off!"

Michael and John gasped. Their dog, Nana, jumped to her feet, too. But Nana wasn't alarmed by Wendy's story. She had heard a strange noise coming from just outside the window.

There it was again! Nana scurried over to the window and poked her head outside.

There, crouched on a narrow ledge, was a redheaded boy dressed in green from head to toe!

Nana froze. Then she slowly leaned toward the boy, growling a low warning growl.

"There, there, Nana," the boy whispered softly. "Please, don't bark."

At the sound of her name, Nana froze again. She tilted her head to one side, wondering if she knew this boy somehow—and how he knew her name.

"You're wondering how I know your name," the boy whispered. "You see, I've come here now and again to listen to Wendy's stories—stories about me!" He stood up straight and puffed his chest out proudly. "I'm Peter Pan, you know!"

Now, Nana was not a mean dog. But there was one thing—well, three things, really—that she was very protective of, and they were the three children inside that nursery. Nana knew it was up to her to make sure they were safe and sound. She also knew that strange boys crouching outside the nursery window—Peter Pan or not—were not to be tolerated.

And so, with another low growl, Nana suddenly lunged farther out the window and snapped her teeth at Peter Pan. The boy flew out of the way just in time, but his shadow was not quite so fast. It struggled to get loose, but it was held tight in Nana's mouth!

Peter Pan laughed merrily and flew off. It was time to begin his journey home to Never Land. But he would be back for his shadow. And *this* time, he would need to go inside. . . .

# Pongo Carries a Tune

"I don't know what we're going to do," Roger Radcliffe told his wife, Anita. "We have all these puppies to feed, and I don't have *one* song to sell!"

"Don't worry," Anita told him. "I'm sure you'll be inspired soon."

"I'm glad *you're* sure!" said Roger. "Because all I've got is a bunch of used paper." He pointed to the overflowing wastebasket.

"Don't give up," said Anita. "I know that you can do it."

After Anita left, Pongo watched his pet pace in front of his piano. "Pongo, old boy, I must have written ten songs in ten days. But they're all terrible," Roger said. "What am I going to do?"

That night, Pongo talked to Perdy about Roger's dilemma. They sat in the middle of the living room, surrounded by puppies.

"Roger has already written ten songs," explained Pongo. "He just doesn't think they're good enough to sell. But I know they are—I've heard him play them, and you don't have a songwriter for a pet without developing a good ear for hit songs."

Perdy saw what he was thinking.

"Do you know the way to the music publisher?" she asked.

Pongo nodded. "I've taken Roger for walks there dozens of times."

After Roger and Anita had gone to sleep, Pongo padded into the music room and gathered up the sheet music from the wastebasket. Then he sneaked out of the house, carrying the music to the publisher's office. Pongo pushed all the pages under the door, then trotted back home.

The next day, the phone rang. Roger answered.

"You what?" Roger said. "You did? You are? But how did you . . . ? Oh, I see. . . . Well, thank you. Thank you very much!"

Anita rushed over. "Who was that?"

"My music publisher," said Roger. "He's buying ten of my songs."

"Ten songs!" cried Anita. "I thought you didn't even have one to sell."

Roger scratched his head in confusion. "I didn't think I did."

"So what happened?" asked Anita.

Perdy looked at Pongo and barked. Her husband sure could carry a tune—all the way across town to Roger's publisher!

# Bird Trouble

It was the height of the rainy season, and the roof of the ant colony had sprung a leak.

"Bucket brigade!" shouted Princess Atta. The ants obediently lined up and began catching the water in cupped leaves, passing them along the length of the line and dumping them into the creek bed.

"There's got to be an easier way," Flik said. "Tomorrow I'm going to invent a way to fix the roof!"

The next morning, Dot found Flik sitting on a daisy. He was looking at a set of plans.

"What are you doing, Flik?" she asked.

"I'm fixing the leak," he said, showing Dot his plans. "See, these leaves will act as rain deflectors. Then the water will run into these hollowed-out flower stems that will act as gutters."

"Wow," said Dot. She was the only ant who thought Flik's inventions were worthwhile.

"The only thing I'm missing is some sort of deflection device for the ant hole itself," he said.

"Aha!" he shouted a moment later. He had spotted a buttercup. "That flower should work perfectly. Come on, Dot. Give me a hand, won't you?"

Together, the two ants dragged the buttercup to the top of the anthill.

"What on earth are you two doing?" asked Princess Atta as she walked up to them.

"Flik figured out a way to fix the leak!" Dot shouted triumphantly.

Flik shrugged modestly. "It's very simple, really," he said. "See, what I did was—"

Suddenly, the ant lookout began shouting, "Bird! Bird! Bird coming!"

Flik, Atta, and Dot dove for cover. Sure enough, a hummingbird was hovering just above the anthill.

"It's going for the flower!" shouted an ant.

The hummingbird pressed its long beak into the buttercup Dot and Flik had dragged onto the anthill.

"Avalanche!" shouted the ants. The delicately built anthill began to collapse. Ants scrambled to get out of the way as the bird flew off.

"Nice work, Flik," said Princess Atta. "This is going to take weeks to rebuild."

Flik sighed and hung his head.

"Don't worry, Flik," whispered Dot. "Someday you'll do great things."

DISNEY·PIXAR
**MONSTERS, INC.**

# The Scare Floor

James P. Sullivan was a professional Scarer. He was famous for collecting more screams than anyone else. That was important, because Monstropolis was having an energy shortage. The city's energy came from human screams, but human kids were getting harder to scare. . . .

Sulley led the Scarers of Monsters, Inc. onto the Scare Floor. Together, these were the best scream collectors in the business. One of them was named Randall. He was a mean, creepy monster who was very jealous of Sulley.

A conveyor belt dropped a door at each station. When the red signals flashed, each Scarer would walk through his door—and into the room of a sleeping child. Hopefully, the child would let out a good scream!

The red signals flashed, and the Scarers went to work. Their assistants collected screams in canisters outside the bedroom doors. When a child's scream had been collected, the Scarer would walk back through the door and then enter a different child's room. Sulley was filling up scream canisters faster than anyone!

Suddenly, an alarm rang out. A Scarer named George had returned from the human world with a child's sock on his back! A squad from the CDA (Child Detection Agency) arrived to decontaminate him.

When work was finished, Sulley's best friend (and assistant), Mike, rushed to meet his girlfriend, Celia. They had planned a special date. But the company's cranky file clerk blocked Mike's way.

"I'm sure you filed your paperwork," Roz rasped.

Mike had forgotten!

Luckily, Sulley offered to help. He went back to the Scare Floor to get the paperwork.

When he got there, Sulley noticed that someone had left a door behind. And the red light was on! Puzzled, Sulley peeked through the door, but there was no one there.

As Sulley closed the door and came back into Monstropolis, he felt something touch his tail. The Scarer turned around and saw . . . A CHILD!

"AAAAH!" he screamed. Everyone knew human children were deadly. What was Sulley going to do now?

# A Lesson in Confidence

"Oh, dear!" said Olivia, a very worried little mouse. She and Dr. Dawson were at the home of Basil, the great mouse detective. Olivia's father had been kidnapped.

"What's the matter?" Dr. Dawson asked.

"My father's been stolen by a peg-leg bat!" Olivia cried. "Have you forgotten already?"

"No, no, dear," Dawson reassured her. "Of course not. I know you must be quite upset."

"Quite upset!" Olivia cried angrily. "I couldn't possibly *be* more upset! What if Basil doesn't want to help me find my father?"

"Why wouldn't he want to help you?" Dawson asked.

"You heard him," Olivia told Dr. Dawson. "'I simply have no time for lost fathers,'" she said, quoting the detective.

"He didn't mean it," Dawson said reassuringly. "Perhaps we caught him at a bad time. But whatever the circumstances, my dear, you must try not to fret."

"I know you're trying to help me, Dr. Dawson," Olivia said, "but I don't know if I can really avoid fretting. My father is out there somewhere, and I just *have* to find him!"

"You're right!" Dawson said. "You *do* have to find him. And in order to do that, you are going to need a clear mind. Now, can you have a clear mind while you're fretting?"

"Well, it probably doesn't help," said Olivia reluctantly.

"Can you work side by side with Basil to save your beloved father while you are *worried*?" Dawson asked.

"No!" Olivia paused as the truth sank in. "No, I can't. I owe it to my father to be levelheaded. I have to be a detective, like Basil!"

"That, young lady, is the smartest thing you could have said. And if you can hold on to that attitude, your father will be found in no time." Dawson smiled at Olivia.

Just then, Basil came swooping back into the room. "Of course he will. I never miss my mark. Your father is as good as found, because I am just that good!"

Olivia smiled and gave Basil a hug. She knew *she* was just that good, too.

# Anyone Can Cook

Remy the rat dreamed of being a chef. His idol was the great chef Auguste Gusteau.

Remy had found his way to Paris, and was looking into Gusteau's restaurant through a skylight. Below him he saw an awkward young man. The man's name was Linguini and he had just been hired as a garbage boy at the restaurant.

Linguini was very clumsy. Remy watched in horror as he accidentally spilled a pot of soup and secretly began adding random ingredients to try to fix it.

"Oh, no!" Remy shouted. "He's ruining the soup!"

Suddenly the skylight fell open. Remy tumbled downward, landing in the kitchen! He quickly scrambled across the floor. Then he smelled Linguini's horrible soup—and stopped short. This was Remy's chance. He could fix the soup!

Remy jumped to the stovetop and started choosing ingredients to put into the pot. Soon the soup was smelling much better!

Suddenly, Linguini noticed Remy. He quickly hid the rat under a colander so the head chef, a man named Skinner, wouldn't see him.

"How dare you cook in my kitchen!" Skinner shouted. He fired Linguini on the spot. But worse things were happening. While Skinner was yelling, a waiter whisked a bowl of the soup off to the dining room to an important food critic!

Word soon came back from the waiter. The critic loved the soup. Skinner couldn't fire Linguini now! He needed him to cook!

Remy made a move for the window, but Skinner spotted him. He made Linguini catch the rat in a jar. But poor Linguini didn't have the heart to throw Remy out. He started talking to him instead. When Remy nodded, Linguini realized Remy understood what he was saying!

"I can't cook," Linguini told Remy. "But you can!" The boy made a deal with Remy. Linguini would let Remy out if he promised to help him cook. This could be Remy's big chance to cook in a real gourmet kitchen! The little rat decided to trust Linguini and give the partnership a try.

# A Robot Kiss

When WALL·E met EVE, he had fallen in love. He had latched on to the spaceship that came to take her away from Earth. Now the spaceship was docking inside an enormous ship called the *Axiom*. This was where all the humans from Earth lived.

The Captain's robot assistant, Go-4, wrapped EVE in energy bands and drove her away. WALL·E raced after her.

As WALL·E chased EVE and Go-4, he accidentally disabled a human passenger's electronic system. The human blinked and looked around. She saw the world around her, instead of viewing it digitally over her holo-screen. She liked it!

Meanwhile, EVE was finally ready to give the plant she had found among WALL·E's treasures to the Captain. By doing so, she would prove that Earth was clean enough that a plant could now grow there. That meant everyone could return to the planet.

But EVE's compartment was empty. The plant had disappeared!

Disappointed, the Captain sent EVE to the repair ward. WALL·E followed behind her, but when they got there, WALL·E thought the robots were hurting EVE, so he helped her escape, along with all the reject-bots from the repair ward.

But there was a problem. Once they ran, they looked like criminals. A warning broadcast their escape throughout the *Axiom*. The ship's stewards tried to catch them.

To avoid being captured, EVE took WALL·E to an escape pod. She would send him to Earth, where he would be safe, and then she could find the plant. Instead, Go-4 appeared. He had the plant! He put it in the escape pod, and WALL·E and the plant were launched into space! But the pod had been set to self-destruct. Luckily WALL·E managed to escape. EVE went to try to help him.

*Whoosh!* WALL·E zoomed up to EVE and showed her that he had saved the plant. Delighted, she leaned toward him, and an arc of electricity passed between their foreheads—a robot kiss.

Soon they were floating in space, dancing and giggling, excited about taking the Earth plant back to the Captain. It was time to go home.

# The Importance of Being a Toy

Woody and Buzz were trapped at Andy's neighbor's house. Buzz had just discovered that he was a toy, not a real space ranger. Now he had a broken arm and was feeling hopeless. But Woody had an idea. He ran to Sid's bedroom window and called out to his friends.

Andy's toys were surprised to see Woody in Sid's bedroom. The cowboy hoped his friends would help him and Buzz escape. But the toys didn't trust Woody. After all, he had tried to get rid of Buzz.

Woody had to show the toys that Buzz was okay. But Buzz refused to come to the window. Pretending that Buzz was beside him, Woody waved the space ranger's broken arm. But the trick backfired. The toys thought he'd hurt Buzz!

Andy's toys walked away from the window. Woody felt terrible. When he turned back into Sid's room, he found that things were even worse than he'd thought. Sid's mutant toys had surrounded Buzz!

Woody tried to fight them off, but they grabbed Buzz's arm.

A moment later, the mutants stepped back. Buzz sat up. His arm was now attached and working perfectly. Sid's mutant toys had fixed him!

Suddenly, the toys heard Sid racing up the stairs. Everyone scattered—except for Buzz, who wouldn't move. He was still upset about being a toy. Sid burst into the room with a rocket, which he strapped to Buzz's back. He would launch it the next day!

All night, Woody pleaded with Buzz to escape. "Next door is a kid who thinks you're great. And not because you're a space ranger. Because you're a toy. You are his toy," Woody said.

Finally, Woody got through to Buzz. The space ranger realized that being a toy was important! But before the toys could escape, the alarm clock rang. Sid jumped out of bed. "Time for liftoff," he yelled, grabbing Buzz and running outside.

Woody knew he had to do something fast. The cowboy gathered the mutant toys and laid out a rescue plan. "We'll have to break a few rules," he told the mutants. "But if it works, it'll help everyone. . . ."

# Finding Ne-who?

"The coral reef is falling down, falling down, falling down . . ."

Nemo was home, brushing up against the anemone, when the most awful singing he'd ever heard in his life made him cringe.

Nemo poked his head out of the golden tentacles to see who was making the awful racket. It was Dory! Nemo should have known.

Nemo swam as fast as he could toward the regal blue tang fish. "Dory! Where have you been?" It seemed like a whale's age since Nemo had seen the fish that helped his dad try to rescue him from the dentist's fish tank.

When Nemo got closer, Dory stopped singing. That was good. But when she looked at him, her face was blank.

"Did you say something?" she asked.

"Dory, it's me. Nemo," he replied.

"Ne-*who*?" She looked at Nemo blankly. "Sorry, kid, don't know you. I was just swimming by, minding my own business, singing a song. Hey, why was I singing? Am I famous? Maybe that's how you know me."

"Dory! We're friends, remember?"

"Friends? I just made friends with a hermit crab . . . I think." Dory swam in a circle looking for the crab, but got distracted and started chasing her tail.

"Please try to remember, Dory," Nemo said. "You helped save me. You helped me find my dad. You know my dad. Big orange guy? Three white stripes? Looks kind of like me?"

"My dad? Looks like you? Sorry, kid, you don't look anything like my dad." Dory looked at Nemo like he was crazy and began to swim away.

Nemo swam after her. "Just think about it for a second," he pleaded. She *had* to remember something. "I'm Nemo!"

Dory did not turn around, but she slowed down. Swimming in a wide circle, she came back. She looked at Nemo sideways, then started laughing so hard, bubbles came out of her nose.

"Had you going, huh?" Dory gave Nemo a big hug and smiled at him slyly. "That was just my little joke. You know I could never forget you!"

Nemo giggled as he swam circles around his friend. "Good one, Dory!" He grinned.

Dory smiled back. "Good one, *who*?"

Nemo groaned. Oh, Dory.

# Boo!

Sulley was a professional Scarer. He worked at Monsters, Incorporated, in Monstropolis. His best friend, Mike Wazowski, trained him.

One night, Sulley found a door that had been left open on the Scare Floor. A child had come through! Sulley didn't know what to do, so he went to find Mike.

Mike was at a restaurant with his girlfriend, Celia. Suddenly he spotted Sulley waving frantically outside the window. Sulley looked terrified.

Sulley told Mike all about the child. Mike was horrified—especially when Sulley showed him the kid, whom he was carrying inside a bag.

Back in their apartment, Sulley and Mike tried not to touch the child, just in case it was poisonous. Then Mike accidentally fell, and the little girl started to giggle. Strangely, her laughter made the lights burn brighter—until they burned out!

Finally, Sulley realized that the child couldn't hurt them. He put her to bed, but she was afraid to go to sleep.

Sulley realized she was terrified that a monster was in the wardrobe. So Sulley stayed with her until she fell asleep.

"This might sound crazy," Sulley told Mike, "but I don't think that kid is dangerous. What if we just put her back in her door?"

Mike didn't like the idea, but what else could they do?

The next morning, the friends disguised the little girl as a baby monster and took her to work with them. In the bathroom, they overheard Randall—a mean monster who was jealous of Sulley—tell his assistant that he planned to "take care of the kid." Sulley needed to get the child home quickly!

Mike had gone to the Scare Floor to pull up the kid's bedroom door.

"That's not Boo's door," Sulley said when he saw it.

"Boo?" Mike couldn't believe Sulley had named the child!

Suddenly they realized everyone on the Scare Floor could hear them talking! When they stopped, they saw that Boo had slipped away. Would they ever be able to find her and take her home?

# Bows and Arrows

"Thanks, Mr. Hood!" Skippy Bunny hopped around holding the bow and arrow Robin Hood had just given him. "This is the best birthday present in the world!"

"Want me to show you how to use it?" Robin asked.

"Yes!" cried Skippy.

"See, you put this here." Robin lined the arrow up with the bow. "Then pull here and let it fly."

The arrow soared through the air and landed in the center of a tree trunk across the yard.

"Wow!" Skippy cheered.

"That's nothing!" Robin said. He handed an apple to Skippy. "Here. Put this on the head of that scarecrow."

"Sure thing, Robin!" Skippy said and hurried off.

As soon as the apple was in place, Robin let another arrow fly. It zipped through the air and hit the apple, neatly slicing it in two.

"Can I try?" Skippy asked.

"All right," Robin said, placing a new apple on top of the scarecrow's head.

Skippy pulled back the bow. But when he let go, the arrow landed only a few inches in front of him.

"That's okay," Robin said. "It happens to the best of us!"

"Even you?" Skippy asked.

"Well, not me. I never miss!" Robin boasted as he pulled back his bow.

Just as he did, Maid Marian's carriage rolled by. Robin's head turned, and his hand slipped off the bow. The arrow fell to the ground a few inches in front of him. Skippy giggled.

"What's so funny?" Robin asked crossly.

"Nothing!" Skippy said, hiding a smile.

"Ahem. As you can see," Robin said, "even the most experienced archers lose their focus occasionally. But it helps if you think of a goal and keep your goal in mind while you draw the string back, aim, and let go. I like to think about setting the sheriff's pants on fire!"

Skippy decided to give it a try. He pulled the string back and then he let it go with a *twang*.

The arrow sailed through the air and split the apple in two. Robin's trick had worked!

# A Race Against Doc

Rookie race car Lightning McQueen was stuck in Radiator Springs. All he wanted to do was get to California for a tiebreaker race—the last race in the Piston Cup championship—but he couldn't leave because he'd ruined the town's road.

The judge, Doc, had ordered him to resurface the road, but selfish Lightning had done a bad job.

"The deal was you fix the road, not make it worse. Scrape it off, start again," Doc ordered.

"I'm not a bulldozer—I'm a race car," Lightning argued.

So Doc challenged him to a race. "If you win, you go and I fix the road. If I win, you do the road my way."

Lightning agreed. He was sure he could beat the old car.

When the race flag dropped, the rookie roared off. But on a sharp left turn, he lost control. Lightning skidded off the road and plunged into a cactus patch.

That night Lightning started over again. When the rest of the cars awoke, they saw Mater—the town's tow truck—driving on a perfectly smooth road.

Lightning, meanwhile, was out on the dirt track, trying again and again to make that tricky sharp left turn—and spinning out of control every time.

"If you're going hard enough left, you'll find yourself turning right," Doc told Lightning.

As usual, Lightning scoffed. What did Doc know about racing?

That night, Mater took Lightning tractor tipping. Mater sneaked up on a sleeping tractor and beeped. The startled tractor woke up and fell over!

The two cars waited a few minutes. Then Lightning revved his engine so loudly that all of the tractors keeled over at once.

Mater and Lightning couldn't stop laughing. It had been a long time since Lightning had just had fun!

As they returned to the Cozy Cone Motel, Mater showed off his amazing backward driving tricks.

Lightning was impressed. "Maybe I'll use it in my big race," he said thoughtfully.

Lightning was starting to enjoy himself in Radiator Springs, but had the race car learned to appreciate the help of others?

# Abracadabra!

Manny was not at his best. Gypsy could tell. Already that day, he had lost two magic wands and stepped on his turban. And with the matinee show at P.T. Flea's World's Greatest Circus about to begin, Gypsy knew she had to be on her toes.

"Ladies and gentlemen," Manny announced, "prepare to be stunned and amazed by the Levitating, Flaming, and Disappearing Water Torture Chamber of Death! You will watch as my lovely and talented assistant, Gypsy, climbs inside this chamber"—Manny motioned toward the empty takeout box at his side— "where I will bind her hands and feet. Then I will fill the chamber with water, seal it, levitate it five inches off the ground, and set it ablaze. And finally, you will watch in awe as the chamber disappears before your very eyes!"

Manny and Gypsy had rehearsed the act thoroughly. Everything was planned down to the last detail. But if one little thing went wrong with the trick, Gypsy could be in big trouble.

As it turned out, one little thing didn't go wrong—three *big* things went wrong!

First Manny tied Gypsy's hands and feet together too tightly. Then he filled the chamber too high with water. Finally, he locked the trapdoor. Together, he and Gypsy had rigged an escape hatch in the back side of the takeout box. Once Manny sealed her inside, Gypsy wriggled out of her bonds, opened the trapdoor, and, unseen by the audience, escaped from the chamber before Manny levitated it, set it on fire, and made it disappear.

Luckily, Gypsy hadn't left anything to chance: she had stowed a sharp shard of glass inside the box. She had learned to hold her breath for ten minutes. And she had put a release latch on the inside of the trapdoor, just in case Manny forgot to leave it unlocked.

She was safely out of the chamber in one minute flat.

At the end of the trick, Manny called Gypsy in front of the audience. "How did you do it, my dear?" he asked dramatically.

"It was magic!" she replied, with a smile and a sigh of relief.

# Eeyore's New Old House

One blustery January day in the Hundred-Acre Wood, the wind blew so strongly that it knocked Eeyore's house right over! So Eeyore went to Pooh's house.

"Well, Pooh," Eeyore said, "it seems that January just doesn't like me. Or my house. So I'm afraid I will have to stay here with you. If you don't mind, that is."

Pooh assured Eeyore that he didn't mind and offered him some honey.

"I'd prefer thistles, if you have any, which you probably don't," Eeyore said. "Oh well. Perhaps Rabbit has some."

Rabbit did have some thistles, so Eeyore settled down to stay with Rabbit. But Rabbit's house was so full of vegetables and gardening tools that there was scarcely room in the burrow for Eeyore.

"I suppose Piglet may have more room, though I doubt it," said Eeyore.

Piglet told Eeyore he was welcome to stay with him, and even made Eeyore a little bed next to the pantry, which was full of haycorns. But Eeyore was allergic to haycorns, and soon his sneezing almost knocked Piglet's own house down.

"One house knocked down today is more than—*ah-choo!*—enough," said Eeyore. "I'll just have to try Kanga and Roo."

But Kanga and Roo's house wasn't quite right, either. Eeyore was about to try Owl's house when his friends showed up.

"Eeyore, we've found you the perfect house to live in!" Piglet cried.

"I doubt that," Eeyore said as they led him through the Wood. "The perfect house would have thistles, and enough room, and no haycorns. But where am I going to find a house like that?"

Soon they arrived at a snug little house made of sticks with a pile of thistles in it. "Here it is, Eeyore," said Piglet.

"That's *my* house," said Eeyore, hardly able to believe his eyes. "But my house got knocked down."

"Piglet and I put it back together again," Pooh said.

Eeyore looked at his house and then at his friends. "It looks like January doesn't dislike me so much after all," he said. "Maybe, that is."

# An Elephant Lullaby

**M**ore than anything else in the world, Mrs. Jumbo had been longing for a baby elephant of her own. Then, one day, the stork brought her one!

The tiny elephant was the most beautiful creature she had ever seen. Mrs. Jumbo was the happiest animal in the circus. Then it happened: her baby sneezed, causing his ears to unfold. They were extremely large ears, and the other elephants laughed at him.

"Instead of calling him Jumbo Junior," one elephant said drily, "he ought to be called Dumbo!" Mrs. Jumbo ignored their taunts and curled her trunk around her beloved baby.

As the days went by, Mrs. Jumbo grew to love her baby more and more. She played hide-and-seek with him, pretending to be surprised when he hid behind her legs. She played peekaboo with him. She sang him lullabies at bedtime and danced around with him when he woke up.

One evening, Mrs. Jumbo found her precious baby looking terribly sad. She tenderly put him to bed, tucking his large ears around him to keep him warm.

"Don't mind what the others say," she whispered softly. "You are going to grow up to be a fine elephant! Shall I sing you a lullaby, darling?"

As Dumbo nodded, Mrs. Jumbo heard the other elephants talking in the next stall. "Honestly!" one of them was saying. "You'd think he was the only elephant left on earth, the way she pampers him!"

But Mrs. Jumbo ignored them and began to sing:

*"Hush, little baby, don't you cry.*
*Mama's gonna sing you a lullaby.*
*And if someone should laugh at your ears,*
*Mama's gonna be here to dry your tears.*
*Just lay your head down and try to rest.*
*You're the one that Mama loves the best."*

Then she continued to hum and rock her son until his eyelids grew heavier and heavier, and finally he fell asleep.

Mrs. Jumbo hummed for a little while longer, then stood up. The stalls had grown very quiet.

Suddenly, Mrs. Jumbo heard a soft snoring. Her lullaby had put all the elephants to sleep!

# Groundhog Day

Winnie the Pooh pounded on Piglet's front door. "Wake up! Wake up!" he called to his friend. "Today is Groundhog Day!"

Piglet dressed quickly, and moments later the two friends were hurrying to the homes of their other friends who lived in the Hundred-Acre Wood.

"Today is Groundhog Day!" shouted Pooh and Piglet together as they woke Tigger, Rabbit, Owl, Eeyore, Kanga, Roo, and Christopher Robin.

Soon the group of friends arrived at the Thoughtful Spot, and everyone sat down to wait.

"Um, exactly what is it that we are waiting for?" asked Piglet.

"Why, groundhogs, of course!" said Pooh.

"But what is it that is supposed to happen on Groundhog Day?" Piglet persisted.

Being a bear of little brain, Pooh was unsure how to answer. He looked expectantly at Christopher Robin.

"There is an old tradition," the boy began, "that says that February second is the day that the groundhog comes out of his hole after a long winter sleep. If he sees his shadow, he decides that there will be six more weeks of winter. If he doesn't see it, he decides that spring will soon be here."

A few more moments went by, and then Rabbit cleared his throat. "Pooh," he said. "Do you expect that the groundhog will take much longer to appear?"

"Oh!" Pooh replied, looking at his friends. "I haven't the faintest idea how long it will take to see a groundhog, as I don't know any groundhogs personally."

Suddenly, Gopher's head popped up from the ground in front of them.

"Aha!" shouted Pooh triumphantly.

"It's only Gopher," said Rabbit.

"I believe Gopher will do quite nicely today," said Christopher Robin. "Gopher, do you or do you not see your shadow?"

Gopher blinked in the sunshine, then looked down at the ground. "I ssssay," he said. "I ssssuppose I do sssseee my sssshadow."

"Well, that's that, then," said Christopher Robin. "Six more weeks of winter. Thank you very much, Gopher."

"You're welcome," replied Gopher. And with that, he went back into his hole.

# Hide, Dude!

"Come on, Squirt!" Nemo cried happily. "Race you to the coral shelf!"

Nemo took off, pumping his mismatched fins as hard as he could. His young sea turtle friend laughed and swam after him. Squirt was visiting Nemo at his home on the reef.

"This way, dude!" Squirt yelled, flinging himself through the water. "I'm catching some rad current over here!"

Nemo hesitated for just a second, watching as his friend tumbled along past some stinging coral. Squirt was so brave! Even after all that Nemo had been through—being captured by a scuba diver, then escaping from a tank to find his way home again—he still got scared sometimes.

With a deep breath, he threw himself into the current. He tumbled after Squirt, fins flying as the water carried him along. Finally, he came out the other end of the current, landing in the still ocean beside Squirt.

He giggled. "Hey, that was fun!" he cried. "Let's do it again! Squirt? Squirt, what's wrong?"

The sea turtle was staring into the distance, his eyes wide. "Hide, dude!"

Squirt cried. Before Nemo could respond, Squirt's head and legs popped into his shell and he landed on the seafloor with a flop.

Nemo started trembling. What had scared Squirt so much? He looked around, expecting to see a shark. But all he could see nearby were a few pieces of coral with a lone Spanish dancer floating along above them.

"Hey," he said. "What is it? There's nothing scary out here."

Suddenly Nemo realized something. "Haven't you ever seen a Spanish dancer before?" he asked.

"A—a Spanish wha-huh?" Squirt asked, still muffled.

"It's a kind of sea slug," Nemo explained. "Don't worry, Spanish dancers are nice."

Finally, Squirt's head popped out again. He smiled sheepishly at Nemo. "Sorry, dude," he said. "I never saw one of those before. It totally freaked me out."

"It's okay." Nemo smiled back. He already knew that new things could be scary—and now he knew he wasn't the only one who thought so. "Come on, let's go play," he said.

# Scaring Sid

Andy's neighbor, Sid, had taken Buzz Lightyear prisoner. The boy had strapped a rocket to Buzz's back and was planning to blast him into space!

Woody knew he had to save his friend, and fast. He gathered Sid's mutant toys and laid out a rescue plan. "We'll have to break a few rules," he told the mutants. "But if it works, it'll help everyone."

The toys sent Legs and Ducky through the air ducts. They came out above the front door and unscrewed the porch lightbulb. Hanging from the hook of Legs's crane, Ducky swung himself toward the doorbell.

While Sid's little sister, Hannah, rushed to open the door, the other toys unbolted Sid's bedroom door. Wind-up Frog, the speediest toy in the house, slipped into the hall. Sid's dog, Scud, jumped up and chased Wind-up Frog all the way to the garden. With Scud busy, Woody and the other toys piled onto Roller Bob's skateboard. They hurtled down the stairs, into the kitchen, and through the dog door.

In the backyard, Sid was preparing to launch Buzz into outer space.

With a cruel grin, Sid leaned over to light the rocket's fuse. "Ten, nine, eight, seven . . ." he began, starting his countdown.

Suddenly, Sid heard a voice. "Reach for the sky!"

It was Woody. He was lying nearby. Sid picked up Woody. How had the cowboy doll gotten outside? he wondered. And was something wrong with its pull string?

One by one, Sid's mutant toys staggered out of the sandbox, splashed out of a mud puddle, and crawled out from under the dog dish! Slowly and steadily, they surrounded the terrified boy.

But Woody wasn't done with Sid. "From now on, you must take good care of your toys. Because if you don't, we'll find out," Woody warned. And then he leaned in very close and looked Sid right in the eye. "So play nice!"

"AAAHH!" Sid threw up his arms and shrieked in terror. Screaming, he ran into the house and slammed the door.

The toys cheered. Their plan had worked! Buzz was saved.

# Child's Play

"This is an outrage!" cried Basil of Baker Street as an evil mouse named Pilfer tied him to a chair. "What is the meaning of this?"

Pilfer smiled. "You'll be sitting here in this shack for a long time, Basil. By the time anyone finds you, our trail will be so cold that even the great Basil of Baker Street won't be able to follow it."

"This is an outrage!" said Basil again.

"Bye-bye, Basil," Pilfer said. "We *won't* be seeing you." And with that, Pilfer and his gang of thieving mice gathered up their loot. As they locked the door behind them, they heard Basil say again, "What is the meaning of this?"

Pilfer and his gang carefully covered their tracks as they emerged from the woods. On the road, a car was waiting for them. They drove down to a quiet section of the waterfront. Then Pilfer raised a torch and waved it three times, signaling to a ship that was waiting in the dark harbor.

The vicious gang of thieving mice was about to row out to make their final escape when they heard someone shout, "Freeze!"

Suddenly, floodlights blinded them from every side. An entire squad of policemice had surrounded them. And Basil of Baker Street was standing beside them!

Soon enough, Pilfer and his gang were handcuffed. As Pilfer was led away, he passed by Basil. "I just don't understand!" Pilfer said angrily. "We left you tied up. It's like you were in two places at once! But that's . . ."

"Impossible?" said Basil. "No, just improbable. You see, I had a feeling that one day some thief would try a stunt like this. So I had toy maker Flaversham build a windup mouse that looked exactly like me. It could even talk, though all it could say was 'This is an outrage!' and 'What is the meaning of this?' Granted, it wasn't the most elaborate trick. But then, you're not a very clever thief, are you?"

"Why, I-I—!" stuttered the thief, astounded at the trick.

"That's really quite brilliant, Basil," the chief inspector said admiringly.

"Nonsense," said Basil. "Thanks to the toy maker, solving this case was child's play!"

# Discovering the Truth

Remy the rat was hiding in a human chef's shirt in the kitchen of Auguste Gusteau's restaurant in Paris. Remy was trying to help Linguini with his cooking.

Suddenly, the ill-tempered head chef, a man named Skinner, burst through the door. Linguini quickly hid Remy in his chef's hat and ducked out—almost colliding with a waiter! Remy tugged on Linguini's hair at the last minute and Linguini jerked backward like a puppet. Could this be their new system for cooking?

The two went home to practice. Remy guided Linguini by tugging his hair to move him. Before long, the system was working. Linguini could even cook blindfolded!

In the meantime, Skinner was reading a letter that Linguini's mother had left for him when she passed away. The letter said that Auguste Gusteau was Linguini's father! That meant the restaurant rightfully belonged to Linguini.

Skinner was horrified. He had always thought the restaurant would be his! He had to do something to make sure Linguini never found out the truth.

The following night, Remy the rat was relaxing in the alley behind the restaurant, enjoying his cooking success, when his brother Emile appeared. They hadn't seen each other since Remy's family had escaped the human house they used to live in. Emile led his long-lost brother to the rat colony's new home. But Remy couldn't stay. He explained that he had new friends, a job, even a new place to live.

Remy's father scowled and tried to convince his son that humans were dangerous. But Remy was sure Linguini was different.

When Remy returned to the restaurant, he found the letter in Skinner's office saying that Linguini was the rightful owner of Gusteau's! Remy grabbed the papers and ran, with Skinner close behind.

By the time Skinner got back, Remy had shown Linguini the truth. The restaurant was his! Linguini fired Skinner on the spot. Remy smiled. He knew he had made the right choice in sticking with Linguini.

# Snake Eyes

"I'm ssstarved," hissed Kaa the python as he slithered across the jungle treetops. "I need a sssnack. . . ."

Suddenly, Kaa noticed a small figure relaxing on a tree limb. It was Mowgli. Kaa slithered over to him.

"Are you feeling sssleeepy?" hissed Kaa. "You look sssleeepy; jussst look into my eyesss. . . ."

Mowgli tried not to look into the snake's eyes, but it wasn't easy. When he turned one way, Kaa was there. When he turned another, Kaa was there, too!

"Ssslip into sssilent ssslumber," Kaa hissed. "And sssleep . . . sssleep . . . sssleep. . . ."

Mowgli's body went completely limp. Kaa had hypnotized him!

Kaa's fangs watered as he coiled his long body around Mowgli. The python opened his giant mouth above Mowgli's head and—

Hey! Someone had jammed a stick into his jaws!

"Hello there, Kaa," said Baloo, leaning one big paw against the tree.

The python's powerful jaws snapped the stick. "You ssshould not inssert yoursssself between a sssnake and his sssnack," he hissed.

"Oh! Sorry!" said Baloo. "I was just admiring how very talented you are."

"Talented?" Kaa said.

"Sure!" said Baloo. "I'm very impressed with how you hypnotized Mowgli there. I bet you could hypnotize almost anything in the jungle."

"What do you mean *almost*?" said Kaa.

Baloo coolly polished his claws on his fur. "Well, let's see," he said. "I bet you can't hypnotize . . . a fish." Baloo pointed to the pond.

"Jussst you watch me," Kaa told Baloo as he slithered toward the pond. Hanging his head over the water, Kaa hissed, "Jussst look into my eyesss. You feel sssleeepy . . . sssleeepy . . . sssleeepy. . . ."

Suddenly, Kaa stopped hissing. And moving. He just stared into the water.

Bagheera stepped up to Baloo and whispered, "What's the matter with him?"

Baloo just laughed. "Kaa was so determined to prove me wrong, he didn't even notice the water was reflecting back his image. That crazy snake hypnotized himself!"

# Making It Home

Woody had saved Buzz from Andy's vicious neighbor, Sid. But the toys had no time to celebrate. There was a moving van in front of Andy's house. If Buzz and Woody didn't hurry, Andy would move without them!

The toys ran toward Andy's house. But Buzz couldn't fit through the fence. Sid had tried to blow up the space ranger, and he still had a rocket attached to his back.

By the time Woody helped Buzz get free, it was too late. The moving van had driven away.

Woody and Buzz raced after the van. Buzz grabbed a loose strap, then climbed onto the van's bumper. He tried to help Woody up, too, but Sid's mean dog, Scud, was right behind them. He leaped up and dragged Woody off the van.

Buzz jumped onto Scud's head to save Woody. Now Woody was safe, but Buzz had been left behind!

Woody rummaged through the boxes in the back of the moving van and found RC Car. Using the remote, he sent RC back to pick up Buzz.

Andy's toys didn't understand. They thought Woody was trying to hurt Buzz and RC, and angrily threw him out of the van! Luckily, Buzz and RC picked up Woody. But before they could catch up with the moving van, RC's batteries ran out!

Woody watched as the moving van chugged farther away. Suddenly he had an idea. Buzz still had the rocket on his back! They could use that to catch up to the van!

The toys lit the rocket's fuse. The rocket's power pushed RC down the street. Soon RC was whizzing so fast that they began to lift off the ground! As they rose upward, Woody let go of RC, who landed in the van. Buzz and Woody whooshed into the sky. Just before the rocket exploded, Buzz snapped open his space wings, cutting the rocket free.

"Buzz, you're flying!" Woody exclaimed.

"This isn't flying," Buzz replied. "This is falling with style!"

Buzz and Woody glided toward Andy's car and dropped unnoticed through the open sunroof. "Woody! Buzz!" Andy shouted. He hugged them close, thrilled to have his two favorite toys back.

Woody and Buzz had made it home.

# Jungle Race

Aladar the iguanodon raced through the jungle, sprinting forward on his powerful legs. His heart pounded in his chest. Tree branches and vines swatted at his face, but he ignored them.

Zini was riding on Aladar's back, clinging tightly with his lemur paws. The two were playing Jungle Race, one of their favorite games.

"Look out!" Zini suddenly cried. But it was too late. Aladar didn't see the thick, ropelike vine across the path. He tripped and fell, sending Zini flying through the air.

Aladar went down hard, knocking against a tree trunk. After catching his breath, he blinked and sat up slowly. For a minute, everything looked topsy-turvy. Then the familiar jungle path swam slowly into view.

The only thing that didn't swim into view was Zini. Aladar got to his feet and looked around.

"Zini!" he called.

Aladar stood completely still and listened. But he heard nothing.

"Zini!" he called again, louder.

Aladar began to search the area, pushing branches and leaves and vines aside. Unlike him, Zini was small. If he didn't search carefully, Aladar might overlook him.

Aladar was several feet down the path when Zini zoomed in, swinging on a vine. He landed on a nearby tree branch.

"That was amazing!" Zini cried in excitement. "First I flew through the air like a meteor. Then I grabbed hold of a vine and swung halfway through the jungle. I practically made it all the way to the ocean!"

Aladar let out a big sigh of relief. "I was worried about you," he said.

Zini leaped onto Aladar's back and wrapped his long, furry arms around his friend's neck. "Sorry, Aladar. But I couldn't resist the opportunity for a flight like that. I felt like a bird! Let's do it again!" he cried.

Aladar rubbed his head. There was a small bump where he'd hit the tree trunk. "I think I need a little rest," he said.

Zini let out a disappointed sigh. "Oh, all right," he said.

Aladar grinned. "But maybe we can do it again tomorrow."

"Excellent!" said Zini.

# Jim's Vow

It had been a very odd night for Jim Hawkins and his mother. A mysterious alien named Billy Bones had crashed his ship near their inn, the Benbow. Before he died, Bones had given Jim a strange treasure map, thought to be the key to finding the riches of the notorious pirate Captain Flint! Jim had just taken the map out of the dying alien's hands when a gang of murderous alien pirates had arrived at the inn, searching for that very same map.

Jim and his mother had barely had enough time to escape with their friend Dr. Doppler before the inn had been destroyed.

At Dr. Doppler's house, Jim had somehow convinced his mother to allow him to accompany Dr. Doppler on the search for treasure. It would be the adventure of a lifetime!

Jim lay in bed, thinking about what he would do if he had all the money in the galaxy.

"Well, for one thing," he said to himself, "I'd buy myself a cool new solar surfer and be the envy of all the other guys."

Jim was an accomplished surfer, but he knew his mother wished he worked as hard at his schoolwork as he did at his surfing.

"And for another," he went on, "I'd buy myself a fleet of private robots and program them to do all my chores without ever talking back to me." Jim's mind was racing now, as he thought of more and more possibilities. He pulled the treasure map out from under his pillow and looked at it closely, thinking hard. Then he replaced it carefully.

"But I don't need any of those things," he said quietly to himself. "If I find any treasure at all on this trip, I'm going to give it to Mom so she can rebuild the inn."

Jim swung his legs over the side of the bed and stood up. He tiptoed to the room where his mother was sleeping. In the dim light, he could see that her face looked pale and lovely. The lines of worry seemed to have smoothed out in her sleep. He bent down and kissed her cool, smooth brow.

"I'm going to make you proud of me, Mom," he whispered to her as she slept. "Just you wait and see."

# More to Life

Lightning McQueen was stuck in a sleepy town called Radiator Springs. He'd crashed there on his way to California and had ruined the town's main street.

The judge, Doc, had ordered him to fix the road. Doc even challenged Lightning to a race—and won! The rookie couldn't understand how the old car had beaten him.

After a lot of grumbling, Lightning finally began to work on the road. The residents of the town were grateful. Sally, the town attorney, offered him a place to stay and Mater the tow truck took him tractor tipping.

Lightning told Mater that winning the Piston Cup tiebreaker race in California meant getting a new sponsor with private helicopters. Mater asked if he could ride in a helicopter someday and Lightning said yes.

Sally overheard their conversation. "Did you mean that?" she asked. Sally was worried that Lightning didn't understand the importance of keeping his promise to Mater.

The next morning, Lightning wandered into Doc's shop and noticed something on a shelf. A Piston Cup! Then he saw two more. Lightning was amazed. Doc Hudson was the "Hudson Hornet"—a racing legend!

Lightning rushed over to Flo's café to tell everyone that Doc was a famous race car, but no one believed him.

Sally surprised Lightning by asking him if he wanted to take a drive. As the two cars zoomed up a winding mountain road, Lightning realized that, for the first time, he was actually racing just for fun. Sally told Lightning how she'd found Radiator Springs.

"I was an attorney in L.A., living life in the fast lane—but I never felt happy. So I left California, just drove and drove and finally broke down right here.

"I fell in love—with this," Sally continued, showing Lightning the view from the mountain. Far below lay a gorgeous valley.

In the distance, Lightning saw cars speeding past on the Interstate. "They don't even know what they're missing," he murmured.

Lightning was finally beginning to understand that there was more to life than winning.

# Banished!

Sulley was the top Scarer at Monsters, Inc. His job was to collect human screams. Mike Wazowski was his best friend.

Now Mike and Sulley were in big trouble. They'd discovered a human girl in Monstropolis! Monsters were very scared of human kids. They thought they were deadly!

But Sulley had grown to like the human child and had named her Boo. He was no longer scared of her. Mike and Sulley had brought Boo to the Scare Floor to send her home—but she had escaped from them! The two monsters had split up to find her, but a mean monster named Randall had cornered Mike. Randall was Sulley's competition for top Scarer! The nasty monster knew all about Boo. He ordered Mike to bring her to the Scare Floor. He said he'd have her door ready.

When Sulley finally found Boo, Mike told him about Randall's plan. Together, they went to the Scare Floor, but Sulley was still worried. "We can't trust Randall!" he told Mike.

Mike disagreed. To prove the open door was safe, he went right through—

and was captured by Randall!

Sulley and Boo followed the monster as he carried Mike to a secret room in the basement. There they learned that he had invented a new machine to capture screams from kids. He was about to try it out on Mike!

Sulley rescued Mike and raced to the training room. He needed to warn his boss, Mr. Waternoose, about Randall. Mr. Waternoose promised he would fix everything—but he was really working with Randall! He shoved Sulley and Mike through a door into the human world. They were banished to the mountains!

Sulley knew Boo was in trouble. He had to get back to Monstropolis. Racing to the local village, he found a door that led home. He rushed to Randall's secret lab and destroyed the machine.

As Sulley raced away with Boo, Mike arrived to help. The two monsters climbed onto the machine that carried doors to the Scare Floor. The power wasn't on, so Mike made a funny face. Boo laughed, and the power surged! It seemed that human children's laughs were more powerful than their screams.

# Look Before You Leap!

Mickey and Goofy were enjoying a game of chess when something soared through the window and landed in the middle of the chessboard! The two friends looked carefully at something that looked right back at them. It was green. It had webbed feet. It said, "Ribbit, ribbit."

It was a frog—a very *jumpy* frog. Goofy tried to grab it. *PLOP!* The frog leaped out of Goofy's hands and right into the kitchen sink.

"You should look before you leap!" Mickey said to the frog.

All of the excitement had made Goofy hungry. He decided to make lunch. Just then, the frog took a giant leap right toward Goofy's sandwich! *SQUISH!*

"Stop!" Mickey cried as Goofy lifted the sandwich to his mouth.

"You really should look before you leap," Goofy said to the frog. "And I should look before I bite!"

Goofy carried the frog outside.

"Hold on tight," Mickey said. "He's pretty slippery."

Goofy yelped as the frog hopped away toward Main Street. He took a great big leap and landed right inside Minnie's goldfish bowl. *SPLASH!* The big wave made the goldfish fly right out. Minnie gently put the goldfish back into its bowl.

Goofy sighed. He hoped they could find a safe place for the frog.

Mickey picked up the frog. Just then he spotted something that made him smile.

"I think I've found just the right place!" The friends walked down the street toward a fountain. Carefully, Mickey placed the frog on the ground. The frog hopped out of Mickey's hands and landed with a *SPLASH!* right next to another frog!

"Ribbit, ribbit," he said.

"Ribbit, ribbit," she replied.

"Maybe we didn't find a pond," said Mickey, "but we did find a good place for him to splash and leap. And a friend for him, too."

Later, Mickey and Goofy got back to their game of chess. "C'mon, Mickey," Goofy said, "you haven't made a move in a long time."

"I know, I know," replied Mickey. "I just want to make sure I look carefully before I leap!"

# Finally Home

On the *Axiom*, the ship where all the humans now lived, a little robot named EVE delivered a special plant from Earth to the Captain. EVE had found it among the treasures of a robot called WALL·E.

The Captain was excited. The plant meant he and all the humans could return to Earth. But the Captain's robot, Auto, wouldn't let them turn the ship around.

Auto snatched the plant and dumped it down the garbage chute. But the plant hit WALL·E. The little bot was climbing up the chute to get to EVE! He happily delivered the plant right back to her. Then Auto sent WALL·E back down the chute with EVE!

The two robots ended up in the ship's garbage bay. WALL·E was injured. EVE tried to help him, but he just kept trying to give her the plant. He still thought she wanted it more than anything else. But WALL·E was wrong. EVE just wanted to help WALL·E.

As the Captain fought to turn off Auto's power, EVE brought the plant to the holo-detector. It would recognize the plant and the ship would set a course for Earth.

But all was not well. WALL·E had been crushed by the giant holo-detector!

EVE wanted to take WALL·E home, where she could find the right parts to fix him.

As soon as the *Axiom* landed on Earth, EVE headed straight for WALL·E's home and repaired him. At last, he powered up . . . and began cubing trash.

Something was wrong. WALL·E didn't even recognize EVE!

Sadly, EVE held WALL·E's hand and leaned toward him. An electric spark passed between their heads—the robot kiss. She was saying good-bye. Then . . . WALL·E's hand began to move. EVE looked into his eyes. He was coming back to life! He recognized her!

"Ee-vah?" he said. After following EVE across the universe, WALL·E had ended up right where he had started—home. But this time he had the one thing he truly wanted—EVE's hand clasped in his own.

# Off-Road Adventure

"Lost toys! Lost toys!" announced Mike the microphone. "Help needed!"

"What's wrong?" said Woody.

"It's the Green Army Men!" Hamm the piggy bank cried from the windowsill. "Andy left them outside and it's raining. Now they're stuck in the mud!"

Buzz and Woody hurried to the window and peeked through the rain-splattered glass.

"How are we going to help them?" Woody cried.

"What about RC Car?" Hamm suggested.

Buzz and Woody climbed inside RC, and the race car took off. RC raced out of Andy's bedroom and down the hall. At the top of the stairs, Buzz and Woody held their breath. "Here we goooo!" Buzz cried as they bounced down the stairs.

"Ouch! Oof! Oww!" yelped Buzz.

RC raced to the kitchen and through the swinging dog door.

"There they are!" cried Woody.

"Situation critical!" shouted the Green Army Men. "Assistance needed immediately!"

RC Car veered into the dirt and parked near the army men. Woody swung his lasso and looped the rope around the Army Men. Then he tied the other end of the lasso around RC's bumper. As he backed up, RC pulled the Green Army Men to safety. When they were all free from the mud, RC Car drove up the pathway and through the dog door. But when he got to the stairs inside, everyone groaned.

"How can we drive back up?" asked Woody.

"Don't worry!" Hamm yelled from the top of the steps. "We're on it."

The toys had put together a train track leading right up the stairs. RC Car gunned his engine and up he went, just as Andy's mother pulled into the driveway. The toys quickly pulled the tracks back into Andy's room and put them back where they belonged.

"That was close!" said Woody. "But I think we got away with it. Andy's mom will never suspect a thing."

Downstairs, Andy's mother scratched her head. "I wonder where all this mud came from," she said.

# Follow That Sound!

C ubby was playing his harmonica on Shipwreck Beach. He was practicing to play at Marina's party.

Nearby, Captain Hook was trying to take a nap. Just as he began to drift off, he was woken up by the sound of music!

"One of those puny pirates is making an awful racket with his blowy music thing!" he cried.

"Why don't you ask the sea pups nicely if they'll be quieter?" said Smee.

"Why would I ask nicely when I can take the thing away!" Hook replied. So Hook used his fishing hook to nab the harmonica right out of Cubby's mouth! But before he could put the instrument somewhere safe, a monkey whizzed past and grabbed it!

Jake and his crew swung through the jungle after the monkey. They thought they had lost him, but then they heard music!

"It's my harmonica!" said Cubby.

"Follow that sound!" said Jake.

The crew soon found the monkey and asked if he would give them the harmonica back. But the monkey wanted to keep it. He wanted an instrument of his very own to play!

The crew made some maracas out of coconuts and little rocks, and swapped with the monkey.

The happy monkey followed Jake and his crew back to Shipwreck Beach, where he and Cubby played together!

Captain Hook wasn't happy.

"What's the matter?" asked Jake.

"The cap'n can't have his nappy-nap with all that music," said Smee.

Jake had an idea. Cubby and the monkey played a lullaby for Captain Hook, who soon fell asleep.

Later that night, Cubby and the monkey played their instruments at Marina's party.

"Cubby, thank you so much for playing," said Marina. "You were amazing!"

"If Hook had just asked us to be quiet, we wouldn't have gone through all that trouble today," said Jake.

"Hook should know better! If you need something, you should ask nicely," said Izzy.

"Yeah, but if the monkey didn't take the harmonica, we wouldn't have been able to jam together!" said Cubby.

# Hide-and-Seek

Dumbo had been the newest baby in the circus for quite a while. Then, one day, the stork arrived with a brand-new delivery—a baby giraffe.

"You know, Dumbo," said his friend Timothy Q. Mouse, "I think we should ask that new baby to play with us."

Dumbo nodded. He loved making new friends!

"Hello, Mrs. Giraffe," Timothy said. "Can your lovely new baby come out to play?"

Mrs. Giraffe agreed and the three new friends set off.

"Okay, kids," said Timothy, "what do you feel like playing? How about hide-and-seek?"

Dumbo and the giraffe nodded happily as Timothy closed his eyes and counted.

"Ready or not," he said finally, opening his eyes, "here I—Hang on! Don't you guys know you're supposed to hide?"

No, actually, they did not.

Timothy sighed. "Okay, let's take it from the top. When I close my eyes, you guys hide. You find a place where you can't see me and I can't see you.

Like this." Timothy ducked behind a popcorn tub. "Get it?"

Dumbo and the giraffe nodded slowly.

"Okay then, let's try this again. One, two, three . . ." Timothy counted to twenty, then opened his eyes.

"No, no!" he groaned. "You can't hide behind the popcorn tub. You're too big. Let's try this one more time."

Again, he closed his eyes and counted. Then, very slowly, he opened them and looked around.

"Much better!" he said, surprised. Of course, it didn't take him long to find Dumbo's nose sticking out of a pile of hay or the giraffe sticking out from behind the clowns' trunk.

"This time, guys, try to find a place for your whole body to hide," Timothy said.

Dumbo and the giraffe waited for Timothy to close his eyes once more. Then they quietly hid again. But this time they picked places that covered their whole bodies.

And do you know what? They hid so well, Timothy Q. Mouse may still be looking for them to this very day!

# The Chase

Things at Monsters, Inc. had become a bit scarier than usual! Best friends Sulley and Mike had discovered a human child in their world and were trying to get her home.

Sulley was the top Scarer at Monsters, Inc. He was the best of the best at collecting children's screams to power the city. But thanks to Boo— the child they'd found—he'd discovered that laughs were just as powerful as screams.

Unfortunately, Sulley's boss, Mr. Waternoose, was working with a mean monster named Randall. They had invented a machine to suck screams out of human kids! Sulley had torn the machine apart and raced away with Boo, but Randall was chasing them.

Mike and Sulley made it to the Scare Floor. But to send Boo home, they still needed to find her door. Mike, Sulley, and Boo jumped in and out of bedrooms. When Randall grabbed Boo, Sulley told him, "She's not scared of you anymore." Then, working together, Boo and Sulley beat Randall once and for all.

But Boo wasn't safe yet. Now Mr. Waternoose and the CDA (Child Detection Agency) were controlling the doors. While Mike distracted the CDA, Sulley escaped with Boo. Unfortunately, Waternoose saw everything.

"Give me the child!" he yelled, running after Sulley. Luckily, Mike recorded Mr. Waternoose as he yelled, "I'll kidnap a thousand children before I let this company die!"

Now everyone knew that Waternoose planned to kidnap children. He was quickly arrested!

It was time for Boo to go home. Sulley followed her into her room. He gently tucked her into bed. Sadly, Sulley returned to Monstropolis. The CDA shredded Boo's door. It wouldn't be used for scaring anymore.

Sulley missed Boo. He had one tiny sliver of her door, but the rest had been destroyed. Before long, Mike surprised his pal. He'd put Boo's door back together! It was missing just one little piece. Sulley inserted the piece, opened the door, and saw . . .

"Boo?" Sulley whispered.

"Kitty!" an excited voice replied.

The two friends were reunited at last!

# Hamm's Heavy Burden

Hamm's head hung low. He had barely moved in days. "Hamm just hasn't been himself lately," Woody said. "He doesn't play with us anymore. And Andy has been paying more attention to him than ever."

Woody stood up and walked over to Hamm.

"Oh. Hey, Woody," the piggy bank said sadly.

"What do you say me and you take a walk down to the toy box and say hi to the Green Army Men?" Woody asked.

Hamm's eyes lit up, but when he looked across the room, his face drooped again. "No thanks," he said with a sigh.

Woody put his arm around his friend. Something was really wrong. Hamm always liked to visit with the Green Army Men.

"Talk to me, Hammy. What's going on? You're not yourself."

Hamm looked at his hooves shyly. "It's just, well . . . uh . . . do I look fat?"

Woody put his hand over his mouth to keep from laughing. "Hamm, you're a pi—" Woody stopped himself when he saw Hamm's hopeful look. "A perfectly proportioned pig," he finished.

"I just feel so heavy lately," Hamm said. "And you know, I should feel great. Andy has been dropping coins in my slot almost every night! I can't remember when he paid this much attention to me. I mean, I'm not you," he concluded.

Woody nodded. He knew Andy paid a lot more attention to him than to most of the toys in the room. But he wasn't sure what to say to Hamm to make him feel better.

The next morning Woody was still worrying about Hamm when Andy raced into the room. He pulled Hamm off the shelf, took the cork out of his belly, and shook him over the bed. Coins rained out of Hamm's stomach.

"Thanks," Andy said, patting the piggy bank. He gathered up his loot and dashed out of the room, yelling, "Coming, Mom! I just had to get my savings."

"Wow, do I feel better." Hamm danced a little jig. "But now maybe I'm a little too empty."

Woody and Bo Peep beamed. "Looking lean there!" Bo Peep said, poking Hamm in the side with her staff.

"Heads up!" cried Woody, tossing Hamm a new coin.

# Lightning's New Friends

Rookie race car Lightning McQueen had been stranded in Radiator Springs after getting lost on his way to a race in California.

Sally, the town's attorney, was telling Lightning why Radiator Springs wasn't the busy place it once was.

"Forty years ago that Interstate didn't exist," Sally explained, looking at the busy highway. "The road didn't cut through the land. It moved with the land. It rose, it fell, it curved."

"What happened?" asked Lightning.

"The town got bypassed just to save ten minutes of driving," Sally replied.

Later that day, as Lightning worked on fixing the town's main street—which he had accidentally ruined—a herd of escaped tractors stampeded through town!

Lightning followed a stray tractor into the desert and saw Doc, the town judge, roaring around the dirt racetrack.

Lightning had just found out that Doc had once been a famous race car. He had even won the Piston Cup!

"You're amazing!" he told the old pro. But Doc just raced off.

Lightning followed Doc to his office. "How could you quit at the top of your game?" he asked.

Doc showed Lightning a newspaper article about a wreck he had been in. After he was repaired, Doc had wanted to return to racing. But he had been replaced—by a rookie. That was why Doc didn't like Lightning—or any other new race car.

The next morning, the road was finished. It was time for Lightning to go to California. But first he wanted to say thank you for the way the town's residents had treated him.

"I'm not sure these tires can get me all the way to California," he said. In a flash, Guido and Luigi proudly fitted Lightning with four shiny new tires!

And that was just the beginning. Before long, Lightning made his way to every shop in town. He filled up on Fillmore's organic fuel, tried out night vision goggles at Sarge's Surplus Hut, picked out a bumper sticker at Lizzie's curio shop, and got a new paint job at Ramone's body shop. Lightning liked helping the town's small businesses.

For the first time, he was realizing how nice it was to have friends!

# A Royal Pain

"**S**ir Hiss, wake up! Wake up!" Prince John shouted into the face of his royal adviser.

Sir Hiss awoke with a start and sat bolt upright in his tiny cradle at the foot of Prince John's bed. "Wha—what is it, Your Highness?" Hiss replied. He shook his head and tried to shake off his sleepiness. "Is everything all right?"

"No, everything is *not* all right!" Prince John snapped. "I don't know how you can sleep while I lie here wide awake, tossing and turning!"

Sir Hiss realized that he would not be allowed to sleep until Prince John fell asleep. So he sprang into action, trying everything he could think of to send the prince off to dreamland.

First he brought the prince a drink from the castle kitchen.

"*Twecchh!*" Prince John spat out his first mouthful. "This milk is warm!"

"Well, yes, Your Majesty," replied Hiss. "Warm milk will help you get to sleep."

"Take it away!" the prince ordered.

Next Sir Hiss tried singing a lullaby. He crooned, "Go to *sssssleep*, little *princccccce. . . .*"

But Prince John scrunched up his face, wiped it with the back of his hand, and yelled, "Say it, don't spray it!"

Sir Hiss was annoyed. But he had one more idea.

"Why don't you try counting sheep?" he suggested.

Prince John did as he was told. But before he had gotten to ten, he had lost his patience.

"Oh, I don't care how many sheep there are!" he thundered.

Sir Hiss was at the end of his rope. And he was completely out of ideas. Then he spotted the prince's money bags, piled high in one corner of the bedroom. Suddenly, he knew just what to do.

"Okay, Sire," said Sir Hiss. "Then how about counting your money?"

Sir Hiss opened one of the money bags and pulled out a handful of gold coins. As he dropped a coin back into the bag, it made a soft clinking sound. He dropped another, and then another. . . . Prince John closed his eyes and began to count each clink.

"One . . . two . . . three . . ."

Before he got to ten, Prince John was fast asleep . . . wearing a huge grin.

# To Play Another Day

Special Agent Oso was at U.N.I.Q.U.E. headquarters, preparing for his fitness test. "I'm ready, Wolfie," he said.

"The wires connect to the computer that will tell us how fit you are," said Special Agent Wolfie.

"I already know I'm as fit as a fiddle," said Oso. "I exercise every day."

"Exercise keeps an agent alert," said Wolfie. "But you have to stick with it. Just like this test, Oso. You have to stick with it all the way to the end."

In a nearby town, a boy called Enzio was at home watching TV. "I want you to think of ways you can get more exercise," his mother told him. "And I'd like you to tell me your ideas before suppertime."

But Enzio didn't know how to get more exercise. He needed Special Agent Oso's help!

Oso soon arrived at Enzio's house. "I'm going to help you get more exercise, Enzio," Oso said. "What's the first step, Paw Pilot?"

"Step one: find activities that interest you," said Paw Pilot.

Oso took Enzio to the park across the street to see what other kids were doing.

"I'd like to play basketball!" Enzio said. "I'll ask my mom if I can join a team."

"Sign-ups end next week," said a girl. "You could be on my team."

"Step one is complete," said Paw Pilot. "Step two is to plan to play for at least one hour every day."

"Being on a sports team will take care of some days, Enzio," Agent Oso told the boy. "But what about the other days?"

"I can ride my bike," said Enzio. "Or play tag in the park!"

"Step two is complete," said Paw Pilot. "Step three is to stick with it!"

"Hey! That's what Wolfie told me to do. 'Stick with it,'" Agent Oso said.

"You will always need to exercise," said Paw Pilot.

That evening, Enzio told his mom all about his new exercise plan.

Meanwhile, Agent Oso went back to U.N.I.Q.U.E. headquarters and completed his fitness test!

"Congratulations, Special Agent Oso," said Paw Pilot. "You have earned your fitness test award!"

# Bad Guys Don't Win Medals

**W**reck-It Ralph worked in the Fix-It Felix, Jr. video game. Every time someone played the game, Ralph would come on-screen and yell, "I'M GONNA WRECK IT!" Then Fix-It Felix, the Good Guy, would arrive with his magic hammer and fix everything.

All the Nicelanders cheered for Felix and gave him pie and a medal. But Ralph? They threw him off the building and into the mud.

Felix enjoyed his work, and the Nicelanders were glad to reward him . . . game after game, year after year. But Ralph was getting tired of that mud puddle. It didn't feel fair. He was just doing his job. Why did Felix always get to be the Good Guy, while Ralph always ended up covered in mud?

On the game's anniversary, Ralph traveled through the power cord to a support group for video game Bad Guys. He told the group that he wished he could be the Good Guy, just once.

"We can't change who we are," the others said. Then they all recited the Bad Guy Affirmation: "I am Bad. And that's good. I will never be Good. And that's not bad. There's no one I'd rather be than me."

Ralph headed home through Game Central Station, the hub for all the games in the arcade. As usual, Surge Protector stopped him for questioning. Ralph knew it was just because he was a Bad Guy.

On his way home, Ralph dropped off treats for the homeless video game characters living in the station. Their games had been unplugged, and they had nowhere to live.

That evening, the Nicelanders held a big anniversary party in their apartment building. Ralph couldn't believe that he hadn't been invited.

"I am going to that party!" he declared.

At the party, Ralph tried to be polite. Then he noticed the cake, with a Felix figurine on top, wearing a medal. Ralph wanted his own figurine to wear a medal, too. But Nicelander Gene said, "Bad Guys don't win medals!"

Ralph was so upset that he accidentally wrecked the cake!

Ralph sighed. Would he ever be able to have his very own medal . . . ?

# A Rave Review

A young man named Linguini had just discovered that the great chef Auguste Gusteau was his father. Gusteau's restaurant now belonged to him and was becoming more and more popular.

Remy the rat was helping Linguini cook. But Linguini was enjoying his success a bit too much. He had stopped paying attention to cooking, and Remy didn't like it. Neither did one of the restaurant's other cooks, Colette.

One day the famous critic Anton Ego visited the restaurant. He was the same critic who had once ruined Gusteau's with a bad review. He gave Linguini a warning: "I will return tomorrow night with high expectations."

Remy was furious that Linguini wasn't more worried about Ego's announcement. He yanked Linguini's hair, hard.

Linguini got angry. He took Remy out to the back and said, "You take a break, Little Chef. I'm not your puppet."

Angry with Linguini, Remy invited the entire rat colony to take whatever they wanted from the restaurant's refrigerator. That's when Linguini returned to apologize.

"You're stealing food?" Linguini asked, furious. "I thought you were my friend. I trusted you! Get out. And don't ever come back!"

Remy felt horrible. He knew Linguini needed help. Remy boldly walked into the bustling kitchen.

"Rat!" shrieked the chefs.

"Don't touch him!" shouted Linguini. "The truth is, I have no talent at all. This rat—he's the cook."

The chefs were horrified and left the restaurant.

Remy's father, Django, had seen Linguini defend Remy! He whistled, and rats instantly filled the kitchen. After going through the dishwasher to clean themselves, the rats began to cook.

Linguini, acting as a waiter, served a delicious dish of ratatouille to Ego. The taste brought back a comforting memory from Ego's childhood.

Ego asked to meet the chef. Linguini waited until all the other customers left the restaurant, and then brought out Remy.

The next morning Ego gave the restaurant a rave review!

# Cruella Sees Spots

Cruella looked around the living room of the old De Vil mansion and rubbed her hands together. Everywhere Cruella looked she saw spots, spots, spots! At last, her dream was coming true!

Cruella thought back to the day this had all started. . . .

It had begun perfectly miserably. Cruella had been shopping for fur coats all morning, but she hadn't found a single thing she liked.

"Too long! Too short! Too black! Too white!" she screeched, knocking an armload of coats out of the shop assistant's hands. "I want something unusual! I want a coat that has never been seen before!"

Cruella stormed out of the shop, slamming the door so hard that the glass cracked. She needed something to cheer her up. Then she remembered that her old school friend, Anita, lived nearby.

Soon Cruella stood at the door, ringing the buzzer impatiently. A pretty brown-haired woman answered the door.

"Oh, Cruella!" Anita cried. "What a surprise!"

"Hello, Anita, darling," Cruella said, walking into the sitting room. At that moment, Anita's husband, Roger, strolled down the stairs.

"Ah, prince charming," Cruella said, smirking. Roger scowled. Suddenly something else caught Cruella's eye. Two black-and-white spotted dogs were sitting in the corner of the room.

"And what have we here?" Cruella asked.

"Oh, that's Pongo and Perdita," Anita explained.

But Cruella wasn't looking at the dogs. She was looking at their coats. Their glossy fur wasn't too long or too short. It wasn't too black or too white. It was perfect!

"Perdita is going to have puppies!" Anita went on.

"Puppies!" Cruella shrieked. Suddenly she had an idea that made her smile even more evilly. "Oh, Anita, you must call me just as soon as the puppies arrive. I think they are *just* what I have been looking for."

Pongo snarled, but Cruella didn't care.

"What a perfectly *marvelous* day," Cruella said to herself as she strode out the door.

And *that* was how it all started.

# This Spells Trouble!

"**W**oody! Bo!" Hamm whispered. "Have you guys noticed anything a little . . . off . . . about Mr. Spell lately?"

"What do you mean?" asked Bo Peep.

"His spelling hasn't been so sharp the last few days," Hamm explained.

Woody looked at Hamm in disbelief. "That can't be right," he said. "Mr. Spell was made to spell. He never gets anything wrong."

Hamm shrugged. "See for yourself," he said.

Woody, Bo Peep, and Hamm walked over to Mr. Spell and asked him to spell *rutabaga.*

"Rutabaga. That's r . . . r . . . r . . ."

Woody and Bo Peep exchanged nervous glances.

"Great, thanks," Hamm said to Mr. Spell, trying to act natural.

"Hey, how about the word 'platypus'?" said Woody.

"Platypus," Mr. Spell repeated. "That's spelled p . . . p . . . p . . . p . . ."

Woody and Bo Peep stared anxiously at Mr. Spell. Could he be losing his spelling edge? It was hard to believe, but how else could they explain what they were hearing? "Okay," Hamm said.

"One more question. How do you spell 'knickknack'?"

"Knickknack," Mr. Spell began, "is spelled k . . . k . . . k . . . k . . ."

This was serious. Mr. Spell was a really, really bad speller!

"Spell?" said Woody, laying a sympathetic hand on Mr. Spell's back. "Are you feeling all right? You don't seem yourself."

"Oh, sure, Woody," Mr. Spell replied. "I feel fine . . . fine . . . fine . . ."

As Mr. Spell continued to repeat the word, Woody suddenly understood the problem.

"Hey! Hamm!" Woody exclaimed. "He's not spelling incorrectly. He just keeps getting stuck. Don't you, Spell?"

But Mr. Spell couldn't respond. He just kept repeating "fine . . . fine . . . fine . . . fine . . . "

Woody gave Mr. Spell a firm slap on the back. It didn't help, so he wound up and gave him a good whack. Mr. Spell fell over on his side. The cover to his battery compartment came loose. Two corroded-looking batteries fell onto the floor.

"Heh, heh, heh," Hamm chuckled. "I guess Mr. Spell just needs some new batteries!"

# Meeting a Hero

Carl and a young boy named Russell were in South America. They had flown there in Carl's house with thousands of balloons tied to it! Carl was there to keep a promise to his wife of many years, Ellie. The two of them had always dreamed of becoming explorers and visiting Paradise Falls.

Since arriving in South America, Carl and Russell had met a strange, huge bird—Russell named him Kevin—and a talking dog named Dug. Dug was on a mission to find Kevin and wanted to take the bird prisoner.

The two were walking to Paradise Falls, holding on to the floating house with a garden hose. That night, they stopped to rest. "Dug says he wants to take Kevin prisoner. We have to protect him!" Russell told Carl while the others slept. Carl agreed that Kevin could come with them to the falls.

The next morning, they found Kevin perched on the roof of the house. The bird was calling toward the distant rocks. "The bird is calling to her babies," Dug explained.

"Kevin's a girl?" Russell asked in surprise.

Soon Kevin set off for her home. Russell wanted to go with her, but Carl was in a hurry to get to the falls. "She can take care of herself," he told Russell.

Suddenly, three fierce dogs burst from the bushes. They were part of Dug's pack. They surrounded Carl, Russell, and Dug and demanded they go back with them to their master.

The dogs led Carl and Russell to a huge cave. An old man stood in the entrance, surrounded by more dogs. When the man saw Carl's house, he laughed. He had thought that Carl and Russell were explorers—but real explorers wouldn't come in a floating house!

"My dogs made a mistake," he told Carl.

Carl thought the man looked familiar. "Wait," he said. "Are you . . . Charles Muntz?"

Carl couldn't believe it—Muntz was his and Ellie's childhood hero!

"My wife and I, we're your biggest fans!" he said, shaking Muntz's hand. Carl wished that Ellie was there—he knew she would have been thrilled to meet the explorer.

# Hero's Duty

Wreck-It Ralph was the Bad Guy in the Fix-It Felix, Jr. video game. At the end of every game, he got thrown in the mud by the other characters, and he was fed up with it. He wanted a medal to prove that he could be a Good Guy, just like Fix-It Felix.

So Ralph did something that no character had done before. He decided to leave his game. He was searching for a medal in another game when a dazed-looking soldier staggered in. He had come from a new game called Hero's Duty, where he'd been battling swarms of cy-bugs. The goal of the game, the soldier explained, was to climb a tower and find the Medal of Heroes.

Suddenly a tiny beetle scuttled across the table and the soldier fainted. That gave Ralph an idea. Maybe *he* could take the soldier's place in the game—and win that medal! Finally he could prove to everyone that he could be a Good Guy for a change!

Ralph borrowed the soldier's armor and snuck into Hero's Duty. Ralph waited with the other soldiers and the first-person shooter—the robot that handled the game player's action! The game started, and huge, hungry cy-bugs attacked! They gobbled up characters, vehicles, and weapons. Then they turned into freakish versions of whatever they ate!

Ralph was terrified! He grabbed the first-person shooter game player and begged for help. But before the girl could wonder why a game character was talking so strangely, a cy-bug chomped her avatar. A loud voice boomed, "GAME OVER!"

Inside Hero's Duty, the game began to reset. Characters went back to their places and a beacon appeared on top of the huge tower in the center of the game. The soldier's leader, Sergeant Calhoun, was furious!

"Never interfere with the first-person shooter!" she yelled at Ralph.

But he wasn't listening. He wanted the Medal of Heroes, up in that tower. This was his chance to prove he could be a Good Guy!

Ralph headed toward the tower. He was determined to get his medal and prove himself, no matter what he had to do.

# Good Luck in California

In the sleepy town of Radiator Springs, rookie race car Lightning McQueen had found some great new friends. He had ended up there by accident while on his way to the tiebreaker race for the Piston Cup in California. At first, he had just wanted to leave. But now he was beginning to realize what it meant to help others. Maybe there was more to life than winning races after all.

Lightning had spent the day helping all of the town's small businesses. Now it was time to go.

Suddenly, a helicopter searchlight swept over the town.

"We have found McQueen!" boomed a voice from a loudspeaker.

News vans swarmed into town. Reporters surrounded Lightning, shouting questions.

"Where are you?" Lightning's agent, Harv, shouted over the speakerphone in the back of Mack's trailer. Lightning tried to tell Harv how great Radiator Springs was, but the fast-talking agent wasn't interested.

"Get out of 'Radiation Stinks' now, or Dinoco is history!" he yelled.

Dinoco was the sponsor Lightning would get if he won the tiebreaker race.

As Lightning's driver, Mack, urged the race car to get into the trailer, Lightning and Sally, the town lawyer, gazed at each other. Neither of them knew what to say.

"Good luck in California," Sally said at last. "I hope you find what you're looking for."

Sally was heading back to her hotel when she heard a reporter thank Doc for letting the press know where to find Lightning. How could Doc do such a thing?

"It's best for everyone, Sally," Doc said.

"Best for everyone? Or best for you?" Sally replied in shock.

Doc didn't like young race cars. He had once been a famous race car, but when he had been involved in a big crash, a rookie had taken his place.

Slowly, Lightning's friends went to their homes and shops. Soon the street was empty. Doc idled alone. Behind him the neon lights blinked off until Radiator Springs was quiet once more.

Doc sighed sadly. The town seemed so much emptier without Lightning around. Had he been wrong about the rookie?

# The Mysterious Backson

One morning, Winnie the Pooh woke up to his tummy rumbling. He was certain a visit to Christopher Robin would turn up some honey. But when Pooh reached Christopher Robin's house, he found a note taped to the door. Pooh couldn't read it, so he brought it to Owl.

"It says, 'gone out, busy Backson.'" Owl looked horrified. "Christopher Robin has been captured by a creature called the Backson!"

Luckily, Rabbit came up with a clever plan to capture the Backson. Pooh and Piglet got straight to work digging a pit. But Pooh's tummy still craved honey, and he wandered off in a daydream. Tigger wandered off, too, to track the Backson on his own.

Pooh's friends were looking for Pooh everywhere when they heard a loud *thud!*

"The plan worked!" Rabbit cried. "We caught the Backson!"

The friends cautiously peered into the pit, only to discover that it was Pooh who had fallen in, not the Backson. They tried to throw in a rope so Pooh could climb up, but instead they all fell in—everyone except Piglet. Now Piglet had to save all of his friends!

As tiny Piglet searched for help, an enormous shadow fell over him. "B-B-B-BACKSON!" he shouted and ran off. But the shadow was only Tigger dressed as a Backson!

Back in the pit, everyone was relieved to see Piglet and Tigger. Soon the friends were able to climb out of the Backson trap.

Back aboveground, Christopher Robin had appeared. Pooh handed him the note. Christopher Robin explained that he had written that he would be "back soon"—not "Backson"!

Relieved, the friends went on their way. There was just one problem. Pooh was still hungry for honey. He got to Owl's front door and pulled the bell rope . . . and realized that it was Eeyore's tail! Pooh decided that returning Eeyore's tail was more important than satisfying his tummy, and he brought his friend the tail right away. Eeyore was so relieved to see his tail that he gave Pooh a big pot of honey. All his honey dreams had come true after all!

# Basil's Blunder

Dawson was just settling down before the fire at 221½B Baker Street when he heard a sharp rap at the door.

Basil put down his microscope and marched to the door. "Yes, yes. What is it?" he asked.

There on the doorstep stood a very young, very wet, and very bedraggled-looking mouse. Water dripped from his whiskers. He had no hat or umbrella to shelter him from the London rain. He wore a book bag over one shoulder, and in his hands was a damp package.

"I'm looking for—"

"No. No. Don't tell me," Basil said. "Let me guess."

He started pacing about the room, as he usually did when he was deep in thought. Basil hated interruptions, but he loved mysteries.

"Come in, dear boy," Dawson said, ushering the boy into the room and taking his worn coat, package, and book bag. "Have a seat by the fire."

"Thank you, er . . ." the boy started.

"That is Dr. Dawson!" Basil said. "And you," he said, "are a university student!"

"Y-yes," the boy stammered.

"I'd say you are a struggling student by the looks of things. You appear to be tired from too much studying. But what are you looking for?" Basil's eyes narrowed.

"I was looking for a—"

Basil put his hand up. "You've lost a parent?" he said. "No! An instructor? Perhaps. But wait. You arrived on my doorstep with something in your hand." Basil whirled and pointed at the damp package. "Aha!"

"Yes, sir. It's for—"

"Please don't tell me!" Basil cried, examining the box. "Why, the address has washed completely away!"

Dawson leaned toward the shivering student and whispered something in his ear. Basil was so busy pacing he did not even notice when the dear lad whispered back his reply.

"I have solved the mystery, Basil," Dawson announced. "The package is for you!"

Basil looked at Dawson. "How do you know?" he gasped.

"It's elementary, dear Basil," Dawson replied. "This student has taken on a job as a delivery boy to pay his school bills. And . . . I asked."

# The Monster of Paradise Falls

Carl Fredricksen was on a trip to Paradise Falls. He had promised his wife, Ellie, he would take her, but they had never found the money. When Ellie passed away, Carl had decided it was time to make the trip. Now Carl was on his way. And he had accidentally brought a young boy named Russell along with him!

Carl and Russell met a large, strange bird. Russell had named it Kevin, but then he had discovered it was a girl! They also met a talking dog called Dug. He had been sent by his pack to capture Kevin. Soon the rest of Dug's pack appeared. They took Carl and Russell to their leader. Much to Carl's surprise, their leader was Charles Muntz—a famous explorer who had been his and Ellie's childhood hero!

Muntz invited Carl and Russell into his giant airship—the *Spirit of Adventure*! It was docked in a gigantic cave. Once onboard, the dogs served dinner while Muntz told Carl and Russell about the Monster of Paradise Falls.

"I've spent a lifetime tracking this creature," Muntz said.

"Hey, that looks like Kevin!" said Russell, noticing a bird skeleton.

"Kevin?" Muntz asked.

"That's my new giant bird pet," Russell explained. "I trained it to follow us."

Muntz became very angry. He thought Carl and Russell were trying to steal the bird from him.

At that moment, they heard a wail outside. Kevin had followed Carl and Russell into the cave! All the dogs began to bark. In the confusion, Carl and Russell slipped away.

"Get them!" Muntz roared.

Carl and Russell untied the house and started to run. The snarling dog pack came racing after them. Kevin scooped Russell and Carl onto her back and raced for the cave opening, with the house still floating behind. But Kevin wasn't fast enough to stay ahead of the pack, and the dogs were closing in.

Suddenly, an avalanche of rocks tumbled down and blocked the pack. "Go on, Master. I will stop the dogs!" someone cried.

It was Dug! He had come to rescue Carl and Russell. But would Carl, Russell, and Kevin be able to escape?

# The Chosen One

The Little Green Aliens looked up as something moved overhead. "Ooh," they cried. Was it the Claw?

The Claw was their master. It descended from the sky and decided who would go and who would stay. But this time it was not the Claw. Instead, the small door on the side of their home opened. Dozens of three-eyed aliens just like them poured in.

"Welcome," one of the original aliens said to the newcomers. "This is the Choosing Place."

Another alien gasped. "Look!" he cried. "One of the new ones is not like us. He is . . . different."

The others cried out in surprise and confusion. One of the new aliens had only *two* eyes on his round green head!

"What is the matter with your face, stranger?" one of the Little Green Aliens asked. "You don't look like us."

"I—I don't know," the two-eyed one said hesitantly. "I have always been this way. A Voice from above once said that—that . . ." His voice trailed off.

A three-eyed newcomer spoke up. "I heard the Voice," he said. "It said that it was a Manufacturing Defect."

Suddenly there was a great whirring sound from above.

"The Claw!" someone cried. "It moves! It descends!"

The aliens waited, gazing upward hopefully as the Claw came closer and closer. Finally, its talons closed over one round green head.

"The Claw has chosen!" they cried.

A child's muffled voice came from somewhere outside. "Cool! I got the best one!"

The aliens watched as the Claw raised the Chosen One above the others. They gasped as they recognized the strange two-eyed newcomer.

"The different one has been chosen!" one of the Little Green Aliens exclaimed. "The Claw has chosen him despite his Manufacturing Defect!"

"The Claw knew that the different one was special," someone else added.

The others nodded solemnly. "We will learn from the Claw," one of them said.

"Yes," another finished. "From now on, we will welcome all newcomers, no matter how different."

The others nodded. The Claw had shown them the way.

# Making Wishes Come True

"Looking good, kid!" the Genie shouted.

Aladdin adjusted his turban and smiled at the sights that surrounded him. Things in Agrabah sure looked different from the back of an elephant—even if that elephant was really your transformed monkey!

Aladdin still couldn't believe he'd found a magic lamp and the Genie inside it. And the three wishes! He'd only used one so far—he'd wished to become a prince. And as he rode through Agrabah dressed in the finest silk and a jewel-encrusted turban— on an elephant—he definitely felt royal. Nobody would call him a "street rat" now!

"Princess Jasmine, here I come," Aladdin said as he rode through the crowded streets. He'd wanted to become a prince for one reason and one reason only—to woo the girl who had won his heart.

Abu trumpeted and the people in the marketplace turned to watch the royal caravan. Aladdin puffed up his chest with pride, then slumped down again as he looked at the people staring up at him. Some of them looked thin. Others were dirty.

Aladdin knew what it was like to be poor. How many times had he been in the marketplace with no money for food? More than he could count.

"Abu, Genie," Aladdin said, "we're making a stop."

"But, kid, we've got to get to the palace," Genie objected. "Princess Jasmine might not know it, but she's waiting for you."

For a moment, Aladdin was tempted to heed Genie's advice and forget about his plan. But one look at a hungry little girl gazing at a roasted-meat vendor changed his mind.

"Stop right here, Abu," he told his elephant. Aladdin got off his mount and proceeded to buy heaps of delicious meats, breads, and fruits from several of the vendors.

"This is for you," he told the hungry little girl as he handed her a loaf of bread and a large piece of warm roasted meat.

Aladdin handed out the rest of his purchases to the hungry people of Agrabah. Then, satisfied, he climbed onto Abu the elephant and continued on his way to the palace.

# Pixie Play

"What do you say, Tink? Can you get it?" asked Peter Pan.

Peter and Tinker Bell were floating high above the streets of London, right outside a large open window. Inside, three children were sleeping soundly.

Tinker Bell nodded and darted through the window.

The last time Peter had visited this house, the children's nurse, Nana, had spied him outside the nursery window. She'd tried to grab him, but all she got was his shadow. Tonight Peter had come to get his shadow back.

Peter watched from the windowsill as Tinker Bell flew around the nursery. First she flew over the eldest child, Wendy Darling, and then her two younger brothers, John and Michael. All three kept right on sleeping.

But when Tinker Bell flew over Nana, the dog awoke with a sneeze! Tinker Bell's pixie dust had tickled Nana's nose.

"Arf! Arf!" barked Nana, trying to grab the fairy. But the poor dog's feet couldn't find the floor! The pixie dust had lifted her off the ground. Now Nana was floating around the room!

Peter started to laugh. The dog obviously didn't know how to fly. Suddenly, the pixie dust wore off and Nana's paws hit the floor again. With an angry growl, she charged at Peter Pan!

"Yikes!" Peter cried, darting back through the window with Tinker Bell right behind him.

"Back to Never Land, Tink!" he said. "We'll get my shadow back tomorrow night."

And with that, Peter and Tinker Bell soared into the sky and vanished.

Back inside the nursery, Wendy suddenly woke up. "What's this?" she cried, touching the window. Her hand sparkled with pixie dust. "Peter Pan must have come back looking for his shadow. I'm sorry I missed him," Wendy told Nana with a frown of disappointment.

"Arf! Arf!" said Nana.

"Yes, I know," Wendy replied. "Time for me to go back to bed."

As Nana licked Wendy's cheek good night, Wendy promised herself that she would be ready to meet the remarkable Peter Pan the next time he paid her a visit!

Bambi

# Rain, Rain, Go Away

*Rrrumble, rrrrumble, BOOM!* The loud clap of thunder startled Bambi and his friends.

"I don't like thunderstorms!" cried Thumper, looking a little scared.

"Bambi!" called his mother as the clouds grew dark and the rain began to fall. Bambi followed his mother out of the open meadow and into the woods. From their warm, dry thicket, Bambi watched sheets of rain pour down.

"I don't like thunderstorms," he told his mother, echoing Thumper's words. "I wish the storm would go away and never come back again."

"Oh, my," said his mother. "Do you mean you never again want to drink the cool, fresh water from the forest stream?"

"Well, no," said Bambi.

"Then do you want the big trees to go thirsty?" asked his mother.

"No! Of course not!" cried Bambi.

"Then do you want the sweet grass to turn brown?" asked his mother.

"No," said Bambi. "We eat the grass. We'd go hungry if that happened!"

"Well, then, my son," said Bambi's mother, "I think you'd better not wish for storms to go away forever. Their raindrops fill the streams and water the trees and grass."

Just then, the rain began to let up. Bambi's friends scampered through the underbrush and into Bambi's thicket.

"Look at the pond!" cried Flower.

Bambi peered through the thicket. The pond was alive with activity. The frogs were leaping and playing. A family of ducks were shaking their feathers and waddling into the water.

"Uh-oh," said Thumper. "That old bullfrog's gonna get a surprise."

Bambi watched the lily pad with the big bullfrog drift closer and closer to the line of ducklings. The last duckling wasn't paying attention, and he waddled right into the bullfrog's lily pad! The sudden collision sent the frog toppling off into the water with a startled *croak!* It surprised the duckling so much that it did an underwater somersault!

Bambi, Thumper, and Flower laughed.

"I guess I like thunderstorms after all," Bambi told his mother.

"You didn't like thunderstorms?" said Thumper. "That's silly! Why would you ever say a thing like that?"

# A New Job

**B**ernard was a simple mouse. He liked his nice, quiet job as a handymouse, he liked to eat a nice hunk of cheese for dinner, and he liked to fall asleep reading a nice book each night. He didn't like the number thirteen, black cats (or cats at all, actually!), or the color green.

Another thing that Bernard didn't like was danger of any kind. He liked to play things safe. Bernard steered clear of all animals bigger than he was, any cheese he had not purchased himself, and anything vaguely resembling a mousetrap.

So when the office he worked in announced it was moving its location from the basement of 1515 Hudson Street to 1313 Hudson Street, he knew it was time to find a new place of employment. One thirteen in the address would have been bad enough, but *two*? Well, it just would not do!

That afternoon, he bought a copy of the *Rodent Report*. Munching on his Limburger sandwich, he read the Help Wanted section.

"'Cheese tester,'" he read. That looked promising! But then he took a closer look at the ad and saw the words *experimental* and *hazardous*.

Bernard shook his head. He was never going to find a new job! He put the paper down next to him, but suddenly an ad caught his eye. *Desperately seeking handymouse*, it read. *Experience required. Apply at United Nations building, subbasement. Rescue Aid Society.*

"That's it!" he cried.

Since Bernard had more experience than any of the other applicants, the job was his!

"Congratulations!" said the French delegate.

That night, Bernard's friends took him out to celebrate his new job.

"The Rescue Aid Society," his pal said. "Wow. Could be exciting, don'tcha think?"

"Oh, no," replied Bernard. "I'm going to be the handyman. No danger. No intrigue. I'll be mopping floors. Fixing leaks. No adventure at all, you can count on that."

His friend raised his glass for a toast. "To your new job," he said.

"To my new job," said Bernard. "May it be safe, quiet, and nonadventurous. Just the way I like it!"

# Quincy's Dream

The Little Einsteins met in the clubhouse after school one day to talk about their upcoming mission. Everyone was excited, except Quincy. He didn't seem to be paying any attention.

"Are you daydreaming, Quincy?" teased Annie.

"I'm really tired," Quincy said. "I had this scary dream last night, and now I'm afraid to go back to sleep. I used to think I was really brave, but now I just feel silly."

"I'm sure even the bravest knight in the world has a scary dream sometimes," said Leo.

"But what should I do if I have another bad dream?" he asked.

"Do what I do," offered June. "Use your imagination to change what happens in your dream. If I have a dream about a big, scary tiger, I just use my imagination to turn him into a cuddly orange kitten."

Annie spotted something she thought could help Quincy. "A dream catcher!" she shouted. "We can use it to catch your bad dream, Quincy!"

Quincy was puzzled. "It looks like a spiderweb with feathers."

"Some Native American tribes believe that if you hang a dream catcher over your bed, you can 'trap' your bad dreams in its web," explained June.

"I've got a plan!" exclaimed Leo. "Catch your bad dream in this dream catcher tonight, and then bring it to the clubhouse tomorrow."

The next morning, Quincy brought the dream catcher to the clubhouse. Leo, Rocket, and the team jumped into his bad dream to show him how to change the ending. With his friends by his side, there was nothing to be afraid of!

Inside Quincy's dream, a famous painting had come to life.

"Yikes!" Annie gasped. "It's a monster!"

"Hey, you can't say I didn't warn you!" Quincy said.

"Okay," June said to the team, "everyone concentrate on the monster. Imagine that instead of stomping his feet in anger, he's actually dancing!"

Suddenly, the angry monster changed into a graceful ballerina.

"We did it!" shouted Leo.

Quincy was proud of himself, too. "You were right, guys. When you use your imagination, anything is possible!"

# Dino-Scare

"I am a failure as a carnivore!" groaned Rex the dinosaur. "I'm just not scary, Woody!"

"Now, now," said Woody soothingly. "Remember what's really important here. The main thing is that Andy plays with you, and you should be happy about that!"

"Red alert! Red alert! Andy's coming!" shouted Sarge, the Green Army Man sergeant. The toys raced back to their positions just in time. The door burst open, and Andy raced in.

"Sheriff Woody, I have a special assignment for you," Andy said, holding Woody in front of his face and assuming a grave look. "You're going to team up with Buzz Lightyear, Space Ranger!" He held Buzz in front of Woody so that they were face-to-face. "Alien dinosaurs from another planet have invaded!" he said.

Dropping Buzz and Woody on the floor with a loud clatter, Andy raced over to where Rex the dinosaur lay next to the toy box. He picked him up and stomped him across the room, roaring menacingly.

"Andy!" Andy's mother called from downstairs.

"Yeah, Mom?" Andy shouted.

"I need you to gather your dirty clothes for me! I'll bring you a basket!" she called.

"Okay, Mom!" Andy called back. Then an idea struck him. With a chuckle, Andy scooped up Rex. He stood next to the door, waiting for the sound of his mother's footsteps on the stairs.

"RAAAH!" roared Andy, jumping into her path as she came in. "I'm an alien dinosaur, here to take over your planet!"

"Oh my," Andy's mom said. "You certainly did scare me! Now, here." She thrust the basket into his arms and went into the laundry room.

Andy did as he was told. Scooping up big armloads of clothes, he tossed them into the basket. "Be back soon, Buzz and Woody," he said to the toys as he staggered toward the door with the basket. "Keep the universe safe while I'm gone, okay?"

As soon as the door had closed and the coast was clear, the toys began to stir. Rex hurried over to Woody. "I scared Andy's mom, didn't I? Didn't I?!" he said excitedly.

Woody grinned. "You bet you did, Rex. I guess you *are* scary after all."

# Milo's Underwater Summer

**M**ilo Thatch loved his new life with Princess Kida in the underwater city of Atlantis. But every so often, Milo found himself thinking of his old life back on the surface.

"I wonder what the weather's like today," he mused to Kida one day as he looked at his favorite photo of himself and his grandfather. "Sometimes in the summer we'd go on these great picnics. . . ."

Kida was afraid that Milo would start missing his former home so much that he might want to leave Atlantis. She decided to try to help him get over his homesickness by creating a little bit of the surface world right there in Atlantis. She planned a dinner party for that very evening and invited some of their Atlantean friends.

"This is nice," Milo said in Atlantean, which he now spoke fluently.

"Goot evoning," one of the guests said in halting English. "Thanks vera much for parting."

"Party," Kida corrected quickly as Milo gave her a confused look.

"What's going on?" he asked.

Kida smiled sheepishly. "We didn't have much time to practice," she explained to Milo. "I thought you'd like to hear English again. To make you feel more at home."

The next morning, Milo awoke to find a bright, glaring light shining directly into his eyes. "Ahhh!" he cried, shading his eyes against the glare. "What is that?"

"It's a crystal," Kida said. "It's meant to remind you of the sun. You know—to make you feel more at home."

"Why do you keep trying to make me feel more at home?" Milo asked.

Kida shrugged. "Because I don't want you to leave."

"Leave?" Milo said. "Why would I leave?"

"Because you're homesick," Kida replied.

"Well, yes, I suppose I am. But that doesn't mean I want to leave!" Milo said.

"It doesn't?" Kida asked.

"Of course not!" Milo said. "Even if I get a little homesick sometimes, I would never trade my wonderful new life in Atlantis for the one I had before." He smiled. "I still have my memories of the surface world, and a few mementos. And that's okay. Because I have much more down here . . . with you."

# The Hero of the Race

The tiebreaker race for the Piston Cup had started. But Lightning couldn't concentrate. He kept remembering the new friends he'd met in Radiator Springs. Somehow, winning no longer seemed that important.

Lightning had ruined the town's road when he had crashed there. Doc, the town judge, had forced him to fix it. But when the work was done, Doc had let the press know where Lightning was.

Doc had once been a racing champion. He didn't like young race cars like Lightning because one had replaced him. But Doc had started to change his mind about the young racing star.

As Lightning's mind drifted from the race, Doc's voice came over the radio: "I didn't come all this way to see you quit."

Lightning's Radiator Springs friends were in his pit—with Doc as his crew chief! "If you can drive as good as you can fix a road, then you can win this race with your eyes shut," Doc said.

Inspired by his friends, Lightning tore around the track, closing the gap.

Chick Hicks tried his usual dirty tricks, but Lightning was ready for him. Soon the rookie race car was winning! Chick and The King—a veteran race car racing his final race—were fighting for second place.

Just then, Chick rammed into The King! The veteran hit a wall. When Lightning saw The King's crumpled body, he remembered Doc's final crash. Lightning screeched to a stop inches from the finish line.

"What are you doing, kid?" Doc asked.

"I think The King should finish his last race," Lightning answered.

As he pushed The King over the finish line, the crowd erupted in cheers. Chick had won the Piston Cup, but Lightning was the hero of the race!

Lightning was offered a great new sponsorship deal, but he politely refused. He had decided to stay loyal to his original sponsor. But he did ask for one favor . . . a helicopter ride for his friend Mater.

Later, Lightning found Sally in Radiator Springs. The pretty car smiled at him. It looked as if the rookie race car had found a new home.

# A Whale of a Tale

"Hop aboard, explorers!" called Nemo's teacher, Mr. Ray.

Nemo, Tad, and the rest of the class jumped on the back of the big manta ray. It was special guest week, and they were going to the Drop-off. When they reached the reef's edge, a royal blue tang fish swam up to meet them.

"Hello, everyone," said the blue tang. "I'm Dory . . . um . . . am I? Yes! Just kidding! I'm Dory, and I'm very happy to be here!"

"Dory, can you teach us something about whales today?" asked Mr. Ray.

"Well, let's see. . . . Whales are very big, but they eat little creatures called krill. And I should know. One whale I met *almost* ate me!"

"Sandy Plankton said Nemo made up that story about how you and Nemo's dad got eaten by a whale!" said Tad.

"I did not make it up!" cried Nemo.

"Well," said Dory, "technically, Sandy Plankton is right. We weren't actually eaten by the whale. . . ." Tad smirked, until Dory added, "We were just in the whale's mouth for a mighty long time!

"You see, the whale was just giving us a ride to Sydney. I find if you talk to a whale beforehand, it clears up most ingestion issues," Dory explained.

"Excellent lesson!" said Mr. Ray. "Now teach us a few words in Whale."

"Oh, okay," said Dory. "Here's a phrase you can use if you're ever in trouble. Now repeat after me: 'Caaaaannnn yooooouuuu heeeeellllllp mmmeeee?'"

"Caaaaannnn yooooouuuu heeeeellllllp mmmeeee?" the class repeated.

"This is stupid," said Tad. "You didn't . . ."

Tad stopped talking. Everyone just stared at Dory in horror.

Slowly, Dory turned around. A blue whale was right behind her!

"Weeeee weerrrrre juuuuusssst praaaactiiiiiccccccinnnng!" Dory told the whale. "Nnnnnnooooo heeeeellllllp nnnnneeeedeeeed. Thaaaaanksssss aaaannnnyyyyywwwaaaaayyyyy!"

With a loud bellow, the whale wished her a nice day, then swam off.

"So, Tad, do you believe Dory now?" asked Nemo.

"Wow, that was *so* cool!" cried Tad. "I can't wait to tell Sandy Plankton how I was almost eaten by a whale!"

Nemo and Dory just sighed.

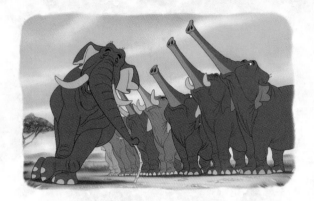

# Dawn Patrol

One day, Mowgli left the Man-village to visit his old friend Baloo the bear in the jungle.

"Why so sad, Mowgli?" asked Baloo.

"It's the dry season, and the river is getting low," said Mowgli. "My friends in the village are worried about running out of water."

"But what about the spring in the jungle?" asked Baloo. "It never goes dry."

Mowgli shook his head. "The spring is much too deep inside the jungle. It would take all day to get there from the village."

Bagheera the panther had overheard the conversation. He had an idea.

The next morning, Bagheera, Baloo, and Mowgli all waited by the spring. Before long, the ground shook with the approach of Colonel Hathi and his elephants.

"Here they come," said Bagheera. "Dawn Patrol."

Quickly, Bagheera, Baloo, and Mowgli hid in the bushes. They waited for the elephants to stop at the spring and take a long drink.

"Ready to try my plan?" Bagheera whispered to Mowgli. The boy nodded, and the two sprang from the bushes crying, "To the river! Quick! Everyone, as fast as you can!"

The elephants looked up in alarm.

"W-what's the m-meaning of this?" stammered the colonel.

"Shere Khan is coming! Run for the river!" called Mowgli.

Mowgli watched as the elephants stampeded through the jungle. They knocked down every tree between the spring and the river.

Now it was time for Baloo to play his part. "Hey, whoa!" cried Baloo, running up to the herd. "False alarm!"

"What's that?" asked Colonel Hathi.

"Shere Khan isn't coming after all," said Baloo.

As the elephants marched off, Mowgli grinned. "With this new path to the spring, my friends will never run out of water."

Bagheera nodded. "Good work," he said.

"Yes, it was," said Baloo with a laugh. "And you know what was good about it? Somebody else did the work for us!"

# Tough Audience

The sticker on the door read *Enter at Your Own Risk*. But Mike wasn't scared. He had never met a kid he couldn't crack up. Tossing his microphone from one hand to the other, Mike sauntered through the closet door to face his audience.

"Hey, how ya doin' tonight?" Mike greeted the kid. The boy in the race car pajamas just glared. "Did you hear the one about the monster who made it in show business? He really clawed his way to the top." Mike paused for a laugh, but the kid was silent.

"All right. I can see you're a tough audience. Enough of the B material." Mike pulled out all the stops. He told his best jokes. He worked the room. But the kid didn't even crack a smile. Mike prepared to let the one about the seven-legged sea monster fly when he heard tapping on the closet door.

Mike pulled the door open a crack. "I'm working here," he whispered.

Sulley poked his head in. "Mikey, you're dying. You've been on for twenty minutes and you're getting nothing. There are plenty of other kids to make laugh tonight. You can come back to this one later."

"No way," Mike hissed. "He loves me. When he laughs he's going to laugh big. I can feel it."

Just then, a rubber ducky sailed through the air and hit Mike in the eye. "See? He's throwing me presents."

"Cut your losses, Mikey. Let this one go." Sulley put a large hairy paw on Mike's head and urged him back through the door.

"I'm telling you, I've almost got him," Mike said through clenched teeth.

"And I'm telling you to give . . . it . . . up." Sulley pulled harder on Mike. Mike grabbed the door frame and braced himself. Suddenly Sulley lost his grip, and Mike flew backward, skidding on the rubber ducky and wiping out.

"Why, I oughta . . ." Mike leaped to his feet, ready to charge Sulley, but was interrupted by the sound of laughing. In fact, the kid was laughing so hard, tears streamed down his face.

Mike high-fived Sulley. "You know, some kids just go for the physical comedy," he said with a shrug.

# St. Patrick's Day Switcheroo!

One morning, Louie had an idea. "Hey," he said to his brothers, "are you two wearing green for St. Patrick's Day?"

"Of course," said Dewey.

"Me too," said Huey.

Louie gestured to the green shirt and hat he wore every day. "I bet we could *really* confuse Uncle Donald!"

The three boys chuckled as they headed toward the kitchen. While Huey and Dewey hid in the hallway, Louie walked in and sat down next to Donald Duck, who was reading the newspaper at the breakfast table.

"Morning, Uncle Donald," said Louie.

"Morning, Louie," Donald replied. "Will you go get your brothers? Breakfast is ready."

"Okay," Louie replied, leaving the room.

Next, Dewey walked into the kitchen and sat down. "Morning, Uncle Donald," he said.

Donald looked up only briefly from his paper. "I thought I told you to go get your brothers, Louie," he said.

"No, you didn't," Dewey replied. "And I'm not Louie."

Donald looked up and scrutinized Dewey's face. "Oh," he said. "I'm sorry, Dewey. Would you go get your brothers?"

"Okay," Dewey replied.

A few minutes later, Huey walked into the kitchen and sat down at the table.

Donald glanced up from the newspaper. "Well, where are they?" he asked Huey impatiently.

"Where are who?" said Huey.

"Your brothers," Donald replied. "I asked you to go get them."

"No, you didn't," said Huey.

"Yes, I—" Donald looked up from the paper and stared hard at Huey. "Oh . . . Huey," he said, realizing his mistake. "I thought you were . . . Hey!" Donald looked at Huey suspiciously. "Are you three trying to confuse me?"

Huey looked up at Donald with a blank stare. "Whatever do you mean, Uncle Donald?"

"It's St. Patrick's Day," said Louie, coming in from the hallway.

"Yeah," said Dewey, following Louie into the kitchen. "That's why we're all wearing green. Happy St. Patrick's Day, Uncle Donald!"

# Out of Order

Sergeant Calhoun, the leader of the soldiers in Hero's Duty, was yelling at Wreck-It Ralph.

"Never interfere with a first-person shooter!" she cried.

Ralph belonged in his own game, Fix-It Felix, Jr., but he wanted to get the Medal of Heroes from Hero's Duty to prove he could be a Good Guy. He was fed up with always being the Bad Guy in his game.

Meanwhile, a girl who was playing in Litwak's arcade moved to play on Fix-It Felix, Jr. She put in the coins to play, but there was a problem . . . Ralph wasn't there to wreck anything!

Luckily, someone had seen Ralph enter Hero's Duty. Felix decided to bring Ralph back. "I can fix this!" he told everyone.

Over in Hero's Duty, Ralph had just climbed the cy-bug tower, which contained the Medal of Heroes. The arcade was now closed for the night, so no game players could see him. The tower contained loads of cy-bug eggs. Every time the game started, the eggs hatched and the soldiers had to battle hundreds of dangerous cy-bugs! Ralph

tiptoed past the eggs. The Medal of Heroes was his!

Just then, Ralph knocked over an egg. It cracked open and a baby cy-bug hurled itself onto Ralph's face. Ralph fell backward into an escape pod. Instantly, the escape pod launched into the sky—with the cy-bug still attached to Ralph's face!

At the same moment, Felix stepped into Hero's Duty. "Have you seen my colleague, Ralph?" he asked Calhoun.

Suddenly, the escape pod zoomed past. They could see Ralph—and the cy-bug—inside! Ralph's escape pod ricocheted through Game Central Station and finally landed in a world made entirely of sweets. Ralph was ejected from the ship, and the cy-bug disappeared in a lake of toffee.

Ralph was in a racing game called Sugar Rush. His medal had landed in a peppermint tree!

Suddenly, a girl named Vanellope showed up. She thought the medal was a gold coin. "Race you for it!" she yelled.

Poor Ralph lost the race—and his medal! How would Ralph ever prove he was a Good Guy now?

# Money Matters

"Greetings, slotted pig," said Buzz.

"Hello, Buzz," said Hamm the piggy bank. "How are you getting used to life here in Andy's room?"

"Life on this planet is interesting," Buzz said. "I look forward to giving a full report to my commander upon my return to base."

Hamm rolled his eyes. Buzz had no idea he was not an actual space ranger. It would be funny if it weren't so . . . annoying.

"So, pig," Buzz continued. "Today I noticed Andy placing several round silvery discs into the slot on your back."

"Yes," began Hamm, "that was . . ."

"And now these silver discs reside in your stomach cavity?" Buzz interrupted.

"Well, yes," began Hamm, patting his full belly. "But . . ."

"Aha!" Buzz cried. "I have determined your power source! What an interesting life-form you are! This will definitely make it into my report!"

Hamm shook his head as Woody and the rest of the toys walked up to join them.

"What's going on?" Woody asked.

"Greetings, cowboy," said Buzz. "I was just inquiring about the pig's power source."

"He's talking about the coins in my belly," Hamm explained.

"No, Buzz," explained Bo Peep. "Those aren't power sources. They're money."

"What's money?" Buzz asked.

"It's what people use to get the things they need—like food, or toys, or comic books," said Woody.

Buzz thought for a moment. "Perhaps I need to procure some of this power source . . . um, I mean money . . . for myself," he suggested thoughtfully.

The rest of the toys started chattering excitedly. They had never thought about what they would do if they actually had some money! Woody started daydreaming about what he would buy. Then he looked around and laughed out loud. "We're toys!" he said. "Toys can't just go to the store and walk up to the counter to buy things!"

"Speak for yourself, cowboy," said Buzz. "Perhaps you've forgotten—I am not a toy!"

Hamm shook his head at the crazy, mixed-up space ranger. "I give up!" he said.

# A Game of Robin Hood

"Let's play Robin Hood!" Skippy shouted to his friends Tagalong, Toby, and Sis.

"All right," agreed Tagalong. "I'll be Robin's best friend, Little John. Toby can be the mean old Sheriff of Nottingham!"

"Well, then, I will be Maid Marian," said Sis.

Robin Hood was loved by the people, because he robbed from the rich and gave to the poor. Nowadays many people were needy, for they were taxed heavily by the Sheriff of Nottingham. Everyone knew that the Sheriff was in league with the evil Prince John, and that they used the tax money for their own gain. Prince John's brother, King Richard, was the true king of England. But King Richard was fighting in the Crusades far away. He couldn't protect his people, so someone else had to—and that someone was Robin Hood!

"Hands up, sirrah!" said Skippy gleefully. He and Tagalong pretended to raid Toby's carriage. "We shall lighten your wallet today and give it away to the worthy citizens you have been taxing so heavily."

"Drat! My evil plans have been foiled again!" snarled Toby, handing over his pretend money.

"One day I'm going to get you, Robin Hood!" Toby continued.

Skippy laughed. "You'll never find me, Sheriff!" he cried. "If you come into Sherwood Forest, we will give you such a whipping that you'll wish you'd never heard of Robin Hood!"

Sis giggled, then ran over to a table and climbed up on top of it. "Oh, Robin! Robin!" she cried. "Help me, my darling, my own true love! That mean old Prince John has locked me up in this high tower! He heard that we are in love, and he intends to prevent us from ever being together!"

Suddenly, the children froze. Someone had chuckled from behind the door of a nearby cottage. "Uh-oh," Skippy whispered. "We're toast. It's got to be the Sheriff of Nottingham!"

"He'll lock us up and throw away the key!" Toby said, his voice shaking.

Just then the "Sheriff" stepped out from behind the door. It was Robin Hood!

"Keep up the good work, kids!" he said with a merry laugh. And then he bounded away into Sherwood Forest.

# The Twilight Bark

The puppies had just finished watching their favorite show, *The Thunderbold Adventure Hour*. Now it was time for bed. And that meant a bedtime story!

Pongo and Perdita had decided it was time to tell the puppies the legend of the Twilight Bark.

"Sounds cool," Pepper cheered.

"What's the Twilight Bark?" asked Freckles.

"Legend has it," Perdy began, "that there's a special way that dogs can send one another messages. It stretches from the farthest side of the city all the way into the countryside."

Penny gasped. "Wow! Why would you need to do that?"

"Sometimes," Pongo began, "you need to communicate information from one place to another quickly and you don't have time to go to the other place yourself."

"I don't need any Twilight Bark!" Patch said. "I can take care of myself."

"Fat chance!" Lucky said under his breath.

"What do you know?" Patch barked back.

"If you ever get into any trouble," Perdy told the pups, "just go to the top of the highest hill you can find and bark out your message, and the members of the Twilight Bark will pass it along until someone can come to help you."

"That sounds like a bunch of baloney," Patch told his parents.

"Patch!" Pongo scolded his son. "That isn't very nice."

Just then, Lucky started howling at the top of his lungs.

"What's gotten into you?" Perdy asked.

"I'm trying out the Twilight Bark," Lucky said, "to get us rescued from Patch."

"Lucky," Perdy scolded him, "I want you to apologize to your brother."

"That's okay," Patch said. "I don't need his apology. I was right, anyway. All that howling and no word from the Twilight Bark!"

Just then, the doorbell rang. All of the puppies gasped and turned to look at Patch.

Perdy and Pongo smiled at each other. It was actually Roger returning from the store, but the puppies didn't need to know that!

# Float Like a Butterfly

One day, Dumbo's best friend, Timothy Q. Mouse, found Dumbo looking sad. "What's the matter, little guy?" the mouse asked the elephant. "Have people been teasing you about your ears again?"

Dumbo nodded. The little elephant looked totally miserable.

Timothy was trying to think of a way to cheer up his dear friend when he saw something. "Look, Dumbo!" he cried, racing over to a nearby fence post. "It's a butterfly cocoon!" Timothy said excitedly.

Dumbo came over to examine it.

"And look—it's about to hatch into a butterfly," said Timothy. He looked thoughtful for a moment, and then he turned to Dumbo. "You know what? You're a lot like the little caterpillar that made this cocoon."

Dumbo looked at Timothy, confused.

"Yep, it's true. You see, a caterpillar is something nobody really wants around much. They think it's kind of plain-looking, and it can't really do anything very interesting. But then one day, the caterpillar turns into a beautiful butterfly, and everyone loves it. And you know what? I think you're going to be that way, too. When you get older, everyone is going to admire you rather than tease you!"

Dumbo smiled gratefully at his friend and wiped away a tear with one of his long ears.

Suddenly, it started to rain.

"Oh, no!" cried Timothy. "The butterfly is going to get its new wings all wet. It won't be able to fly if it gets rained on. What'll we do? We need an umbrella!"

As Timothy looked this way and that for an umbrella, Dumbo smiled and unfurled his long ears. He draped them over the fence post so that they made a lovely roof for the insect, protecting it from the falling droplets of rain.

"Great idea!" said Timothy admiringly. The two friends stood there during the downpour, which didn't last very long. While they waited, they watched the beautiful new butterfly emerge from its cocoon and unfurl its colorful wings. When the rain stopped, the butterfly spread its wings (which were quite dry, thanks to Dumbo) and flew away.

# A Difficult Decision

Carl Fredricksen and Russell had flown to South America in Carl's house. Carl was an old man who had dreamed of being an explorer since he was just a boy. His wife, Ellie, had shared this same dream. But they never managed to save enough money to go anywhere, and sadly, Ellie had passed away.

Carl was so close to fulfilling Ellie's dream of seeing Paradise Falls. While walking toward the falls with the floating house in tow, he and Russell had met a strange female bird named Kevin and a talking dog named Dug. Dug was part of a pack of dogs who wanted to capture Kevin for their leader—the great explorer Charles Muntz!

Muntz thought Carl and Russell were trying to steal the bird from him, and he sent his pack of dogs after them. Dug blocked the other dogs' path with some rocks. But he couldn't stop the pack for long.

Luckily, Carl and Russell were holding on to the house by the garden hose. The wind lifted the house into the air, taking Carl and his friends with it! Muntz's dog grabbed Kevin's leg, but he lost his grip as they floated away.

Carl and his friends had escaped, but Kevin's leg was badly hurt. Russell realized that the bird needed help to get back to her babies.

Out of nowhere, a spotlight appeared and shone down on the bird. Muntz had followed them in his airship, the *Spirit of Adventure*!

Before Kevin could escape, a net shot out from the airship and trapped her. Carl tried to set her free.

"Get away from my bird!" Muntz snarled. Then he set Carl's house on fire!

Carl couldn't let his house go up in smoke—it held all his memories of Ellie. He quickly made the decision to give up Kevin instead.

The dogs dragged the wounded bird onto the airship. As Muntz lifted off with his prize bird, Carl ran to his house and beat back the flames.

"You gave away Kevin," Russell said.

Carl felt terrible, but what could he do?

"I didn't ask for any of this!" he snapped. "Now, whether you assist me or not, I am going to Paradise Falls."

# Buzz's Backpack Adventure

It was space day at school. Andy couldn't wait! He put Buzz in his backpack and set off for school.

In class, the teacher taught Andy and the other students about the solar system. Just then, the lunch bell rang. Andy and his friends went to eat lunch, leaving their bags behind.

With the kids gone, Buzz stepped out of Andy's backpack. All around him were models of the stars and planets. Buzz was thrilled! He loved anything having to do with space.

Just then, Buzz spotted a large cage. Inside was a hamster. Buzz had never seen one before. "Greetings, strange creature," he said. When the hamster didn't reply, Buzz lifted the lid off the cage so he could go inside.

Startled, the hamster jumped out of the cage! It ran into Buzz and sent him flying.

Andy and his friends still weren't back, so Buzz looked inside some of their desks. He found old chewing gum, broken yo-yos, and moldy sandwiches, but no sign of the hamster. He put down a desktop and made his way over to a table. There he spotted some creatures from space!

Or at least, he thought they were from space. They were actually toy aliens that Andy and his friends had made from clay.

"Greetings," Buzz said. "Have you seen a strange, furry creature?"

When the clay aliens didn't answer, Buzz tried to shake hands with one of them to show that he was friendly. But as he moved the alien's arm, it fell off.

"Sorry about that!" Buzz cried.

Buzz looked around. The room was a mess. Buzz knew he had to clean up—and fast!

The bell rang just as Buzz finished cleaning. The space ranger quickly hopped back into Andy's backpack. Buzz looked at the cleaned-up classroom. No one will ever know what happened, he thought.

Suddenly, Andy's classmates pointed at the chalkboard ledge. The hamster was sitting on it.

"How did you get out?" the teacher asked, bringing it back to its cage.

The hamster smiled at Buzz. The space ranger smiled back. He couldn't wait to tell Woody and the others about his exciting day. . . .

# Don't Be Alarmed

"CUT!" yelled Felipe from behind a video camera. "This film just doesn't have the razzle-dazzle I'm looking for. We need costumes, glitter, music—perhaps a few dancing nuts and bolts?"

"Or maybe all your film really needs is a new director!" Turner sneered.

"This is serious, Turner!" cried Felipe. "If we're going to be on the *Sheet Rock Hills Today* show tomorrow, we have to be prepared!"

Manny and the tools had been asked to talk about the importance of fire safety.

The next morning, Manny and the tools arrived on the set of *Sheet Rock Hills Today*. All the tools were excited, except for Rusty. He was a bit nervous.

The presenter of the show, Dwayne Bouffant, spoke into the camera. "Good morning, Sheet Rock Hills! Today, Manny Garcia and his tools are here to show us how to change the batteries in a smoke alarm."

"Thanks for having us here, Dwayne," said Manny. Then he turned to the audience. "We're here to remind everyone to test your smoke alarm each month."

"Press this button, like so," Pat said, tapping the button on the alarm. "If it beeps, it means your batteries are working!"

"You should change the batteries in your alarm at the same time each year," added Dusty.

All the tools looked at Felipe. It was his turn to show everyone how to put the new battery in the smoke alarm, but he just stared at the camera.

Rusty knew what to do. He picked up the new battery and explained how to insert it.

After the show, Dwayne shook Manny's hand. "Thanks again, Manny. That was a great segment!"

When Dwayne left, Manny and the tools gathered around Felipe.

They could tell he was upset about freezing up during the show.

"Aw, cheer up, Felipe," Squeeze said brightly. "I don't think anyone noticed."

"Do you really think so?" asked Felipe.

Squeeze nodded. "Besides, Rusty came to the rescue and put out the fire—so to speak!"

# Dawson Takes the Case

"My little boy is missing!" a sobbing Mrs. Mousington cried to Basil, the great mouse detective. "Can you help me find him?"

"I'm terribly sorry," said Basil. He was examining a brick wall very closely, looking for clues. "But I'm working on an important case for the queen. I don't have time."

"No, wait!" cried Dr. Dawson, Basil's partner. "Madam, if the great mouse detective is too busy, then perhaps I can offer you my services."

"A splendid idea!" said Basil.

Before Dawson left with Mrs. Mousington, Basil stopped him. "Don't forget this," he said, handing Dawson an umbrella.

"But it's a sunny day," said Dawson, puzzled. "Why would I ever need an umbrella?"

"A sunny day can turn dark quicker than you think," advised Basil.

Dawson shrugged and took the umbrella.

Mrs. Mousington took him to a shop with a tall tree in front of it. Dawson searched the area and found a long white hair. But a closer look told him this was not just any hair. It was a cat's whisker! Calling to a nearby bird, Dawson asked for a lift up.

On the shop's roof, Dawson saw a cat dozing. Beneath its paw was a tiny mouse's tail.

As the bird set Dawson down on the roof, he wondered how he was going to lift the cat's heavy paw. Then he remembered the umbrella! Using one end as a lever, he heaved. Beneath it he found Mrs. Mousington's terrified son.

Dawson pulled the little boy free. With relief, he waved at the boy's mother, who was waiting on the sidewalk below. But before Dawson could signal another bird for a ride down, the cat woke up.

Dawson opened his umbrella, scooped the little boy mouse in his arms, and jumped. The umbrella filled with air and slowed their fall until they landed gently on the sidewalk.

Back at the great mouse detective's house, Basil was delighted to hear how Dawson had saved the little boy.

"It was easy," Dawson told Basil. "Thanks to your umbrella, I'd call it an open-and-shut case!"

# Friday Night Fun

Mater looked out at all the sleeping tractors in the field. Then, as Lightning watched, he quietly drove up to one and honked. *Beep!* The startled tractor woke up, tipped over, and moaned as its wheels spun helplessly in the air.

Suddenly, headlights shone in the two friends' faces. It was Sheriff.

"You should know better," he said. "I'll see you both in traffic court tomorrow."

The next morning at court, Lightning and Mater were sentenced to community service.

"Why don't you help Ramone clean his shop?" Sheriff suggested.

"You bet," answered Lightning.

But as they cleaned, Mater accidentally knocked over a can of pink paint. The lid flew off, and the paint splattered Lightning.

"You sure do look purty in pink," said Mater.

"Let's see how you look in it!" shouted Lightning. He threw an open can of paint at Mater. After a few minutes, they were covered in paint!

When Ramone peeked in, he got splattered, too. "Look at my shop!" he cried. "Get out!"

The friends left the shop and drove to Doc's garage. "Boys, boys . . ." Doc sighed when he heard what they'd done. He gave them one last chance. "Go find Bessie and surprise Flo with a new paving job."

The friends started paving, but then they decided to race. They had so much fun that they forgot all about the paving job at Flo's. By the time they remembered, it was dark.

The next morning, Mater and Lightning drove over to Flo's. Just about everyone in Radiator Springs was hard at work, trying to finish the paving job. No one had been able to drive in for their breakfast fill-up!

Mater and Lightning knew they had made a mistake. It was up to them to fix the road.

A few hours later, they were done. The V8 Café looked fantastic, and everything finally went back to normal—until Friday night rolled around again. . . .

"Hey, buddy," whispered Mater to Lightning. "How 'bout a little tractor-tipping fun ternight?"

# A Rainy Day Adventure

It was a rainy day. Suddenly, a clap of thunder shook the Clubhouse. *BOOM!*

"Aw, phooey. I didn't think it was going to storm," said Donald. "Now we'll be stuck indoors with nothing to do!"

"There must be things we can do," said Mickey. "And we can get help from some Mouseketools! Oh, Toodles!"

Toodles showed up with four ceramic frogs, some striped napkins, a toy pirate ship, and the Mystery Mouseketool.

"What is that noise?" said Mickey.

"Oh, pickle juice!" said Donald. "It's water dripping through a leak in the roof!"

"We need a Mouseketool," said Mickey. "Let's use the ceramic frogs to catch the drops of water in their open mouths. We've got ears! Say cheers!" said Mickey. Everyone grabbed a ceramic frog and placed it under a leak.

"I'm hungry," said Goofy. "Let's go to the kitchen and get a snack!"

Everyone hurried to the kitchen. Dirty bowls and baking trays were everywhere! They decided to clean up before their snack. Donald carried dirty dishes to the sink. Daisy put away ingredients. Mickey turned on the water to start washing the dishes.

"Gee, with all the rain and the water from washing the dishes, it feels like we've had a boatload of water today!" said Mickey.

"Being on a boat would be fun," said Goofy.

"Or a pirate ship!" said Minnie.

"That's it!" said Donald. "Let's be pirates!"

Mickey flipped the Silly Switch and the bathtub appeared. Everyone took a turn sailing their toy pirate ship.

"We're looking for sunken treasure!" said Donald.

"It's time for the Mystery Mouseketool!" said Mickey. "It's gold coins. Super cheers!" said Mickey. "I'm going to hide these coins throughout the Clubhouse. Each one of you has to find a coin and bring it back."

The friends played and played.

"Who cares about the rain?" said Daisy. "We pirates know how to have fun no matter where we are!"

Mickey smiled. No one even realized that the rain had stopped.

# The Den of Doom

"Where are we going, Baloo?" Mowgli asked. He and Baloo had been traveling through the jungle for a while now.

"Have you ever heard of the Den of Doom, Man-cub?" replied Baloo in a hushed voice.

Mowgli gasped. "The Den of Doom? They say that the Den of Doom is a giant cave filled with bears who will eat anything—or anyone! They say that even Shere Khan is afraid of them!" he exclaimed.

"Mmm-hmm," said Baloo. "They do say that. They also say that all of the bears in the Den of Doom are over eight feet tall, that their teeth are green and razor-sharp, and that their battle cry is so loud that the whales in the ocean hear it and shake with fright."

"And we're *going* there?" Mowgli squeaked. "We can't!"

"Too late, Man-cub," Baloo said with a grin. "We're already here!" He picked Mowgli up and strode right into a thicket. The boy looked around in surprise.

Mowgli had expected to see tons of fierce, angry bears. Instead, he saw hundreds of relaxed, happy bears having a really good time. Bears were swimming in a small pond, splashing and laughing. Bears were resting in the cool shadows of the cave. Bears were playing tag out in the clearing and chomping on piles of ripe, delicious fruit. It was, in short, a bear party.

"I don't understand," Mowgli said to Baloo. "This is the Den of Doom?"

"Yep," Baloo said happily, grabbing a palm frond and fanning himself with it. "It used to be called the Den of Delights, but we had to change the name. See, everyone in the jungle knew that the Den of Delights was the most fun place around. We bears never turned anyone away from our party. But then it got so crowded that it just wasn't fun anymore. So we spread a few rumors, changed the name, and presto—it's the Den of Doom! Now no one bothers us bears anymore."

"But what about me?" Mowgli said anxiously. "I'm not a bear."

"You're an honorary bear, Mowgli," Baloo replied with a smile. "You sure have enough fun to be one."

## MARCH
# 30

# The Best Gift Ever

Other than Dumbo's mother, Mrs. Jumbo, all the elephants at the circus made Dumbo feel like a nobody. But Timothy Q. Mouse was different. Since the day he and Dumbo had met, Timothy had encouraged Dumbo. Dumbo was so happy to have a friend like Timothy! He wanted to do something nice for him.

Dumbo decided to give Timothy a gift. At feeding time, he put aside a bale of hay. Then he lugged the hay behind the Big Top and looked around for Timothy. He found him lounging in the shadow of the lion's cage and plopped down the hay bale.

"Hiya, Dumbo!" said Timothy. "What's with the hay?"

Using his trunk, Dumbo nudged the hay bale closer to Timothy.

"For me?" Timothy said. "Wow. Uh . . . thanks."

Dumbo's heart sank as he realized that mice didn't eat hay.

The next day, Dumbo came upon a patch of flowers. He picked a nice big bouquet and took it behind the Big Top to Timothy.

"Shucks, Dumbo," said Timothy. "You shouldn't have." Tiny Timothy took the

bouquet from Dumbo's outstretched trunk and promptly fell over, dropping the flowers everywhere.

Sadly, Dumbo realized the bouquet was too heavy for Timothy to enjoy.

The next day, under the Big Top, Dumbo spotted a bunch of balloons tied to a seat. Those wouldn't be too heavy for Timothy. They stayed up all by themselves. So Dumbo untied them and brought them to Timothy.

But when Timothy took hold of the balloon strings, the helium-filled balloons lifted him right off the ground! Dumbo quickly reached out with his trunk and pulled Timothy back to the ground.

With a disappointed sigh, Dumbo took the balloons back. Would he ever find a good gift for Timothy? he wondered.

"Dumbo," Timothy said, "I wanted to thank you for giving me the best gift ever."

Dumbo's eyes widened in surprise. What could Timothy mean? Every gift he had given him had been wrong.

"You're my best friend," Timothy said. "And that's the best gift I could ever ask for."

# The Game

'Hey, guys!" said Woody as he gazed out Andy's window. "Check this out."

In Andy's backyard, Andy and his friends were playing a game of football.

"So *that's* what this thing's for," said Rex, picking up a small blue football.

"I have an idea," said Woody. "Why don't we play our own game of football in here?"

The toys agreed. Andy's bed would be the field, and Woody and Buzz would each be a captain. Woody chose Rex, Hamm, Slinky Dog, and Bo Peep. Buzz ended up with Sarge, Jessie, and Bullseye. But who else should he pick? Buzz looked around Andy's room at all the eager toys . . . and then he saw it! The bobble-head football player that Andy had brought in just the other day. A real football player, with a helmet and everything!

"I pick him!" Buzz declared. "C'mon, Number Three. You're gonna win me a football game!

"Okay, team," Buzz said as they gathered in their huddle. He pointed to a play drawn out on Etch-a-Sketch. "Number Three . . . could you stop nodding for one second? You run straight and watch for me to throw you the ball. Got it?"

The football player nodded eagerly. But no sooner had Buzz fired a pass than he realized Number Three was never going to catch it. His head was bobbing so much, he couldn't see the ball—much less the players. Bo Peep snatched the ball out of the air and brought it back for a touchdown.

"Okay, team," Buzz said as they huddled together again. "This time let's really show 'em what we're made of. Sarge, you block Rex and Hamm. Jessie and Bullseye, you block Bo Peep and Slinky Dog. Don't worry about Woody. I'll take care of him. Then, Number Three, I'll hand the ball off to you."

Again, the football player nodded like crazy.

But instead of taking the ball when Buzz tried to hand it to him, all the bobble-head football player did was nod . . . and nod . . . and nod. He probably would have kept nodding all day if Slinky Dog hadn't run up and accidentally knocked him over on his face.

Buzz sighed. "Anybody up for a game of checkers?" he asked.

# And They're Off!

"What are you doing, eh?" Kenai looked up to see Rutt and Tuke standing and staring in disbelief. The two goofy moose were trying to determine just what Koda, the young bear cub who was traveling with Kenai, was doing.

"Koda is watching those centipedes," Kenai replied.

Koda looked up. "They're racing," he said.

Rutt looked surprised. "Gee, I didn't think centipedes knew how to race."

"Everybody knows how to race," Tuke told Rutt. "Even a hoof-for-brains like you."

Koda's eyes sparkled. "That's a great idea!" he said. "You guys should have a race! Ready—set—go!"

Both moose stood still, staring at him.

"Where are we going?" Rutt asked.

"You're just supposed to go!" Koda cried. "You're racing, remember?"

Tuke stepped forward. "Come on, Rutt. Keep up."

"No! You're not supposed to tell him to keep up!" Koda cried. "You're supposed to run away from him!"

So Tuke took off at a gallop. But Rutt just stood there watching them.

"Well?" Kenai said. "Aren't you going to run after him?"

"Run after him? Why would I do that, eh?" The moose looked confused.

Koda growled with frustration. "Because that's what you do in a race!"

Rutt nodded. Then he ambled off after Tuke.

The two bears glanced at each other. "Even the centipedes could beat those two," Koda whispered to Kenai.

Kenai laughed. "Let's follow them."

First the bears came upon Tuke, who had stopped to eat twigs. Then they found Rutt rolling in the mud. When Tuke caught up to Rutt, the two started gossiping about some squirrels they knew.

"Maybe some animals just aren't meant to race," Koda said sadly.

Kenai could tell the little bear was disappointed. "You may be right," he said. "But I have an idea."

"What?" Koda asked.

Kenai grinned. "Race you to the river!" he cried. And he took off with Koda chasing him happily, laughing all the way.

# The Sweetest Songs of All

"Why is Quasimodo so sad?" asked Hugo.

"Judge Frollo has commanded that he never leave Notre Dame Cathedral," answered Victor. "He's lonely because he has no friends."

Just then Quasimodo appeared.

"Good morning, Quasi!" Hugo cried. "Nice day for ringing bells."

"I guess so," Quasimodo replied, staring at the people far below.

"Cheer up! What do they have down there that we don't have up here?" Hugo asked.

Quasimodo frowned. "I don't know, because I've never been there. But I hear people laughing and singing."

Then Victor spoke. "The sweetest songs of all can be heard in this tower, if you do what I tell you to."

"I will!" Quasimodo cried.

"Then fetch a piece of firewood and a knife from the kitchen," Victor commanded.

Quasimodo quickly returned with both.

"I want you to carve statues of lots of different birds," said Victor.

Quasimodo nodded. For two days, he worked. On the third day, he showed Hugo his first carving.

"Wow, that really looks like a dove," said Hugo.

"I'm going to carve a finch next," Quasimodo vowed.

Over the next few weeks, Quasimodo carved hundreds of birds out of wood—larks and thrushes and robins and sparrows. Each statue was better than the last. He worked so hard that he nearly forgot he was lonely.

Finally, he showed Victor and Hugo a carving of a beautiful nightingale.

"It is your best work of all," said Victor.

Quasimodo was so proud that he set his bird on the highest tower so they could all admire it.

The next morning, he was surprised to see two real birds perched next to his statue. More birds soon arrived. Some even built nests. Soon, hundreds and hundreds of birds lived in Notre Dame. They woke Quasimodo with their songs in the morning and they sang him to sleep at night.

Victor had told Quasimodo the sweetest songs of all could be heard at Notre Dame, and he was right. Since that day, birds have always lived in Notre Dame Cathedral.

# A True Adventure

Carl Fredricksen was in South America with a young stowaway named Russell. They had flown there in Carl's house, with thousands of balloons tied to the roof! Since arriving in South America, Russell had made a new friend, a bird he called Kevin. They had also met a talking dog called Dug, whose mission it was to capture Kevin.

Although Carl did not like Kevin, he promised Russell he would look after the bird.

One morning, the bird left for home. It turned out that Kevin was a mother! She had to get back to her babies. Kevin had not been gone long when three fierce dogs burst from the bushes.

"Where is the bird?" snarled their leader. The dogs were part of Dug's pack. When they found out that he had lost the bird, they insisted on taking Carl and Russell back to their master.

The dogs led Carl and Russell to a huge cave. Inside, Carl got a surprise. The dogs' master was famous explorer Charles Muntz, Carl's childhood hero!

Muntz thought Carl and Russell were trying to steal the bird from him. "Get them!" he told his dogs.

With Kevin and Dug's help, Carl and Russell escaped. But Muntz tracked them down, and he set Carl's house on fire! Carl couldn't let his house go up in smoke. As he ran to beat out the flames, Muntz's dogs grabbed Kevin. Russell was horrified.

Carl felt terrible, but he didn't know what to do. He pulled the house the rest of the way to Paradise Falls without Russell's help. Carl had finally kept his promise to his wife, Ellie, but he still felt sad. He wished Ellie could have been on the adventure with him.

Inside the house, Carl found his wife's adventure book. He turned through the pages. To his astonishment, they were filled with photos of their life together! At the end was a message from Ellie. It read: *Thanks for the adventure. Now go have a new one.*

Carl realized that Ellie had gotten her wish after all. Their life together had been her true adventure. And now it was time for his next adventure—to help Russell save Kevin!

# Tigger's Moving Day

Tigger loved to bounce. But he kept bouncing into things in his house.

"Tigger, you don't have enough bouncing room in this little house," said Rabbit. "We've got to find you a bigger house. That's all there is to it!"

Soon Tigger and Rabbit found a wonderful new house. "It *is* a bouncy house," said Tigger. "The kind of house tiggers like best!" He bounced, and he didn't bump into anything. "But," he said, sighing, "I won't live next door to little Roo anymore."

"I know you'll miss being so close to Kanga and Roo," said Christopher Robin, "but now you'll live much closer to me. Just think of the fun we can have being neighbors."

Kanga told Tigger she would bring Roo to visit. Tigger felt better and invited everyone to stay awhile. But Rabbit put his paws on his hips. "We aren't finished yet. We need to move all your things from your old house to this house," he explained. Rabbit told everyone to bring all the boxes they could find to Tigger's old house.

Soon everyone arrived with their boxes. "Wow! Boxes are fun!" cried Roo as he and Tigger bounced in and out of the boxes everyone had brought.

"There'll be time for fun later," grumbled Rabbit.

Tigger packed all his games and his stuffed animals in a box. Rabbit packed Tigger's dishes. Kanga packed Tigger's hats and scarves. Pooh and Piglet packed Tigger's food. Soon Eeyore arrived with his donkey cart. Christopher Robin and Owl hoisted Tigger's bed and table and chairs onto the cart.

After his friends had gone, Tigger put his things just where he wanted them. When he was finished, he sat down to rest.

Hmmm. Seems like an awfully quiet house, he thought to himself.

Just then, Tigger heard a little voice.

"Halloo!" the voice called.

"Roo!" cried Tigger. "Kanga! Come on in!"

Tigger soon heard all his friends calling outside his new door. They had all had brought housewarming presents!

"Our work's all done," said Rabbit at last. "Now it's time for fun!"

# Moon Mater

Mater and Lightning McQueen were looking up at a large full moon.

"Yep," said Mater, "I've been up there."

"Pffft! You have not," Lightning said.

But Mater insisted. He began to tell a story about the time he went to the moon. A moon buggy named Impala Thirteen was stuck on the edge of a crater!

"He needs a tow!" cried one of the forklifts who worked at NASCA. Just then Roger the space shuttle saw Mater driving by. Mater happily agreed to help.

On the day of his flight, Mater rolled onto the space shuttle and strapped himself in. Smoke spilled out of the booster rockets at the base of the launchpad. Finally the shuttle rocketed into the sky.

"We have liftoff!" Mission Control announced.

As Roger flew into space, he whooped with joy. "Wooooooo-hooooooo!" Inside the shuttle, Mater looked out the window. "See ya later, Earth."

Soon Roger's rockets had carried them deep into space. They were nearly at the moon!

"Operation Tow Mater is a go!" Mission Control said over the radio. It was time for Mater's moon landing. He floated out of the shuttle and into space.

"Good luck," Roger said. "See you on Earth." The shuttle began the trip home. The rescue mission was up to Mater now.

Using his jets, Mater steered himself toward the surface of the moon. Slowly, he bounced over to the Impala Thirteen.

"Connect your rescue apparatus to the frontal structural component of the linear axle assembly," Impala Thirteen instructed.

"Uhh," Mater replied. "How 'bout I just give you a tow?" He fastened his tow hook, blasted his jets, and pulled the moon buggy free!

"Mission accomplished!" Impala Thirteen said. "Now take us home!"

Mater fired his jets and rocketed toward Earth with Impala Thirteen on his towline.

In Radiator Springs, Mater had just finished his story. "Oh, come on," Lightning said. "That did not happen."

Suddenly, Roger the space shuttle set down next to them. "Suit yourself," Mater said, and then he drove up a ramp into the shuttle.

# Market Day

Abu sat at the window gazing longingly toward the village.

"What's wrong, Abu?" asked Aladdin. "Do you want to go to the market?"

Abu nodded happily, and the pair set off. They had a wonderful afternoon visiting old friends. Abu played with Salim the goat, joked with Kahlil the ox, and teased Gamal the camel.

Aladdin saw how happy Abu was in the hustle and bustle of the busy marketplace. "You know, Abu," he said, "you can invite your friends from the marketplace to the palace anytime you'd like."

The next day, Abu disappeared at sunrise. When he returned, Salim and Kahlil were with him.

"Welcome," said Jasmine. "Please, make yourselves at home." But they already had. The goat was chewing on the curtains and the ox was eating the flowers in the garden.

"We can always buy new curtains or plant new flowers. The important thing is that Abu is happy again," Aladdin said.

The following day, Gamal and several other camels arrived. Jasmine was not pleased when they spat on the new carpet.

"Think of Abu," Aladdin told her.

The day after that, the fruit seller rolled through the palace with his cart. Next came the lady who sold dates, and the man who sold pottery.

"Isn't it wonderful that Abu has so many friends?" said Aladdin.

"It is," Jasmine agreed. "But have you noticed that we only see his friends coming and not going?"

"Hmmm . . . let's find out what's going on," Aladdin said.

The couple followed Abu as he led his guests out to the garden. The entire marketplace was there!

Aladdin burst out laughing. "I guess the next time Abu is feeling homesick, he doesn't need to go any farther than his own backyard!"

Jasmine sighed. "Aladdin, these people can't stay here." But when Jasmine saw the sad look on Aladdin's face, she added, "Well, maybe they could come back next month."

And so began a new tradition— "Palace Market Day," which happened once a month. And *that* made little Abu *very* happy!

# Buzz to the Rescue

"There you go, pardners," Andy said as he packed Woody, Jessie, and Bullseye into his backpack. He was taking them to Cowboy Camp. Jessie couldn't wait!

Just then, Andy's mom poked her head into his room. "You know the rules. You can only take one toy to camp with you."

Andy sighed. He lifted Jessie and Bullseye out of the bag and placed them on the windowsill. Then he left his room. Jessie climbed down from the window and flopped into a box full of books.

Suddenly, a Green Army Man yelled, "Red alert!" Someone was coming. It was Molly's babysitter. She picked up the box of books and took it to the attic. The toys looked at each other in shock. Jessie was still inside the box!

"We've got to do something!" Buzz cried.

In the attic, Jessie looked for a way back to Andy's bedroom. But the attic door wouldn't budge. Suddenly, she had an idea. She found a jump rope, made a lasso, and threw the loop over the window lock. Jessie opened the window

a few inches and crawled outside.

Just then, she heard someone fiddling with the attic doorknob. Oh, no, she thought. The babysitter! Jessie grabbed the rope and jumped.

But the noise wasn't the babysitter at all. It was the other toys opening the attic door to rescue Jessie. Buzz gasped when he spotted the open window. Then he saw Jessie hanging on to a jump rope.

"Don't let go, Jessie!" he shouted. "I'm coming for you!"

Buzz spread his wings. Then, taking a deep breath, he dove out the window. Jessie looked up and saw her friend falling toward her. Thinking fast, she swung her legs out and caught Buzz. The two toys swung forward—right through Andy's open window! The rest of the toys raced down the stairs to Andy's room.

"We saved Jessie!" Buzz announced.

Jessie laughed. "Saved *me*?" She was the one who had rescued Buzz!

Jessie looked at her friends. They were all smiling. "Thanks, everyone!" she said. "Even though I didn't get to go to Cowboy Camp, this has been the best adventure ever! Yee-hah!"

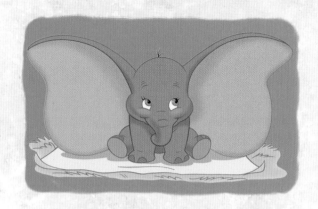

# 'Ears a Job for You, Dumbo!

It had been a hard day for little Dumbo. It was bad enough that everyone made fun of his ears. But now they had put his mother in a cage!

What made things even worse was that Dumbo didn't have anything to do. It seemed that he was the only creature in the circus who didn't have a purpose.

Dumbo heaved a sigh and went for a walk through the circus tents. Soon he found himself among the refreshment stands. Everyone here had a job, too. Some were squeezing lemons to make lemonade. Others were popping popcorn or roasting peanuts. Wonderful smells filled the air.

Finally, Dumbo came to a little cotton candy wagon. Dumbo wanted a taste, but there were so many customers that he couldn't get close enough.

Suddenly Dumbo heard a loud buzzing. Then all the customers waved their hands over their heads and ran away from the wagon. The smell of sugar had attracted a swarm of nasty flies!

Dumbo reached out his trunk to smell the delicious cotton candy.

"Not you, Dumbo!" the cotton candy man cried. "It's bad enough chasing away flies. Do I have to chase away elephants, too?"

Poor Dumbo was startled. With a snort, he sucked cotton candy right up his nose.

*Aaaachoo!* When he sneezed, Dumbo's ears flapped and something amazing happened.

"Remarkable!" the cotton candy man cried. "All the flies are gone. They think your ears are giant flyswatters!" The cotton candy man patted Dumbo's head. "How would you like a job?"

Dumbo nodded enthusiastically and set to waving his ears. Soon the cotton candy wagon was the most popular refreshment stand in the circus—and had the least flies. But best of all, Dumbo now had something to do to take his mind off his troubles. He was still sad, but things didn't seem quite so bad. And who knew? Perhaps soon he'd have his mother back.

"I wonder what other amazing things those big ears can do," said the cotton candy man, giving Dumbo a friendly smile. "I'll bet they carry you far. . . ."

# Dishes, Dishes, Dishes

"Hmmph." Jim Hawkins grabbed another plate from the enormous pile of dishes he was scrubbing and dunked it into the sudsy bucket. "This is not the adventure I had in mind," he said grumpily.

Jim had been dreaming about finding Treasure Planet since he was a kid. And he was finally doing it! But somehow, working in the galley doing dishes for some crazy cyborg had never been a part of his fantasy.

With a sigh, Jim rinsed the plate he was holding and grabbed another one. He wished he was allowed to do something (besides mopping) up on deck. But no. He was stuck in the kitchen, washing dishes. Alone.

Being alone was practically the worst part of it all. It was getting to be that Jim even looked forward to Silver's company. Sure, he was a weird old guy with a creepy cyborg eye. But at least he told some good tales of spacers, and he was better than no company at all.

Yawning, Jim dipped the last dish in the bucket, scrubbed it, rinsed it, and wiped it dry. Then he added it to the pile of clean dishes. "There," Jim said with a sigh. But when he looked back, another dish was sitting beside his washtub.

"Hmm. Must've missed one," he said, picking up the plate. "Now *that's* got to be it," Jim said, drying his hands on a towel. He leaned back on his stool. But what he saw nearly caused him to fall over. Another dirty dish was waiting to be cleaned!

"I *know* I got the last one!" Jim rubbed his eyes. Maybe he was more tired than he thought. But when he opened his eyes, the dish was still there. "I've been in the kitchen too long," Jim mumbled.

By the time he cleaned it, another had appeared in its place! Jim had to get out of the kitchen. He was starting to go crazy.

Suddenly, the dish he was washing slipped out of his hands. A pink blob burst out of the soapy water, sputtering and giggling.

"Morph!" Jim couldn't help but smile at the little blob of protoplasm and his practical joke. "Thanks for all of your help with the dishes," he said with a laugh.

# Nemo and the Ghost-Light Fish

Nemo loved school. So did his friends Tad, Pearl, and Sheldon. Their teacher, Mr. Ray, made everything so much fun! He took his students all over the reef.

One day, Mr. Ray took his students exploring and gave them an assignment. "Okay, explorers," he said. "Let's see if each of you can find a shell."

Nemo was searching through some seaweed when he heard an odd noise. He looked up and saw his friends bolting out of a nearby cave, screaming loudly.

"What's the matter?" Nemo asked.

"It's a g-g-ghost fish!" Sheldon replied fearfully.

"Yeah, right," Nemo replied.

Just then, Tad realized he had lost the shell he'd found. "I must have dropped it in there. But I'm not going back for it!"

"Don't worry," said Nemo. "I'll find it." Nemo swam bravely into the cave. "See?" he said to himself. "Nothing to be afraid of."

Then Nemo froze. On the cave wall was a huge fish-shaped shadow! He took a deep breath. "Uh, excuse me, Mr. Ghost Fish?" he asked.

"A ghost fish?!" a tiny voice said nervously.

Nemo followed the voice. To his surprise, the ghost fish was actually a tiny glow-in-the-dark fish!

"Don't be afraid," Nemo said. "My name's Nemo. What's yours?"

"I'm Eddy," replied the little fish. "You mean there's no ghost fish?"

Nemo explained the whole funny story.

"By the way," said Nemo. "How do you glow like that?"

Eddy shrugged. "I just do," he replied.

Nemo thought of someone who would know more about Eddy's glow—Mr. Ray! So Nemo invited Eddy to meet everyone.

Outside, Nemo rejoined his friends.

"I didn't find your shell," Nemo said to Tad. "But I did find your ghost fish!"

Everyone wanted to know what made Eddy glow. "Good question," Mr. Ray replied. "There are tiny glow-in-the-dark organisms inside these patches on either side of Eddy's jaw."

Everyone *oohed* and *aahed*.

Mr. Ray smiled at Nemo. "I think you deserve an A in Exploring today, Nemo!" he said.

# The New Kid

It was a beautiful morning in Sheet Rock Hills, and Manny and the tools were getting ready for their first big job of the day. "We're going to help out our new neighbors, Mr. and Mrs. Ayala," said Manny. "They just moved to Sheet Rock Hills and need our help setting up their son Marcelo's seesaw."

When Manny and the tools arrived at the Ayalas' house, Marcelo looked very sad. Mr. Ayala explained that Marcelo missed his friends back in Argentina. Marcelo was worried about meeting new people.

"You'll make lots of new friends, Marcelo!" cheered Squeeze. "The first time I came to Manny's Repair Shop, I was worried that nobody would like me. But then I met Rusty. He's a lot like me, 'cause we both turn things with our teeth."

"Marcelo, I think you will be surprised to learn just how much you have in common with the kids in Sheet Rock Hills," Manny said. "I bet you'll discover that you're not so different from them after all."

"Well . . . maybe you're right," said Marcelo.

With Marcelo's help, Manny and the tools put the seesaw together. Then Manny saw Nelson playing in the yard next door. It gave him an idea.

"Marcelo, I have a bit of a problem. I want to make sure the seesaw is the right height for you," Manny began, "but I can't do it without someone sitting on the other end."

The tools called Nelson over. "*Hola*, Nelson," said Manny happily. "This is your new neighbor, Marcelo."

Nelson smiled. "Hi, welcome to the neighborhood! Hey, that's a neat seesaw."

Marcelo grinned. "Thanks! Um, would you like to try it out with me?"

"Sure!" exclaimed Nelson, climbing onto the seesaw. "Wow, you're so lucky—moving to a different place, getting introduced to new people."

Marcelo was surprised. "Lucky?"

"Yeah, I bet everyone can't wait to meet you," Nelson explained. "Being the new kid in town must be really exciting!"

Marcelo gave Manny and the tools a wink as he rode on the seesaw. "Well, it certainly has its ups and downs!"

# A Deal with Vanellope

Wreck-It Ralph was in a racing game called Sugar Rush. He had just lost a race to a little girl called Vanellope, who had won his Medal of Heroes from him!

Ralph had left his own game and gotten the medal from a game called Hero's Duty to try to prove that he was a Good Guy. In his own game, he was the Bad Guy . . . and he was fed up with it. He just wanted to be treated well for once.

At the Sugar Rush Stadium, the Random Roster Race was about to begin! King Candy explained that each racer needed a coin to enter. The top finishers would appear as game characters in the arcade the next day.

Vanellope stepped out of the shadows and tossed Ralph's medal into the pot. She held her breath. Would the medal get her into the race?

Vanellope's name appeared on the list of racers! The crowd gasped in shock. To them, Vanellope was a glitch, a mistake in the game's programming. No one wanted Vanellope and her rickety little kart to race.

King Candy quickly ordered the Donut Police to take her away.

Just then, Ralph burst onto the track, desperate to find his medal. "Thief!" he cried at Vanellope. He chased after her, accidentally wrecking everything in his path.

Vanellope escaped, but Ralph was taken to King Candy's castle. The King told Ralph that the medal would belong to the winner of the next Random Roster Race, to be held later that night, when the racetrack was fixed. Then he ordered Ralph to leave Sugar Rush. But Ralph had other plans. . . .

Ralph tracked Vanellope through the Lollistix Forest. Just as he was about to confront her, a group of other racers arrived. They demanded that Vanellope drop out of the race. Then they smashed her kart and tossed her in the mud! That made Ralph mad! He chased the mean racers away.

Afterward, Vanellope promised that if she won the race, she'd give Ralph back his medal. But to win, she would need a new kart. Reluctantly, Ralph agreed to help. Would he finally get his medal back . . . ?

# A "Snappy" New Ship

It had not been a good day for Captain Hook. Peter Pan and the Darling children had stolen his ship. Now Hook was stranded on an island with Smee and the other pirates.

"It's a nice island, Captain," offered Smee, trying to cheer up his boss. "And you could use a vacation. Why, look at those dark circles under your eyes."

Captain Hook turned to Smee with a furious look on his face. "Pirates don't take vacations!" Hook boomed. "Pirates seek revenge! Which is precisely what we are going to do as soon as we have a new ship to sail in."

Smee looked around. "Where are we going to find a ship around here, sir?" he asked.

"We aren't going to find one," Captain Hook answered. "You and the rest of this mangy crew are going to *build* one!"

For weeks, the pirates chopped trees and cut them into planks for the ship. Finally, the ship was done.

"It's ready, Captain!" Smee announced.

Even Hook had to admit the ship was magnificent. Shaped like a gigantic crocodile, it was painted a reptilian shade of green. "No one will dare come near this ship. Not even that pesky crocodile. He won't want to tussle with anything this terrifying," Smee assured him.

Captain Hook was delighted. "We set sail tomorrow!" he crowed.

That night, Smee couldn't resist putting one finishing touch on the ship: he painted a row of eyelashes on the crocodile's eyelids.

The next morning, Captain Hook and the crew climbed aboard and pushed off. The ticking crocodile soon appeared.

"Smee!" yelled a terrified Captain Hook. "I thought you said he wouldn't come near us!"

"But look how calm he is," said Smee, puzzled. "He's even smiling!" Smee leaned over the side of the railing. "You know, it might be those eyelashes I painted. Maybe the croc thinks the ship is its mother."

Hook lunged at the first mate. "You made my ship look like a *mother* crocodile? This vessel is supposed to be terrifying!"

"Mothers *can* be terrifying, sir," said Smee. "You should have seen mine when I told her I was going to become a pirate!"

# Come Out, Whatever You Are!

The toys in Andy's room were in a panic. There was something in the closet—and it was alive! Passing by the slightly open door, Rex had seen some red lights blinking in the darkness.

"What do you think it is?" asked Jessie. She picked up Lenny and pointed the binoculars at the closet door, but it was too dark to see.

Woody walked right up to the closet. "Hello in there, and welcome to Andy's room," he called. "Come on out. There's nothing to be afraid of."

But the thing with the blinking red lights stayed right where it was.

"I get it, a shy type," Hamm guessed. The piggy bank jingled the coins in his body. "Show your face and there's a reward in it for you."

Buzz tried next. "In the name of Star Command, I, Buzz Lightyear, Space Ranger, demand that you show yourself! I have a laser out here, and I'm not afraid to use it," he said in an official-sounding voice.

The stranger in the closet didn't budge. Buzz turned to Rex, who looked like he might faint. "Clearly, the intruder is not threatened by the

sheriff or myself. It's up to you as the dominant predator to go in and get him."

"Me?" Rex asked, his knees shaking.

"Yes, you," insisted Buzz. "Just use the techniques I've been teaching you. You can be very intimidating if you set your mind to it."

"Go on, you big lizard!" Hamm yelled. "Make him wish he was extinct!"

"Oh, all right," Rex said. "Here goes." He ventured into the darkness of the closet and gave a spine-chilling roar.

"I got him!" shouted Rex. He emerged from the closet pulling on a shoelace. Everyone stared at him in disbelief.

"It's—a sneaker," Buzz said.

"With lights in the heel," added Woody.

Rex burst into tears. "My big moment, wasted on a shoe!"

"Well, look on the bright side," said Hamm.

Rex looked hopeful. "There's a bright side?"

"Yeah," the pig assured him. "At least it didn't stick its tongue out at you!"

# Patch's Plan

"Whoa!" Patch said. "Look at all these Dalmatian puppies!"

Patch's brothers and sisters were still whimpering with fear. They had just been dognapped! Now Patch was trying to work out a way to get back home.

The puppy looked around the large, shabby room where they were being held. He had never seen so many dogs in one place.

"Hey," Patch asked the closest stranger, "where are we?"

The spotted puppy smiled at him. "Oh, you must be new!" he said. "Which pet shop did you come from?"

Patch scowled at the strange new puppy.

"We're not from a pet shop," he told him. "We were stolen from our house."

Several other puppies heard him and moved closer. "Stolen? Really?" they exclaimed.

The first puppy shrugged. "Well, bought or stolen, we're all stuck here now."

"Maybe *you're* stuck here," Patch said boldly. "But our parents will be here soon to rescue us, just see if they don't!"

"I hope so," Patch's sister Pepper said. "I wonder why someone would want to steal us, anyway."

"I guess Cruella just really likes puppies," one of the other puppies told Pepper.

Patch gasped. "Cruella?" he cried. "Do you mean Cruella De Vil?"

His brothers and sisters shuddered. Their parents had told them scary stories about that nasty woman.

"Yes, she's the one who bought us," said one of the puppies.

The other puppies nodded their heads.

This changed everything! "We have to get away," Patch declared. "Cruella is bad news—that's what Dad always says!"

Patch gestured to the entire group of puppies, bought and stolen. It didn't matter where they'd come from. What mattered was they were in this mess together.

"We have to work as a team," he said.

The first puppy smiled at him. "I'm with you!" he exclaimed. "Let's teach Cruella a lesson!"

"Yeah," said another puppy. "When we're done with her, Cruella will be seeing spots!"

# The Sleepover

"Comfortable, Piglet?" Pooh asked. The two friends were having a sleepover at Pooh's house.

"Oh, yes," Piglet replied. "Good night, Pooh Bear."

Piglet lay in the darkness of Pooh's room. The darkness at Pooh's house was much, much darker than it was at Piglet's house. Pooh's bedroom was also much quieter than his own room at night.

"Pooh Bear?" Piglet whispered. There was no answer.

Piglet heard a soft, low rumbling. The sound grew louder and then softer, over and over again! Is that the sound of a heffalump? Piglet wondered.

"Oh dear!" Piglet shouted, running to Pooh's bed. "Wake up! P-p-please, P-P-Pooh!"

"Hmm?" Pooh said drowsily, sitting up. Piglet was hiding under the covers in Pooh's bed. "Why, Piglet," said Pooh. "What's the matter?"

"It's that horrible n-n-noise, Pooh," he stammered. Piglet listened for the noise, then realized he couldn't hear it. "That's funny," said Piglet. "The noise stopped as soon as you woke up, Pooh."

"Hmm," said Pooh. He shrugged. Then he yawned. "I guess that means we can go back to sleep."

"Pooh Bear," said Piglet timidly, "could we, well, have the rest of our sleepover another night? I'm just used to sleeping in my own house."

Pooh put his arm around Piglet. "I understand, Piglet," he said. He helped Piglet gather his things and then, hand in hand, they walked to Piglet's house.

Piglet was happy to be at home. "Thank you so much for understanding," he said. "I suppose you'll need to get home to bed now?"

"That does sound like the thing to do," Pooh replied. "But first I might sit down for a little rest."

While Piglet put away his things, Pooh sat down in a chair. By the time Piglet came back, Pooh was making a soft, low rumbling sound. But in the comfort of his own house, it didn't strike Piglet as anything other than the sound of one sleeping bear snoring.

"Sweet dreams, Pooh Bear," he whispered. Piglet climbed into his own bed and drifted off to sleep. It seemed that he and Pooh were having their best-friend sleepover after all.

# Up, Up, and Away!

**D**onald and his friends were standing outside of the Clubhouse on a bright day.

"Shhh!" Donald whispered. "Don't make a move! Something is following me!"

Daisy giggled. "Oh, my!" she said. "There *is* something following you! It's wearing a sailor's cap—just like yours. And when you move, it moves, too."

"Aw, phooey," Donald quacked as he turned around and saw his shadow. "That is a fine-looking shape, but I still don't trust it!"

"Cheer up, buddy," Mickey said. "Why don't we all leave our shadows on the ground and go for a ride in our hot-air balloon?"

Soon the friends were floating high above the Clubhouse. But they had a problem. They were headed straight for the top of a mountain!

"We need help," cried Mickey. "Oh, Toodles!" he called.

Toodles appeared with a ladder. Mickey dropped it over the side of the balloon, and the friends headed down one by one. Everyone was happy to be standing on firm ground again. But they had to hike back home! The friends trudged along, growing more and more tired.

"I think we've been walking in circles," Mickey finally said. "I'm sure I've seen this tree before. We need help! Oh, Toodles!"

Toodles appeared and showed Mickey three pictures. Mickey shared them with his friends.

"I'm standing in front of the Clubhouse, and my shadow is different in each picture. In the morning, my shadow falls in front of me. At noon, I have no shadow. In the evening, my shadow falls behind me. Do any of you know what this could mean?"

"I've got it!" Donald shouted. "Right now, it's late and the sun is setting behind us. Toodles shows that in the evening, our shadows point toward the Clubhouse. If we follow them, they'll lead us back home."

Donald was correct. The shadows helped the friends head in the right direction. Soon they arrived back at the Clubhouse.

"Well, Donald," Daisy said, "do you trust your shadow now?"

But Donald and his shadow had already settled down for a nap!

# Surprise!

Basil of Baker Street looked up from his newspaper. He sniffed the air. A mysterious smell was wafting through the room. There had also been some strange noises in the hallway, and the front door had been opened and closed an unusual number of times.

"That doesn't smell like Mrs. Judson's usual tea," he muttered grimly. "I sense there's trouble afoot. . . ."

Basil hurried to the kitchen. His housekeeper was standing near the oven.

"Er—what is it, Basil?" she asked quickly.

Basil narrowed his eyes. Just then, he noticed a dab of a mysterious blue substance on the counter. "Nothing," he told Mrs. Judson, quickly wiping up the substance. "Nothing at all."

Basil retreated to his study, his mind churning. Could this be a mystery—in his own house? He quickly set up a complicated array of beakers and test tubes, then dropped the blue substance into his new contraption. The little dial at the end spun around. The arrow landed on the words UNKNOWN SUBSTANCE—EDIBLE.

"Confound it," he muttered. "That doesn't tell me anything!"

Tiptoeing into the hall, Basil heard voices.

"Oh, dear, I'll never be ready!" Mrs. Judson cried.

"Nonsense, madam. Everything will be fine," someone replied.

Just then, the door opened. Basil's friend Dawson walked through it. Basil was caught! Or so he thought.

"There you are, old chap," Dawson said. "There's something that requires your attention in the drawing room, if you don't mind."

"There is?" Basil asked suspiciously.

Dawson chuckled. "Yes, I need to have a word with you in the drawing room."

Aha! Basil thought. Perhaps now I will get to the bottom of this mystery!

Dawson threw open the doors of the drawing room. "Surprise!"

Basil stared in shock. His family and friends all stood there, smiling at him. Mrs. Judson was holding a bright blue cake with candles on it!

Basil laughed out loud. What kind of detective am I? he thought. I didn't even remember my own birthday!

# Yard Sale

"Ready to go to Cowboy Camp?" Andy asked Woody, bursting excitedly into his bedroom.

Woody was very excited about camp, but he couldn't tell Andy that. Toys were supposed to stay very still whenever people could see them.

Andy had a few minutes before he had to leave for camp, so he grabbed his two favorite toys for a quick adventure.

"Never tangle with the unstoppable duo of Woody and Buzz Lightyear!" he shouted, linking the toys' arms together.

Suddenly, there was a loud *RIIIPPPP!* Woody's shoulder had torn open! Andy's mom suggested fixing Woody on the way to camp, but Andy shook his head. "No," he said with a sigh. "Just leave him."

Andy's mom put Woody on a high shelf. The cowboy watched sadly as Andy left for camp without him.

As he looked around, Woody spotted his old friend Wheezy the penguin. Andy's mom had put Wheezy on the shelf when his squeaker broke. She had meant to fix him, but that had been months ago.

Woody was worried. Would he be forgotten on the shelf, too?

Suddenly, the toys saw something truly terrifying. Andy's mom was putting up a sign for a yard sale!

Andy's mom came into Andy's room looking for some items to sell. She felt around the shelf and finally chose Wheezy.

Once Andy's mom was out of sight, Woody whistled loudly for Buster, Andy's puppy. Together, Woody and Buster snuck outside. They grabbed Wheezy and headed back to safety. But Woody's broken arm made it hard for him to hold on to Buster. The cowboy lost his grip and tumbled to the ground!

Just then, a strange man noticed Woody. The man picked up the cowboy . . . and stole him! From their upstairs window, the other toys watched in horror as the man threw Woody into the trunk of his car.

Buzz couldn't let Woody be stolen! He raced to rescue his friend, but he was too late. All Buzz saw was the car's license plate. It said LZTYBRN. A few feathers floated out of the car.

Buzz had to find Woody and bring him home!

# June's Shoes

Annie, Leo, and Quincy were waiting for their friend June. When she finally appeared, Annie noticed that something was different about her.

"Are you wearing new ballet shoes?" asked Annie.

"Yes, I just got them this morning," June said, beaming. "Wearing new shoes feels a bit strange, but I'll get used to them. Don't you just love to dance? One, two . . . OUCH! Oh, dear. Every time I try to leap or twirl, I fall!"

"Don't worry, June," said Annie. "Just take your time, and you'll be dancing before you know it."

"It takes time to get used to new things," Quincy said.

Leo agreed. "I remember the first time I wore my glasses. I knew I needed them to help me see things clearly, and they felt really strange at first, but now I don't know what I'd do without them!"

Suddenly, Rocket sent a signal.

"Team, we have a mission," said Leo. "Cow is stuck on the moon, and we have to help get her down!"

"How did she get up there?" asked Annie.

"Aha! Rocket is showing us Mount Everest—the tallest mountain in the world," replied Leo. "Cow must have leaped from the very tip of the mountain, but instead of jumping *over* the moon, she landed right *on* it!"

Rocket raced the team to the moon. But when they got there, Leo realized that Cow was too big to fit inside Rocket. The team needed a plan.

"I've got it!" exclaimed Leo. "June, you're the only one who can show Cow how to jump back down."

"It's true, June," agreed Quincy. "You're the best dancer we know. You can do it!"

"I'm not so sure," replied June. "Do you really think I can do it?"

"We sure do," her friends cheered.

June took a deep breath and . . . they did it! June and Cow landed safely on Mount Everest.

"Hooray!" said June. "I've gotten used to my new shoes. Thank you all for believing in me!"

"Cow is back home!" cheered Leo. "Mission completion!"

"I think it's time for a celebration!" shouted Quincy.

"Let's sing a song," said Annie.

"And have a dance!" added June.

# Mater's Jukebox

"Yeee-ha! Ready or not, Radiator Springs, my jukebox is ready!" Mater hollered. He had made a fantastic jukebox and he couldn't wait to show all of his friends.

Mater hooked the jukebox up to his towline and off he went. The first car he saw was Ramone, but Ramone didn't have time to listen to the jukebox. Little tractors were messing up his body paint shop! "I've got to clean up this place!" Ramone cried.

Next Mater passed by his best friend, Lightning.

"Sorry, Mater!" Lightning called. "I've got to round up these little tractors." Lightning zoomed after another little tractor as it darted away.

At Casa Della Tires, Luigi had no time to hear Mater's junkyard jukebox, either. "No-no-no-no!" Luigi cried. "Look at Luigi's Leaning Tower of Tires! Now she is just Luigi's Pile of Tires!"

Mater knew he had to help, but how?

Mater rounded the corner and found Sheriff. "Hey, Sheriff, you'll never guess what I made. . . ."

"Mater! I've got no time today for lollygagging. I need to round up these little rascals." Sheriff turned on his siren and drove away after the tractors.

For such cute little fellas, those tractors sure are causing a load of trouble! Mater thought. I gotta put away my jukebox so I can help my friends.

As Mater headed back to his scrapyard, he cranked up his jukebox and began to sing along with the music.

A tractor followed him shyly. Soon the other tractors started trailing after Mater and his jukebox! To his surprise, Mater noticed the music was attracting all of the little tractors. He turned up the sound and started a little tractor roundup.

"Well, lookee here!" Mater shouted. "These little fellas like my music!"

"Mater rounded up the tractors!" cried Sally.

The whole town cheered. "Hip hip hooray for Mater!"

"That's music to my ears!" Sheriff sighed.

Everyone was happy. The tractors were out of trouble, and the music was great!

# Telephone

"Did you hear the news, my dear?" one of the circus elephants said to another.

"What is it?" the second elephant asked.

The first elephant looked around carefully to make sure that no one was listening.

"Well," she whispered in the second elephant's ear, "you know Mrs. Jumbo's son, Dumbo? A little bird told me that his first show was a hit! Everyone loved the 'Building on Fire' act. Dumbo leaped off a platform twenty feet high. And they're going to raise it up much higher next time!"

"But don't tell a soul!" the first elephant warned.

As soon as the first elephant turned away, the second elephant turned to another of her friends. "Listen, dear," she said. "You'll never believe what I just heard!"

"What is it, dear?" the third elephant asked.

The second elephant lowered her voice to a whisper. "It's Dumbo—twenty clowns had to hit him with a tire to get him to leap off a platform!"

The third elephant gasped. "Oh, my! That is big news!"

"But don't breathe a word to anyone!" the second elephant exclaimed.

Soon the third elephant was talking to another friend. The fourth elephant gaped with amazement as she listened.

". . . and so Dumbo set the platform on fire, and it took twenty clowns to put out the flames," the third elephant confided.

The fourth elephant told a fifth, and the fifth told a sixth. Soon the whole circus was buzzing with the news of Dumbo's first clown show.

A little bird was flying over the Big Top when he saw a pair of elephants chattering below. "Good day, ladies," he said. "What's the word around the circus this evening?"

"It's Dumbo," one elephant said excitedly. "It seems he fell off a platform in the last show and hit twenty clowns. Now they're talking about setting him on fire next time!"

The little bird didn't stick around to hear the end of the discussion. "I can't wait to spread this news!" he squawked, fluttering back up into the sky. "Wait until everyone hears—they'll never believe it's true!"

# Woody's Roundup Gang

Woody was in trouble. He had tried to save Wheezy the penguin from being sold at Andy's mom's yard sale, and had ended up being stolen by a stranger!

The stranger's name was Al. He brought Woody to his apartment and put him inside a glass case.

"You, my little cowboy friend, are going to make me big buck-buck-bucks!" he laughed.

When he was alone, Woody opened the case. He ran to the apartment door and pushed, but it was no use. He was trapped.

Suddenly, a cardboard box burst open, and Woody was knocked off his feet by a galloping toy horse.

"It's you! It's really you!" shouted a cowgirl, hugging Woody tight. The cowgirl told Woody that her name was Jessie. The horse was Bullseye. Then she introduced the Prospector, a mint-condition toy who had never been out of his box.

"We've waited countless years for this day," said the Prospector.

Woody didn't understand why the toys were so excited to see him. How did they know who he was?

Bullseye turned on the lights to reveal a room filled with items showing Woody's picture. Then Jessie showed him an old TV show, *Woody's Roundup*. Woody was the star!

"Now it's on to the museum!" the Prospector exclaimed.

"Museum?" Woody asked.

The Prospector explained that the Roundup toys had become very valuable. Al planned to sell the whole set to a Japanese museum for a lot of money.

Woody told Jessie he couldn't go to the museum. He had to get back to Andy.

Jessie told Woody that she had had an owner once, too—a little girl named Emily. But as Emily grew up, she had played with Jessie less and less. Finally, she had abandoned Jessie.

"You never forget kids like Emily or Andy," said Jessie. "But they forget you."

Woody began to worry that Andy would forget about him one day, too. Maybe he would be better off at the museum after all. . . .

# Hide-and-Sniff

Little Koda had been talking . . . and talking . . . and talking for hours. In fact, he had been talking for so long that Kenai had stopped listening.

"So?" Koda said. "What do you think?"

"Hmm?" said Kenai, who had been sleepily digging berry seeds out of his teeth.

"I said," said Koda, bouncing up and down, "what do you think?"

"Oh, I don't know." Kenai didn't have the least idea *what* Koda was talking about. "Whatever you say, I guess."

"All right!" exclaimed Koda. "I *knew* you were ready to play a game. Tag! You're it. Close your eyes and count to twenty-seven—'cause that's all I can count to—and then try to find me. Good luck! You'll need it—I'm an excellent hider!" And with that, Koda raced off.

"Excuse me?" Kenai exclaimed. But Koda was already out of view.

Playing hide-and-seek with a bear cub was the *last* thing Kenai wanted to do. But he did need Koda. And unfortunately for Kenai, that meant he had to find him.

"Now," Kenai said to himself, "if I was a pain-in-the-neck, blabbermouth bear cub, where would I hide . . . ?"

He raised himself up on his two rear legs and scoped out his surroundings. Finally, he began to search the bushes, since they were the closest option, but the only things he found there were an irritable badger and two friendly chipmunks.

"Sorry," said Kenai, backing away.

"And just what are you doing nosing around in other creatures' business?" demanded the badger. "You big old bears think you own the whole country!"

"I said I was sorry," said Kenai. "I was just playing a game. You haven't seen a cub about so high hiding here, have you?"

"Seen a cub? Thank heavens no!" replied the badger. "But I sure did smell one over yonder. *Whoo!* Can't you?"

Smell? Kenai gave a big sniff and was suddenly aware of how strong his sense of smell was. Yes, indeed, he *could* smell the little cub.

"Gotcha!" he soon hollered, poking his shaggy head into a cave. "You should know better, Koda, than to play hide-and-seek with a bear!"

# Bananas Are Forever

Special Agent Oso was standing at the edge of a cliff, ready for a training exercise. "It looks like the only way to get to the other side is by walking across this narrow beam," he said.

"This exercise will test your balance," said Dotty. "Just watch where you put your feet."

"If I go one step at a time," Oso whispered, "I'm sure I can do it!"

Meanwhile, a girl named Keira was excited that her friends were coming over. "Let's make a snack for them!" she said. But Keira wasn't sure how to make a healthy snack. She needed help.

The message was soon sent to Agent Oso, who headed straight to Keira's house.

"I'm here to help you make a healthy snack," Oso told Keira. "Paw Pilot, what's the first step on the checklist?"

"Step one," said Paw Pilot, "is to look at the foods you have!"

"Most of the food needs to be cooked," Keira said. "And I don't use the oven."

"Right," Oso said. "Your healthy snack should be a safe snack. No cooking and no sharp knives."

Oso found some healthy food in the refrigerator. Step one was complete.

"Now for step two," said Paw Pilot. "Decide on one thing to make."

"We can make frozen cinnamon bananas on a stick!" shouted Keira. "They're yummy!"

"Great job," said Paw Pilot. "You're ready for step three—prepare your healthy snack."

Keira and Oso began making the snacks. Whoops! Oso dropped a banana peel and then slipped on it!

"Watch where you put your feet, Oso!" said Keira.

"Watch where I put my feet?" said Agent Oso. "That's what Dotty said!"

Agent Oso cut the bananas into two pieces. Keira put a lollipop stick in each piece and sprinkled them with cinnamon.

"They have to freeze for one hour," Keira said. "That's when my friends will be here."

"Step three completed," said Paw Pilot.

"Thank you, Agent Oso!" said Keira.

Back on the beam in the mountains, Agent Oso remembered what Dotty and Keira had told him. By watching where he put his feet, he completed his training exercise with ease.

# Funny Faces

Hugo, Victor, and Laverne were gargoyles at the great Cathedral of Notre Dame. Most of the time they were stone, but they came to life in the presence of Quasimodo, the cathedral's bell ringer.

Although they were all good friends, Hugo and Victor were always finding something to bicker over, and today was no exception.

"That's ridiculous!" Hugo snapped.

"No, *you're* ridiculous!" Victor shot back.

Victor had suggested that Quasimodo tell his master that he wanted to take some time off. Hugo had pointed out that Frollo would sooner become a gypsy than give Quasimodo a vacation.

"Guys, there's no need to argue," said Quasimodo.

"Well, he started it," Hugo said.

"*I* started it?" Victor asked.

Suddenly, a loud whistle interrupted them. They turned around to find their friend Laverne.

"May I have your attention, please?" Laverne said. "I would like to propose a way for you to settle this dispute like gentlemen."

"What is it?" Quasi asked.

"A face-making contest," Laverne said. "Here are the rules: you two take turns making faces at each other, and the first to make the other laugh wins!"

"I'm going first!" declared Hugo, sticking his tongue out at Victor.

"Child's play," said Victor scornfully. He crossed his eyes at Hugo.

"Ha!" said Hugo. "Try resisting *this*!" Hugo crossed his eyes, flared his nostrils, and stuck his lower jaw out, baring a crooked row of teeth in a hideous grimace.

Victor managed to keep a straight face at this, but Quasimodo couldn't help but laugh out loud.

"Shh!" Laverne said. "Frollo's coming!"

"Frollo?" Hugo and Victor grew pale and quickly turned back to stone.

Frollo marched in. "What's going on up here?" he asked Quasimodo.

"Nothing, sir," Quasi said, trying not to laugh.

"Hmm," said Frollo suspiciously. As he turned to go, Victor and Hugo began making funny faces at Frollo's back. When he was out of sight, all four friends collapsed in laughter.

"You know what?" Quasi said to them. "Being with you is more fun than a vacation any day!"

# A Rescue Mission

Buzz and the other toys were very busy. Woody had been stolen, and it was up to them to get him back.

Buzz thought about the clues he had found: a license plate that said LZTYBRN and a chicken feather. Just then he saw a commercial for Al's Toy Barn. The owner, Al, was dressed in a chicken suit. Buzz realized that Al had stolen Woody!

Buzz decided to lead a rescue party to the toy store. "Woody once risked his life to save me," he told the other toys. "I couldn't call myself his friend if I wouldn't do the same."

With a little help from Slinky Dog, the toys jumped off the roof. "To Al's Toy Barn . . . and beyond!" Buzz cried as they set off.

The toys slowly made their way across town. By early morning, Buzz and his rescue team had almost reached Al's Toy Barn. They just needed to cross one last, very busy street. Luckily, Buzz noticed a pile of orange traffic cones.

One by one, the toys ventured across the street, hiding under the cones. Soon the street was filled with skidding, honking, crashing cars. They were all trying to avoid the strange, moving traffic cones. But the toys didn't notice. They'd arrived at Al's Toy Barn.

Inside, aisles of shiny new toys seemed to stretch as far as they could see. The toys knew their best hope was to split up. Soon Buzz discovered an aisle full of updated Buzz Lightyear toys! He gasped when he saw each figure's fancy new utility belt.

As he reached out to touch the belt, a hand clamped down on his wrist. It was a new Buzz Lightyear. The toy thought he'd caught an escaped space ranger! He quickly tied Buzz into a box. Then New Buzz ran to join Andy's toys.

The toys had found Al and were going to rescue Woody. They didn't realize that they had a new Buzz with them!

Buzz struggled free from his box just in time to see his friends head out the front door, inside Al's bag! Racing to catch up, he crashed into the automatic doors. He was too light to open them. How would he ever catch up with his friends?

# A New Day

Chicken Little started to cross the street. *Squish!* He stepped on a piece of chewing gum.

He tried to move, but he was stuck. Suddenly, the light turned green. Cars were headed straight for him! Quickly, he pulled a lollipop from his pocket and licked it. Then he slapped the lollipop onto a car's bumper and held on tight. The car pulled him out of the gum, but his pants had stuck to the ground!

When he got to school, Chicken Little hurried into gym class wearing a pair of origami pants he'd cleverly made out of his math homework. The class was playing dodgeball. Suddenly, Foxy's sidekick, Goosey, grabbed Chicken Little and threw him across the room. As he started to fall, he grabbed a handle on the wall.

*Riiiiiiiiinnngg!* He'd pulled the fire alarm.

Things were not going Chicken Little's way.

Chicken Little had an idea. Maybe things would change if he joined the baseball team. But it was no use. The coach wouldn't let him play. Game after game, Chicken Little sat on the bench.

Finally, it was the last game of the season. The game was on the line, and there were only two batters left: Chicken Little and Foxy Loxy. The announcer looked at the lineup card. "Up next, Chicken Little," he said.

No one expected Chicken Little to even hit the ball. The pitcher threw the first pitch. Chicken Little swung at the ball. "Strike one!" called the umpire.

The pitcher threw the second pitch. Chicken Little missed again. The pitcher wound up for the third pitch. If Chicken Little missed this ball, his team would lose the game.

"Today is a new day," Chicken Little told himself. As the ball came toward him, he closed his eyes and swung his bat hard. *Craaack!*

Chicken Little's eyes flew open. He'd hit the ball!

Chicken Little slid into home base just as the throw came from the outfield. After the umpire dusted off the plate, he saw Chicken Little's foot and made the call. "The runner is safe!" Chicken Little had won the game!

Chicken Little was thrilled. Maybe, he thought, things were changing after all.

# Smitten

Robin Hood straightened his hat and smoothed his whiskers. "How do I look, Little John?" he asked.

"You look like you always do," John replied with a wave of his hand. "Like a regular Casanova."

Robin grinned. "Let's hope Maid Marian agrees with you." He put a hand over his heart. "I just hope she still remembers me."

Robin Hood was nervous. Maid Marian was the cleverest and most beautiful maiden in the land. And she'd been in London for several years. What if she didn't remember her childhood sweetheart?

"Get going," Little John said.

Robin nodded and set off through the forest. Soon he was outside the castle gate. He could hear voices— female voices—laughing and talking. Maybe one of them was Marian's!

Robin's heart pounded in his chest. He had to see! He looked around and spotted a large tree with branches that reached inside the castle grounds. Perfect!

Robin leaped gracefully up to the first branch, grabbed hold, and began to climb. When he was nice and high, he worked his way out onto a branch. Now he was inside the castle grounds. Robin moved a branch and leaned forward to see who was talking.

It was Marian! She was playing badminton with Lady Cluck. And she was a good shot!

"Nice one, Maid Marian," Lady Cluck said as Marian won a point.

Robin gazed down at the sight below. Marian was so lovely, and so talented!

"Oops!" Marian said as the birdie sailed off the court completely.

Robin saw it fly toward his hiding place. It landed in the tree just above him! He got to his feet and reached up to retrieve it for Marian. But he lost his balance and fell just as the birdie came loose. The two landed on the ground at the same time.

"Ooof!" Robin didn't mean to make an entrance like this!

"What was that?" Lady Cluck asked as Robin scrambled away, leaping over the fence.

"I do believe it was an outlaw," Maid Marian said with a smile.

# The Spooky Sleepover

It was a quiet morning at Monsters, Inc. Sulley had arrived early to catch up on paperwork when he got a phone call from dispatch.

"Annual slumber party at Shannon Brown's house. Waxford is out sick. We need a replacement."

"Piece of cake," Mike said when Sulley told him the situation.

Shannon Brown's door slid into his station on the Laugh Floor and Mike walked through the closet into the girl's room. It was empty. "Uh . . . hello?" Mike called. Just as Mike turned to leave, he heard the sound of laughter.

Suddenly, thunder cracked across the sky. Mike ran to the closet door to return to the factory. He jiggled the doorknob, but it just opened into the closet, not the Laugh Floor! Mike realized that lightning must have struck the door and broken it. He took a deep breath and headed into the hallway.

Meanwhile, back at Monsters, Inc., Sulley was working at his desk when the floor manager came running over.

"Sulley!" he shouted. "Mike hasn't returned from the slumber party. He's never been gone this long!"

Sulley went to check on the door and found that it was broken. He immediately called someone to fix it.

Back at Shannon's, Mike heard laughter down the hall. When he found the right room and went in, it was quiet. Slowly, Mike entered the silent room. All of a sudden, a light went on.

Mike jumped. Shannon Brown and all her friends roared with laughter! They thought Mike looked funny sneaking into the room.

At that exact moment, the closet door opened and Sulley burst into the room. Sulley was so surprised to find Mike screaming that all he could do was scream, too! Then he and Mike huddled in fright. Shannon and her friends laughed even harder.

"Looks as if our work here is done," Sulley said to Mike as they headed back into the closet.

"I was never scared for a second," said Mike.

"Me neither, buddy," Sulley replied, his fingers crossed behind his back. "Me neither."

# The Prospector

Woody had been kidnapped by a toy store owner named Al. He wanted to sell the cowboy and the rest of the *Woody's Roundup* dolls to a Japanese museum.

At first, Woody only wanted to get home to Andy. But after talking to the rest of the *Woody's Roundup* gang, Woody had started to think that maybe he'd be better off at the museum. Andy would be grown up soon and might stop playing with him. When Andy's toys showed up to rescue Woody, the cowboy refused to go with them.

"You are a toy!" said Buzz, who had caught up with the other toys after escaping Al's toy store. "Somewhere in that pad of stuffing is a toy who taught me what matters is being loved by a kid!"

But Woody still wouldn't go with them. Sadly, Buzz was forced to leave Woody behind.

Later, as Woody watched a TV commercial of a boy hugging his toy, he realized that Buzz was right. Woody belonged with Andy. He ran to the vent and called for his friends to come back. Then he turned to the Roundup gang.

"Come with me," he told them. "Andy will play with all of us."

Jessie and Bullseye were excited, but the Prospector blocked their path! After a lifetime in his box, he was determined to go to the museum.

"No hand-me-down cowboy doll is gonna mess it up for me!" he shouted.

Suddenly, the toys heard footsteps. Al was coming!

Al packed Woody and the Roundup gang into a case and dashed out the door. He was late for his flight to Japan.

"To the elevator!" shouted Buzz, who had come back when he heard Woody call to him. The toys rushed to the elevator's emergency hatch. Al was still inside.

While Buzz held on to his legs, Slinky stretched down to Al's case. Swinging close, he undid the latches and grabbed hold of Woody's arms.

But before they could save the cowboy, the Prospector popped up and yanked Woody back down again! A moment later, the elevator doors opened. Al hurried outside, with the Roundup gang still in his case.

Andy's toys sprinted into the parking lot, but Al was already gone. They were too late. How would they rescue Woody and his friends now?

# Lend Me Your Ears

"I think I can, I think I can, I think I can," chugged Casey Junior the circus train. The train moved slowly around a bend. "I think I can. I think I . . . *Achoo!*" he sneezed. Suddenly, he came to a halt. "I know I can't," he admitted finally.

The animals and the performers poked their heads out of their train cars, wondering what was wrong.

"Casey Junior here has a very bad cold," the engineer said. "He's going to need some rest before he can take us any farther."

The Ringmaster frowned. "But we're due at the fairground in a few hours. What will we do? After all, the show must go on!"

The engineer just shrugged and turned his attention back to the sneezing, coughing, and spluttering little engine.

The Ringmaster went down the train, swinging open the doors to all the cages and cars. "Come on, everyone," he said. "Might as well stretch your legs."

Dumbo the elephant and his mother, Mrs. Jumbo, took a drink from the bucket of water the Ringmaster had set out. Mrs. Jumbo gazed around. "Looks like we're in the middle of nowhere," she said. "I do hope poor Casey Junior is feeling better soon."

"Me too," Dumbo's friend Timothy Q. Mouse said hopefully.

Just then there was a clap of thunder. Rain began to fall from the sky. The animals and performers ran for the shelter of the circus wagons. Dumbo held on to his mother's tail. Suddenly the wind picked up. The gust caught Dumbo's huge ears and sent him flying backward!

"That's it!" yelled the Ringmaster over the howling wind. "Dumbo, come with me!"

He led Dumbo over to the train, climbed onto the front wagon, and motioned for the little elephant to join him.

"Now spread out those great ears of yours!" the Ringmaster said. Dumbo's ears billowed out, catching the wind like giant sails and pushing Casey Junior along the tracks.

"The show will go on!" the Ringmaster shouted happily.

"I know I can. I know I can. I know I can," chanted Casey Junior. And then he added, "Thanks to Dumbo!"

# Dory's Surprise Party

**D**ory's birthday was coming up, and Nemo wanted to throw a surprise birthday party for her.

"What kind of food should we have?" Nemo asked his friends.

"Kelp cake and algae ice cream," Sheldon replied.

"How about music?" Nemo asked.

"We could be the band," said Pearl. "I'm great on the mussel tambourines."

"Yeah, and I play the clamshell drums," said Sheldon.

"Great!" cried Nemo. "Let's meet here tomorrow after school to practice."

The next day, Nemo and his friends were carrying their musical instruments when they bumped into Dory.

"Hi, Mimo! Hi, kids!" Dory exclaimed. She had trouble remembering Nemo's name. "What are you up to?"

"Music class homework," Tad piped up.

"I didn't know you played instruments," said Dory. "Well, have fun!"

The friends looked at each other. "Whew, that was close!" said Nemo.

The day of the party arrived. Nemo and his friends got up early and started decorating. Then Nemo suggested they practice singing "Happy Birthday."

Just as they finished the line "Happy birthday, dear Dory," Dory appeared!

"How did you know it was my birthday?" she exclaimed.

"You told me," said Nemo.

"Really, Pluto?" asked Dory.

"Now the surprise is ruined," said Nemo sadly.

"What surprise?" said Dory.

It sure was helpful that Dory's memory wasn't very good! "Another close call," said Nemo to his friends.

A few hours later, the guests arrived. They all hid and waited. When Dory and Nemo swam in, everyone shouted, "Surprise!"

"Look, Pluto, it's a party for you!" Dory cried.

"No, Dory, it's for you," Nemo said. "It's your birthday."

"It is? Cool, a party for me!"

Later, she swam over to Marlin and Nemo. "I sure am glad your dad and I found you, Nemo. This is the best birthday I've ever had."

"Hey, Dory!" said Nemo. "You remembered my name."

"What's that, Flipper?" asked Dory.

"Oh, nothing," Nemo said with a sigh. "Happy birthday!"

# Rabbit's Frightful Garden

Rabbit woke up bright and early. He had a lot of work to do in his garden. There was just one problem. Rabbit had lent all his tools to his friends—and they hadn't returned them.

Meanwhile, Pooh and Piglet were enjoying breakfast with Kanga when Roo bounced in with a bunch of wildflowers.

"Thank you, Roo!" Kanga exclaimed, giving him a kiss. "Let me just trim these."

She rummaged around in a kitchen drawer, where she came across Rabbit's gardening shears. "Oh, no," Kanga said. "I never returned these to Rabbit after I borrowed them."

"That reminds me," said Piglet, "I still have Rabbit's rake. And, Pooh, I'll bet you still have Rabbit's shovel."

The friends decided the neighborly thing to do would be to return Rabbit's tools right away. When they arrived at Rabbit's house, though, their friend was not at home. He was on his way to *their* houses to get his tools back!

"Rabbit's garden could use some work," Kanga said. "Why don't we take care of it for him as a way of saying

that we're sorry for keeping his tools for so long?"

Everyone agreed that this was a splendid plan.

When they had finished working, they spotted some birds hungrily eyeing the harvest.

"This garden needs a scarecrow!" cried Roo.

The work crew sprang into action, and soon a towering scarecrow was planted right in the middle of the garden. "Won't Rabbit be surprised?" Piglet said proudly.

When Rabbit returned home a few minutes later, he couldn't quite believe his eyes. First he looked at the vegetables, all neatly picked. Then he looked at his garden tools, which had mysteriously reappeared. Finally, he looked at the strange scarecrow, which seemed to be looking right back at him!

"D-d-d-did you do this?" he stammered to the straw man. Just then, a gust of wind knocked over the rake resting on the scarecrow's arm.

Convinced his garden was haunted, Rabbit turned and ran for his life.

"Ahhhhhhhhh!" he screamed as he rushed past his friends.

"I *told* you he'd be surprised," said Piglet.

# Something for Felix to Fix

Wreck-It Ralph was a bad guy from the arcade game Fix-It Felix Jr. He was in a racing game called Sugar Rush where everything was made of sweets. Ralph had left his own game to find a medal and prove he was a Good Guy, but had ended up far from where he belonged!

Now Ralph was helping his new friend Vanellope make a new kart. She was a racer in Sugar Rush and wanted to win.

Elsewhere, Felix from Ralph's game and Sergeant Calhoun from Hero's Duty were searching for Ralph. When Ralph crashed in the game, he had accidentally set free a dangerous cy-bug! Felix was looking for Ralph, and Calhoun was looking for the cy-bug. Calhoun asked Felix why Ralph would leave his own game.

"I wish I knew," Felix replied. "I never thought he'd go Turbo. . . ."

Years ago, there had been a racing game in the arcade called Turbo Time. Its star, Turbo, was very popular . . . until a newer racing game arrived. Overcome with jealousy, Turbo had left his own game and tried to take over the

new one. But when Turbo appeared in the wrong game, everyone thought it was broken. In the end, both games were unplugged and hauled away.

"We have to fix this mess and get Ralph home, or the same thing's going to happen to my game," said Felix. Together, the two headed farther into Sugar Rush.

Not far away, Vanellope led Ralph to the Sugar Rush kart bakery. The two sneaked inside and baked a kart.

Just then, King Candy—the king of Sugar Rush—arrived. Vanellope and Ralph ran away! At Vanellope's home, Ralph realized the girl needed a place to practice driving. He wrecked the rocks around the lake she lived by to create a racetrack. Soon Vanellope was speeding along! Ralph thought Vanellope might be a natural, if only she could stop all the twitching and glitching that she did.

Vanellope was excited. She and Ralph were heading for the big race! She was happy to have a friend at last. The other racers thought she was just a glitch in the game, but she was going to prove them wrong!

It's your Uncle Ricky's Birthday!

# Al's Sky-High Adventure

Al Oft, the Lightyear blimp, was hovering over the big stadium when he witnessed an amazing sight: superstar rookie Lightning McQueen was pushing a broken-down race car—The King himself!—across the finish line.

Everyone at the racetrack knew who Al was. The fans always cheered when he flew overhead. But he was lonely up in the sky all by himself. Al couldn't help admiring Lightning's pit crew. It was filled with the rookie's close friends. They had come all the way from Radiator Springs to support Lightning at his big race.

When the season ended, Al decided to travel the countryside. One day, Al saw a town below him that looked like the place Lightning had described. He flew low and spotted Lightning!

"Hey, Lightning!" shouted a rusty old truck. "Lookee there! It's that Lightyear blimp from your big race!"

"Al! How are you doing, buddy? Good to see you. Welcome to Radiator Springs!" the race car called up.

"My name's Mater!" said the rusty truck. "Wanna help us round up a stray tractor that busted loose, Mr. Blimp?"

"Yeah," said Lightning. "We can't see where the lost tractor went. But I'll bet you can from up there!"

Sure enough, from high in the sky, Al soon found the lost tractor. He lit up his sign to show Lightning that he had found him.

"Hey, that's great, Al, but we can't get over those big rocks!" Lightning shouted. "Can you see a way for us to get around them?"

Al looked down and all around. He soon found a path the two cars could take to reach the lost tractor. Within minutes, Mater and Lightning were guiding the tractor home.

"Now, this calls for a celebration, Al!" Lightning shouted. "We're having one of our neon cruises tonight. Why don't you join us?"

As the cars in Radiator Springs cruised down the road, Al hovered over them. "That's my friend Al Oft, the Lightyear blimp," Lightning said. "Just look at him. He's got the best neon you've ever seen."

Al smiled. He was having the most fun he'd ever had. And with all his new friends, he knew he'd never be lonely again.

# Alien Invasion

Chicken Little was tired of everyone laughing at him and calling him "that crazy little chicken." Life was just getting back to normal when part of the sky fell—right into Chicken Little's bedroom.

Chicken Little called his friends Abby, Runt, and Fish, and they came over.

"I'm sure there's a simple explanation," Abby said.

While the others tried to figure out a plan, Fish climbed on top of the piece of sky. To everyone's surprise, it floated off the floor and zoomed out the window!

"Come on!" cried Chicken Little. He and his pals chased after Fish. The panel came to a stop over the town's baseball stadium.

Suddenly, a spaceship appeared! Chicken Little, Runt, and Abby ran for shelter in the dugout. While the friends watched, two spidery-looking aliens dropped out of the hatch and scuttled off.

Chicken Little, Abby, and Runt climbed aboard the spaceship. It was dark inside. The only friendly sight was a cute orange creature floating in a beam of light.

Chicken Little stopped and winked at it, and it winked back. Then it hopped down and followed Chicken Little.

Suddenly, Fish jumped out from behind a screen.

"All right, let's get out of here," Abby ordered. But now Runt was missing! Fish pointed to a room down the hall. Runt was staring up at the ceiling with a terrified look on his face. There was a giant picture of the entire solar system. Several planets were crossed out, but Earth was circled. It looked like the aliens were going to destroy the planet!

Chicken Little, Abby, Runt, and Fish left the ship and ran into the forest. The aliens were right behind them!

"We've got to ring the school bell to warn everyone!" Abby cried. They raced to the school and rang the bell. *Ding-dong! Ding-dong!*

The aliens fled back to their ship just as the alarmed townspeople gathered at the school. Everyone thought Chicken Little had imagined the whole thing—just like he had imagined that the sky was falling.

Chicken Little just knew that he had to find a way to make everyone believe him.

# Red Alert!

"Nice work with the wheat husker," Flik said. He smiled with satisfaction as he watched a troop of ants lower the contraption that lightly smashed the wheat kernels.

"How's it going with the berry masher?" called a voice. It was Atta, the colony's queen.

"I was just heading over to take a look," Flik said, smiling at Queen Atta. "Care to join me?"

"Sure," Atta said as she led the way to the berry-mashing area. Mashing berries was messy, so the ants did it in a special part of the anthill.

"Cowabunga!" called a large ant. Ten dozen ants leaped off a rock and onto a giant lever. The lever lowered, pressing a flat rock onto a pile of berries. Sweet red juice squirted out from the sides and dripped into carved wooden bowls.

"With your new invention, we should have plenty of juice for this year's feast," Atta said. "As long as Dot and the Blueberries don't drink it all first," she added.

Flik laughed. Dot and her Blueberry friends loved berry juice and were always trying to dip into it before the feast. They had been shooed away from the berry masher more than once in the last week.

"Good work, masher ants!" Flik called to the horde that was climbing back up to their jumping rock.

Nearby, another group was making a fresh pile of berries. They had nearly finished piling up a huge mound of berries when an alarm sounded.

"Alert, alert!" a guard ant called through a megaphone made from a rolled-up leaf. "Red fire ants are storming the colony!"

Flik, Atta, and the masher ants fled the food area as fast as their legs could carry them. Sure enough, they soon ran into six red ants.

Flik was about to charge when he heard a familiar voice.

"Flik, it's me!" it said. The voice sounded like . . . Dot's.

"Hold on!" Flik shouted. The ants stopped. Flik quickly wiped the first red ant's sticky face. "These aren't fire ants," Flik explained. "They're Blueberries—covered in berry juice!" He smiled at Atta. "Maybe we should call them Redberries instead!"

# An Airport Rescue

Woody had been stolen by a toy store owner named Al. Now he was on his way to the airport to be sold to a Japanese museum. But Woody's friends were close behind. They had stolen an empty Pizza Planet truck and were driving to the airport, too.

When they got to the airport, Buzz spotted a pet carrier. The toys piled inside. Sticking their legs through the bottom, they followed Al and his green suitcase. When Al put his bag on the conveyor belt, Buzz and the other toys hopped on, too.

"Once we go through, we just need to find that case," Buzz explained, nodding at the door to the baggage area.

The toys gasped as they entered a huge room full of conveyer belts. Buzz quickly found Al's case. But when he opened it, the Prospector jumped out and punched him!

"No one does that to my friend," Woody yelled, tackling the Prospector.

With his pickax, the Prospector started to rip open Woody's shoulder! He was about to drag Woody back into the case when the rest of Andy's toys arrived. With the toys' help, Buzz tackled the Prospector and tied him to a little girl's backpack. The toys helped Bullseye get free of the bag, but they didn't get to Jessie in time. The case fell into a baggage truck and she was carried away.

"Ride like the wind, Bullseye!" Woody yelled as he and Buzz jumped on the little horse's back. By the time they caught up to the baggage truck, Al's green case was already being loaded onto a plane! Woody hid inside another bag and was tossed onto the plane, too. He found the scared cowgirl. "C'mon, Jess," he said. "It's time to take you home."

Just then, the plane's doors closed! The toys crawled through a hatch, down to the wheels. The plane was speeding down the runway and Woody slipped! Jessie caught him, but his arm was starting to tear. Woody lassoed his pull string onto the wheels of the plane. Then he held Jessie's hand and, together, they swung down and landed right behind Buzz, who was galloping along on Bullseye!

The toys were safe. It was time to go home.

# A Major Mess

High in the bell tower of Notre Dame cathedral, the gargoyles Victor, Hugo, and Laverne were playing hide-and-seek.

"Ready or not, here I come!" called Victor. "And no one had better be hiding in Quasimodo's underwear drawer!" And with that, he leaped over a pile of rumpled clothes and began searching among stacks of books and games and other scattered objects.

Quasi had asked them to please look after his things—particularly his carvings and precious bells—while he was away. "And of course," Quasi told them, "feel free to make yourselves at home." And, boy, had they ever!

They had tried on his clothes and left them scattered all over the floor. They had leafed through his books and played all his games. They had even used his pillows for pillow fights!

So it was with some shock and horror that Victor suddenly stopped their game and shrieked, "Do you know what day it is?"

"Excuse me?" said Hugo, peeking out from behind a pillar.

"It's Friday!" said Victor. "The day that Quasi returns home!"

"Oh!" Hugo gulped, gazing at the mess. "He's not going to be happy with us, is he?"

"Oh, but he *is*," said Victor. "We're going to clean all this up. If we don't, he'll never trust us to be home alone again."

"Maybe he shouldn't," muttered Hugo.

"Where is Laverne? Laverne!" Victor called. "Come out, come out, wherever you are! We have work to do."

And work they did. They folded the clothes. They made the bed. They put the books back on the shelf. They washed the dishes and scrubbed the floor. They even polished every one of Quasi's bells.

"You missed a spot on Big Marie!" Victor called to Hugo . . . just as Quasimodo arrived.

"Guys! I'm home!" he shouted.

"Quasi! We missed you. How was your vacation?" the gargoyles asked.

"Great!" said Quasimodo, giving each of the gargoyles a hug. "You should try it sometime."

The gargoyles agreed. After all the work they'd just done, a vacation was exactly what they needed!

# Something Different

Sulley groaned and shifted in his reclining chair. "Ate too much again," he said.

"Oh, me too," Mike moaned, reclining beside him in front of the fire. "I feel like all we do is sit around and eat."

"And eat and sit around," Sulley agreed. "Ain't it great?"

"Great if you like the same thing all the time," Mike said glumly. Then his tone changed. "What we need," he decided, "is to get away. We need to go someplace, do something different. What do you think, buddy?"

"Sit down. Have another chocolate." Sulley waved a box of candy at Mike.

But Mike was insistent. "Someplace with snow!" Mike pounded his fist in his palm. "That's it!"

\* \* \*

"I don't know how you talked me into this," Sulley said a short time later. He and Mike stood at the top of a steep hill with snowboards strapped to their feet. "Can't I use a sled instead?"

"Come on," Mike said. "Sleds are for old monsters. Are you old? No! So don't worry. You'll be great!"

Mike took off down the hill. He did turns, he caught air, he went fast, and in a spray of snow he came to a halt. "Your turn," he called up to Sulley.

"How do I know I will live to regret this?" Sulley asked under his breath, looking down the hill. "Actually, how do I even know I'll *live*?"

He slid slowly across the top of the mountain. He was moving. This wasn't so bad! But when he tried to turn down the hill, things got tricky. His board had a mind of its own . . . and it had decided to go back to the lodge!

\* \* \*

Sulley groaned and shifted in his chair. He propped his sprained ankle up on a pillow and rubbed his stomach. "Ate too much again," he said. He sighed and rubbed his belly.

"Me too," Mike groaned from his reclining chair beside him. In front of them a glowing fire hissed and popped. "All we do is sit around and eat." He sighed happily.

Sulley smiled sleepily. "Ain't it great?"

"Sure is." Mike sipped his hot chocolate. "I told you we needed to get away and do something different!"

# The Parr Family

**D**uring the golden age of the Supers, Mr. Incredible was the world's greatest hero. Mr. Incredible's greatest fan was a boy named Buddy. He wanted to be a Super like his hero. Buddy decided to change his name to Incrediboy, and he even invented some rocket boots that allowed him to fly. He asked Mr. Incredible if he could be his sidekick, but Mr. Incredible told Buddy that fancy boots didn't make someone a Super. Supers were born, not made.

Mr. Incredible married another Super, Elastigirl. The future seemed bright for them . . . until disaster struck.

People started to sue the Supers and claim they hadn't wanted to be saved! The government told the Supers to stop being heroes. They had to go into hiding and live like normal people. So Mr. Incredible became boring, average Bob Parr, and Elastigirl became Helen Parr. They had a shy daughter, Violet, who could turn invisible and create force fields, a Super-fast son named Dash, and a baby, Jack-Jack, who seemed to have no Super powers at all.

Helen adjusted very well to normal life and focused all her efforts on the kids. Bob worked in a boring job at an insurance company and desperately missed being a Super.

Bob couldn't stop dreaming of the past. One night, Bob went out with his friend Lucius.

Lucius Best was a Super known as Frozone, literally the coolest Super of all! The two friends tuned in to the police radio, listening to reports of crimes in progress. Bob was hoping to save someone—just like in the good old days. When he heard about a fire at a nearby apartment, Bob convinced Lucius that they should go and help.

"We're gonna get caught," Lucius said.

The two Supers saved several people—but in order to escape the fire, they had to break into the jewelry shop next door. A policeman thought they were thieves! Lucius used his Super powers to freeze the policeman, and the two Supers escaped.

But someone had seen them! What would become of Mr. Incredible?

# Oscar's House of Smoothies

**H**andy Manny and the tools were at Oscar's House of 18 Smoothies. Oscar had accidentally dropped a blender that morning and cracked his counter.

"Thanks for coming to help so quickly," Oscar said.

"*De nada*, Oscar. You're welcome," Manny said as he inspected the damaged counter.

Oscar smiled, pointing to the sign above his counter. "I have eighteen different fruit smoothies customers can choose from!"

Stretch looked, and realized Oscar actually only had seventeen flavors on his menu!

"What am I going to do?" cried Oscar. "I came up with all the smoothie flavors I could possibly think of!"

Dusty chimed in. "We can help you come up with another flavor!"

"I have a plan," said Manny. "I'll go to Kelly's to buy the supplies we need to fix the counter. While I'm gone, you guys can help Oscar come up with another flavor."

The tools were excited. "Guys, it would be smart to check out Oscar's kitchen," Turner said. "Let's look around and see

if there's an ingredient he hasn't used yet." So the toys and Oscar looked at the seventeen smoothies already on the menu, and realized the only ingredient Oscar hadn't used was peanut butter!

Just then, Mr. Lopart—who owned the sweet shop—burst into Oscar's kitchen. He was zooming around on his new office chair with wheels and crashed into the ingredients!

Manny returned to find Mr. Lopart on the floor of Oscar's kitchen, covered in food.

"Are you okay?" Manny asked.

Mr. Lopart wiped some of the food from his face and licked his fingers. "Hmm, it's quite tasty! Is that peanut butter and banana mixed together?" Mr. Lopart said.

Stretch jumped up and down, excited. "Peanut butter and banana could be a new smoothie flavor!" he said.

Oscar grinned. "That is a wonderful idea!"

While Oscar cleaned his kitchen and made his brand-new smoothie, Manny and the tools fixed the counter. When they were done, everyone tried the Peanut Butter Banana Smoothie. It was delicious!

# A Tight Squeeze

It was early one morning and Andy had just left for school. The toys were ready to have some fun, so Woody told them all about a game they could play. "It's called 'sardines,'" he explained. "It's like hide-and-seek, except when you find the hider, you hide with them and wait for someone else to find you both. The next toy to find you hides with you, too, and so on and so on. Get it?"

"So, by the end of the game, we are all hiding together in one spot?" Jessie the cowgirl asked.

Woody nodded. "Right," he said, "except for the last toy, who is still looking for the hiders. In the next game, that toy is the one who hides!"

The toys decided that Hamm the piggy bank would be the one to hide. Woody told the other toys to close their eyes and count to twenty-five. Meanwhile, Hamm hurried off to find a good hiding place. With seconds to spare, he spotted one of Andy's old lunch boxes, hopped inside, and closed the lid.

The first toy to open the lunch box lid was Woody. His eyes lit up when he saw Hamm inside. Making sure no one was watching him, he hopped inside and shut the lid. Soon the lid opened again. It was Jessie. She wedged herself between Hamm and Woody and shut the lid again.

Buzz opened the lunch box next and hopped inside. But he couldn't get the lid to close, no matter how hard he tried.

By the time Rex found the hiders, the lunch box was completely full. Soon the rest of the toys were hurrying toward the overstuffed lunch box.

"Oh, well," said Woody with a laugh. "They've found us. I guess this game is over. Everybody out!" One by one, the toys tumbled out of the lunch box and gathered around Hamm.

"Gosh, Hamm, couldn't you have picked a bigger hiding place?" Rex asked.

"Well, yeah," Hamm replied, "but isn't the point of the game to get squished? Like sardines in a can?"

The toys thought that over. They realized he was right. From then on, every time the toys played "sardines," the hider made sure to pick a small hiding place—just to keep things interesting!

# Mater Private Eye

Lightning McQueen drove up to the air pump. "My tires are going flat," he said.

Just then, Mater popped out of nowhere. "Flat tires, ya say? I thought I done solved that crime. I was a private eye," Mater explained. Then he told his friend about his detective days. "It was a Friday night . . ." he began.

Mater sat behind the desk in his office reading an article about accidents caused by tires blowing out. "I was on to something real big," Mater explained. "There was some kind of counterfeit-tire ring."

Suddenly, a car named Tia drove into Mater's office. "I need you to find my sister, Mia," Tia cried. "She's been carnapped! She was working for Big D at his club, the Carpacabana."

Big D was a sedan who had recently opened a nightclub. That night, Mater went to the club. A singer was performing. After her song, she came to Mater's table. "I'm looking for Mia. Have you seen her?" Mater asked.

"I saw her a couple of days ago with Big D. She smelled salty, like the ocean," the singer said. But before he could find out any more, Mater was thrown out of the club.

Mater headed to the docks, where he found Mia on a cargo ship. Just then, a crane grabbed Mater and hoisted him up over the water.

Back in Radiator Springs, Lightning was on the edge of his bumper. "WHAT DID YOU DO?" he cried.

Mater laughed aloud. "Like you don't know, Lieutenant!"

Police Lieutenant Lightning McQueen drove onto the docks with a group of squad cars. "Looks like we finally caught you, Big D," he said. With Big D distracted, Tia hit a switch on the crane and lowered Mater to the ground. Mater threw his tow hook at another crane, which dropped its crate—right on Big D!

The crate split open, and tires spilled all over Big D.

"Aha! Just what I thought. Counterfeit tires," Mater said.

Now that Mater had uncovered Big D's scam, the police stepped in.

"You led us right to him, Mater," Lightning announced gratefully. "Take him away, boys!"

# Lemur Love

Early one morning, Plio the lemur sat on a branch, trying to groom her daughter. Suri was very fidgety. She was itching to join her friends. But Plio wouldn't let Suri go until her fur was combed and clean.

"Why do I have to be groomed every single day?" Suri groaned.

"Would you rather I let you swing around with dirty fur?" Plio said.

"Yeah!" Suri exclaimed.

Plio sighed. "All right, all done," she said, giving Suri's fur one last stroke. In a flash, Suri jumped up and hurried off to join her friends.

Plio shook her head as she watched her daughter go. "Every morning, it's the same thing: an out-and-out struggle to get that girl groomed," she said to herself. "But if I didn't, I bet she'd get so tired of being messy that, after a few days, she'd be begging me to groom her!"

That gave Plio an idea. The next morning, Plio didn't say a word about grooming.

Just as Suri was about to leave her mother's side to go off and play, she hesitated.

"I guess you have to groom me first, huh, Mom?" Suri said glumly.

Plio shrugged. "Not if you don't want me to," she replied.

The next day, Suri happily left without being groomed. Then, on the third day, Plio caught Suri looking over at her wistfully.

"Suri?" Plio said. "What's wrong?" But she thought she knew what was wrong.

Just as Plio expected, Suri said, "Mom, would you groom me this morning?"

"Groom you?" Plio said, pretending to be surprised. "But, Suri, I thought you hated being groomed. Let me guess: you're tired of having messy fur, aren't you?"

Suri shook her head. "No," she said.

"No?" said Plio.

"No," repeated Suri. "I miss being fussed over."

Suri hung her head bashfully and wrapped her arms around her mother.

Plio's face softened into a smile as she hugged Suri back. Then Plio gave Suri a long and careful grooming.

And do you know what? Suri didn't fidget at all.

# Sidetracked

"All right," Kenai told Koda. "No more getting sidetracked. We're heading to the place where the lights touch the earth, and I mean pronto!"

Koda gave Kenai a sideways glance. "I guess that means you're not interested in tasting the sweetest honey on the face of the earth," he said.

"What has that got to do with anything?" Kenai asked.

"Nothing," Koda said, "except for the fact that I just happen to know where to find the sweetest honey in the entire world, and it isn't far from here at all."

"The sweetest-tasting honey in the world, huh?" Kenai asked.

"That's right," Koda said.

"Prove it!" Kenai said.

"It's this way!" Koda said and took off running. Koda led Kenai to a tree with a beehive hanging from it.

"It's right there!" Koda pointed. "All we have to do is get it down."

Bees buzzed in and out of the hive.

"That looks a little dangerous," Kenai said.

"Nothing to it," Koda said and began clawing his way up the tree.

But as he reached out his paw to grab the hive, a swarm of bees flew toward him. "Maybe we could use some help."

"I have an idea," said Kenai, pointing to Rutt and Tuke, who were browsing in a field not far from them. "Just don't wander too far from that tree."

Kenai crouched down as low as he could and began crawling toward Rutt and Tuke.

"This is the life, eh, Tuke?" Rutt said.

"Nothing could ruin this day," Tuke replied.

Just then, Kenai jumped out at them. He chased after the moose, leading them right in the direction of the tree. Rutt looked up just in time to skid to a halt, but Tuke was less fortunate. He was headed right for the tree. At the last moment, he turned so that he slammed into the tree with his shoulder. The hive flew off, landing right in Koda's waiting paws.

"Aren't you going to have some?" Koda asked Kenai, honey smeared all over his face.

Kenai dipped his paw into the honey.

"What do you think?" Koda asked.

Kenai smacked his lips. "That's the best-tasting sidetrack I've ever had!"

# Happy Campers

It was a warm, sunny day on Ant Island—the perfect day for Princess Dot and her fellow Blueberries to go on a campout! Flik volunteered to be their leader.

"This is gonna be so much fun, Flik!" said Dot, marching behind him. "Pitching our tents! Making a campfire! Telling ghost stories all night long!"

"Well, we've got to get to our campsite first," Flik reminded her. "The perfect campsite for the perfect campout!"

"Where's that?" asked Dot.

"I'm not exactly sure," said Flik. "But don't worry! I'll know it when I see it."

So on they hiked, until they came to some soft moss beside a quiet stream.

"Is this it?" asked Daisy excitedly.

Flik shook his head. "Definitely not," he said. "Too out in the open."

"We're getting tired," Dot said.

"Chins up, Blueberries," said Flik. "We'll find the perfect campsite soon. I'll bet it's just across that stream."

Flik guided the Blueberries onto a broad leaf. Together they rowed across the water. But the other side of the stream was not quite perfect enough for Flik, either.

"No worries," Flik said. "See that hill over there? I'll betcha the perfect campsite is just beyond it."

The Blueberries followed him up the grassy hill and down the other side.

"We made it!" the Blueberries cheered.

"Not so fast," said Flik, frowning. "The ground is too damp here. We'll have to keep looking."

"But, Flik! We can't go any farther," they complained.

"Nonsense!" said Flik, tightening his backpack. "You're Blueberries! C'mon!"

And so, with the Blueberries dragging their poor, tired feet, Flik hiked on. Then, just when the Blueberries thought they couldn't walk another inch, Flik suddenly froze in his tracks.

"The perfect campsite! We've found it! Let's pitch those tents, Blueberries, and get a fire started!"

But instead of cheers, Flik heard only silence. He turned around and saw that those poor Blueberries, still wearing their backpacks, were already fast asleep!

# Oliver's Sleepover

Oliver couldn't wait. At last, Jenny's limo pulled up to the docks. Even before the chauffeur could open the door, Oliver leaped out the window and began racing toward the barge. Then, remembering Jenny, he stopped, turned around, and waved his paw in her direction.

"Good-bye, Oliver!" she called. "Have a fun sleepover!"

Don't worry, thought Oliver. I will!

This was the first time, you see, that Oliver had been back to the barge since he'd gone to live in Jenny's mansion. And though he loved Jenny dearly, boy, did he miss his friends!

"Tito! Einstein! Francis! Rita!" Oliver called as he ran in to find his four-footed friends waiting for him.

"Hey! What about me?" barked a voice from the back of the barge.

"Dodger!" yelled Oliver. He leaped up on the shaggy dog and gave him a friendly face rub. "It's so good to see you!"

"So how's life in the mansion?" Dodger asked.

"I can't complain," said Oliver.

He told his friends about his latest cruise on Jenny's yacht. "All those fish!" he said dreamily. Then he told them about her house in the country. "The best part is just lying out in the sun! You've got to come with us someday!"

Just then, Fagin walked in with a great big tray. "Oliver, my good friend! Welcome back! I do hope you're hungry!"

Oliver's eyes grew wide as he took in the piles of hot dogs, chicken fingers, and fish sticks (his favorite!) on Fagin's tray. Oliver and the dogs dug in and ate . . . and ate . . . until they could not eat another bite. Then it was time for games!

Fagin dealt out some playing cards.

"I'm gonna stay up all night!" Oliver cried.

"Whatever you say, little buddy," Dodger said. "It's your night."

So they played a little Go Fish, then some Duck, Duck, Goose. Then Fagin told them some of Oliver's favorite spooky stories. When he was done, Dodger turned to Oliver.

"So, what's next, little buddy?" he asked.

But Oliver didn't answer. . . . He was fast asleep!

# Spring Time

Outside, it was a beautiful spring day. Inside, most of the toys were helping Bo Peep find her sheep.

"Did you try the closet?" asked Hamm.

"How about under the bed?" said Jessie.

Just then, Buzz pulled Woody aside.

"I could use some advice," he said. "How about we go sit outside for a few minutes?"

Woody thought for a moment. "It *is* nice out," he said. "Let's sit on the roof. Andy and his mom shouldn't be home for a while, anyway."

The two toys climbed onto the roof and sat down. But Buzz had barely opened his mouth when the toys saw a flash of lightning. Suddenly the sky opened up.

"Help!" Woody cried. The pounding rain swept him into the rain gutter!

"I'm coming," cried Buzz. But the space ranger wasn't coming to *help*. He was being washed down the gutter, too.

Woody and Buzz sped through the gutter and down the drainpipe. Woody was sure they would hit the ground soon, but the force of the water sent them flying all the way to the curb.

"Storm drain!" he cried as he was swept forward.

At the last moment, the toys grabbed on to a twig that was blocking the mouth of the drain.

Luckily, up in Andy's room, Lenny the binoculars had been watching the sudden spring storm. He called the other toys, who gathered at the window.

"We have to do something," cried Hamm.

Slinky Dog had an idea. With Rex holding his feet, Slinky dropped himself out of the window. Then he stretched his spring as far as it would go.

"He can't reach!" Jessie cried. "We need to form a toy chain!"

Bo Peep held on to Rex. Hamm held on to Bo Peep. The Green Army Men held on to Hamm—and each other— and Jessie grabbed the last of them. Finally, Slinky was long enough. Buzz and Woody grabbed ahold of his ears and let go of the twig. *Boing!* They flew through the air and landed in a heap in Andy's room.

"So much for the nice spring weather today," Buzz said to Woody.

The cowboy smiled. "Thank goodness we had a nice spring to save the day!"

# Trusting Trusty

"Tramp!" cried Lady one morning. "One of our puppies is missing!"

"Don't worry," said Tramp with a yawn. "Scamp is always getting into mischief."

"It's not Scamp," said Lady. "It's little Fluffy! Tramp, what should we do?"

"You look inside. I'll look outside," said Tramp worriedly.

From a neighbor's porch, Trusty the bloodhound called, "Howdy! Whatcha looking for?"

"My daughter, Fluffy! She's missing," said Tramp.

Trusty's long floppy ears pricked up. "A missing puppy—now that's serious! I should know; I used to help my grandpappy track down missing persons through the swamps!"

"I know," said Tramp. He'd heard Trusty tell that story a hundred times.

"Have you found a trail yet?" asked Trusty.

Tramp shook his head.

"Well, let me at it!" Trusty loped back to Tramp's garden. He put his big nose to the ground. *Sniff, sniff, sniff . . .*

"Tramp, have you found Fluffy?" Lady called from the dog door.

Tramp ran over. "No," he replied. "But Trusty offered his . . . uh . . . services."

"He can't smell anymore," Lady whispered.

"He helped us once," said Tramp. "I think we should trust him again."

Just then, Trusty shouted, "Look at this!" He had spotted a bluebird's feather below a window.

"That's the window the puppies look out," said Lady.

"Look! A bit of puppy fur," said Trusty. "And footprints!" Trusty followed the trail of footprints to the back of a shed. And wouldn't you know, that's where he found the missing puppy! Fluffy was fast asleep under a big tree.

"Fluffy! What happened?" Lady cried.

"I woke up and saw a bluebird," said Fluffy with a yawn. "I didn't want Scamp to bark and scare it away, like he always does. So I didn't wake anyone. I followed the bird all the way to this tree. Then I guess I got sleepy."

Lady walked over and gave Trusty a kiss. "Thank you," she said.

"Aw, shucks," said Trusty, blushing. "It weren't nothin'."

As the bloodhound trotted home, Tramp turned to Lady. "See that?" he said. "I told you we should trust Trusty!"

# Laughter Is the Best Medicine

"I hope Quasi is okay out there!" Laverne said fretfully.

The other two gargoyles in the bell tower, Hugo and Victor, nodded in agreement. Their friend Quasimodo had just left Notre Dame to help the young soldier Phoebus search for the Court of Miracles. It was sure to be a dangerous mission.

"The only things we can do are stay strong and be hopeful," Victor said solemnly.

Hugo smirked. "How can we *not* be strong?" he said. "We're made of stone, remember?"

"Good one!" Laverne giggled. "Rock solid."

"You know that's not what I meant." Victor frowned at his friends. "And both of you—don't you have any sense of the seriousness of this situation? Our dear compatriot is out there somewhere, facing grave peril . . ."

"*Grave* peril?" Laverne said. "Way to be optimistic, Victor—you've already got poor Quasi in his grave!"

"I see," Victor said sternly. "So you two would rather mock me and crack bad jokes than join me in my concern for poor young Quasimodo."

Laverne stood up and brushed herself off. "Why does it have to be an either-or thing, Victor?" she asked. "Just because we're laughing, it doesn't mean we're not worried, too."

Hugo nodded. "If we spend all our time thinking about how terrible everything is, we'll go nuts."

Waving his arms to help make his point, Hugo accidentally hit a bird's nest that was tucked into one of the eaves. The occupant of the nest squawked and flew upward. Laverne ducked just in time to avoid having the bird fly straight into her face, but then she tripped and fell and wound up on the ground. The bird banked upward, still squawking as it flew over Hugo.

Hugo leaped backward—and landed on Laverne's hand! She yelled and yanked her hand out from under him. Hugo lost his footing and landed in a heap on top of Laverne.

Victor stared at his friends, who were trying to untangle themselves. Then he started to laugh. He laughed harder and harder, until he could hardly speak.

"You know," he said finally, "I think you just might be right. I feel much better already!"

# A Bear-y Tale

It was time for Mowgli, Bagheera, and Baloo to go to bed. But Mowgli couldn't sleep. He needed a bedtime story. And so Baloo began. . . .

"Once upon a time, in a house not far from this very jungle, there lived a clan of men. This clan, they cooked their food, and one day, don't you know, they made a mighty tasty stew. Only thing was, when they sat down to eat, it was just too hot. So the mother got an idea. They'd go for a walk in the jungle, and by the time they got back, their stew would be nice and cool. But do you know what happened next?"

"No," Mowgli said.

"Well, that family had barely been gone a minute when an old bear came wandering up and stuck his nose into the Man-house."

"He did?" gasped Mowgli.

"Well, now, can you blame him? That stew just smelled so awfully good. And the next thing you know, he was tastin' it—startin' with the biggest bowl, but that was still too hot. So next he tried the middle bowl, but that was too cold. So he tried the littlest

bowl, and, don't you know, it was just right! That old bear ate the whole thing right up!"

"What happened next?" said Mowgli.

"Oh, well, after that, this bear, he started to get tired. And don't you know that right there in that house, looking so soft and comfortable, were three cushy-lookin' pads . . . I think men call them 'beds.' Anyway, that bear, he had to try them, too. Naturally, he lay down on the biggest one first, but it was too hard. So he tried the middle one, but that was much, much too soft. So he tried the littlest one, and let me tell you, that thing was so comfortable, he fell asleep right then and there! And he would have slept clear through the next full moon . . . if only that family hadn't returned and—"

"And what?" Mowgli asked. "Don't stop now!"

"And startled that bear so much, he ran back into the jungle . . . full belly and all."

Mowgli smiled and tried to cover a big yawn. "Is that a true story, Baloo?"

The bear grinned. "Would I ever tell you a tall tale, Little Britches?"

# What a Crab

Nemo was having trouble at school—and its name was Ruddy. The big crab was mean to Nemo and the other kids whenever he got the chance. The trouble was, he was crafty and never did it when the teachers were looking.

One day, he shoved Nemo into a tide pool and made him late for their coral lesson. Another time, he taunted Nemo by saying, "My dad's bigger and stronger than your dad!"

"I have tried everything," Nemo complained to his shark friends, Bruce, Chum, and Anchor. "But he won't leave me alone. What do *you* think we should do?"

"Just leave it to us!" said Bruce. "We're experts in behavior modification."

The next day, three huge shadows fell over Nemo's classmates as they played in the school playground.

"Hello," Bruce said to the crab. "You must be Nemo's new little friend."

While Ruddy trembled, Bruce snarled, "We just wanted you to know that any friend of Nemo's is a friend of ours. You are a friend of Nemo's, aren't you?"

Everyone looked at Ruddy. "Oh, yeah!" he managed to splutter. "Nemo and I are buddies."

"Good!" Anchor said. "Because you don't want to know what happens to anyone who's not nice to our little pal here."

Chum cleaned a piece of seaweed from between his razor-sharp teeth with a spiny urchin. "You should stop by for lunch sometime," he said to Ruddy with a wink, and then swam away.

Ruddy sidled up to Nemo. "You're friends with three sharks?" he said. "Wow! That's pretty cool! I wish I had friends like that. In fact, I wish I had any friends at all."

"How do you expect to have friends when you're so . . . well, *crabby* all the time?" Nemo said.

Ruddy admitted that he had decided to pick on everyone else before they had a chance to pick on him.

"If you promise to stop acting mean, I promise to be your friend," Nemo said.

"Deal," Ruddy agreed. "Besides, I guess I'd better be your friend if I don't want your shark pals to eat me."

Nemo didn't say a word. Bruce, Chum, and Anchor were vegetarians, but Ruddy didn't need to know that!

# Lessons

In the depths of the woods somewhere in England, Merlin the magician was waiting for a very special visitor. His name was Wart, a clever but reckless young boy.

Wart soon tumbled into the room and landed on a chair in front of Merlin.

"A great destiny awaits you, my boy," Merlin said to Wart. "But first you need to learn a few things. There's no great destiny without a great teacher—and I will be that person! Just let me pack my case and then we'll be off."

First lesson: the world of water. Merlin touched his wand to Wart's head, and the boy transformed into a fish! Merlin transformed himself, too, and they swam in the moat around the king's castle. Wart waved his fins and made bubbles, enjoying his lesson.

Suddenly, a monstrous fish swam straight for them! Quickly, Merlin changed back into human form and saved Wart from the jaws of the pike.

Second lesson: exploring the forest in the form of a squirrel! Wart immediately made a friend—a charming female squirrel who really liked him. But just when a wolf was about to attack him, Wart changed back into a child.

"What's the third lesson?" he then asked his teacher.

"Flying through the air!" answered Merlin, transforming him into a baby bird.

In the company of Archimedes, a grumpy old owl, Wart launched himself into the air. What fun it was to fly! But danger lurked in the air, too: an eagle appeared and threatened the two friends!

Panic-stricken, Wart fled from the eagle and flew into a chimney. He fell into the house—and the clutches—of mad Madam Mim, a wicked sorceress who lived in the forest!

Luckily, Merlin appeared in the cottage. To overpower the sorceress, he changed himself into a germ and gave her the measles!

Later, as he walked home, Wart came across a mysterious sword thrust into an anvil. Engraved on the sword were the words WHO SO PULLETH ME OUT WILL BE KING OF ENGLAND.

To everyone's astonishment, the boy effortlessly pulled the sword out of the stone! Wart—or rather, Arthur—was to be King of England. And what better king than one who had learned his lessons?

**MAY**
# 26

# Three Cheesy Wishes

**L**ong ago, before there was an Aladdin, a Jasmine, or even a Sultan, a traveling merchant bought a lamp, along with some other "junk." Not knowing its value, he traded the lamp to a cheese seller for some lunch.

Hassan the cheese seller looked at the lamp skeptically. He sighed and began to shine it up. In a puff of smoke, the Genie appeared.

"Hello there! I'm the one and only magical Genie!" the big blue spirit announced.

"Excuse me?" said Hassan.

"Nice to meet you," said the Genie. "And what do you do here in Agrabah?"

"My name is Hassan, and I'm a—"

"Wait!" cried the Genie. "Let me guess!" The Genie put his hand over his brow as he secretly looked around the man's shop. "You sell . . . cheese! Am I right or am I right?"

"You are right," said Hassan. "But that's an easy guess."

"You're very observant, Hassan," said the Genie. "So I'll give you three wishes."

"Three wishes, eh?" Hassan thought for a few minutes. Then he said, "It's hard to get enough good milk to make the best cheese. I wish I had many, many goats so I would always have enough milk."

*Poof!* In a flash, thousands of goats filled the streets of Agrabah. Goats were everywhere!

"Goodness!" Hassan cried. "I would have to wish for the biggest cheese shop in the world to sell the cheese from so many goats."

*Poof!* All of a sudden, Hassan's store began to grow and grow! His cheese shop was even taller than the highest sand dunes outside the city.

"This is terrible!" Hassan cried. Far below, the people looked like tiny ants. "I can't live and work in such a monstrosity. All I wanted was to make the finest cheese in Agrabah." Hassan turned to the Genie. "I wish I'd never met you!" he cried.

*Poof!* The Genie disappeared and Hassan found that his shop had returned to normal. Outside, the marketplace was completely goat-free. Hassan searched high and low for the lamp, but it was gone, too.

"It must have all been a crazy dream," said Hassan. But from that day forward, everyone said Hassan's cheese was the finest in all of Agrabah!

# Stay Loose, Moose!

Two moose named Rutt and Tuke were grazing on some grass on a plateau when Rutt lifted his head and moved it from side to side, stretching his neck.

"Tuke," he said to his brother, "you gotta try some of these new stretches I learned. They're just the thing to get your mind, body, and spirit back into balance, eh."

"My balance is fine the way it is," Tuke said.

"Aw, come on," said Rutt. "We've been on our hooves all day. Don't tell me you're not feeling a tweak in your back."

Tuke didn't reply right away. "Well . . ."

"Aha! I knew it," said Rutt. "I promise these stretches will fix you right up."

Tuke hesitated, but finally he agreed. "Oh, all right," he said. "But nothing too strenuous."

"Excellent!" Rutt exclaimed, demonstrating the first posture. "Try this one: the Downward-Facing Dog." Rutt moved his front and back hooves closer together and raised his rear end high into the air. Tuke did the same.

"How does that feel?" Rutt asked as he held the pose.

"Good," Tuke replied. "Really good."

Rutt smiled. "Let's try something more advanced," he suggested. "This one's called the Resting Lizard."

Rutt crossed his right back leg over his left back leg, like a pretzel. Then he placed his two front hooves together. He closed his eyes so he could really concentrate and breathed in and out deeply.

Tuke did the same. He was doing fine for the first few seconds. Then he lost his balance.

Tuke fell over onto his side and rolled onto his back, coming to rest with his legs pointed straight up in the air.

Rutt was concentrating so hard on his Resting Lizard pose that he didn't notice what had happened—until he opened his eyes.

"Hey, all right." Rutt smiled. "You're already getting creative and coming up with your own poses, eh? What do you call that one?"

Tuke scowled. "I call it the Mad Moose," he replied sarcastically. "Now help me up!"

# Not Just a Glitch

Wreck-It Ralph, from the computer game Fix-It Felix, Jr., had agreed to help his new friend Vanellope build a racing kart. Vanellope was a character in the Sugar Rush game. She had won Ralph's Hero's Duty medal from him and used it to enter the game's race. Ralph wanted his medal back. That meant he would have to help Vanellope. And right now what she needed was his help winning!

As the pair headed out to race, the little girl hit the brakes. "Forgot something!" she said. "I'll be right back."

Just then, King Candy, the leader of Sugar Rush, appeared. He told Ralph that Vanellope was in danger. She didn't belong in the game. If players in the arcade saw her glitching, they'd think Sugar Rush was broken and switch off the game. And because Vanellope was a glitch, she wouldn't be able to escape the game. She'd be switched off along with it! King Candy gave Ralph's medal back and asked for his help. He told Ralph he had to stop Vanellope from racing.

After King Candy left, Vanellope returned with a homemade medal, just for Ralph. On the back, it read "To Stink Brain," and on the front, "You're MY HERO!"

Ralph knew it was up to him to save Vanellope. He told her that she would confuse the players if she raced. And if the game was switched off, she would be doomed. Vanellope refused to listen. Ralph had no choice. He wrecked her kart so she couldn't race.

Sadly, Ralph returned to his own game. He threw a medal against the game's front window. The glass shook and the OUT OF ORDER sign slipped. Ralph could see the Sugar Rush console . . . with Vanellope's picture on it! Ralph gasped. Vanellope *did* belong in Sugar Rush!

Ralph hurried back to Sugar Rush to get some answers. He found King Candy's sidekick, Sour Bill. Sour Bill explained that King Candy had reprogrammed Sugar Rush and stolen Vanellope's computer code. But if she ever crossed the finish line, she'd become an official racer again!

Ralph rushed off to find his little friend. He had to help Vanellope cross that finish line.

# Tokyo Mater

One afternoon three flashy modified cars roared past Flo's V8 Café.

"I used to be an import," Mater said. Mater described driving through Carburetor County and seeing an older car. . . .

Mater pulled up. "Looks like you could use a tow somewhere," he said.

"It is very far," replied the older car. His name was Ito-San.

"Well, no tow is too far for Tow Mater!" Mater exclaimed. And so Mater towed Ito-San all the way to Tokyo!

Mater had never seen so many tall buildings. Then Mater accidentally bumped into Kabuto, the leader of a gang of ninja cars.

"You scratched my paint," Kabuto snarled. "We will race at midnight."

Kabuto had challenged Mater!

"You need modification," Ito-San said. With the help of some other cars, Mater soon got a slick blue paint job and a large rear spoiler. At midnight, he pulled up to the starting line.

"Race to the top of Tokyo Tower. First one to seize the flag will become king of all drifters," Ito-San explained.

Kabuto and Mater zipped through the streets. Mater was driving so fast that he missed a turn. Then Mater went the wrong direction on a one-way street and sped down an alley. He saw Kabuto up ahead and drove up next to him.

"Good," said Kabuto. "But not good enough. Ninjas, attack!"

Suddenly, a group of Kabuto's ninjas appeared. Mater was forced to slow down while Kabuto sped off laughing.

Back in Radiator Springs, Lightning asked, "What did you do?"

"Well, shoot. You oughta know," Mater replied. "You was there, too!"

Mater was surrounded by ninjas. Suddenly, Dragon Lightning McQueen was there. With a kick of his rear tire, Lightning sent each ninja flying.

Meanwhile, Kabuto was nearly to Tokyo Tower. Just then, Mater landed in front of him. "Well, hey!" Mater shouted. He took off down the highway, driving backward. Kabuto chased after him. Then Kabuto pushed Mater over the railing.

Mater quickly threw his tow hook onto the tower and pulled himself up to the top. He had finished the race first! "I win!" Mater said proudly.

# Dumbo's Parade Pals

When Dumbo's circus came to town, the animals and circus folk marched in a big parade. The crowd loved seeing all the circus animals marching down the street.

Suddenly, Dumbo noticed a peanut on the ground. He picked up the peanut with his trunk and ate it. Then Dumbo saw another peanut, and another.

Leaving the parade, Dumbo followed the trail of peanuts all the way to a playground.

"See, the peanuts worked!" exclaimed a little girl with pigtails. "Now we have our own elephant to play with."

"Let's have our own circus," said a boy.

"I'll be the ringmaster!" cried the little girl. "Ladies and gentlemen! Presenting our star attraction—the Little Elephant!"

Dumbo knew just what to do. He stood up on his two back legs. Then he juggled some balls with his trunk. The children cheered.

Soon Timothy Q. Mouse appeared. "Here you are!" he said to Dumbo. "We have to get back to the circus camp to get ready for the show!"

Dumbo nodded and waved good-bye to his new friends.

"I wish I could go see him in the circus tonight," one of the children said. "But I don't have enough money for a ticket."

Dumbo was sorry that the nice children he had met would not be able to go to the circus. That night, he felt very blue as he put on his stage makeup and warmed up his ears. He tucked Timothy into the brim of his hat and climbed onto a tall platform.

"Ladies and gentlemen!" the Ringmaster cried. "I give you *Dumbo, the Flying Elephant!*"

Dumbo leaped off the platform, and his giant ears unfurled. The crowd cheered as Dumbo flew around the tent.

Far below in the crowd, Dumbo spotted his playground friends sitting in the first row! He swept by them, patting each child on the head with his trunk. The girl with pigtails waved at Dumbo. "Your mouse friend gave us free tickets!" she cried.

Dumbo smiled and reached his trunk up to the brim of his hat, where Timothy was riding. He was the luckiest elephant in the world to have such wonderful friends!

# A Mission for Bob

**B**ob Parr had a boring job. Nobody knew that he was actually Mr. Incredible, a Super who used to save people from disaster!

One day at work, Bob wanted to help someone who was being mugged outside, but his boss wouldn't let him go. Bob was so frustrated at not being allowed to help that he gave his boss a tiny push. Unfortunately, it carried all of Bob's Super strength. *WHAM!* Bob's boss crashed through five walls, and Bob lost his job.

At home, Bob was clearing out his briefcase when a computer fell out! On the screen was a woman who had secretly watched Bob save people from a fire the night before.

Bob's wife, Helen, didn't know, but Bob had started using his Super powers again.

"My name is Mirage. I represent a top secret division of the government," said the woman on the computer. "A highly experimental prototype robot has escaped our control . . ." The woman had a very special top secret mission for Mr. Incredible!

The robot was called the Omnidroid.

Mirage told Bob that if he could stop the malfunctioning Omnidroid battle robot before it caused any damage, he'd be paid three times his yearly salary!

Bob accepted. He needed the money—but more importantly, he needed the adventure.

Bob knew Helen wouldn't approve, so he told her he was going on a business trip. He was taken to the island of Nomanisan, where Mirage told him to shut down the robot, and quickly. "And don't die," she added.

Mr. Incredible soon met the robot, and the fight began. The Omnidroid was a fast learner. The more Mr. Incredible fought, the more it learned about how to protect itself. Finally, Mr. Incredible tricked the Omnidroid into destroying itself.

Mirage and her boss watched the robot's defeat. "Surprising," said her boss. After a celebration dinner with Mirage, Bob flew home. He was excited about getting back into Super work. He began to lose weight, bought a new car, and even played with the kids more!

Things were looking up.

# A Team Again!

Wreck-It Ralph, the Bad Guy from the Fix-It Felix, Jr., computer game, was on a mission to help his friend Vanellope, a racer from the game Sugar Rush.

Vanellope had become a glitch in the game. The other racers had tried to tell her it was because she didn't belong, but Ralph had discovered the truth. The leader of Sugar Rush, King Candy, had reprogrammed the game and stolen Vanellope's unique computer code! That was why she glitched. Ralph had learned that if Vanellope ever crossed the race's finish line, she'd become an official racer again!

Ralph soon learned that his friend Fix-It Felix and Vanellope were being held prisoner in King Candy's castle dungeon. Ralph wrecked his way into Felix's cell and told him about Vanellope. Felix agreed to fix her broken racing kart right away.

Next Ralph rescued Vanellope. They were a team again!

The big race had already started, but Ralph pushed Vanellope onto the track anyway. She quickly glitched and twitched past almost everyone. Finally, she pulled up next to King Candy.

"This is my kingdom!" he snarled.

"Race you for it!" Vanellope replied.

King Candy tried to make Vanellope crash her kart, but she concentrated very hard and glitched away just in time! As Vanellope glitched, so did King Candy! The crowd watched on the screen as the king flickered and turned into . . . TURBO!

Turbo had been a very popular racing character long ago, until a newer racing game had arrived. Feeling jealous, Turbo had left his own game and tried to take over the new one. But when Turbo appeared in the wrong game, everyone thought it was broken! In the end, both games were unplugged and taken away.

"You've ruined everything!" Turbo screamed at Vanellope. But Vanellope zoomed forward.

Ralph cheered as his friend raced toward the finish line. "She's going to do it!" he cried.

Finally, Ralph felt like he *was* the Good Guy.

Bambi

# First Impressions

Bambi was just discovering the wonders of the forest. His mother had brought him to a little clearing in the woods. While his mother grazed nearby, Bambi began to explore. He found a patch of green grass and clover, and he bent down to eat. When his nose was just a few inches from the tips of the grass, he suddenly leaped backward in alarm. A leaf had just sprung up from the patch of grass and landed a few feet away.

Bambi looked around to where his mother stood, still grazing. She seemed to think they were in no great danger. So he followed the leaf all the way to the edge of the clearing, where a wide brook babbled over craggy rocks.

Bambi's fascination with the hopping leaf faded as he approached the brook. Water cascaded smoothly over the rocks, bubbling and frothing in shallow pools. He took a step closer and felt his foot touch a rock at the edge of the water.

Suddenly, the rock moved! It shuffled toward the water and then—*plop!*—jumped right in and swam away.

Bambi was dumbfounded as he watched it dive beneath the surface and vanish. He stared at the spot where the rock had been for a moment, and then stooped down to have a drink.

Bambi jumped in surprise. There in the water, staring right back up at him, was another little deer! Cautiously, he approached the water again. Yes, there it was!

Bambi turned and bounded back across the clearing to his mother.

"Mama! Mama!" he cried. "You will never guess what I have seen today!"

His mother lifted her head and gazed at him with her clear, bright eyes.

"First," he said, "I saw a jumping leaf. Then I saw a rock with legs that walked right into the water and swam away! And then," he continued in amazement, "I saw a little deer who lives right in the water! He's right over there, Mama!"

His mother nuzzled her son's face, thinking over what he had said. Then she laughed gently.

"Darling," she said, "I think you have just seen your first grasshopper, your first turtle, and your very own reflection!"

# Wild West Showdown

A train rumbled across the desert. Suddenly, the roof exploded and the outlaw One-Eyed Bart climbed out, carrying bags of stolen money. Luckily, Sheriff Woody was there to stop him!

"You've got a date with justice, One-Eyed Bart!" cried the sheriff.

But One-Eyed Bart wasn't alone. "Ai-ai-yah!" came a cry from behind Woody. It was One-Eyed Betty, One-Eyed Bart's karate-chopping wife! With one kick, she knocked Woody right off the train.

Suddenly, Jessie the cowgirl sped up on her trusty steed, Bullseye. She caught Woody and together they raced after the villains.

One-Eyed Bart wouldn't be stopped that easily. He pulled out a detonator and blew up a bridge that crossed a giant canyon. Bart and Betty jumped into their getaway car.

"It's me or the kiddies!" yelled One-Eyed Bart. "Take your pick!"

As the outlaws sped away, Jessie saw that the train was filled with orphans. And it was heading right toward the broken bridge! Woody had to save the orphans before going after One-Eyed Bart.

Woody leaped back onto the train. He quickly found the brake. The train squeaked as it slowed down. But Woody had been too slow. The train plunged into the canyon with Woody and the orphans still on board!

Suddenly, Buzz Lightyear appeared! He caught the train and lifted it out of the canyon.

Jessie cheered as Buzz carried the train to safety.

Suddenly, a giant shadow appeared overhead. A pig-shaped spaceship beamed One-Eyed Bart, One-Eyed Betty, and their sidekicks to safety.

With a wicked laugh, One-Eyed Bart dropped an army of vicious monkeys onto Woody, Jessie, and Buzz.

"Buzz!" shouted Woody. "Shoot your laser at my badge!"

Buzz aimed his laser beam at Woody's badge and fired. The beam bounced off the badge and hit the spaceship.

*BOOM!* The ship crashed and the villains plunged to the ground. With the help of his fearsome dinosaur, Sheriff Woody quickly tied them up.

"Good job, deputies!" Woody shouted. The sheriff and his friends had saved the day again!

# Easy Come, Easy Go

One day, Robin Hood was boasting to his friends in Sherwood Forest about his skills with a bow and arrow. "I can take from the rich and give to the poor using only a single arrow," said Robin. "And I'll defeat the greedy Sheriff with that same arrow, too."

"With one arrow?" asked Little John. He knew his friend was talented, but that seemed impossible.

"One arrow is all I need," said Robin. "And it won't even *touch* the Sheriff."

"Now, that really is impossible!" Little John laughed. He was sure Robin was teasing.

But Robin was serious. "Look," he said, "here comes the Sheriff to collect taxes from the poor villagers. I'll show you how easy it is."

Little John and Robin followed the Sheriff to the village. They watched as he went from house to house collecting taxes. Soon the Sheriff's leather bag was bulging with the poor villagers' savings.

As the Sheriff prepared to leave, Little John whispered, "Robin, the Sheriff is taking everything they have.

We can't let him get away with this."

"No, we can't," agreed Robin.

Drawing back his bow, Robin took aim.

"You're going to shoot him?" asked Little John.

"No need," said Robin.

Instead, Robin shot the arrow at the bag of coins, putting a hole in it. The Sheriff didn't even notice.

"Why did you do that?" asked Little John.

"Just watch," Robin said with a smile.

As the Sheriff mounted his horse, the coins began to drop out of the hole in the bag. By the time he'd trotted out of the village, all the tax money he'd collected had spilled out onto the ground. Robin and Little John collected the money and returned it to the delighted villagers.

Little John slapped Robin on the back. "You did it, Robin! You robbed from the rich and gave to the poor— and with only one arrow, just like you said."

"Sure." Robin grinned. "And, as the Sheriff is about to learn, easy come, easy go!"

# The Power of Reading

Princess Kida and Milo were helping the fishermen pull their nets to shore after a long day of fishing for tuyeb.

"You actually eat these ugly things?" Milo asked.

"They are very delicious!" the princess insisted. "The meat is sweet, and the tentacles are excellent when fried. We will have some for dinner tonight."

"I think I'll stick to tuna!" said Milo.

Milo and the princess went back to work. It took a long time to drag the nets to shore—so long that most of the tuyeb slipped through the nets and swam away.

"There has to be a better way." Milo sighed, wiping the sweat from his brow.

When they got to shore, Milo yawned. "I'm tired. Let's take a break."

They sat down next to a great big statue of a tuyeb with long, metal tentacles.

"What's this thing for?" Milo asked.

"I do not know," Kida replied. "There are many of these statues along the shore, but no one knows why they are here, because no one can read the words written on the statues."

"I'll bet I can," Milo declared.

He adjusted his glasses and began to read the ancient words. "This is amazing!" Milo cried. "This thing is a machine."

"But what does it do?" Kida asked.

"You'll see!" said Milo. "But first you have to power it up with your crystal."

Kida plugged her crystal into a slot in the statue's head.

"Now, watch!" said Milo. He pressed a few buttons and the statue began to hum.

"It's moving!" Kida cried.

"Look out!" Milo warned.

Fishermen on the beach scattered as the mechanical tentacles shot out over their heads, grabbed nets full of squirming tuyeb, and dragged them to the beach.

"It is incredible!" Kida cried, clapping her hands. "This machine will make catching tuyeb much easier!"

To Milo's surprise, the princess gave him a big hug. "You have given us a wonderful gift. Thank you," she said.

"It was nothing," Milo replied, blushing. "All I did was read the instructions. That's the power of reading—if you can read, you can learn anything!"

# I'm Syndrome

Bob and Helen Parr were Supers, but they had stopped using their powers when people started complaining about them—some people didn't want to be saved! Bob had missed his life as a Super and had secretly started Super work again. A woman named Mirage had given him a mission to defeat an evil robot called an Omnidroid, and Bob had succeeded!

Bob was feeling good. He started exercising more and even had a new Super suit made by fashion designer Edna Mode. The new suit arrived just in time. Mirage had a new assignment for Bob.

Bob told Helen he had to go to a business conference, and instead he flew to the island of Nomanisan to meet Mirage. But Helen had discovered a blond hair on his jacket. She wondered where her husband was really going. . . .

Mr. Incredible got quite a shock when he arrived for his briefing. A new and improved Omnidroid attacked him! This time the robot was unbeatable. As it defeated the hero, a stranger in a black costume appeared.

"It's too much for Mr. Incredible," the stranger gloated. "I went through quite a few Supers to get it worthy to fight you. But you are worth it. After all, I am your biggest fan."

"Buddy?" Mr. Incredible said. Buddy had once been Mr. Incredible's number one fan. As a boy, Buddy had asked to be the Super's sidekick. But Mr. Incredible had explained to him that Supers were born, not made.

"My name's not Buddy anymore!" Buddy cried. "And now I have a weapon that only I can defeat!"

Mr. Incredible tried to escape, but the villain froze him in his immobi-ray.

"I am Syndrome!" he yelled. Then he lost control of the ray and accidentally flung Mr. Incredible off a waterfall.

Mr. Incredible found safety in an underwater cave. The hero hid behind the remains of Gazerbeam, a Super who had died battling the Omnidroid.

Meanwhile, Helen had found Bob's newly mended suit. She knew that Edna must have fixed it, so she went straight to her to find out what Bob was doing—and where he was! It was up to Helen to help her husband now.

# Raptor Attack

"Everyone, stand up," said Aladar. "There are raptors around here, and you need to stay with the group, where you'll be safe."

The dinosaurs were traveling to the Nesting Grounds. Although Aladar was young and healthy, he had chosen to stay in the back of the herd with the very old and very young dinosaurs, who needed help to keep up. The leader of the pack, an iguanodon named Kron, had little sympathy for the old and weak. He was more concerned about getting to the Nesting Grounds. If they lost a few of the herd along the way, so be it.

"My feet are so sore, my blisters have blisters," Baylene complained. "I know I won't have the strength to get through any more sand bogs like the ones we just got through."

"You girls are doing great," said Aladar encouragingly. He tried to sound cheerful, but he was exhausted, too.

Aladar gave two little iguanodons playful nudges with his nose. "Catch up, guys," he said. "Nobody lags behind."

Aladar heard some rapid footsteps behind him. Wheeling around, he saw three raptors coming over the ridge. "Run and catch up with the herd!" Aladar yelled to the little dinosaurs. "I'll keep them distracted!" The two little dinosaurs scampered away in terror.

"RAAAAAH!" Aladar roared. But the raptors looked ravenous and ready to fight. "Think, think," Aladar said to himself, trying to keep a clear head. And then he had an idea.

"Let's see how fast you are!" he roared at the raptors, and took off, back in the direction that the herd had just gone. The raptors pursued him.

Suddenly, Aladar made a quick turn and doubled back the way he had come. The raptors followed, but then the sound of their footsteps stopped.

Aladar looked back. They were caught in the sand bog and were starting to sink. Aladar wasted no time rejoining the herd. He looked back to see the raptors barely managing to struggle out of the wet sand. For now, the herd was safe.

# Dumbo's Daring Rescue

"All right, kid. You're on," Timothy Q. Mouse said from the edge of Dumbo's trunk. Dumbo was ready. He knew what he had to do, because he did the same thing every night. When the firefighter clowns called, Dumbo would leap from the platform and plummet toward the ground. Then, at the last possible moment, Dumbo would spread his tremendous ears and fly. The audience would cheer, and the show would be over.

Taking a step forward, Dumbo began to fall. He sped faster and faster toward the floor of the tent. The audience swam into view. They were screaming and laughing.

Then Dumbo saw something else. There, in the first row, was a little girl sitting all by herself. She was crying and holding on to a stick of cotton candy.

In an instant, the little elephant forgot all about the act. Spreading his ears, he swooped away from the shouting clowns. He scanned the seats intently. Why was the girl all alone? Where were her parents?

"Dumbo! What are you doing?" Timothy clung to Dumbo's trunk as he soared toward the peanut and popcorn sellers. "We don't have time for a snack now!"

Dumbo ignored his friend. The little girl needed help!

At last, Dumbo saw what he was looking for. There, next to the cotton candy stand, were two very worried-looking parents.

"Clara, where are you?" the father called. His voice was lost in the busy crowd. His daughter would never hear him calling!

Dumbo circled the tent again, turning back toward the bench where the little girl sat sobbing.

Swooping low, Dumbo stretched out his trunk and scooped up the little girl.

"Dumbo, what are you doing?" Timothy cried again.

Dumbo sailed back and placed the girl gently beside her parents. Immediately, the little girl's tears were dried. She was safe in her parents' arms!

The crowd went wild as Dumbo soared high over the arena. Even the clowns were smiling.

"Nice work, kid," Timothy said. "Good show."

# The Last Laugh

Feeling funny today?" Sulley asked Mike on the Laugh Floor one morning.

Mike smiled. "You bet!"

Just then, laughter filled the floor, catching Mike off guard. A group of employees were standing around another monster.

"Who's the comedian?" Mike asked.

"Stan, our newest recruit," Sulley replied. "I'll introduce you."

"Good morning!" Stan said when he saw Sulley.

"Hey, there's someone I'd like you to meet." Sulley turned to Mike. "Mike Wazowski, this is Stanley Stanford. Mike here is our top Laugh Collector."

Mike and Stan shook hands. "What were you guys laughing about before?" Mike asked.

"I was just telling them about the time I met the Abominable Snowman and his mother. I said to him, 'Hey, Mr. Snowman, where's your mother from?' And he said, 'Alaska.' And I said, 'Hey, don't bother. I'll ask her myself!'"

Everyone burst out laughing all over again—everyone except Mike, who couldn't help feeling green with envy. Mike felt like his position as best Laugh Collector was being challenged!

"Hey, good one, Stan," Mike said when the laughter had died down. "But have you heard the one about the skeleton who decided not to go to the party?" All eyes turned to Mike. "He had no body to go with!" Mike exclaimed.

Everyone laughed. He was back on top!

Soon Mike and Stan were having an all-out joke war. The employees gathered around the two jokesters. Then, suddenly, Mike's mind went blank! He began to jump up and down, hoping to jump-start his brain. As he jumped, Mike landed on the edge of a wheeled cart.

"Waaaaaaah!" Mike cried as the cart took off, rolling across the room and carrying him with it! The employees watched as Mike rolled wildly across the Laugh Floor. They fell down, laughing their heads off! When Mike landed in a pile of cardboard boxes, the joke-off was over. Mike was the winner.

# Piglet's Night-Lights

Winnie the Pooh knocked on Piglet's door. "Ready for our campout, Piglet?" Pooh called.

Piglet opened the door and looked around anxiously. "It's getting awfully dark out there."

As Pooh and Piglet walked to meet their friends, Piglet got more and more frightened. "What's that?" he asked suddenly, pointing to a scary-looking shape in the trees.

"Hello!" called a voice from above. Pooh and Piglet both jumped, startled.

"Who's there?" Pooh asked.

"Why, it's me—Owl," the voice answered. "I thought you two might need a little help finding the others. We owls can see quite well at night."

By the time the friends reached the campsite, it was completely dark.

"Have no fear, Tigger's here—with illuminagination!" Tigger said, holding up a lantern.

The friends set up the tent, and Piglet climbed inside and began to unpack. A few minutes later, he poked his head back out. "Oh, no!" he wailed. "I forgot my night-light!"

"Don't worry, buddy boy," Tigger said. "You can use my lantern!" But just then, the lantern flickered out.

"Can't have a campout without a campfire," Eeyore said. The friends went to gather some sticks. Minutes later, a fire was burning.

"Campfires certainly are pleasant," Piglet said. "They make a very good sort of light."

The friends played shadow puppets until bedtime. Piglet wouldn't leave the light of the fire, though, so Pooh kept him company. Soon the fire began to fade. "Maybe we should go to sleep now, Piglet," Pooh said, yawning.

"I can't sleep without a night-light, Pooh," Piglet replied.

Looking up at the night sky, Pooh thought of something. "The stars are night-lights, Piglet," he said, pointing up at the sparkling stars.

Piglet looked around. "You're right, Pooh!" he cried. Piglet pointed to the moon. "And look how bright the moon is tonight. I feel much better."

"Do you think you might be able to sleep now, Piglet?" Pooh asked with a huge yawn. "Piglet?"

But Piglet was already fast asleep.

# Lilo's Riches

**S**titch stretched his blue arms and folded them behind his head, soaking up the rays on the wide Hawaiian beach.

*Flash!* Lilo snapped his photo. *Flash!* Lilo turned and snapped a picture of Nani and David riding their surfboards.

Suddenly, Stitch stood up. He grabbed Lilo's camera. Lilo struck a hula pose and—*flash!*—Stitch caught it on film.

"Let's take some more!" Lilo giggled, running toward the shoreline. Stitch was right behind her, but he wasn't looking where he was going. He smashed into a bald man holding a mint chocolate chip ice cream cone. The man dropped the cone.

"Sorry," Lilo muttered. She grabbed Stitch's arm and tried to lead him away, but Stitch strained against her, pulling her closer to the melting green blob.

With one swipe of his tongue, Stitch lapped up the mess. "Ptooey!" He spat it out all over the man's feet. It was too sandy! "Ptooey! Ptooey!"

As soon as he stopped spitting, Stitch pointed at the snack shack.

"Sorry, Stitch. I don't have any money for ice cream," Lilo explained. "How about some music instead? Here, you play." Lilo tossed Stitch the ukulele. "I'll dance."

At first, Stitch just plucked a few sour notes. But soon the rhythm got him and he was playing like a real-life rock star.

Lilo was enjoying dancing so much, she didn't even notice that the tourists had begun to toss coins to them! When the song ended, the two took a bow. Quickly, Lilo gathered the coins.

"We've got enough! Come on!" Lilo took off running toward the snack shack. "Three mint chocolate chip cones, please," Lilo said.

Lilo handed one cone to Stitch. She took a quick lick of the second one as she scanned the beach. Spotting the bald man, she hurried over and thrust the third cone toward him.

"Here," she said. "Sorry about before." The man smiled and took the cone. Then Lilo handed him her camera. He snapped a picture— *flash!*—of Lilo and Stitch eating ice cream.

# Rocket Launchers

"All clear!" Woody the cowboy doll announced. "Andy's off to school."

The toys gathered around a mysterious box in the middle of the room. Andy had brought it home yesterday. Woody opened the box and looked inside. He pulled a piece of paper out of the box and began to read. After a couple of minutes, he smiled.

"It's a rocket launcher!" he said.

Soon the toys had put the rocket together. All of the toys lined up to try launching the rocket.

"Looks like we have a tie," Buzz said when all the toys had taken a turn.

"Yep," Woody agreed. "Hamm and Slink both made it all the way to Andy's door."

"We need a tiebreaker!" Jessie said.

The toys decided that Hamm and Slinky would each get one final stomp. Slinky Dog was first. He walked over to the rocket and loosened up. The other toys fell silent. Slinky pushed down on the pump as hard as he could, but the rocket didn't move!

Next up was Hamm. He stomped his foot on the pump, but the rocket still didn't move. The toys knew that something must be wrong.

Buzz looked over the rocket. "I think we have some space invaders," he said with a smile. A small door on the rocket opened up and three Little Green Aliens hopped out! Slinky Dog swung the door shut and stomped on the pump as hard as he could. The rocket flew across the room.

"Ooooh!" the Aliens said as they watched.

Hamm stomped on the pump and his rocket shot into the air. It landed in the same place Slinky Dog's had!

The toys decided to call it a tie and give the Aliens a ride instead. For the rest of the morning, the Aliens took turns riding in the rocket.

When the other toys got tired of playing, Buzz and the Aliens sat beside the globe. Woody joined them. "Slinky and Hamm were just saying that they think if they work together, they could launch all three of you in one go."

"What a great plan," Buzz said. "Teamwork will get us out of the galaxy, to the moon—"

"To infinity and beyond!" Woody finished.

# Time to Come Clean

**M**anny had just opened his repair shop when the phone rang. "*Hola!* You break it, we fix it! This is Manny."

"Hello, Manny. This is Mrs. Ayala. We have a problem with our tub. It seems to be clogged. Do you think you can help us?"

"*Absolutamente*, Mrs. Ayala. We'll be right over!"

Mrs. Ayala was relieved to see Manny and the tools. "Thanks for coming so quickly," she said.

"No problem," said Manny. "When did you first notice a problem?"

"This morning, when I started the shower. The water just filled up the tub instead of going down the drain. That's when I knew there was a clog."

"Who was the last person to use the tub?" Dusty asked.

Mrs. Ayala thought. "Let's see . . . my son Marcelo took a bath right before bed last night."

"Okay, tools," said Manny, "let's get to the bottom of this clog."

Felipe unscrewed the drain top, and then Manny lowered the snake into the drain. "I think I feel something," said Manny. "Yes, got something!"

"Hey, I know that toy. It's Diver Davy, the scuba-diving action hero!" exclaimed Squeeze.

"Well, I don't want to jump to conclusions," Dusty said, "but there's only one person in the house who has action figures."

Just then Marcelo came into the room. "Is there something you want to tell us, Marcelo?" asked Manny.

"I'm sorry, Manny. I tried to make Diver Davy dive down the drain for a special mission after my bath last night, but then I couldn't get him back out!"

"Why didn't you just tell your mom and dad?" asked Pat.

"I was afraid they'd be mad at me," Marcelo explained.

"You have to tell your mom when you make a mistake. Honesty is the best policy!" insisted Manny.

Manny and the tools followed Marcelo into the kitchen, where he confessed what had caused the clog.

"Telling the truth is always the right thing to do," said Mrs. Ayala. "You've learned a very important lesson today."

"That's right," said Dusty in her most serious voice. "It's always important to come clean."

"Especially after a bath!" joked Felipe.

# Unidentified Flying Mater

In Radiator Springs, a hubcap flew past Mater and Lightning McQueen. "Hey, look, a UFO!" Mater shouted. "And I know, 'cause I done seen one once."

Mater began to tell his friend a tale about the time he saw a spaceship. He had pulled up to a railroad crossing in the desert when suddenly he saw a UFO floating right in front of him! "Well, hey there," he said. "My name is Mater."

"My name is Mator," the UFO replied.

That sounded a lot like his own name, the tow truck thought. "Should I take you to my liter?"

"Your leader," the UFO echoed. Mater led the UFO to the spot where he kept his oil cans. "Here are all my liters," he said.

The UFO looked excited. Mater grabbed a can and drank the oil through a straw. When he glanced over, the UFO was slurping from a large oil drum.

Suddenly, a giant magnet dropped from the sky. *ZINGGGG!* It grabbed the UFO and pulled him upward. "Mator! I'll save you!" Mater yelled. He secretly followed Mator through the desert to a military base and snuck inside. Several

military and science vehicles were examining the UFO.

"Dadgum!" the UFO exclaimed.

"He's trying to communicate!" one of the scientists said. "Where's Dr. Abschleppwagen?"

Mater quickly put on a scientist disguise. "Here I am!" he announced.

"What does 'dadgum' mean?" asked one scientist.

"It means . . ." Mater began. As he stalled, he quickly flicked a switch, turning off the magnet! Mater and Mator flew away at top speed.

"Do you really expect me to believe that?" Lightning asked.

"You should," Mater said. "You was there, too!" Then he continued his story. Except this time, Mater described Lightning zooming across the desert, too. Suddenly, an enormous mother ship appeared. It pulled Mater, Mator, and Lightning aboard in a beam of light. Then the ship blasted off. After a quick ride through space, it was time for Mater and Lightning to get back.

"Thank you!" Mater called when they were safely home. He would miss his new friend, Mator, but he was glad the little UFO was safe.

# The Good Spot

"I'm tired. Where are we going to stop for the night?" Koda whimpered.

"You're the one who's supposed to know where we're going," Kenai growled in response. Kenai wished he could get away from Koda, even if it was only for a few hours. "Hey, is that a cave ahead?" he asked.

Koda scampered ahead to check it out. "It *is* a cave!" Koda shouted, suddenly full of energy. He ran inside and trotted back, twining around Kenai's feet and nearly tripping him. "And it's empty. Can we stop there? Can we?"

Kenai lumbered inside and slumped against the wall at the back.

"It's not very big, is it?" Koda said. "My mom and I had a huge cave. We always slept in the back, too. It's warmest there. My mom called it the 'good spot.' Are we going to sleep in the good spot, Kenai?"

Koda crawled on top of Kenai and started to make himself comfortable. "I am," Kenai growled, shoving Koda off. "You're going to sleep over there." He pointed a paw toward the cave entrance.

For once, Koda was quiet. He walked slowly away without looking back and lay down alone.

Kenai snorted and closed his eyes. A second later, they were open again. His ears twitched. Something was clicking. It was Koda's teeth. The cub was shivering by the cave opening.

"Fine. You sleep here, and I'll sleep over there." Kenai stood and swept Koda toward the back of the cave with his paw.

"You're giving me the good spot? Thanks!" Koda grinned and curled up in the warm spot where Kenai had been lying.

Kenai grumbled and lay down. He was willing to do almost anything to keep Koda quiet. Kenai closed his eyes. But he couldn't sleep.

In the back of the cave, Koda rolled over, snoring peacefully.

Kenai shivered. He glanced at Koda. The cub looked so warm that the big bear crawled to the back of the cave. Being careful not to wake him, Kenai lay down beside the cozy cub.

"I guess you're right sometimes, little bear," Kenai whispered to Koda. "This *is* the good spot."

# Just Like Dad

"Dad, when I grow up, I want to be just like you," Simba said to his father.

Mufasa nuzzled his son's head. "All in good time, son," he said.

Simba's friend Nala bounded up to them. "Come on, Simba!" she called. "Let's go play by the river!"

On their way, Simba stopped abruptly. "Listen to this," he said. He threw back his head and roared as loudly as he could. Then he looked at her expectantly. "Do I sound like my dad?"

Nala tried to suppress a giggle. "Not quite," she said.

Simba was eyeing a tree branch that extended over the raging river. "I may not be as big as my dad yet, but at least I'm as brave as he is!" he shouted, and he raced up to the tree. Climbing its gnarled trunk, he began walking along the branch over the water.

Nala hurried over. "Simba!" she yelled. "Come back here! The branch is going to break!"

But Simba couldn't hear her over the loud waters. As Nala bounded away to get help, Simba felt the branch begin to sag. "Uh-oh," he said to himself.

Suddenly the whole thing broke off and Simba tumbled into the water! The current was strong, and he struggled to swim to the shore. He was running out of strength, and he realized he might not make it.

Then he felt himself being lifted out of the water and tossed onto the bank. Dripping and coughing, he looked up— right into the angry eyes of his father.

"Simba!" thundered Mufasa. "There's a big difference between being brave and being foolish! The sooner you learn that, the better chance you will have of growing old!"

Simba hung his head. Out of the corner of his eye, he saw Nala. She was pretending not to overhear. "I'm . . . sorry, Dad," he said softly. "I just wanted to be brave like you."

His father's gaze softened. "Well," he said. "As long as we're soaking wet, why don't we go to a quieter part of the river and do some swimming?" He looked over to where Nala was sitting. "Come along, Nala!" he called.

"Yippee!" cried the cubs, and they all went off together.

# A Feather in His Cap

Peter Pan and Tinker Bell were off on an adventure, and the Lost Boys were bored.

"Never Land is a dull place without Peter Pan," Slightly complained.

Then Rabbit spoke up. "We can play Pirates! That's always fun."

"Can't," said Slightly. "I lost the feather off my pirate hat."

"We could find another feather," Tootles suggested.

"An extraordinary feather," Cubby said. "Like Captain Hook's."

"That's it!" Slightly cried. "I'll steal Captain Hook's feather!"

A short time later, the Lost Boys were sneaking aboard Hook's pirate ship. Luckily for them, the pirates were taking a nap!

There, hanging from a peg on the mast, was Captain Hook's hat.

"There it is," whispered Tootles. "Get it!"

Just then, Smee, Hook's first mate, awoke with a start. He turned and spied the Lost Boys. "Ahoy!" he cried, waking up the other pirates. Quick as a flash, the Lost Boys were caught.

Captain Hook burst from his cabin. "Lash them to the mast!" he commanded. "We'll catch Peter Pan when he comes to save his friends."

Floating high on a cloud, Peter Pan and Tinker Bell saw their friends being captured. They flew down to Pirates' Cove and landed on the ship's mast. Peter cupped his hands around his mouth and made a most peculiar sound: "Tick tock . . . tick tock!"

Down on deck, Captain Hook became very frightened. "It's that crocodile!" he cried.

"Tick tock . . . tick tock!" Peter could hardly keep from laughing.

"Man the cannons!" Hook cried. "Shoot that crocodile!"

The Lost Boys tied to the mast were forgotten. As the pirates ran in circles, Tinker Bell began to flap her wings. Fairy dust sprinkled down onto the Lost Boys. Soon they floated right out of the ropes and up into the clouds. On the way, Slightly snatched the feather from Hook's hat.

Peter Pan, Tinker Bell, and the Lost Boys met on a drifting cloud.

"Thanks for saving us!" said Tootles.

"You helped me scare old Hook!" Peter Pan said. "That's a feather in all your caps."

# Elastigirl Returns

Mr. Incredible and Elastigirl—now known as Bob and Helen Parr—were Supers. But the government had made them stop saving people. Now the couple were trying to live a normal life with their three children.

Bob was bored of the day-to-day grind of an ordinary life. A woman named Mirage had brought him to an island where he'd been asked to fight an Omnidroid robot. The owner of the island turned out to be Buddy, a man who was once Mr. Incredible's biggest fan. When Buddy was a boy, he'd wanted to be Mr. Incredible's sidekick. Mr. Incredible had told him Supers were born, not made—but Buddy hadn't listened. He now called himself Syndrome, and he had built a weapon that only he could defeat.

Bob's wife, Helen, was trying to find out where her husband was. She had found Bob's newly mended suit and knew that fashion designer Edna Mode must have fixed it. She went straight to Edna to find out what Bob was up to.

Edna was thrilled to see Helen. She'd so enjoyed making and testing Bob's new suit that she'd made one for Helen, too—and one for each of their children, Violet,

Dash, and Jack-Jack! Each new suit came with a homing device for handy tracking.

But Helen was very upset. "You helped my husband resume secret hero work behind my back?"

"I assumed you knew, darling," Edna protested.

Helen phoned Bob's work—and found out that he'd been fired almost two months ago. Where was he? Edna passed Helen the homing device that would locate him.

Meanwhile, Bob sneaked into Syndrome's base. He hacked into Syndrome's computer and discovered that the villain planned to set the robot loose in the city. No one would be able to stop it—except for Syndrome himself.

Suddenly—*BLEEP, BLEEP*—Mr. Incredible's homing device went off! Now Helen knew where he was—but so did the island's security. Mr. Incredible was trapped!

Back on the mainland, Helen knew she must find her husband. She realized she would only be able to do it if she became Elastigirl!

It was time for the Parrs to become Supers once more. . . .

# Tuned In

Andy's toys were gathered around the TV in Andy's room. "This again!" Bo Peep said as a super hero show came on. "We watch this every day."

"So?" said Hamm. "He's the defender of the universe! What could be better? I love this show."

Rex picked up the remote control and pressed a button. Suddenly, the channel changed to a real dinosaur show.

"Aggh!" Rex cried, diving under the covers. "Save me!"

The Green Army Men sprang into action. "Eliminate the enemy!" Sarge ordered. "Go! Go! Go!"

The soldiers jumped on the remote, and the channels began to change.

"Oooooh!" cried one of the Aliens as the channels flew by in a blur. "Perhaps this machine can help us return to our planet," they all said together. Bo Peep chuckled.

Buzz walked over. "Sheriff, I think we need to put an end to this channel surfing," he said. Woody agreed.

Sarge called off his troops, and Buzz marched over to the remote control. He told the Aliens that the television couldn't take them back to their home planet. "But the TV *can* take you to plenty of new and exciting places," Buzz said.

This made the toys start talking about their favorite shows. They couldn't decide what to watch, so Bo Peep suggested they watch a little of each channel.

The toys watched super heroes for Hamm. They watched the Animal Channel for Slinky Dog. Then they turned to the Military Channel for Sarge and the Green Army Men. They watched the Cooking Channel for Rex and the Sheepherding Channel for Bo. Then, finally, they turned to the Cowboy Channel for Jessie.

"Howdy, partner!" the toys suddenly heard.

"Could ya keep it down, Woody?" said Hamm. "We're trying to watch something."

"Huh?" said Woody. "I didn't say anything."

"Well, would you look at that!" said Jessie. "Woody and I are on TV!"

The TV was showing an episode of *Woody's Roundup*!

"Now there's a show!" said Woody. Everyone else had to agree!

# How Bad Could He Be?

Wreck-It Ralph was the Bad Guy from the Fix-It Felix, Jr. computer game. But he was fed up with playing the Bad Guy. He wanted to be a hero! So he left his game and found the Medal of Heroes in the Hero's Duty game. But Ralph had accidentally released a dangerous cy-bug, which had multiplied. The cy-bugs were now attacking Sugar Rush, where Ralph's new friend Vanellope was trapped! She couldn't leave because she was a glitch. An old game character called Turbo had stolen her computer code!

Ralph knew that he needed a bright light to defeat the cy-bugs. He headed straight for Diet Cola Mountain. On the way, a cy-bug attacked him. Ralph fell and smashed into the mountain. Beneath him, a Mentos stalactite broke loose and fell toward the hot diet cola below . . . along with Ralph. At the last minute, someone appeared and grabbed him. It was Vanellope!

The sweets from the mountain hit the cola and exploded! A glowing tower of cola spewed out of the mountain. The cy-bugs turned and flew into the light!

When the cy-bugs were gone, Fix-It Felix—the Good Guy from Ralph's game—repaired the broken Sugar Rush racetrack. Ralph pushed Vanellope gently across the finish line. The whole game glitched and then returned to normal.

But one thing had changed. Vanellope had transformed into a princess! At last, everyone knew the truth. Turbo had stolen Vanellope's royal identity, and now she had it back.

It was almost morning, and the arcade was due to open. Everyone needed to return to their games. Vanellope gave Ralph a hug. "You could just stay here and live in the castle," she said. But Ralph knew he had to go home.

Back in the arcade, Mr. Litwak was just about to unplug Fix-it Felix, Jr. when a little girl shouted that the game was working. The kids lined up to play. Ralph was back and the game was saved!

Ralph still worked as a Bad Guy, but now he knew he didn't need a medal to be a Good Guy. A little girl like Vanellope liked him. How bad could he be?

# Island Adventure

**M**ickey, Minnie, Donald, and Daisy were on a seaside vacation.

"I'm going to relax right here!" Minnie declared as she spread out her blanket.

"Me too," said Daisy, opening her umbrella.

"Those waves are just perfect for surfing," said Donald.

"You boys run along," Minnie said.

"We're happy right here," said Daisy.

Mickey and Donald surfed and swam until the sun went down.

The next day was sunny, too. On their way to the beach, Mickey and Donald spied a boat for rent. "Let's go fishing!" cried Donald.

But Daisy and Minnie shook their heads. "We want to relax," they said. So Donald and Mickey went fishing alone.

On the third day, Mickey and Donald wanted to go for a long swim.

"No, thanks," said Minnie. "I want to take it easy."

"Me too," said Daisy. "We're going to the cove to relax."

The boys went off to swim. Daisy and Minnie headed for the cove.

While she and Minnie were lounging under the palm trees, Daisy spied a bottle floating in the water. There was a map rolled up inside. She waded into the water to get it. "It's a treasure map!" she exclaimed.

"The treasure is on an island!" cried Minnie, pointing to a big X on the map.

Minnie and Daisy decided to follow the map. They went up one hill and then down another. They crossed a stream and reached a dock with a boat tied to it.

"That's the island," said Daisy, pointing out to sea. They hopped into the boat and started to row. They rowed and they rowed until they reached the island. Minnie and Daisy were very tired and very hungry.

"Look!" Minnie cried. "I see a fire!"

"Pirates!" exclaimed Daisy.

But there were no pirates. Just Donald and Mickey, waiting for Daisy and Minnie to arrive. A campfire was roaring, and fish sizzled on the grill.

"Looks like they found our map!" Donald exclaimed.

"*Your* map?" cried Minnie.

"It was the only way to get you two to have an adventure with us!" Mickey replied.

"Now, sit down by the fire," said Donald. "Lunch is served!"

# The Good Thing About Rain

"**R**ise and shine!" cried Pongo. One by one, he nudged each of his fifteen Dalmatian puppies with his nose. Most of the puppies yawned and stretched. But Rolly just rolled over and slept on.

"Aw, come on, Rolly," Pongo whispered in the pup's ear. "It's morning! Don't you want to go out?"

At the mention of the word *out*, Rolly was instantly wide awake! And he was not alone. As if by magic, the sleepy group had become a pack of jumping, barking puppies. They raced together through the kitchen to the back door, where they jumped up and down, waiting for Nanny to let them out into the garden.

"Okay, here I come," said Nanny as she made her way across the kitchen. Then she flung the door open wide and stepped out of the way to let the puppies race past. But they didn't move. It was raining!

"Oh, go on," said Perdita, trying to nudge the pups out the door. "It's only a little water."

But they wouldn't budge!

The next morning, Patch awoke with a start. With a few sharp barks,

he helped Pongo wake the other puppies. Within seconds, all fifteen were crowding around the back door. Nanny again rushed to let them out. And once again, the puppies were very disappointed to see raindrops falling.

When Nanny opened the door the next morning, the puppies were so surprised to see the sun shining that they didn't know what to do! Then, springing into action, they tumbled over one another in their rush to get out the door. They raced off in different directions, ready to explore.

But then, almost at once, all fifteen puppies froze in their tracks. They looked around at one another, then down at themselves. What was this stuff getting all over their spotted white coats? It was brown. It was wet. It was squishy. It was mud! And it was *fun*!

From the doorway, Pongo and Perdita looked out at their muddy puppies and laughed.

"You know what this means, don't you?" Pongo asked Perdita.

Perdy nodded. "Baths."

Pongo smiled, watching the frolicking puppies. "Let's not tell them just yet," he said.

JUNE
23

# Monster Truck Mater

Mater and Lightning were at Flo's one day when a monster truck drove by. "I used to wrestle trucks bigger than that," Mater said. He began to tell Lightning about being a wrestler called the Tormentor.

An ice cream truck with monster wheels rolled into the ring. The Tormentor wasn't sure how to wrestle such a big truck. He put on a hat, hoping to trick his opponent. "Can I have one double-dip dipstick sundae?"

"Huh?" said the I-Screamer. "Oh, sure." When the ice cream truck reached for a sundae, the Tormentor grabbed his bumper with his tow hook and flipped him. The referee announced that the Tormentor had won.

After his first win, the Tormentor became unbeatable. He soon made it all the way to the world championship against Dr. Frankenwagon's Monster! Each of the Monster's tires was bigger than the Tormentor's entire body. The monster had a giant scoop on one side and a claw on the other. A wrecking ball on his back could crush a truck with one direct hit.

Back in Radiator Springs, Lightning interrupted the story. "Whoa!" he cried. "What did you do?"

Mater looked over at his friend. "Don't you remember nothin'? We was a tag team."

Mater continued his story, except this time, Lightning was also in the ring, wearing his own wrestling outfit.

The Monster lunged for the race car, ignoring the tow truck. Lightning saw their opponent coming straight at him. He raced around the ring to avoid the Monster's wrecking ball. When the Tormentor heard Lightning call for help, he ducked back into the ring. He had a plan.

While the Monster's wrecking ball was on the ground, the Tormentor quickly snagged it with his tow hook. Then he zipped under one side of the ring and out the other. With a wink at his fans, the Tormentor yanked his towline. He flipped the entire ring—trapping the Monster underneath!

"The winners!" the referee announced. "The Tormentor and . . ." He turned to Lightning. "What's your name?"

"Lightning McQueen," he replied. "And Frightening McMean!"

# Toys in Paradise

Andy ran around his room, throwing clothes into a bag. His best friend's family was going on a vacation to Florida and they had invited him along.

When Andy left the room, his toys came to life.

"I'd give anything to go on a tropical vacation," said Bo Peep. "Just think of it. The sandy beaches, the warm sunshine . . ."

"Hey, I've got an idea," said Jessie. "Why don't we make our own tropical paradise, right here in Andy's room?"

The toys searched the house for the things they needed. Sarge and the Green Army Men found a potted plant. Hamm and Rex raided the kitchen for Buster's water dish and some sponges. Bo found a doll's umbrella in Molly's room. Soon all of the supplies were gathered in Andy's room.

"Next stop: paradise!" Jessie exclaimed.

The toys got to work. In no time at all, they had created their own tropical paradise. Woody and Buzz stretched out on the lounge chairs they had made out of shoe box tops and sponges.

"Aah. This is the life," Woody said.

But something was missing—an ocean breeze! Jessie climbed onto Andy's dresser and flipped a switch. Within seconds, the wind picked up, blowing Andy's things everywhere. It was a storm! The toys ran for cover as the beach chairs flew across the room.

"It's okay!" Jessie called. She flipped off the switch and the wind stopped. "It was just the fan. I wanted to make our palm tree sway in the breeze. Is everyone okay?"

"Almost everyone," Woody said. He pointed toward the bed, where Rex's tail was poking out from under the bedspread. It took a while for the toys to convince Rex to come out of his hiding place. He was still trembling with fear!

"Don't worry, Rex," Woody said. "There won't be any more storms here today."

The toys put the umbrella back in its place, shading the lounge chairs from the sun.

Rex walked back over to the beach. "I hope Andy has a great trip," he said. "Paradise can definitely be fun . . . as long as you're with good friends!"

# A Real Sleeper

"Time for bed, Nemo," said Marlin. "It's a school day tomorrow," he added. "You need to get your rest."

"Okay," said Nemo. "But can you tell me a story, Dad? How about one from when you were younger?"

"Well, just one," said Marlin, swimming back over to his only child. He thought for a moment, then smiled broadly. "Did you know that when I was younger—much younger, actually—did you know that I wanted to be a comedian?"

"But, Dad," said Nemo, "you aren't funny at all."

"Hey now! Wait just a minute!" Marlin said a bit huffily. "In my day, I was known as quite the jokester! Let me see. I'm sure I can remember some of my old routine, if I just think about it for a moment." He thought for a moment. "All right, it's all coming back!"

He cleared his throat. "Good evening, ladies and jellyfish! The ocean sure is looking *swell* tonight. Would you like me to give you a coral report about the latest happenings on the reef? Get it?" he said, looking down

at Nemo. "You see, there's something called an oral report, and the words *coral* and *oral* sound quite a bit alike."

Nemo gave his father a pained look.

"So, the other day, my appendix nearly burst," Marlin went on. "So I decided I'd better go to a sturgeon!"

Nemo blinked. "Dad, these really aren't that funny," he said with a yawn.

"A *sturgeon*. Get it? Rather than a surgeon?" Marlin sighed and continued his routine. "A funny thing happened on the way to the show tonight. I met a guy, nice fish and all, but he seemed to be a bit down on his luck. He told me he was living on squid row."

Nemo's eyes were starting to droop sleepily.

"Do you know why the whale crossed the ocean?" Marlin continued. "Now, don't try to guess. I'll tell you: the whale crossed the ocean to get to the other tide. The other *tide*."

Nemo's eyes were now completely closed, and a tiny snore escaped from him. Marlin smiled at his sleeping son.

"Works every time," he said with a chuckle.

# The Bear Facts

Koda the cub loved to tell stories. But sometimes he got a little carried away. One day, he was telling a group of cubs about the fishing expedition he and Kenai had been on the day before.

"And then we caught about a hundred fish! I mean, that pile of salmon must have been as tall as a tree. Of course, I caught most of them, but Kenai caught some, too," he said.

"What did you do with all of them?" asked one little grizzly.

"We ate them all. Yup, we were mighty hungry after all that work," Koda declared.

Just then, Kenai lumbered up to the circle of cubs. "Hey, Kenai," asked one, "is it true that you and Koda caught a hundred fish?"

Kenai shot Koda a stern look. "Well, not exactly," he said.

Later that day, Kenai and Koda went walking in the woods. After a while, it became clear that they were lost.

"Kenai," Koda said, "we're goners."

"Koda! Would you please stop exaggerating all the time?" Kenai scolded. "We're not dead, we're just lost!"

"Look . . . over . . . there," said Koda, gesturing. A strange male grizzly was approaching, and he did not look friendly.

"You're right," said Kenai. "We're goners."

"Not yet we aren't," Koda answered, suddenly sounding brave. The cub sprang into action. "Look out, you big lug . . . I'm a ragin' ball of fur!" The cub darted back and forth, throwing kicks and punches at the air. He shrieked and whooped. He jumped up and down and spun around.

The grizzly stood absolutely still, completely confused by the cub's odd behavior. Eventually, he turned and walked off.

"Koda, that's the craziest thing I ever saw," said Kenai, shaking his head in disbelief. "Thank you for saving us."

Safely back at the bear camp that night, Koda recounted their hair-raising adventure to the rest of the group.

"Kenai, did it really happen that way?" one of the cubs asked.

"Yes," said Kenai, smiling. "That's exactly how it happened, believe it or not!"

# Things Go Better with Friends

Not long after the dinosaurs reached the Nesting Grounds, new dinosaur babies were born. Among the happy parents were Aladar and Neera. Zini the lemur wanted to give them a special gift. He decided to pick them a juicy melon.

When Zini told the other lemurs of his plan, everyone wanted to help.

"No way!" Zini cried. "It's my idea, and I'm going to pick the fruit myself!"

The walk to the melon vines was long. When he finally reached them, Zini was almost too tired to lift up the huge leaves of the melon vines. He had to, though, because every lemur knows that the best melons grow under the biggest leaves on the vine.

But the leaves were also slippery! Zini would get a leaf lifted almost high enough, but when he let go to grab the melon underneath, the leaf would slip right back down again!

"What am I going to do?" Zini said.

Suddenly, Zini spotted a dinosaur coming toward him. She was a big dinosaur—the biggest of them all— Baylene! And spiky old Eema was not far behind.

"Are you having trouble?" Baylene asked, her long neck bent low.

"I can't lift the leaves high enough to pick fruit for Aladar and Neera," Zini complained. "And even if I could pick a melon, I don't think I'm strong enough to carry it home."

"That's why Yar sent us," Baylene explained. "He said you were too stubborn to ask for help, but you needed it anyway."

"Will you help me?" Zini asked.

"What are friends for?" Baylene replied. She took the edge of a leaf in her teeth and moved it up off a huge, ripe melon.

"This is easy! And fun, too," said Zini as he scampered under the leaf and rolled the melon out from under it.

"I'll carry that, Zini," said Eema. "I may be slow, but I'm not too old to handle one melon—even a melon as big and ripe as this one!"

Before sunset, the three friends had returned to the Nesting Grounds with their prize.

"So you got it on your own?" Yar asked when he saw the melon.

"I had help," said Zini. "And I figured something out. Things go better when you have friends!"

# A Talented Mouse

"Look, Dumbo," Timothy Q. Mouse said, pointing to the newspaper. "There's another article about us in here!"

Mrs. Jumbo, Dumbo's mother, peered over Timothy's shoulder. "What a nice story," she cooed. "Too bad the picture isn't better—why, I can hardly see you, Timothy!"

Timothy peered at the paper. "Hey," he said, scanning the story. "This article doesn't mention me at all!"

"It's all right," Mrs. Jumbo said soothingly. "Everyone knows how important you are."

But Timothy wasn't so sure. "Am I really that important?" he said. "It's Dumbo who has the talent—not me."

Timothy wandered away sadly. "I have to figure out a way to get famous on my own," he muttered. "But how?" Suddenly, he snapped his fingers. "I've got it!" he cried. "I'll learn to fly, too! That way Dumbo and I can be famous together!"

Timothy climbed to the top of the tallest circus tent. Dumbo had learned to fly by jumping off things. Timothy just hoped it would work for him, too. He rubbed his hands together.

"Here goes nothing," he muttered. He leaped off the tent and looked down. The ground seemed very far away.

"Uh-oh!" Timothy gulped. What had he done?

The ground got closer and closer. Timothy squeezed his eyes shut. . . .

Suddenly, he felt himself being whisked upward. Opening his eyes, he saw that he was clutched in Dumbo's trunk.

"Whew!" he gasped. "Thanks, buddy!"

Dumbo smiled at his little friend. He set Timothy in his cap. Timothy settled into the familiar spot. Flying was much more fun when Dumbo's ears did all the work!

Soon they landed beside Mrs. Jumbo.

"Oh, Timothy!" she cried. "You're safe! When I saw you fall, I was so worried. . . . Dumbo and I don't know what we'd do without you."

Timothy blinked. "Never thought of it that way," he mused. "Maybe I'm not front-page news, but who cares? I know I'm important, and my friends know it, too. That's what matters!"

Timothy smiled. He had plenty of his own talent, and that was good enough for him!

# A Fine Feathered Friend

One afternoon, Woody was watching his favorite TV show—*Woody's Roundup*. On the show, Sheriff Woody was repainting the old jailhouse. His horse, Bullseye, whinnied and stomped the ground.

"Not today, partner," Woody said. "I've got to finish painting and then I'm helping Miss Tilley with her errands."

Bullseye snorted and wandered off to find Jessie. She was feeding peanuts to a squirrel. Bullseye bent his front legs so she could climb on his back.

"Oh, sorry, Bullseye," she said. "I promised to help this little guy gather some nuts for his friends. Some other time."

Bullseye sadly lowered his head to munch some grass. He felt very lonely. Suddenly, he saw something sitting among the weeds. It was a brown speckled egg. Bullseye looked around for a mother hen, but there wasn't one in sight. So Bullseye found an old basket nearby and used it to carry the egg back to town.

Bullseye cared for the egg just like a mother hen. He tucked hay around it to keep it warm and checked on it every hour. Finally, one afternoon, Bullseye heard a tapping sound. *Tap-tap-tap.* It was the egg! He watched it closely. A little beak poked through, then the egg broke open! A tiny yellow chick with spots on its back appeared. Bullseye named him Horsefeathers.

One day, Bullseye and Horsefeathers met Woody and Jessie at the corral. Horsefeathers trotted around the ring. "Neigh!" he said.

Jessie looked worried. "Horsefeathers should be learning how to be a chicken, not a horse," she said quietly.

"You've done a fine job, partner," Woody told his horse. "But Horsefeathers needs to be with his real family."

Just then, a mother hen and her chicks passed by. Woody heard the strangest sound. "Peep! Peep! Peep!" It was Horsefeathers, chirping like a chicken for the first time!

Horsefeathers ran over to his real mother and she tucked him under her wing.

"He is one unique bird," Woody said, shaking his head.

"And Bullseye is one unique horse," Jessie added. She gave Bullseye a hug. "Good job, partner!"

# The Four-Legged Festival

Quasimodo was a kind young man who was always quick to offer help to anyone in need. It wasn't surprising, then, that Quasimodo had a growing collection of orphaned animals. First he had taken in a stray kitten, and then an abandoned puppy. Next he adopted a lamb, an old donkey, a baby bird, and an ox.

Esmeralda and Phoebus helped him build a pen. But they weren't sure how he could afford to continue feeding so many pets.

"I'll find a way—somehow," Quasimodo told the couple. "They're counting on me!"

The Festival of Fools was coming up, and Quasimodo was a little worried about how his pets would react to all the noise and excitement.

"While you're helping with the puppet show at the festival," said Esmeralda, "why don't we have Djali keep an eye on the animals?" Djali was Esmeralda's clever little goat. He was used to crowds and often danced with Esmeralda in the village square.

"Why, thank you, Esmeralda!" replied Quasimodo. "That's a wonderful idea."

Soon the day of the festival arrived. Esmeralda brought Djali and put him inside the pen with the other animals.

When Djali heard the tinkling of Esmeralda's tambourine on the far side of the square, he nibbled at the latch of the pen. The gate flew open and Djali took off running. The other animals followed—even as the goat crashed through a stall full of masks for sale!

Everyone turned to see the animals, which were now disguised as jesters and kings, songbirds and queens. The masked animals danced right past the puppet wagon and onto Esmeralda's stage.

Quasimodo watched in amazement as Djali and the others joined in the gypsy's merry dance. The crowds cheered and showered the performers with coins.

When the show ended, Esmeralda climbed down from the stage and delivered the money to Quasimodo. "This should take care of whatever food you need to buy your pets," she said happily.

Quasimodo felt like dancing for joy—but he decided to leave that to the animals!

# Eeyore Beats the Heat

Eyore sighed.

"Something the matter, Eeyore?" asked Roo.

"Oh, it's just that it's so terribly hot," replied Eeyore. "If I weren't stuffed with sawdust, I think I would melt."

"Well, come with me!" squeaked Roo. "I'm going to the swimming hole to cool off."

But Eeyore shook his head. "Can't do, Roo," he said. "Not with my sawdust and all. . . . I'd probably just sink. And that's if I'm lucky."

So Roo, who felt sorry for Eeyore, but who was also eager to swim, continued on his way.

Soon another friend came along. And this friend was Winnie the Pooh.

"You're looking a little warmish, Eeyore," Pooh said.

"Same to you," said Eeyore with a sigh. "Same to you."

"Ah," said Pooh, "but I am off to catch a breeze—and pay a call on some bees—with my trusty balloon here. Care to join me?"

"No, thanks, Pooh," said Eeyore. "I never did like feeling like the ground was missing. And I expect that with my luck, the balloon would probably pop."

"I understand completely, Eeyore. Wish me luck, then, won't you?" Pooh replied.

"Good luck, Pooh," said Eeyore. "As if anything I ever wish comes true."

The next friend to come upon Eeyore was little Piglet.

"Hello there, Eeyore," said Piglet. "Whoo! Are you as uncomfortably hot as I am?"

"Oh, no," said Eeyore. "I'm sweltering."

"Poor Eeyore," said Piglet. "Why don't you come play in the cool mud with me?"

But once again, Eeyore shook his head. "Afraid mud is not an option, Piglet," he said. "Once I get dirty, I'll never get clean. No. Go enjoy yourself on this hot day like everyone else. All except me. As usual. I'll just suffer."

And suffer poor Eeyore did . . . until not too terribly much later when his friends all returned with something sure to cool off even Eeyore on this sultry day.

"Guess what we've brought you, Eeyore!" Roo squealed with delight.

"It's ice cream," whispered Pooh.

"Ice cream, huh?" Eeyore sighed. "I suppose I'll have to eat it all before it melts."

And do you know what? He did!

# Sleep Tight, Nemo

It was late at night at the bottom of the sea—but little Nemo was wide awake.

"Nemo," said Marlin, poking his head into the anemone, "you should be asleep!"

"But I can't sleep," said Nemo. "I need another story."

"No more stories," said Marlin. "I told you five already."

"Then maybe another snack?" said Nemo.

Marlin rolled his eyes. "No, Nemo. What you need is to close your eyes and go to sleep!"

"Okay, Dad," said Nemo. Then he did as his dad told him and closed his eyes. But seconds later, they popped open again.

"Dad!" Nemo called out. "Daaaad!"

"Nemo!" Marlin groaned. "I'm beginning to lose my patience!"

"But, Dad," said Nemo, "I . . . I . . . I heard a noise."

"What kind of noise?" Marlin asked.

"Um . . . a . . . a spooky noise," Nemo answered.

"Hmph." Nemo could tell Marlin did not like this reason for being awake, either. But still, Marlin stopped and listened . . . and listened . . . and listened.

"I don't hear anything, Nemo," he said after a moment. "Go to sleep."

So Nemo tried his best to shut his eyes really tight and get comfortable. He wiggled this way . . . then that way . . . then this way again. But nothing worked.

Now, Nemo knew his father well, and he knew when Marlin was just a teeny-tiny, itsy-bitsy bit angry with him. But Nemo also knew that when you can't go to sleep, you can't go to sleep. And no matter how many moonfish or angelfish or sea stars you count, no matter how tightly you close your eyes, no matter how mad your dad gets, you'll never go to sleep until you're absolutely, positively, no-doubt-about-it ready. And Nemo wasn't.

Suddenly, Nemo bolted up. "Dad!" he shouted. "Dad! Oh, Daaaaad!"

"All right. That's it, Nemo!" Marlin said.

"But, Dad," Nemo said. "There's one more thing I really, really, truly need. Then I promise, I'll go to sleep."

And with that, he snuggled into Marlin's fins for a great big good-night hug.

"I love you, Dad," he said. "See you in the morning." Then Nemo closed his eyes and fell right to sleep.

# Mater the Greater

Lightning McQueen and his friends were enjoying a few oil cans at Flo's V8 Café when Mater sped backward over a ramp and crashed into a pile of cans.

"I used to be a daredevil," he told his friends. Mater began to tell the story of his days as a daredevil. One of his events had been at a sports arena.

"Ladies and gentlecars, Mater the Greater!" the announcer called.

It was nearly time for Mater's big stunt. He would try to jump over a long line of cars!

"And he's off!" the announcer called out. Mater's wheels burned rubber as he drove toward the ramp.

THUD! Mater the Greater landed on the second car past the ramp. Each car in the lineup groaned as Mater the Greater tiptoed down the row.

"Scuse me!" he said. "Pardon me! Comin' through!" At last, Mater the Greater rolled over the last car.

"He did it!" the announcer cried. The crowd went wild! Mater the Greater had made his way over all the cars. It didn't matter to them how he had done it.

Mater explained that he had done all kinds of stunts. He had been shot from a cannon through a ring of flames, dived from a high platform into a tiny pool of water, and jumped Carburetor Canyon.

Lightning was starting to doubt Mater's story.

"Jumping Carburetor Canyon? No way!"

"Yes, way," Mater replied. "You remember. You was there, too."

Mater continued his story, except now Lightning was with him.

Lightning had a fancy new paint job. Three huge rockets were strapped to his roof. He even had on Mater the Greater souvenir false teeth!

"Ready, buddy?" Mater the Greater asked.

But Lightning didn't have a chance to answer. Someone lit his rockets and pushed him down the ramp!

Lightning shot down the ramp and launched into the air. He was about halfway across the canyon when his rockets sputtered . . . and went out. By this time, everyone at Flo's V8 Café was listening. They were all waiting to hear the end of Mater's story.

"Well, what happened?" Lightning asked.

"You didn't make it," Mater replied. "Well, see ya later!"

# The Fireworks Show

Andy had been gone all day. He was out with his family, celebrating the Fourth of July.

"The Fourth of July is the United States' birthday," Woody told Buzz. "People celebrate by going on picnics in the afternoon and watching fireworks at night. That must be where Andy and his family have gone."

"It's too bad he didn't take us with him," said Buzz. "I'd like to see fireworks myself. I'm told they look something like Space Ranger Rockets!"

"Well," Woody said thoughtfully, "last year we were able to see the fireworks from the roof. Maybe we could climb up there again tonight."

Sure enough, the toys were able to use Woody's lasso to pull themselves up on the roof. As the sun sank, the toys settled into their seats for the fireworks show.

"Wow," said Buzz, "there sure is a lot of stuff up on this roof." He looked around and saw a football, a Frisbee, a hula hoop, an old sweatshirt, and a shiny red balloon.

"That's because Andy's not allowed on the roof," Woody explained. "Every time he throws something up and it gets stuck, it stays here."

Suddenly, there was a flicker and a boom. The toys looked up as the fireworks began. Lights exploded across the sky, colors flashed, and there was a deep rumbling sound.

"Why don't Andy and his mom set off their own fireworks in the backyard?" asked Buzz. "That way the fireworks wouldn't have to be so far away!"

"Fireworks are very dangerous," said one of the Green Army Men. "If one goes off near you, it makes a huge explosion, and a tremendous banging noise, and you could really get hurt."

Just then, there was a tremendous banging noise—right on the roof! The toys jumped. But there was no explosion—just Rex, looking embarrassed, with a deflated balloon hanging from the end of his tail.

"Sorry," he said, "I accidentally sat on the balloon. Did I scare everyone?"

The toys laughed. They agreed that, for once, Rex the dinosaur had actually scared them. They also all agreed that they were glad the real fireworks were far, far away.

# Young Mike Wazowski

Mike Wazowski couldn't wait. His class was going on a trip to Monsters, Inc.

Mike was the smallest monster at Frighton Elementary—and the least popular—so it was not surprising that when his teacher told everyone to pair up, Mike ended up alone.

"Well, Michael, looks like it's you and me again," said the teacher, taking Mike's hand.

A tour guide met the class and took them inside. "We're entering a very dangerous area," he warned. "This is where we collect the scream energy to power our whole world."

The guide warned the little monsters to stay in the viewing area and never cross the red safety line marked on the floor. But that didn't stop Mike. He followed one of the Scarers into the human world!

Mike watched as the Scarer crept up to the sleeping child and frightened him. It was the most exciting thing the little monster had ever seen!

It was then that Mike decided he wanted to be a Scarer when he grew up.

The years passed and Mike grew old enough to attend college. He decided to go to Monsters University to study Scaring.

On Mike's first day, a group of monsters called the Smile Squad greeted Mike happily. They helped him to register and told him all about the university. Soon Mike was touring the campus.

As Mike walked through the quad, the Greek Council handed him a leaflet. "We sponsor the annual Scare Games. It's a super-intense scaring competition where you get a chance to prove you're the best!"

Mike liked the sound of that!

Finally he reached his dorm. Inside, he met his roommate, Randy. He was a friendly eight-legged monster who could disappear without warning. It was a great talent, even if his glasses *did* give him away.

Mike started to unpack. His dream was about to come true. All he needed to do now was graduate with honors and become the greatest Scarer ever.

"Aren't you even a little nervous?" Randy asked.

"No," said Mike. He had been waiting for this moment his whole life.

# Let's Get Jumping

Jake and his crew were playing on the beach when they saw a package. Inside was a pogo stick!

"Let's get jumping!" said Izzy.

*Boing, boing!* The crew took turns jumping.

Nearby, the wind had blown Captain Hook's hat into a tree. Just then, Hook heard a sound. *Boing, boing.* Jake was jumping on the pogo stick.

"Did you see that?" Hook asked Smee. "That puny pirate has a sproingy thing! If I had that, I could get me hat!"

Using his plunger hook, Captain Hook grabbed the pogo stick.

"That sneaky snook took our pogo stick!" said Cubby.

Captain Hook jumped on the pogo stick all the way to the tree and grabbed his hat! But then he hit his head on a big bunch of bananas, and he dropped his hat again.

"Cap'n, where are you going?" called Smee as Hook started bouncing away.

"To get me hat!" called Hook.

Meanwhile, Jake and the crew were wondering where Captain Hook could be. Then they heard a noise. *Boing, boing!*

"I hear Hook, but I don't see him anywhere," said Izzy.

"Look!" said Jake, pointing at the ground. "Pogo-stick tracks. If we follow them, I bet we'll find Captain Hook!"

Finally, they came across Smee. "Thank goodness you sea pups are here," said Smee. "Here's your pogo stick. Sorry for all the trouble."

"That's okay, Mr. Smee," said Jake.

"Um, there's just one little problem," said Smee. "I'm afraid the Cap'n is, well . . . up a tree."

"Oh, no," said Cubby. "He's going to fall!"

"We have to help him!" said Jake.

Izzy sprinkled some Pixie Dust on everyone, and they rescued Captain Hook.

"You know," said Jake, "if Hook had just asked for help in the first place, he wouldn't have gotten into all that trouble."

"And we wouldn't have lost our pogo stick," said Skully.

Now that they had the pogo stick back, Cubby practiced and practiced. Soon he was a pogo master!

"I knew you'd get the hang of it!" said Jake.

# Hakuna Matata

'W'hy are you so sad?" Pumbaa asked Nala.

"I'm not sad," Nala said. "I'm just a little more on the serious side than the two of you."

"I think you could use a little *hakuna matata*," Pumbaa said.

"A whona mawhatta?" Nala asked.

"You really think she can handle it?" Timon whispered to Pumbaa out of the side of his mouth.

"Of course I can handle it!" Nala said, raising her voice. "I just need to know what it is first."

"Ahhhh, *hakuna matata*," Pumbaa said dreamily. "It's the problem-free way of dealing with all of life's ups and downs."

"It means 'no worries,'" Timon explained.

"*Hakuna matata* helps you relax," Pumbaa offered.

"It sounds like your *hakuna matata* is just another way of saying 'uninspired and lazy,'" Nala continued.

"I think she just might have insulted us," Timon whispered to Pumbaa.

"There you are." Simba came walking toward them. "What are the three of you up to?"

"I was just learning about a strange little notion called *hakuna matata*," Nala explained.

"Isn't it great?" Simba said with a grin.

"Well, sure," Nala said. "If you don't ever want to get anything done."

Simba frowned. "It's not like that. *Hakuna matata* helps you get through things."

"Sure," Nala continued. "*Hakuna matata*—I don't have to worry or try."

"I guess you could look at it that way," Simba said. "But to me it means 'Don't worry about it right now. It's okay.' It gives me the strength to get through the bad times."

"Wow, I hadn't thought about it like that," Nala said.

"So, are you ready to join us now?" Timon asked.

"Absolutely!" Nala smiled.

"Bring on the crunchy beetles!" shouted Pumbaa.

"Everyone to the mud hole for a mud fight!" Simba yelled, and he, Timon, and Pumbaa started off.

"Oh, dear," murmured Nala, "this isn't exactly what I had in mind." But she smiled and ran after her carefree friends. "Last one to the mud hole is a rotten egg!" she cried.

# Spaghetti and Meatballs

Tramp had just escaped from the dogcatcher—again. He'd taught that dogcatcher who was boss! Tramp could smell wood burning in fireplaces and dinners cooking. . . . His stomach suddenly rumbled. Escaping from the dogcatcher always worked up quite an appetite!

But where would he go for dinner tonight? He usually stopped by the Schultzes for some Wiener schnitzel on Monday, and he had corned beef and cabbage with the O'Briens on Tuesday . . . but what he was really craving was some spaghetti and meatballs. So Tramp headed to Tony's Restaurant. He scratched at the back door, as was his custom.

"I'm coming! I'm coming!" Tony shouted. He appeared at the door, wiping his hands on a towel. He pretended not to see Tramp, as he always did.

"Hey, nobody's here!" Tony shouted.

Tramp couldn't take it anymore. He was so hungry! He barked.

"Oh, there you are, Butch my friend," said Tony. Tramp—whom Tony called Butch—jumped up and down. "I'll get your dinner," said Tony. "Relax, enjoy yourself."

Tramp sat down and looked around the cluttered alleyway. This was the life!

Tony reappeared with a plateful of pasta. He had given Tramp two—no, make that three—meatballs! This was quite a special night.

Tony stood and chatted with Tramp as he ate his meal, telling him about his day: the late delivery of fish, the customer who had complained that the tomato sauce was too garlicky, the trip that he and his wife were planning to take . . .

Tramp finished eating and gave the plate one last lick. It was sparkling clean.

"That reminds me," said Tony. "There's something I've been meaning to talk to you about. It's time you settled down and got a wife of your own."

Tramp gave Tony a horrified look and began to back out of the alleyway. Tony laughed so hard his sides shook.

"Good-bye, Butch!" he called. "But mark my words: one of these days, you're going to meet the dog you can't resist. And, when you do, I have a good idea—you bring her to Tony's for a nice romantic dinner!"

# Supers to the Rescue

Bob Parr—aka Mr. Incredible—had become bored of pretending to be normal, and had secretly taken up Super work again. He'd kept this secret from his wife, Helen, and had ended up as a prisoner on the island of Nomanisan—owned by Syndrome, who was Mr. Incredible's ex–number one fan, Buddy. Buddy had built an Omnidroid robot, which only he could defeat.

Meanwhile, Helen had discovered where her husband was. She knew the only way to help him was to become Elastigirl once more.

In a borrowed jet, Elastigirl followed the homing signal on Mr. Incredible's suit. She soon found that her Super children, Violet and Dash, had left Jack-Jack at home with a babysitter and stowed away on the jet! They had found the Super suits that Edna Mode had made for them, and wanted to help save their dad!

As they approached the island, missiles attacked the jet. Elastigirl told Violet to create a force field around the plane, but Violet didn't think she could make one that big.

In his prison cell, Mr. Incredible listened to the attack on his family with horror.

"We have a confirmed hit," said Mirage.

But Mr. Incredible's family was still alive! Elastigirl had stretched herself around Violet and Dash to protect them just as the missile blew the jet out of the sky. Next she had made herself into a parachute and floated down to the water below with her children. Then Elastigirl stretched into the shape of a boat. Dash pushed her and Violet to shore by kicking his speedy legs. They soon found safety in a cave.

Elastigirl told her children that she was going to go look for their father. "If anything goes wrong, use your powers. When the time comes, you'll know what to do."

After Helen left, the cave suddenly filled with a huge ball of fire. Dash and Violet fled. The fire was the rocket exhaust from Syndrome's base. He had launched the Omnidroid toward the city!

The Parr family was going to have to use all their Super strength to save the city—and one another—from Syndrome.

# Adventures in Babysitting

Aladar and Neera the iguanodons loved being parents. Their son was adorable and sweet and funny—and very active!

Zini the lemur came by to visit often. "Anytime you want me to babysit, you just say the word, and it'll be Uncle Zini to the rescue!" he said.

One day, the couple finally took him up on his offer.

Zini looked up at the baby dinosaur, who towered over him. "What do you say you and I go find some lunch, little guy?" he suggested.

Instead, the baby made a beeline for the mud hole.

The lemur took a running leap and belly flopped in. Zini tried to grab on to the baby, but the dino was way too slippery. While the babysitter flopped and flailed, the baby climbed out of the puddle and wandered toward some vegetation.

"Go ahead and start on lunch without me!" Zini called. "I'll be right there."

By the time Zini managed to pull himself over to the trees, Aladar and Neera's son had already eaten halfway through a tree trunk. The lemur settled in under the shade of the tree with a nice bunch of leaves.

All of a sudden, Zini heard a loud *creak* and a *crash!* as the tree fell to the ground. The baby had eaten right through the tree trunk! Fortunately, the tree had fallen away from the baby iguanodon and the lemur.

Zini breathed a sigh of relief. That was a close one! "You know what, little guy? After the refreshing mud bath and that big lunch, I could use a nap. How about you?"

The baby dinosaur's lower lip stuck out. It began to tremble. Then he stamped his foot as hard as he could. The ground shook.

"Waaaaaah!" he wailed. "Waaaaaah!" Zini did everything he could to calm him down, but nothing he did helped. Finally, the baby wore himself out and collapsed on the ground, snoring.

When Aladar and Neera returned, their son was still sleeping peacefully. "Would you look at that?" said Aladar. "Zini, how did you manage to get him to nap?"

"Nothing to it," said the exhausted lemur. "I just have a way with children!"

# Redfinger

Juan, a young boy, had lost his football in the playground.

"It must be in here," he said as he reached into a rosebush and felt around.

Then, suddenly, "OUCH!" he shouted. Juan had forgotten that rosebushes have very sharp thorns!

"Oh, no!" Juan cried when he saw the cut on his finger. "Now what should I do?"

A special alert was sent out to Special Agent Oso, who raced to the playground to help Juan.

"Three special steps, that's all you need!" said Oso's Paw Pilot.

"Special Agent Oso!" Juan cheered. "Thanks for coming to the rescue."

"Glad to help out, Juan."

Oso motioned toward the bathroom. "There's no time to waste. Let's see to that finger!"

Special Agent Oso consulted his Paw Pilot for instructions.

"Step one: Wash the cut with warm, soapy water," guided Paw Pilot.

"Oh, no, this water is too cold," Oso said.

Juan quickly turned on the hot tap. Soon the water was warm.

"Ahhh, my finger feels better already," Juan said with a sigh.

"Step two: Use a towel to dry off your hands," explained Paw Pilot.

"Then add a dab of antiseptic cream to prevent the cut from getting infected," continued Oso.

Oso scratched his chin. "Gee, there's one more step, but I just can't remember what it is."

Oso thought and thought. Finally he remembered. "We need to put a bandage on the cut! The bandage will keep out dirt and germs and will help the cut heal."

Oso looked at the flowers. "Now it's time to tackle this rosebush."

Oso slipped on some heavy-duty work gloves and quickly found Juan's football hiding in the thorny branches.

"Touchdown!" Juan cheered. "Great play, Coach Oso!"

"Now make sure you wash your finger and change your bandage every day," advised Oso. "Before you know it, that cut will disappear completely!"

Juan smiled. "Thanks, Special Agent Oso! I'll remember!"

"Assignment complete!" shouted Paw Pilot.

# Showdown

One afternoon, Jessie was watching *Woody's Roundup* on TV. In the old Wild West, Sheriff Woody and Jessie were talking about who was the best cowpoke.

"I can out-cowpoke you any day," Jessie said with a grin.

Woody knew Jessie was a great cowpoke. But he didn't think she was better than him.

Just then, the Prospector walked over with Woody's horse, Bullseye. Jessie told the Prospector what they were talking about.

Woody sighed. "How about we just say you're as good a cowpoke as I am?"

Jessie grinned. That was all she wanted to hear. She knew Woody was a fine cowpoke.

"Whoa, hold on a rootin' tootin' minute," the Prospector said. "A true cowpoke never backs down from a challenge, Sheriff. How will you prove you're the roughest, toughest cowpoke in the West?"

Jessie suggested they each try to teach Bullseye a trick, but Bullseye wouldn't budge.

"This contest stuff is dumb," Woody said. "What if. . . ."

"Woody! Jessie!" the Prospector said. "The new calf just fell into the Rushing River."

The two cowpokes quickly climbed onto Bullseye's back and raced to the river. They soon spotted the calf wedged against a rock, struggling and mooing.

Jessie grabbed her lasso and threw it neatly around the calf's neck. Woody carefully climbed down, hopping from one slippery rock to the next. He patted the calf and led it back across the river. Meanwhile, on the riverbank, Jessie and Bullseye held the rope so the calf wouldn't be swept downstream.

"Woody saved the day!" Jessie exclaimed when the calf was safely onshore. "He's the bravest cowpoke ever."

"Jessie's the real hero," said Woody. "She lassoed the calf like a great cowpoke."

"Seems we still don't know who is the roughest, toughest cowpoke in the West," said the Prospector.

"Yes, we do," said Woody, grinning at Jessie.

"We're both great cowpokes!" they cried.

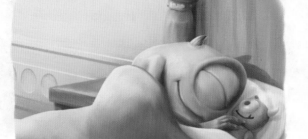

Disney·PIXAR
MONSTERS, INC.

# Mike's Worst Nightmare

"AAAAAAIEEEE-AHHHH!" Sulley sat bolt upright in bed. The anguished yell was coming from his roommate Mike's bedroom. Sulley raced out of his bedroom and threw open Mike's door.

"Hi," said Mike in a shaky voice. "I guess I must have had a bad dream."

Sulley nodded.

"Uh, Sulley, do you want to hear about it?" Mike asked with a hopeful grin.

Sulley came over and sat down on the edge of his friend's bed. "Okay," he said.

"I dreamed . . ." Mike began. "This is going to sound really, really crazy, I know, but . . . I dreamed that there was a kid, a human kid, in my closet over there!"

"Now, now," said Sulley, smiling at Mike. "Maybe it was the movie you watched tonight."

"*Kidzilla*?" Mike scoffed. "Nah. I've seen it a dozen times and it's never bothered me before."

"Well, why don't you try to go back to sleep?" said Sulley, suppressing a yawn.

Mike cleared his throat shyly. "When I was little, my mom would bring me a sludgesicle when I had a bad dream," he said.

Sulley sighed patiently, then went and brought Mike a sludgesicle from the kitchen.

"She would sing me a little lullaby, too," said Mike.

In his low, scratchy voice, Sulley began to sing: "Rock-a-bye, Mikey, Googly-Bear, with sharp little fangs and shiny green hair! Morning will come when the sun starts to rise, and you'll wake up and open those googly eyes!"

"That googly *eye*," Mike said, snuggling under his blanket. "Uh, my mom also always checked the closet."

With another patient sigh, Sulley opened Mike's closet door and stepped inside. "Nope. Nothing in here!" he called. Suddenly, there was a loud clatter and a landslide of junk spilled out of the closet door. A yellow mop fell out. It looked just like blond hair!

"AHHHH!" shrieked Mike, leaping out from under the covers. Then he relaxed. "Oh, sorry, pal. In this dim light, I thought that mop was, you know, a human child!"

Sulley chuckled at the idea. "Don't be silly, Mike," he said. "A kid will never get loose in Monstropolis—what a disaster that would be!"

# Laugh, Cobra Bubbles!

Lilo thought she was a pretty lucky girl. She had a bunch of good friends whom she loved to laugh with. Stitch had a funny, scratchy laugh to go with his scratchy voice. Pleakley giggled, and Jumba shouted out big guffaws.

But as for Cobra Bubbles, well, the truth was that Cobra Bubbles just didn't laugh. Ever. And Lilo was dying to find out what his laugh sounded like.

So Lilo tried to get Cobra Bubbles to laugh. She showed him the latest episode of *The World's Funniest Lobster Videos*, but he didn't crack a smile, even when a lobster ate an entire jar of pickles. She made funny faces at him until her face hurt, but he just looked at her, expressionless.

Clearly, something had to be done. It just wasn't healthy for a person to never laugh.

"Nani, Cobra Bubbles is one of my best friends. He's practically family! But he never laughs. I think I need to help him," Lilo said.

"Well," Nani said thoughtfully, "what have you tried?"

Lilo ticked off the things she had tried.

"Hmm," said Nani, "I think I see the problem. Do you think those things are funny?"

"Well, no," Lilo admitted. "I'm scared of lobsters, and my face still hurts from making funny faces."

"Maybe Cobra Bubbles feels the same way," said Nani. "You know, he might laugh if he's having a good time. Why don't you start out by doing something fun?"

The next day, Lilo enrolled Cobra Bubbles in her hula class. He did his best to follow the complicated steps of the dance, and Lilo did her best to keep a straight face. But it was impossible. Cobra Bubbles in a grass skirt was the funniest thing she'd ever seen. The other kids in the class thought so, too. Soon they were all laughing—even the hula teacher!

To Lilo's surprise, Cobra Bubbles began to smile. And then he chuckled. And soon enough, Cobra Bubbles was actually laughing!

Lilo thought that Cobra Bubbles's laugh was perfect. It was somehow both quiet and big, and very nice. Just like him. What a nice surprise!

# Happy to Help

Dumbo was walking toward his train car, looking forward to a long nap, when suddenly he heard someone shout, "Oh, no! My beautiful balloons!"

Dumbo looked up. A bunch of colorful balloons were drifting away from a balloon seller. The elephant quickly sprang into action. He flew after the balloons, grabbed the strings with his trunk, and flew back to the ground.

"You're the best!" the balloon seller said.

Happy to have helped, Dumbo continued to make his way toward his train car to take his overdue nap. As he walked, he saw a crowd gathering. Using his trunk, he politely nudged his way in to see what was going on. A little girl stood crying in the middle of the crowd.

"I think the poor kid is lost," said a magician. "We must help her. But how?"

Dumbo walked over and tapped the girl on the shoulder with his trunk.

"Great idea, Dumbo!" said the juggler. "You could spot the little girl's mom from above!"

He picked up the girl and put her on the elephant's back. Dumbo and the little girl flew up above the circus tents. They looked down at the crowds of people.

"Mommy! There's my mommy!" the girl shouted.

Dumbo landed gently. The girl climbed off his back and ran into her mother's arms.

"Thank you, Dumbo! Thank you!" said the girl's mother.

Dumbo was glad to have been able to help.

Suddenly, a pie went whizzing by!

Dumbo turned to see some circus clowns throwing pink cream pies at one another. They were covered from head to toe!

"What a mess!" said one of the clowns.

"I think it's time for a shower," said another.

Dumbo had an idea! He flew over to the water tank and filled his trunk. Then he sprayed water all over the clowns! The clowns laughed as Dumbo rinsed away the gooey pink pie. Then, smiling, Dumbo went off to finally take his long-awaited nap!

# A Never Land Story

It was a cold winter night, and John and Michael just couldn't get to sleep. They climbed onto the bed of their older sister, Wendy.

"Oh, tell us a story, Wendy!" said Michael.

"Yes, please. A Peter Pan story!" pleaded John.

"Certainly," said Wendy. "Have I told you about the time that Peter Pan outsmarted the evil Captain Hook?"

"Yes!" said Michael eagerly. "And we want to hear it again!"

Wendy laughed and began her story. "Well, one night, Captain Hook moored his ship in a secret cove close to the island of Never Land. He and his men rowed ashore quietly, for he was intent on discovering the hiding place of Peter and the Lost Boys.

"Fortunately for Peter Pan," Wendy continued, "his dear friend Tinker Bell learned of Captain Hook's evil plan ahead of time. She flew to Peter and warned him that the pirate was coming.

"'Oh-ho!' laughed Peter. 'We shall be ready for him then!'

"Peter found a clock just like the one the crocodile who ate Hook's hand had swallowed. He whistled up into the trees, and a group of his monkey friends appeared. 'Here's a new toy for you!' Peter shouted, tossing the clock up to them.

"When Hook came to the clearing, the first thing he heard was the ticking clock. The sound seemed to be coming at him from all sides! The monkeys were having a grand time, tossing the clock back and forth among the trees and creeping up behind Hook.

"Seized with terror, Hook and his men raced to their boat and rowed madly back to their ship."

Just then, the Darling children's parents came in to check on them. "You're not telling more of those poppycock stories about Peter Pan, are you, Wendy?" their father asked.

"Peter Pan is real, Father!" cried the children. "We know he is!"

As the parents kissed their children good night, they didn't see that a boy in green was crouching just outside the nursery window. He had been listening to the story, and he would be back again—soon.

# Little Lost Sheep

**W**oody was relaxing on Andy's bed when Bo Peep came running over. "Oh, Woody! It's my sheep!" Bo cried. "I can't find them anywhere!"

"Are you sure?" asked Woody. "Where did you see them last?"

Bo explained that her sheep had been with her earlier that day, but now they were missing.

Woody put his hand on Bo's shoulder. "We won't rest until those sheep are safe with you! Right, everyone?" he called. All the toys in Andy's room shouted their agreement.

Soon the toys were searching the whole house. "Please, find them!" called Bo Peep. Then she sat down. She looked like she was about to cry.

Suddenly, the baby monitor crackled on the dresser. Andy's mother had left it in his room when she picked up the laundry that morning. The sound of Sarge's voice came from the speaker.

"This is Sarge reporting from the baby's room. There are not any sheep in here. Over and out."

"Oh, dear," said Bo. "Where could they be?"

Woody and Buzz came back into Andy's room with RC and Wheezy behind them. "Kitchen is clear," Buzz said. "No sheep there."

At that moment, the toys heard the sound of bleating sheep. Bo Peep gasped. Then she looked at the sheep more closely. "These aren't my sheep," she said.

Woody lifted a cotton ball off a little green head. It was the Aliens! They had just wanted to help.

Bo Peep thanked them, but she was still upset that her sheep were missing.

Suddenly, Hamm called out, "Andy's mother is coming!"

All the toys went limp as Andy's mom walked into the room. She placed a basket on the bed and started folding Andy's clothes. After a few minutes, she laughed. She'd found Bo Peep's sheep in her basket!

"Hey there, little guys!" she said. "I hope you enjoyed your bath." Finding Bo Peep on the shelf, she placed the sheep beside her. "I bet you missed these," she said, laughing. "Little Bo Peep has lost her sheep," she sang.

When the toys knew it was safe to move, they burst out laughing!

# Abu's Wild Ride

It was midnight in Agrabah, and all the kingdom was fast asleep—all, that is, except little Abu. The little monkey simply could not fall asleep. And so, while the rest of the palace slept, Abu was out looking for something to do.

He could make himself a midnight snack, but he really wasn't hungry. Or he could play with Rajah's tiger toys, but they were covered with tiger slobber. Yuck! There was, it seemed, nothing at all in the whole, entire palace for a wide-awake monkey to do. . . .

Then Abu spied a patch of bright wool hovering in the moonlight. It was the Magic Carpet!

Now that, Abu thought to himself, was something to do! With a happy little squeal, Abu hopped aboard.

*Whoosh!* Before Abu even knew what was happening, the Carpet was off, zipping toward the ceiling, then zooming to the floor. Abu clung to its fringes for dear life—and grinned. This was great!

The Carpet carried the little monkey through the castle corridors . . . whizzing in and out of doorways, twisting around columns, skidding down staircases, zooming as fast as it could

fly . . . until at last it soared right out an open window.

Uh-oh, thought Abu. This wasn't good. Where in the world was the Magic Carpet going? Soon the palace was just a tiny dot behind him. Where would he end up?

Just as Abu was really starting to worry, a giant blue hand appeared.

"Whoa, now, pardners!" a hearty voice boomed. "Slow down!"

It was the Genie. Abu sighed with relief.

"Taking a little joyride, are we?" he said.

The Carpet nodded, and if it were possible for a carpet to look sheepish, it would have looked very sheepish indeed.

"Well, time to go home now, oh Flat, Fuzzy One," the Genie said, giving the Carpet a gentle little pat. "Hmm, I can't say I blame you, Abu. I've always wanted to drive one of these, too. Whaddya say we take her home together?" He gave Abu a wink. "Scoot over! And, hey, Abu, I won't tell Aladdin about tonight if you don't."

Abu shook the Genie's hand. It was a deal!

# Blue Ramone

'Dum-da-dee-dum," Ramone hummed to himself in his body shop.

"Hey there, buddy! Are you painting yourself again?" It was Lightning, and he had Mater with him.

"I'm painting myself blue for Flo's birthday. It's her favorite color," Ramone replied. "And I plan on staying this color for an entire week!"

"Gee whiz!" said Mater. "I've never even seen you stay one color for a whole day!"

That night, the town gathered for a cruise down Main Street for Flo's birthday. Suddenly, the door of Ramone's body shop popped open, and a very blue Ramone emerged, driving low and slow.

"Oh, Ramone!" Flo exclaimed. "You painted yourself blue! Now, are you going to take me on a birthday cruise or what?"

Ramone and Flo slowly cruised down Main Street together as the rest of the cars watched.

The next day, Ramone got up early and started cleaning his shop. But after a few hours, he was finished. He was tempted to paint himself a new color.

Then he remembered his promise, so he went over to Flo's instead.

"Hey, baby, you want a quart of oil?" Flo asked.

"Yeah, thanks," Ramone said. Then he added, "Do you want me to give you a new paint job?"

"Oh, honey, thanks, but no," Flo said. "I have all this work to do."

Ramone stayed blue the next day and the next. He kept asking all the cars in town if they wanted paint jobs, but no one did.

"Ramone! What's wrong with you, baby?" Flo said. "Listen to me. If you want to paint yourself a new color, just go right ahead and do it."

"But I made a promise," Ramone said sadly.

"No. A happy, freshly painted Ramone made that promise," Flo said with a sigh. "I miss that Ramone. Just be yourself."

"Yeah," said Mater. "Just be yourself. We like ya that way."

Ramone turned around. It seemed as if the whole town was there to encourage him. So, Ramone happily went to work painting himself every color he could find!

# Nighttime Is for Exploring!

"Bambi! Oh, Bambi!"

Bambi slowly opened an eye. "Thumper?" he whispered. "Why aren't you asleep?"

"Asleep? Come on!" cried Thumper. "Sleep is for the birds! How can you sleep when there's so much to see and do at night?"

"But everybody knows that nighttime is for sleeping," Bambi said.

"Oh, brother," Thumper said. "Do you have a lot to learn! Follow me, Bambi, and Flower and I will show you how the night is a whole new day!"

At the prospect of a new adventure, Bambi's sleepiness disappeared. He stood up quietly and let his friends lead the way.

Thumper was right—the forest was as busy at night as it was during the day, but with a whole new group of animals. Owls, raccoons, and badgers—all those animals that Bambi thought spent most of their lives asleep—were now as lively as could be.

"Wh-wh-what's that?" Bambi exclaimed as a dot of light landed on his nose.

"Don't worry, Bambi, it's just a firefly," Flower said with a giggle.

"Firefly," Bambi said. Suddenly, the little light disappeared. "Hey, where'd it go?" the little deer asked.

"There it is!" cried Thumper.

Happily, the three friends chased the firefly as it flitted all around the forest.

But their game was soon interrupted by a flurry of sound. Thousands of leathery wings were suddenly beating overhead.

"Duck, Bambi!" hollered Thumper just as the whole group of flying animals swooped around their heads.

"Boy, that was close!" said Flower.

"Were those fireflies, too?" Bambi asked.

"Naw." Thumper laughed. "They didn't light up! Those were bats."

"Bats," repeated Bambi. "They're really busy at night."

"You can say that again," agreed Thumper, trying to stifle a yawn. And, since yawns are contagious, Bambi's own yawn was not far behind.

"This was fun," Bambi told his friend. "But what do you say we go home and go to bed?"

But there was no answer. . . . Thumper and Flower were already fast asleep!

# Scary Solar Surfing

Things were busy at the Benbow Inn—and B.E.N. wasn't helping much! The clumsy robot had already spilled purp juice on a whole family of Cyclopes, broken a whole set of Mrs. Hawkins's Alponian chowder bowls, and was now chasing a healthy serving of Zirellian jellyworms across the dining room floor.

"Don't you worry, Mrs. H.," B.E.N. assured the innkeeper. "Tell those spacers their lunch will be on the table in just one minute . . . *whoops!* Better make that two minutes."

"Jim!" Mrs. Hawkins cried, seeing her son. "Going surfing, I see. Wouldn't you love to take B.E.N. out for a ride with you?"

"Oh boy, oh boy! I've always wanted to do this!" said the robot as Jim unfurled the solar sail and they took off. "Where's the steering wheel? Where's the ON button?"

"Hang on, there, B.E.N.," said Jim. "There is no steering wheel. All you have to do is lean—like this. And there is no ON button. In fact, whatever you do, do not touch this button here!"

"Roger that!" said B.E.N. "Stepping on button a no-no. I completely understand and will not, under any circumstances—*Aghhhhhh!*"

To Jim's dismay, B.E.N. kicked the very button he had warned him not to. Instantly, the sail retracted, and the solar surfer began to fall.

"Help! Help! Help!" cried B.E.N., leaping onto Jim's back and holding on with all his might.

It was all Jim could do to balance himself as the surfer spiraled out of control! Luckily, there was no better surfer in all the greater galaxy than young Jim Hawkins, and after a few heart-stopping seconds, they were back under control.

"Phew!" sighed B.E.N., wiping his metal brow. "That was a close one, huh?"

"Yeah," muttered Jim.

"But it was pretty cool, too," B.E.N. went on.

Jim started to smile. "Yeah," he said. "It was."

"Wanna do it again?" asked B.E.N.

Jim's smile widened. "Absolutely!" he said.

And off they went.

# The Wrong Shortcut

It was summertime in Sherwood Forest. Birds were singing, bees were buzzing, and wildflowers covered the fields.

The day was so beautiful that Robin Hood and Little John went into the woods to pick berries. Maid Marian came along, too.

"The sweetest berries can be found on the other side of the creek," Little John declared. "And I know how to get there."

A little while later, the three reached the creek. It was wide and deep. A rickety bridge went over the water.

Little John stepped onto the bridge. The wood groaned under his weight. Little John took each step carefully, but in the end, it didn't matter. Halfway across the bridge, a board broke under his feet. Little John landed in the creek with a big splash! Sputtering, he swam to the other shore.

"I made it across!" he called.

"But you weren't supposed to get wet!" called Robin, laughing. "Luckily, I'm more clever than you. I can cross the bridge and stay dry, too."

"Oh, Robin, let me do it," said Marian. "I'm sure I can cross without falling into the water!"

But Robin Hood just shook his head. "It's too dangerous," he said. "Don't worry, I'm too clever to fall into the creek."

Very carefully, Robin stepped onto the bridge. He tested each plank before he put his foot on it. But before he reached the other side, there was a loud crack. Robin broke through the bridge and plunged into the cold water. Shivering, he swam to the other side. "The bridge is far too dangerous!" Robin called to Marian. "Don't cross. You'll only fall into the water."

But Marian just smiled. Cautiously, she tiptoed her way onto the bridge. Since she was lighter than Robin and Little John, she made it all the way to the other side—without getting a drop of water on her dress!

"How did you do that?" Robin asked later as they danced.

Maid Marian smiled. "Bigger and stronger doesn't always work better," she said. "Sometimes you need a Marian to do a Merry Man's job!"

# Toys that Go Bump in the Night

Andy was at a friend's house for a sleepover, and the toys had the whole night to themselves. Woody watched as lightning lit up the sky. It was the perfect night for telling scary stories!

Buzz, Rex, and Jessie took turns telling stories. Finally, it was Woody's turn. His story was so scary, it made the other toys shake with fear.

"All right, gang," Woody said when he saw that the toys were afraid. "I think we've had enough stories for tonight. Let's get some sleep."

Woody had just fallen asleep when he felt a nudge. It was Rex. "I heard something! It's coming from under Andy's bed," the dinosaur said.

"You're going to make me get up, aren't you?" Woody asked.

"If it wouldn't be too much trouble," Rex answered.

So Woody and Rex went to check under Andy's bed. *GRRRRRR*, went something beneath the bed. Woody was starting to feel a little nervous, too. He decided to wake Buzz.

"I think we have an intruder," Woody whispered to the space ranger. Just then, another rumbling sound came from under the bed. Rex wailed and then fainted in fright.

Rex's cry had woken the other toys, who gathered in the center of the room. Buzz tried to crawl under the bed, but his space wings shot out and he got stuck. Sarge and his men pulled Buzz back out.

"There's something under there," Buzz said. "And it was definitely moving."

"We'll take over from here," Sarge announced.

The soldiers stormed under the bed. "Halt!" boomed Sarge's voice. "It's one of our own! Switch to rescue-mission protocol!"

The other toys looked at each other, confused. Suddenly, RC shot out into the room!

"What was he doing under there?" Woody asked.

"His batteries are nearly out of juice," Sarge reported. "He just sat there revving his engine, spinning his wheels, and going nowhere."

"I knew there had to be a simple explanation," Rex said. "I don't know what Woody and Buzz were so worried about."

# Tools for Toys

Handy Manny and the tools were at Mr. Singh's house. They were inspecting a swing set that needed to be repaired, when a little girl pushed her wobbly doll carriage toward them.

"Hello, Leela." Mr. Singh smiled. "This is Manny. He's come with his tools to fix your swings."

Leela was thrilled. "Goody! That means we can play on them right after the tea party with my dollies. Right, Daddy?"

"I would love to, sweetheart," said Mr. Singh. "But I have a very busy day."

Leela was very sad to hear this. While Manny and Stretch went to inspect the swing with Mr. Singh, the rest of the tools offered to fix Leela's wobbly carriage.

"Hi, Mister Tool!" Leela exclaimed to Turner. "Would you like to play with me? I think you'd make a really nice dolly!" And with that, she carried Turner away.

"Uh, excuse me, little girl," said Rusty. "We've come to get our friend Turner."

The tools told Leela they had to get to work, and they needed Turner's help.

Leela frowned. "My dad always says he's very busy, too."

The tools felt bad, so they drank make-believe tea with Leela. Before long, Manny, Stretch, and Mr. Singh arrived. Manny was surprised to find that the carriage was still broken.

"We took a little tea break to play with Leela," confessed Dusty.

"Well, taking a short break is fine," Manny began, "but now it's time for my tools to get back to work, Leela."

Seeing Leela sad made Mr. Singh feel bad. "Don't worry. I'll play with you, Leela."

"B-but you're too busy!" cried Leela.

"Too busy? Is that what you think, sweetie?" Mr. Singh hugged his daughter. "I can't think of anything more important than spending special time with you."

So Mr. Singh and Leela went off to play while Manny and the tools finished their repairs.

When it was time to leave, Leela gave Turner a little pink bow.

"You know, Turner, you look pretty good when you're all dolled up!" teased Felipe.

# Mike Meets Sulley

**M**ike Wazowski had been the smallest monster at Frighton Elementary School, and the least popular. Now Mike was all grown up. He was still small and he was still unpopular, but he didn't care. He had made it to Monsters University and was about to begin studying at the best Scare Program in the world!

On the first day of classes, Mike and his roommate Randy entered the Scare School lecture hall. As their teacher, Professor Knight, was greeting them, Dean Hardscrabble swooped in. The Dean was in charge of the Scare Program.

"At the end of the semester, there will be an exam," said Hardscrabble. "Fail that and you are out of the program."

After Dean Hardscrabble left, Professor Knight asked, "Who can tell me the properties of an effective roar?"

Mike's hand shot up. He was giving his answer when an enormous "*ROAR!*" erupted from the back of the classroom.

It was James P. Sullivan—Sulley for short. Sulley was a huge blue monster, and the son of legendary Scarer Bill Sullivan.

"I expect big things from you," Professor Knight told Sulley.

After class, Mike went back to his room, but his peace was disturbed by a creature flying through his window. It was Archie the Scare Pig. Archie was the mascot of rival university Fear Tech. Sulley had stolen him!

Mike just wanted to be left alone, but Archie grabbed his lucky hat. Mike took off after him, with Sulley close behind.

Finally Mike caught the Scare Pig. Sulley scooped them both up and held them triumphantly above his head. Everyone thought Sulley was a hero!

The top club on campus, Roar Omega Roar, was impressed. They wanted Sulley to join them. Mike tried to explain what had really happened, but the RORs wouldn't listen. Their president told Mike to go and hang out with the losers' club, the Oozma Kappas. Sulley laughed and told Mike that ROR was for Scare students who had a chance.

"My chances are as good as yours!" Mike said angrily, and he promised Sulley he would out-scare him in every way in coming year. The challenge was on!

# Red's Tune-Up Blues

Red the fire engine thought it was the perfect day to plant a garden. He started his engine. *Rrrrrr.* Red's engine sounded funny. *Pop! Pop! Pop!* Loud noises were coming out of his tailpipe!

As his engine sputtered, Red tried to shrug it off. He didn't want to go to Doc's clinic. Red didn't like the idea of being poked and prodded. Instead, he headed into town to work on his garden. The fire engine soon passed Lightning McQueen.

"Hey, Red!" Lightning greeted him. "How's it going?"

"Fine," Red replied shyly. *Bang! Bang!*

"Whoa!" Lightning exclaimed. "That can't feel good. You okay?"

"Mmm-hmm," said Red. *Pop!* Red continued driving toward town.

Lightning headed into town, too, to find his friends. The race car found the others at Flo's V8 Café, filling up on breakfast.

"Red's not running right," Lightning explained. "But he's afraid to go to the clinic."

"Aw, shucks," said Mater the tow truck. "I know how the poor fella feels.

I was scared my first time, too! But Doc's a pro. He'll have Red fixed up before he knows what hit him!"

Mater and Ramone tried to convince Red to visit Doc. Ramone even offered him a new coat of paint, but nothing would convince Red to go to the clinic.

"We had better get over there," Lightning said to Sally, who had just rolled up. The two cars sped over. Mater, Luigi, Guido, Fillmore, and Flo followed.

"Listen, Red," Sally said. "We all know going to get a tune-up for the first time can be scary. But whatever is wrong could be easy to fix. If you don't go now, it could turn into a bigger problem later. None of us wants you to need a complete overhaul. We care too much about you."

Red looked back at his friends. He knew what Sally said was true. "Will you go with me?" he asked Sally.

"Of course I will," she replied.

Later that day, Red rolled out of the clinic. His friends were waiting for him. Red revved his engine. *Vroom!* It sounded smooth as silk. It was great to be running on all cylinders again!

# Roo's New Babysitter

I don't want to be babysitted!" cried Roo. Roo's mama, Kanga, was going shopping, and Pooh was going to babysit. "I want to go shopping!" cried Roo. He had a large bag and was filling it with cans of food when Pooh arrived.

"Hello, Pooh," said Roo. "I'm shopping!" He put more cans in his bag.

Roo and Pooh said good-bye to Kanga. Then Pooh gave Roo a hug.

"How about a nice smackerel of honey?" Pooh said, rubbing his tummy.

"I want to go shopping," squeaked Roo. "I don't want to eat."

"Hmmmm," said Pooh. "*Now* what do I do?"

"You don't know how to babysit?" asked Roo. "I'm good at babysitting. I'll tell you how. The first thing a babysitter does is climb!"

Pooh, who was starting to think there was not much *sitting* involved in babysitting, said, "Okay, let's find a good climbing tree."

They climbed the old apple tree in Roo's backyard. Roo hopped from branch to branch, and Pooh climbed up behind him. "Babysitters always pick apples for dinner," said Roo.

And so Pooh picked some apples.

Next Roo showed Pooh how babysitters poured a whole bottle of bubble bath into the bathwater. Roo disappeared under the bubbles. *Wffffffff.* Pooh blew on the bubbles, but he couldn't see Roo!

"Look at me jumping!" squeaked a little voice. Roo was jumping on his bed, all wet! Pooh dried Roo off, then helped put on his pajamas.

"Time for your Strengthening Medicine," said Pooh, a little more sternly than when poohs usually say such things. But Roo didn't want it. He folded his arms across his chest.

"Oh well," said Pooh, slumping into a chair. "Why don't you give me a spoonful? I think I could do with it!"

"Now, Pooh, dear, here's your medicine," said Roo in a cheerful, grown-up sort of voice.

"Ahhh!" said Pooh. "Thank you, Roo. You are a good babysitter."

Just then, Kanga opened the door and saw Roo and Pooh snuggled together in the chair.

"Mama!" cried Roo. "I'm babysitting Pooh!"

"Of course you are, dear," said Kanga.

# A Prizewinning Pair

**M**ax and his dad, Goofy, were sitting at the breakfast table. Max looked at the funny pages, while Goofy leafed through the other sections of the newspaper.

"Listen to this!" said Goofy. "Channel Ten is sponsoring the Father and Son of the Year Contest. The father and son who can prove that they have achieved something truly incredible together will appear on national TV."

"Too bad Bigfoot ruined that video we took of him last summer," said Max. "Hey, I know! Why don't we go back and find him again?"

"Okay, Maxie. Count me in!" said Goofy.

Goofy and Max reached the campsite that night, pitched their tent, and went to sleep. Soon they were awakened by a loud crash.

"It's him!" cried Max. "Get the camera!"

But when they poked their heads out, they saw it wasn't Bigfoot at all, but Pete and P.J.

"I'm sorry," said P.J. "I told my dad about your trip, and now he wants us to win that prize. We're out here looking for

Bigfoot, just like you two are."

The next day, Pete set up a barbecue with several juicy steaks.

"This will lure him out for sure," he told P.J.

The trick worked. In a matter of minutes, Bigfoot crashed through the trees and made a beeline for the meat. "Tackle him, P.J.!" yelled Pete.

Though he was scared, P.J. did as he was told. Bigfoot threw him around while Pete turned on the camera. "The judges are going to love this!" cried Pete.

"Help!" P.J. begged.

Goofy and Max heard P.J.'s cries and came running from the lake. Without saying a word, Goofy jabbed the monster in the backside with a fishing lure while Max threw a fishing net over the monster's head. "You were awesome," Max told Goofy.

"Right back at you, son," Goofy replied.

Back at home, Pete turned in the video. The judges had decided Goofy and Max deserved the award! But on the day they were to appear on TV, Goofy and Max decided to go to the beach together instead. They realized they didn't need anybody to tell them what an incredible father-and-son team they were.

They knew it already!

# Mr. Incredible's Greatest Adventure

The evil genius Syndrome had just launched a deadly robot toward the city. Syndrome had once been a normal boy and Mr. Incredible's number one fan, but when Mr. Incredible had told him that Supers were born, not made, the boy had decided to prove his hero wrong.

Syndrome had lured Mr. Incredible to his island and held him prisoner. Mr. Incredible's wife, Elastigirl, had discovered where her husband had gone and set off to save him. Without her knowledge, two of their Super children, Violet and Dash, had stowed away on the jet.

At headquarters, Mirage—who was working for Syndrome—had decided to set Mr. Incredible free.

Suddenly Elastigirl burst in!

"Where are the kids?" asked Mr. Incredible.

"They might've triggered the alert," said Mirage. "Security's been sent into the jungle!"

Syndrome's guards had indeed found Violet and Dash. They chased the two young Supers. Vi protected herself and Dash with a force field. Then Dash began to run. Together, the two young Supers raced through the jungle. Finally Mr. Incredible and Elastigirl found them. The family fought off Syndrome's guards. Then Syndrome arrived and locked the Incredibles in his immobi-ray!

"Looks like I've hit the jackpot!" Syndrome gloated when he saw the whole family. Then he took them to his base and suspended them in an immobi-ray cell.

The family stood by, helpless, as Syndrome described his evil plan. "The robot will emerge dramatically, do some damage," the villain explained, "and just when all hope is lost, Syndrome will save the day!" He sneered at Mr. Incredible. "I'll be a bigger hero than you ever were!"

"You killed off real heroes so that you could pretend to be one!" said Mr. Incredible.

Syndrome cackled and took off for the mainland.

Vi created a force field, allowing her to escape the energy beams and set her family free. Soon the Incredibles were back in action! It was up to them to stop the Omnidroid before it attacked the city.

# The Longest Day

"Could I have everyone's attention, please?" called Woody. "Today is Andy's last day of school. And you know what that means. . . ."

Summer meant the toys would get to play with Andy all day. They wanted the fun to start right away, but they had to wait until Andy came home. One by one, the toys suggested ways of passing the time. Buzz Lightyear made up a game of laser tag.

"But it's still only morning," Rex protested when the game was over. "This is the longest day of my life!"

"Don't worry, Rex," Buzz said. "There are plenty of other things we can do."

The toys decided to play knights-and-dragon in the castle Andy had built the night before. Rex played the dragon and pretended to attack the castle, letting out a roar. Then, suddenly, Andy's puppy, Buster, came skidding into the room and attacked it for real!

"Bad Buster!" Woody said as the dog ran out of the room. He hurried over to the mess. "We're going to have to rebuild the castle so it looks exactly like it did before."

The toys worked together restacking the blocks. When they were done, the castle looked as good as when Andy had built it!

By three o'clock, the toys were all waiting anxiously for Andy. "I'm positive this is the last day of school," Woody said, climbing onto Andy's desk. Then he spotted a note. "Oh, I'm sorry, guys," he said. "It appears there's a party after school."

"So what time will Andy get here?" asked Rex.

Woody didn't know the answer.

Suddenly, the toys heard the happy shouts of children playing. Woody looked out the window and saw lots of kids in Andy's backyard. Andy's entire class was here for the end-of-school party! No wonder it had taken him longer to get home, Woody thought.

Footsteps thundered up the stairs, and Andy and his classmates burst into the room.

"Wow! Great toys!" a boy shouted as he picked up Buzz and Rex. The other kids grabbed more toys until Woody and all his friends were part of the celebration.

This is going to be the best summer ever! Woody thought happily.

# The Show Must Go On

The wind whistled around the Big Top, pulling the canvas tent that Dumbo was holding out of reach of his small trunk.

"I'll get it," Dumbo's mother said as the tent flapped over their heads.

If the weather hadn't been so terrible, Dumbo thought, he could have flown up to grab the edge of the tent. But the whipping wind was too much, even for Dumbo's winglike ears.

At last, standing on her back legs, Mrs. Jumbo caught the canvas in her trunk. She pulled it taut and let the workmen tie it off. But Dumbo noticed several new rips in the fabric.

The Ringmaster had noticed the rips, too. He ordered the clowns to sew them up. "The repairs must be finished by showtime!"

Dumbo felt terrible. All the circus performers, animals, and workmen were working hard in the storm. He had made even more work by letting the canvas get torn. And now the Ringmaster's mood was as foul as the weather!

A blast of cold air blew across the field and whirled the Ringmaster's black top hat off his head.

"That does it!" the Ringmaster yelled.

"There will be no show tonight!"

Dumbo could not believe his ears. The announcement was even enough to wake Timothy Q. Mouse from his nap in a nearby bale of hay.

"No show? I can't believe it!" the little mouse cried.

The rest of the circus folk couldn't believe it, either. They silently continued to set up.

Suddenly, Dumbo noticed something. The Ringmaster's hat was caught on the flagpole, high over the Big Top. Perhaps he could get it for him?

Bravely, Dumbo took off. The wind was strong, but he tucked his head down and flapped his ears hard. When the wind calmed for a moment, the small elephant saw his chance. He grabbed the top hat and quickly flew to the ground.

Shyly, Dumbo held out the hat to the Ringmaster.

"Thank you, Dumbo." The Ringmaster took his hat gratefully. He looked around at all the people and animals still hard at work. He looked a little embarrassed. As he placed the hat on his head, he shouted, "The show must go on!"

# Sarge's Boot Camp

"First gear!" Sarge shouted. Guido and Luigi started moving slowly. "Second gear! Third gear! Fourth gear!"

Luigi raced down Main Street with Guido close behind. Sarge had decided to start a training camp for all the 4x4s that he was sure would soon be arriving in Radiator Springs.

"Hey!" Sheriff yelled. "Slow down, fellas!"

Just then a big, brand-new 4x4 rolled into town. "Hi," said the 4x4. "I'm T.J."

"Welcome to Radiator Springs, T.J.!" Sarge shouted to the newcomer. "You've reached the home of my boot camp!"

"Car camp!" Luigi shouted happily. "It will be tough! But don't worry. Guido and I are fully prepared to change your tires at any time."

"You mean I might get a flat?" T.J. said.

"You will if you don't change that attitude!" exclaimed Sarge. "Now, let's get going!"

Sarge led the group out of town to a rocky dirt road.

"Oh, no!" T.J. complained. "I've already got dirt in my grille!"

"No talking!" shouted Sarge. "Now . . .

first gear! Second gear! Third gear!"

"Come on, T.J.," said Luigi. "If Guido can do it, so can you!"

"Okay, team!" said Sarge. "We're going down that slope and across that big, muddy puddle."

T.J. gasped. He could lose control going too fast down the hill! But down, down, down they went.

"I'm gonna flip over!" T.J. cried.

"Hit the brakes!" Sarge called out. "Show a bit of courage, soldier!"

Soon they were at the bottom of the hill, crossing the mud puddle. T.J. hesitated. "Come on!" Luigi called to T.J. "You're a 4x4! This should be no problem."

T.J. thought about it and began to laugh. "I'm dirty, my paint is scratched, and I'm tired. But I can do it! Thanks, Guido. Thanks, Luigi."

"Now hit the showers!" Sarge shouted. "We've got a big day tomorrow!"

"Sir! Yes, sir!" T.J. yelled.

Luigi and Guido looked up the steep hill in front of them. "Come on, guys! Hop onto my roof rack! I'll give you a ride," T.J. offered.

Together the cars raced up the hill and back to town—excited about the next day of Sarge's boot camp!

# Knock, Knock! Who's There?

Standing in her brand-new bedroom, Lilo grinned. Lilo wasn't quite sure that the closet was in exactly the right place, but she loved everything else.

Lilo walked out into the living room to join Nani, her sister. Nani was worried. Cobra Bubbles, their social worker, was coming today to see how they were doing.

"Lilo, I want you to stay out of the workers' way," Nani said. "And keep an eye on Stitch! He keeps licking our nice new windows!"

"We'll stay out of trouble." Lilo smiled angelically.

Stitch wasn't exactly staying out of trouble. He had a tool belt around his waist, and his mouth was full of nails. With amazing force, Stitch spit the nails into the floor, accidentally fastening the end of his own belt to the ground.

Lilo shrugged. "That'll keep you out of trouble." Then there was a knock at the door. Lilo opened the new front door. Cobra Bubbles filled the door frame.

"Hey, come on in and see our new digs!" Lilo cried, happy to see her friend.

Cobra Bubbles stepped over a power cord and walked around a pile of flooring. "You don't actually live here yet, do you?" he asked slowly.

"Not yet," Lilo chirped. "It's supposed to be finished next month."

"And where is . . . Stitch?" Cobra Bubbles peered around the room.

Lilo frowned. Stitch was no longer nailed to the floor.

Suddenly, they heard a knock. Lilo and Nani looked at each other. It wasn't coming from the front door—in fact, it sounded like it was coming from Lilo's room!

"Who is it?" Lilo asked quietly.

With a monumental crash, Stitch burst through one of the new walls in Lilo's bedroom.

"Here he is!" Lilo shouted.

"Yes," said Nani nervously. "Stitch sure is, uh, helping out with the construction. Why, here he's decided on a new spot for Lilo's closet. We didn't really want it where it was, anyway."

Nani gave Cobra Bubbles a weak smile, then turned to look at Stitch's handiwork.

"Actually," Nani said with a real smile, "this is a much better spot for the closet. Thanks, Stitch!"

# Doctor Doppler, Daredevil

Dr. Delbert Doppler didn't know how he had gotten himself into this mess. There he was, standing atop a cliff on a solar surfer with fifteen-year-old Jim Hawkins, who was about to launch them into the etherium on a narrow plank of metal powered by energy-panel sails.

"Hold on, Doctor," said Jim. "Here we go!"

Jim launched the surfer off the cliff. In a flash, they were sailing through the etherium.

Ever since they had both returned from their amazing adventure on Treasure Planet, the two had become quite close. Doppler had thought solar surfing would be a fun bonding experience. But now he wasn't so sure it was a good idea.

Jim, an expert solar surfer, was in complete control. In fact, he was going easy on Dr. Doppler. If Jim had been surfing on his own, he would have been free-falling, rolling, and twirling through the air. But he didn't want to scare his passenger.

Dr. Doppler wanted to put on a brave face. "Wow, Jim," he said

through clenched teeth. "This is awful . . . er . . . *awesome!*"

"Really? You like it?" Jim replied. "Well, then, maybe we should try some more advanced moves. Like maybe a barrel roll?"

"No, no, no, no!" Dr. Doppler cried out anxiously. "I mean . . . m-maybe not today. Perhaps never . . . er . . . *next* time."

"Okay," Jim said with a shrug.

Five minutes later, Jim landed the surfer smoothly on a level patch of ground behind the inn.

For Dr. Doppler it was none too soon. He leaped off the surfer and stooped to kiss the solid ground. Then, realizing that Jim was looking at him funny, he straightened up and cleared his throat.

"Thank you, Jim," he said, a slight quiver creeping into his voice. "That was really intimidating . . . I mean, *exhilarating!*"

Jim smiled. "So maybe I'll take you solar surfing again sometime?"

Dr. Doppler flushed, unprepared for the question. "Uh . . . er . . . that sounds terrifying . . . er . . . terrible . . . I mean, *terrific!*"

# Woody's Hat

It was Saturday morning, and the toys in Andy's room were waking up. Jessie yawned and stretched. "It's time for *Woody's Roundup!*"

On the show, Woody's hat flew off and Bullseye trampled it! Jessie picked up the hat. It looked pretty ragged.

"I have lots of hats," Jessie told Woody. "Maybe you can find a new one."

Jessie brought Woody all the hats she could carry. There were so many, they tumbled out of her arms.

Woody picked up one of the hats and put it on his head. "What do you think?" he asked.

Jessie smiled. "It looks mighty fine."

"I don't know," Woody said. "Do you think it's too brown?"

"How about that one?" Jessie said, gesturing toward a hat with buttons on the band. "It's a lighter brown."

"That one's not brown *enough*," Woody said.

"Hmm," Jessie sighed. She piled more and more hats onto Woody's lap. "There must be a hat here that you like. Keep trying. How about this one?"

"That one is pink!" Woody said. "I'm sorry, Jessie, but none of those are right for me."

Jessie couldn't believe that Woody couldn't find *one* hat he liked in the huge pile she had brought.

"What we really need is a plan," she told Woody. "Why don't you tell me just what kind of hat you're looking for, then we can try to find it in the pile."

Woody leaned against the fence and thought. "I'd definitely like a brown hat," he said. "Not too dark or too light, but brown is best. It would be nice if it had a wide brim. And it should have stitching around the edge. But I don't think we'll find anything like that."

Sheriff Woody looked hopeless. Then Bullseye pulled Woody's old hat from the pile!

Jessie laughed when Bullseye held up the hat.

"Woody, I think Bullseye found just the right hat!" Jessie called out.

Woody grinned. "This is *exactly* the kind of hat I wanted! How does it look?" he asked.

"It's the best hat in the West!" Jessie replied.

# Mickey's Choo Choo Express

It was a hot day at the Clubhouse. Mickey and his friends were trying to think of ways to stay cool.

Minnie started dreaming about snow. "Brrr. . . . I feel better already," she said.

"I have a supercool idea!" Mickey said. "Do you remember Professor Von Drake's Icy Cold Easy-Freezy Snow?"

"You mean the snow that stays cold and never, ever melts?" asked Minnie.

"Yup," Mickey answered. "If only there were a way to bring the snow to the Clubhouse!"

"But Mistletoe Mountain is far away," Minnie said. "How can we get there?"

"Let's look in the garage," Mickey said. "We might find something to help us out."

In the garage, Mickey and his friends found a train!

"Let's get choo-choo-chooing," Donald said. "All aboard!"

"But Choo Choo needs tracks to ride on," Mickey said.

"I found a box," Donald called. "Aw, phooey," he said as he dropped the box and a bunch of springs fell out.

"We need to get these springs back into their box," Mickey said.

Mickey called Toodles. "Oh, Toodles!"

Toodles brought Mickey and his friends a magnet, which they used to pick up the springs.

"Choo Choo is ready to go," Mickey said. "All aboard!"

"There's nothing better than choo-chooing!" Minnie sang as they took off.

Suddenly, the train stopped. "We're almost at the mountaintop," Daisy said. "Why did Choo Choo stop?"

"There's a river in the way," Goofy said. "We have to cross it."

Mickey called Toodles again. Toodles brought a ladder, which Mickey laid across the river like train tracks.

"Hiya, Professor," Mickey said when they reached the top of Mistletoe Mountain. "It's such a hot day, we thought we could bring your Easy-Freezy Snow to the Clubhouse."

Soon Mickey and his friends were scooping snow into Choo Choo.

"My snow never melts, so you can play in it anytime," the Professor said.

When Choo Choo got back to the Clubhouse, Mickey and his friends spread the snow around. Goofy made a snow angel. Minnie and Daisy made a snowmouse. And Mickey just enjoyed being cool.

# Kuzco's Guide to Life

**H**ellooooo, all you underlings out there! The name is Kuzco. *Emperor* Kuzco to you, pal.

Welcome to Kuzco's Guide to Life, otherwise known as rules to live by—*if* you're me! I wouldn't try to follow these rules at home if I were you.

See, I'm an emperor, which means that, besides being rich and powerful and full of charisma, I have everybody in my kingdom doing *exactly* what I want them to do. You, on the other hand, probably don't have that kind of pull at your house.

So here are my personal rules. Read 'em and weep, and wish that you, too, were a rich and powerful emperor like me!

**Rule 1:** Do not allow anyone or anything to mess up your groove. By *groove* I mean the rhythm in which you live your life. For instance, when I feel like dancing around my throne room, that's what I do. Of course, a weird thing happened today when I was dancing. Several enormous stone statues fell over and nearly crushed me. Freak accident, probably.

**Rule 2:** Never consider anyone's feelings except your own. The other day, this huge, folksy peasant guy came by the palace and tried to talk me out of building my summer palace on the top of a hill where his family has lived for six generations. Boo-hoo, right?

**Rule 3:** Always put your own needs first. When you're hungry, clap your hands and your servants will bring you a meal. When you're tired, snap your fingers and they'll bring you a bed. And when you're bored, lift a pinkie finger and they'll bring in a circus show. Of course, the other day, when my servants brought in my food, I first fed a piece to my dog and he turned into a rhinoceros. And while I was sleeping in my royal bed, I was sure I heard someone sawing a hole in the floor all around me. And the day the circus came to entertain me, my royal adviser Yzma "accidentally" dropped the snake charmer's cobra into my lap! But maybe I'm just imagining things.

So those are my rules. Hey, you don't think people are out to get me, do you? Nah. That's a crazy idea, isn't it?

# The Great Garden Mystery

For the first time in many years, the Sultan of Agrabah had spare time. With Jasmine and Aladdin helping him run the kingdom, the Sultan could spend his afternoons in his vegetable garden. He grew eggplants, chickpeas, parsley, cucumbers, tomatoes, and lettuce.

One day, the Sultan came out to his garden and found that there was not one vegetable left in it! The chickpea plants were bare, the lettuce was gone, and the tomatoes had vanished. There wasn't even one lonely sprig of parsley!

The Sultan, Jasmine, Aladdin, and Rajah searched high and low for any clues. Finally, they found one: a set of muddy claw prints. The prints could only belong to one creature—Iago!

The group followed the claw prints over the garden wall and into the city. Finally Aladdin recognized his old neighborhood.

"I wonder why Iago would bring those vegetables here?" he said. As they turned the corner, they saw a poor family having a picnic. And in the middle of it all was Iago.

"Iago!" cried Jasmine. "You gave my father's vegetables away?"

The father of the family stood up.

"My apologies, Your Highness," he said. "We did not know that the vegetables belonged to the Sultan. This parrot saw how hungry we were and said he would give us something to eat. We would give them back, but we have already made falafel out of the chickpeas and parsley, and baba ghanoush out of the eggplants. However, there is plenty to go around, if you would like to join us."

Jasmine thought she had never received such a nice invitation. So they all sat down and dug in.

The baba ghanoush was rich, and the falafel was tasty and went very well with the Sultan's tomatoes and lettuce.

"I am delighted," said the Sultan, "that my garden is such a success. I think, however, that it would be even better if the garden was in the city and belonged to everyone. Perhaps I will move the garden to this very courtyard."

Everyone thought that was a wonderful idea, except for Iago.

"Vegetables, yuck!" he said.

# Robin Lends a Hand

It was a hot day in Sherwood Forest—a very hot day! So hot that the Sheriff of Nottingham had decided not to collect taxes for fear the coins would burn his greedy hands.

As for Robin Hood, he was trying to keep cool in the shade of Sherwood's oaks. Taking off his hat, he stretched out under the tallest, broadest tree, closed his eyes, and waited for a breeze.

Suddenly, he heard someone coming. "Halt! Who goes there?" he shouted loudly, jumping up. "Oh! Skippy, my good man. Forgive me. I didn't mean to scare you."

Robin helped to pick up Skippy's twigs, which he had dropped when Robin jumped out at him. "Now, then," he said. "That's better."

But Skippy didn't seem to agree. Robin didn't think he had ever seen him look so unhappy.

"Why so glum, old chum?" Robin couldn't help but ask.

"Oh, Robin." Skippy sighed. "It's so very hot, and all the other children have gone to the swimming hole. But Mother has so many chores for me to do, I don't think I'll ever be able to join them."

"I see," said Robin, nodding. "That could get a fellow down, now, couldn't it?"

"I'll say," said Skippy.

"Unless," Robin went on with a big grin, "a fellow had a friend to help him out!"

Skippy's sorrowful face grew brighter. "Do you mean . . . ?"

"Indeed!" Robin answered, bending to pick up a handful of sticks.

"Hooray for Robin Hood!" Skippy cheered, nearly dropping his sticks once again. "Hip, hip, hooray!"

And so, working together, Robin Hood and Skippy gathered firewood. They wrung out the laundry and hung it to dry. They picked a peck of juicy plums and a basketful of lettuce, weeded the garden, and built a scarecrow. By lunchtime, in fact, not only was every one of Skippy's chores done, but he and Robin had washed all the windows and swept Skippy's cottage floor, as well.

"Robin Hood, how can I ever thank you? I'd still be hard at work if it weren't for you!" Skippy asked when they were through.

Robin scratched his head and thought for a moment. "I have it!" he declared at last. "Take me swimming with you!"

# Bedtime for Billy

Mike and Sulley were excited about their evening. They were monster-sitting for Mike's nephew, Billy.

"Everything will be fine, Sis," said Mike. "Sulley and I will take good care of the little guy. You don't have to worry about a thing."

Billy's parents kissed him good-bye and hopped in the car. Then the three monsters went inside and ate pizza and popcorn while they watched classic movies like *Gross Encounters of the Kid Kind*.

After the movies were over, Sulley, Mike, and Billy listened to music, sang, and danced. Soon it was bedtime.

But putting Billy to bed wasn't going to be easy. There was one very important detail that Billy's mother had forgotten to tell her monster-sitters. Billy was scared of the dark!

"Aaaaaaahhhhh!!!!" screamed Billy when Mike turned out the light.

"Wh-wh-what is it?" shouted Mike as he and Sulley ran back into the bedroom.

"There's a kid hiding in the c-closet," stammered Billy. "It wants to g-get me!"

Mike and Sulley searched for human children.

"There aren't any kids in the closet," said Mike.

"All clear under the bed," announced Sulley.

"See, there's nothing to worry about," Mike said. "You can go to sleep now."

But Billy was still frightened. Mike and Sulley quickly realized they had to come up with another plan to help him get over his fear. How could they show Billy that children weren't scary?

"I've got it!" exclaimed Mike. "The scrapbook!"

Mike brought out the scrapbook, and the three monsters looked through it. It was filled with photographs of monsters with children, newspaper clippings of them together, and laugh reports.

"See, Billy?" said Mike. "Human kids aren't dangerous, and they love to have fun, just like you."

"You know, Billy, sometimes human kids get scared of us," said Mike. "But once they see that we're funny and friendly, they realize there's no reason to be scared of monsters."

Billy soon fell fast asleep as Mike and Sulley watched from the doorway.

"Another job well done, Mike," said Sulley.

# How to Unpack for a Vacation

One morning, Donald Duck heard a knock at his door. When he opened it, he found his friend Mickey Mouse standing there. "Today is the day!" exclaimed Mickey.

"Today is *what* day?" asked Donald with a yawn.

"Don't you remember?" said Mickey. "You're driving me, Minnie, and Daisy to the beach for a week's vacation."

"Oh, no!" cried Donald. He hadn't packed yet.

"Calm down," said Mickey. "You have time to get ready. Just pack your things now."

While Mickey relaxed on the porch in a rocking chair, Donald went back inside. "What do I pack?" Donald muttered to himself as he raced through his house. "I'll need books and toys, of course, in case I get bored."

Donald ran to his playroom and placed all his books and toys in boxes.

"What else should I pack?" Donald asked himself. "Clothes!" He ran to his bedroom and took out every suitcase he owned. Then he emptied all his drawers and filled his suitcases.

Finally, Donald calmed down. "That should do it," he said, looking at his pile of boxes and suitcases.

Mickey couldn't believe his eyes when Donald began packing up his car. When Minnie Mouse and Daisy Duck arrived, they were each carrying one small suitcase. They took one look at Donald's car and gasped. Boxes and baskets were crammed into the back and front seats. Daisy opened the trunk and found it overflowing with Donald's suitcases.

"There's no room left for *our* suitcases!" cried Daisy.

"Forget our suitcases!" exclaimed Minnie. "There's no room for us!"

Mickey put his arm around Donald. "It's okay, Donald," he said. "It's hard to pack for a vacation. You have to leave some things behind—even some of your favorite things."

"And besides," added Daisy, "don't you want to leave room in your car to bring back souvenirs, like seashells and T-shirts and saltwater taffy?"

Donald brightened. "Seashells and T-shirts and saltwater taffy!" he cried excitedly. "Oh, you bet!"

"Good," said Mickey. Then he pointed to Donald's overflowing car. "Now let's all help Donald *unpack* for this vacation!"

# A-Ropin' and a-Ridin'

"Yippee-ki-yay!" Jessie whooped as she twirled her lasso. "I'm going to show Woody that he's not the only cowpoke who can do fancy rope tricks! All I need is something to rope."

Bullseye walked over to Andy's open window and stomped his hoof.

"Good idea, pardner!" said Jessie. "I'll lasso some acorns on that tree."

Jessie stood on the edge of the bedroom window. There was a lone acorn hanging on a nearby branch. Jessie twirled her lasso over her head. Up went the rope—just as a hungry squirrel reached for the acorn.

"Oops!" Jessie cried. She had lassoed the squirrel instead of the acorn! With a squeak, the squirrel ran away, dragging Jessie along with him!

As the squirrel raced up the tree, Jessie held on tight. When the squirrel hopped from the tree to the roof, Jessie found herself being pulled across the shingles.

"Now that's just about enough!" she cried. Pulling herself to her feet, she planted one foot against the edge of a shingle and tugged hard. The squirrel jerked to a stop.

"Sorry, Mr. Squirrel, but I don't want to lose a good rope!" And in a flash, she was sitting on his back. "Time to break this bronc!" she cried.

The squirrel bucked up and down. Finally, he got tired and sat down to catch his breath.

Jessie hopped off the critter's back and slipped the lasso off his neck. "Now that I've got my rope back, can you give me a ride back to Andy's room?" Jessie asked the squirrel.

But the squirrel just raced away.

Jessie looked around. The roof was too steep, and her rope was too short. She was stuck!

What Jessie needed was a sure-footed creature to help her out. She thought for a moment, then whistled loudly. A few minutes later, Bullseye burst out of the attic window and trotted to her side.

"Good horse," said Jessie as she climbed into the saddle. "I just did some fine bronco bustin'."

Bullseye whinnied.

"That's right, Bullseye," Jessie said with a chuckle. "Woody can brag about his lasso tricks, but I'll bet he never won a squirrel rodeo!"

# Kida's Surprise

Although it was Kida's 8,500th birthday, she honestly didn't want anyone to make a big deal about it. There were much more important things to think about. Rebuilding the city, for one thing! And yet, as the day wore on and Milo still had not even said "happy birthday" to her, Kida began to feel a little down. If Kida didn't know better, she'd think Milo had completely forgotten.

Just then Kida realized, she *did* know Milo! And come to think of it, he probably *had* forgotten. And not just him. For the first time in her life, Kida sadly realized, no one in Atlantis had remembered her birthday.

Kida tried the best she could not to feel sorry for herself. Instead, she concentrated on tuning up her Ketak speeder.

It was hard, though, when Milo finally came up to her later that afternoon and asked if she'd like to help him take his sluglike ugobe for a walk.

"Oh, I don't know," Kida said with a sigh. "I'm a little tired."

"Ah, come on, Kida," Milo said. "I thought it would be such a fun thing to do on this special day."

"Special?" said Kida, suddenly perking up. Had Milo remembered her birthday after all?

"Of course." Milo grinned. "It's exactly eight and a half months since we met!"

"Oh," Kida replied.

"So are you coming?" Milo asked her.

Finally Kida agreed. Milo put a leash on his ugobe and took Kida by the hand. He led them through the palace courtyard, out onto the street. But instead of turning right, Milo went straight, heading toward the city center.

"Where are you going?" Kida asked. "There's no place for an ugobe to run this way."

"No?" said Milo. "Are you sure?"

"Positive," said Kida. "There's only—" "SURPRISE!"

Kida's mouth fell open as thousands of smiling Atlanteans greeted her with a thunderous cheer and a cake the size of a Ketak. The entire kingdom had gathered beneath the great crystal Heart of Atlantis to surprise her!

"Happy birthday, Kida," said Milo. "You didn't really think we'd forget it, now, did you?"

# Leo's Baton

The Little Einsteins were inside their clubhouse. Suddenly Leo noticed that Rocket's antenna had lit up.

"We have a mission!" he exclaimed.

The team quickly headed to Rocket's Look-and-Listen Scope to discover their mission.

"I think it's a flower trying to push its way through the snow," guessed Quincy.

"Ooh, it's a crocus—the first sign of spring!" June exclaimed.

"Our mission must be to help spring arrive!" Leo said. "And to do that, we'll need to get the crocus to bloom."

Suddenly Leo realized something was wrong. "My baton is missing!" he shouted.

"Oh, dear!" exclaimed Annie. "You'll need it to conduct the crocus. We have to go back to the clubhouse and find it!"

Quincy was puzzled. "There has to be a clue around here somewhere."

"What do all these pictures mean?" asked Annie, looking at their clue.

Quincy looked intently at them. "Hmm . . . maybe it's a code we need to crack."

June had an idea. "Let's write down the first letter of each pictured word to see if it spells out a sentence."

"Let's see," said Leo. "If we write in an *F* for frog, an *I* for ice cream, an *N* for nail, and a *D* for dog, we have the word FIND!"

"Awesome job, Leo!" said June. "Let's look at the next word: a *Y* for yo-yo, an *O* for owl, a *U* for umbrella, and an *R* for rabbit—YOUR!"

"The final word is FOOTPRINTS!" shouted Quincy. "Find your footprints."

"Leo just needs to track down his footprints to find his baton," said June.

"Leo, didn't you have it on our last mission, in Vermont?" asked Annie.

"You're right, Annie!" exclaimed Leo. "And my footprints should be easy to find in the snow. Let's go!"

When they reached Vermont, the team followed Leo's footprints to a tree.

"Here it is!" June called, picking up Leo's baton.

"Following our footprints really worked!" exclaimed Quincy. "We found Leo's baton and now we're ready to wake up spring."

"Look!" exclaimed Annie. "The snow is melting, and leaves and flowers are popping up everywhere!"

"Great job, team!" exclaimed Leo. "Mission completion!"

# Heavy Metal Mater

Everyone was gathered at Flo's V8 Café for karaoke. Lightning McQueen looked over at Mater. "Why don't you get up there and sing?" he asked.

"I don't want to steal the show," Mater replied. "I was a big rock star."

"What?" Lightning couldn't believe it.

Mater nodded. "I started out in a garage band. . . ." he said, describing how his rock band, Mater and the Gas-Caps, had gotten their start.

Soon Mater and the Gas-Caps had a gig at the Top-Down Truck Stop. When the band finished, all the trucks cheered.

"That so rocked!" called a waitress named Mia. "Do you guys have a record?" The guitar player shook his head, but Mater smiled. He had an idea.

Not long after, Mater and the Gas-Caps were in a recording studio. Mater sang so loudly that everyone in the recording studio heard him. Doors began to open. Cars peeked out. "What's that sound?" someone asked.

A music agent named Dex knew the answer. "Sounds like angels printing money to me!"

Dex rolled into Mater's recording booth. "Say, you boys are good," Dex told

the band. Then he noticed the name on the drums. "All you need is a new name."

At that moment, a delivery car entered the studio. "Where do you want this heavy metal, Mater?" he asked.

That was it! Heavy Metal Mater! The band was an overnight success. They packed stadiums and had thousands of fans. A giant Mater balloon with wings lifted up from behind the stage and floated over the audience.

Back in Radiator Springs, Lightning interrupted the story. "You were Heavy Metal Mater?"

"No," the tow truck replied. "*We* was Heavy Metal Mater!"

At Mater's concert, a platform rose up. Lightning was on it, wearing sunglasses.

"Are you ready to rock?!" Lightning yelled.

At Flo's V8 Café, Lightning stopped Mater's story again.

"I'm sorry," he said with a laugh, "that did not happen."

"Well, suit yourself," Mater replied, motioning to the sky.

Lightning looked up. The balloon from the concert was flying overhead! Had Mater been telling the truth. . . ?

# Thrown Out

Mike Wazowski was determined to do well at Monsters University. He had dreamed of becoming a Scarer his whole life, and he was willing to do whatever it took to make his dream come true.

Mike worked harder than anybody else. He read every book he could find on scaring. He practiced making frightening faces in the mirror and studied every Scare technique. His competition, James Sullivan, hardly worked at all. Johnny Worthington, the president of the ROR fraternity, told Sulley that if his grades didn't improve, he would be kicked out of ROR.

On the day of the Scare final exam, Professor Knight explained that each student would enter the scare simulator and perform a Scare on a robot child. Dean Hardscrabble would then decide who would move on in the Scare Program.

While they were waiting, Mike and Sulley began to fight. Before they knew it, they were in a Scare-off. Suddenly, Sulley stumbled into Dean Hardscrabble's record-breaking scream can, knocking it to the floor. The can flew around the room, releasing the scream as it went.

"It was an accident!" Sulley insisted.

Dean Hardscrabble remained calm, but when Mike and Sulley finished their exams, she announced that neither of them would be continuing in the Scare Program.

Mike begged for another chance, but Dean Hardscrabble's decision was final. Mike and Sulley were enrolled in the Scream Can Design Program instead.

"Some say a career as a Scream Can Designer is boring, unchallenging, and a waste of a monster's potential," droned Professor Brandywine.

Mike and Sulley agreed. They had to find a way back into the Scare Program.

Back in his dorm room, Mike threw a book against the wall in frustration. His calendar fell down, revealing a Scare Games flyer. Mike thought back to the day he had been given the flyer.

"It's a super-intense scaring competition where you get a chance to prove you're the best!" a monster had told him.

Mike smiled and grabbed the flyer. The Scare Games were the answer to his problems!

# The Supers Work Together

Bob and Helen Parr—Mr. Incredible and Elastigirl— and their children were Supers. Mr. Incredible had been lured into a trap by Syndrome, a self-made Super who had created a robot that only he could defeat.

The Incredibles were trapped on Syndrome's island. Syndrome had launched his deadly robot toward the city and had left to "save the day." Luckily, Violet—Mr. Incredible's daughter—had created a force field, allowing her to set her family free. The Incredibles were back in action!

The family escaped from the island in a rocket and flew toward the city, where the robot was already destroying everything it could find. The people of the city were terrified.

"Someone needs to teach this hunk of metal a few manners!" Syndrome told the crowd. Sneakily he worked the robot's remote control and removed the Omnidroid's arm.

The crowd cheered, and Syndrome loved it.

But the Omnidroid was a learning robot, and it realized Syndrome was controlling it. It knocked Syndrome out!

The Incredibles crash-landed in the city, and Mr. Incredible announced he would fight the robot alone. When Elastigirl objected, Mr. Incredible begged her to stay out of the fight. "I can't lose you again," he said. "I'm not strong enough."

Elastigirl smiled. "If we work together, you won't have to be."

The Supers fought as a team. Mr. Incredible's old pal Frozone helped them, too. Still, the Omnidroid proved to be too powerful for them—that is, until Mr. Incredible remembered that the only thing that could defeat the Omnidroid was itself.

He grabbed the arm that had fallen from the robot. Elastigirl, Frozone, and the children pushed buttons on the remote while Mr. Incredible aimed the arm so it pointed at the Omnidroid. Finally, Elastigirl found the right button . . .

The rocket on the robot arm ripped the robot apart. The city was saved!

Syndrome recovered to find everyone cheering the Supers! No one cared about him!

Furious, he crept away . . . determined to get revenge on the Incredibles.

# The Race

"Good morning, young Prince," Thumper greeted Bambi one bright and sunny day.

"Good morning, Thumper," Bambi said.

"I have a great idea, Bambi. Let's have a race," Thumper said. "Whoever makes it to that big pine tree over there first wins the race."

"But it would be silly for us to race," Bambi told his friend.

"Why's that?" Thumper asked, confused.

"Because I'll win," Bambi said.

"What makes you so sure?" Thumper challenged, puffing up his chest.

"Because I'm bigger and faster than you are," Bambi explained.

"If you're so sure you'll win," Thumper said, "why are you afraid to race me?"

Bambi paused. He didn't want to hurt the little rabbit's feelings. "Fine," he said at last. "Let's race."

Flower, who had just joined the friends, agreed to judge.

"On your mark. Get set. Go!" cried Thumper. They both took off as fast as they could.

Bambi, with his long legs and big, wide stride, immediately took the lead.

But Thumper's small size helped him to dart through the underbrush and slip through some bunches of trees. When Bambi looked back, he saw that Thumper was right on his heels. Bambi paused to jump over a tree that had been knocked down, blocking the path. Thumper was able to wiggle under it. He popped up in front of Bambi and took the lead.

Bambi took longer and longer strides, running faster and faster. Soon he had passed Thumper. But in his hurry to go as fast as he could, he got tangled up in a bush. As Bambi struggled to free himself, Thumper hopped past him again.

They were quickly approaching the big pine tree. Bambi was running as fast as he could, jumping over logs and bushes. Thumper, too, hopped as quickly as his bunny legs would carry him, ducking and weaving through whatever obstacles were in his way. And as they crossed the finish line, they were in a neck and neck tie.

"See?" Thumper said, panting. "Little guys can keep up!"

"You are absolutely right!" Bambi said, also panting.

And the two friends, both winners, sat down together to catch their breath.

# All Wet

Timon pounded his tiny chest and gave a mighty yell as he swung out over the lagoon. He let go of the vine and threw his arms out wide, hitting the water with a small but very satisfying smack. He popped to the surface, shouting, "Ta-da!"

Pumbaa was next. "Look out below!" he called. He backed up on the rock ledge, then charged. The warthog's splash sent water flying high into the air.

"Not bad," Simba said. "But I bet Nala could do better."

"Ha!" Nala laughed. "You know I don't like to get wet."

"Oh, come on, Nala. Give it a try. The water's fine!" Simba said.

"The water *is* fine," Nala replied slowly, rolling over and licking her paw. "For drinking."

Simba frowned. Nala was making him look silly in front of his friends. Was he king of the Pride Lands or not?

Using his most commanding voice, Simba gave Nala an order. "You will come swimming with us right now, or else!"

Nala didn't even lift her head. She closed her eyes. "Or else what, Your Mightiness?"

Simba couldn't come up with anything, so the argument was over. Nala, as usual, had won. Accepting his defeat, Simba ran to the edge of the rocky ledge, sprang high in the air, and tucked his paws in for a royal cannonball.

Pumbaa and Timon were drenched. Slinking slowly out of the water, Simba signaled to them. He pointed at his dripping mane and then up at Nala's rock.

Timon winked, and he and Pumbaa began a noisy mock–water fight to distract Nala. Simba walked quickly but silently. Drawing closer, he crouched, his legs coiled to pounce.

With a triumphant roar, Simba jumped onto Nala's rock and gave his sopping mane a mighty shake. Nala was drenched.

Nala leaped to her feet with a snarl. Simba rolled onto his back, laughing.

"What happened, Nala? You're all wet!" Timon laughed.

Pumbaa was laughing so hard, he could barely breathe.

Nala tried to glare fiercely at Simba, but she couldn't. She had to laugh, too. "King of the practical jokers," she said.

# Superhero for a Day

Lucky sat glued to the television set. He was watching his favorite show, *The Thunderbolt Adventure Hour*. "I'm going to be just like Thunderbolt when I grow up," Lucky announced.

Patch laughed at his brother. "Thunderbolt can jump clear across a river," he said. "You can barely climb up the stairs!"

"Just wait!" Lucky said.

While the other puppies went outside to play, Lucky practiced his leaping. He leaped from the arm of the sofa onto the chair. Then he leaped from the chair . . . right into a lamp. *CRASH!*

Nanny came running.

"Lucky!" she scolded. "Go outside while I clean this up!"

When Lucky got outside, he found Rolly with his head stuck in the bushes. "Don't worry!" shouted Lucky. "I'll save you!" He ran up to Rolly, grabbed him by the leg, and pulled.

"Ow!" yelled Rolly as he and Lucky collided. "What did you do that for?"

"You were stuck!" answered Lucky. "I was trying to save you."

"I didn't need saving!" complained Rolly. "We were playing hide-and-seek!"

Lucky's brothers and sisters came over to see what all the fuss was about. "Come on," said Patch. "Let's go inside before Thunderbolt Junior tries to save anybody else!"

Lucky stayed behind. He'd show Patch! He climbed to the top of the doghouse to practice leaping some more.

Below him, Penny had returned to fetch her bone. But she found it had already been snatched by Bruno, the neighborhood bully. Lucky watched from above as the bulldog growled and bared his teeth.

Suddenly Lucky lost his balance and tumbled off the roof.

"Ahhhhhh!" Bruno howled when Lucky landed on his back. The bulldog dropped the bone in terror, turned, and ran off.

By now the other puppies had come running from the house.

"What happened?" asked Rolly.

"Lucky saved me!" Penny said. "You should have seen him! He flew right through the air and scared Bruno away—just like Thunderbolt!"

Lucky puffed out his chest with pride.

"Wow!" said Patch. "Can I have your autograph?"

# Pooh's Neighborhood

"I say, it's a splendid day in the neighborhood!" cried Owl.

"Which neighbor wood are we talking about?" asked Pooh.

"*Neighborhood*," said Owl. "The place where we live and where all our neighbors live and are neighborly."

"Oh," said Pooh. "It is a splendid day in it, isn't it?"

"Now I'm off for an owl's-eye view!" Owl said as he flew away.

As Owl flew off, Pooh began to think about what it means to live in a neighborhood. He thought perhaps he would bring a neighborly present to his closest neighbor, Piglet. Pooh went inside his house and took a honey pot out of his cupboard.

When he reached his Thoughtful Spot, Pooh suddenly had a thought: I could take the path straight to Piglet's house. Or I could go up the path and around the whole neighborhood. And sooner or later the path would take me to Piglet's house, anyway. So that's what he did.

As he walked the long way to Piglet's house, Pooh came across each of his neighbors in turn. He joined Kanga and Roo for a snack at the picnic spot and collected some carrots from Rabbit. After lunch and a longish snooze at Christopher Robin's house, he soon reached Eeyore's Gloomy Place.

Eeyore was feeling sad, so Pooh offered him a nice lick of honey. But the honey pot was empty! Pooh had eaten all the honey on his journey through the neighborhood.

Pooh walked away from Eeyore's house glumly. Before long, Owl flew over.

"I've seen our whole neighborhood today," Pooh told him. "But now I have no neighborly present left for Piglet."

"The bees have been quite busy at the old bee tree lately," said Owl. "Perhaps you can get a fill-up there."

So they walked together until they came to the old bee tree. Up, up, up Pooh climbed. Owl had a thought, and he told Pooh to go to the very top of the tree and look around.

"Our neighborhood!" cried Pooh. "Our beautiful home!" The Hundred-Acre Wood was spread out below him.

"That's the owl's-eye view," said Owl grandly.

Then Pooh filled the honey pot once more, and he and Owl went to Piglet's house for supper.

# Finding Flicker

"*Vámonos!* Let's go!" shouted Felipe.

Manny and the tools were packing for a trip to one of their favorite spots—Lake Nochanailin! Someone else was going, too. Abuelito was riding his motorcycle to the lake and meeting them at the cabin.

Just then Manny noticed he was out of batteries for Flicker, his flashlight.

"I need to go to Kelly's," he said.

"That's the trouble with tools that need batteries," said Pat. "I don't need them. I'm a hammer!"

When Manny returned from Kelly's hardware store, the tools were in a tizzy. Flicker was missing!

"I think someone hurt his feelings," Turner said.

"I know you didn't mean it, Pat," said Manny. "Let's find Flicker. Pronto!"

The toys tried Mr. Lopart's sweet shop first, but Flicker wasn't there. Next, they headed to Mrs. Portillo's bakery. Flicker wasn't there, either!

Manny and the tools wondered where to look next.

"Flicker loves story time at the library," said Felipe.

"Good idea," said Manny. But Flicker wasn't at the library, either! Manny was worried. Where was Flicker?

Just then the phone rang. It was Abuelito. "If you are looking for Flicker, he is safe with me!" Abuelito said.

"*Bueno!*" replied Manny. "That is so good to hear. How did you find him?"

"He found *me*," said Abuelito. "When I got to the cabin, I found Flicker hiding in my motorcycle bag!"

Manny was relieved. Finally he and the tools set out for the lake. They arrived just after sunset.

"Ooh, the cabin looks very dark," said Rusty.

"*Sí,*" said Manny. "I wonder if something is wrong."

"Manny," said Abuelito. "You got here just in time. The electricity went out. My homemade *dulce de leche* ice cream will melt!"

"It's a good thing you found Flicker," said Manny. "I can't fix the electricity without him. I need your light, Flicker!"

Manny and tools went outside the cabin to fix the fuses. Thanks to Flicker, they were able to save Abuelito's ice cream. It was delicious.

"Hooray for Flicker!" the tools shouted.

# Potion Commotion

Emperor Kuzco's royal adviser, Yzma, was down in her secret laboratory, mixing potions. She had enlisted her enthusiastic but dim-witted right-hand man, Kronk, to help her in her work.

"Kronk, I need spider legs, one eye of newt, and elderberry juice . . . and quickly!" Yzma directed.

Kronk hurried across the laboratory to the cupboard that contained all of Yzma's potion ingredients.

"Let's see," Kronk said to himself as he pored over the containers. "Legs, eye, juice. Legs, eye, juice." He found the Legs section. "Newt legs! Check!" Kronk said to himself, confusing Yzma's instructions.

Then he found the Eyes section. "Spider eyes! Got it!" he said, grabbing the jar.

"Kronk!" shouted Yzma. "I said spider legs and eye of newt! Not newt legs and eye of spider! And where's the elderberry juice? Hurry, hurry!"

Kronk hurried back to the cupboard. "Spider legs . . . eye of newt . . . spider legs . . . eye of newt," he recited as he went. This time, he managed to keep them straight and took down the right

containers from the cupboard. But what was that third ingredient?

"Juice!" Kronk remembered. "Berry juice." He found a small vial of blueberry juice and brought everything to Yzma.

"Not blueberry juice, you numskull!" Yzma screamed. "ELDERBERRY!"

"Right," Kronk said. He hurried back across the laboratory and quickly located the Juice section. "Boysenberry . . . cranberry . . . " he read, moving alphabetically through the containers.

"ELDERBERRY!" Yzma shouted at him. "Get it over here! And step on it!"

Kronk finally located the right bottle. "Got it!" He rushed it across the laboratory.

Yzma reached out to take the bottle from him. But Kronk didn't hand it to her. Instead, he gently placed the bottle on the floor. Then he lifted his right foot and stomped on it—hard— shattering the bottle and splattering juice everywhere.

"KRONK!" Yzma screamed in surprise. "What are you doing?"

Kronk was confused. "I did just what you said," he explained. "I got the elderberry juice, and I stepped on it."

# A Tramp Tale

It was a warm evening, just about the time that the first star comes out to shine, and *long* past the time for Lady and Tramp's puppies to go to sleep.

"Just one more story, Dad," begged Scamp.

Tramp rolled his eyes. "Well," he said, "okay, but just one."

Happily, the puppies snuggled down onto their cushion. Tramp stretched out beside them.

"Did I ever tell you kids about the time I stole my very first sausage?" he asked.

"*Tramp!*" Lady warned him from her seat across the parlor. "That hardly sounds like a proper story for the children."

"Oh, tell it, Dad!" Scamp urged him.

"Well, maybe *stole* isn't exactly the right word," Tramp reassured his wife. "And besides, it's got a great moral!" And with that, he began his tale:

"Now, this all happened way back when I was just a little pup, already living on my own in the big city.

"Well, one day I was especially hungry, and my nose was picking up all sorts of savory scents. So you can imagine the interest I developed in a certain spicy smell coming from the butcher shop. Well, I followed my trusty nose, which has still never let me down, and sure enough, there was a heaping tray of steaming sausages. Can you believe it?"

"So you jumped up and gobbled them all up! Right?" Scamp broke in.

"That's my boy!" Tramp laughed. "But no. Don't forget, I was just a little guy. Couldn't reach the tray. All I could do was think about how to get that sausage. After a few minutes, up walked a lady with a kid in a stroller. Well, at first I was irate. Competition! But then I noticed the crumbs all over the kid in the stroller. Hey! I thought to myself. This might be the ticket—this kid obviously can't hang on to anything. Sure enough, when the lady handed the kid a piece of sausage, the kid dropped it, and down it fell into my waiting mouth! Delicious!

"See, Lady?" Tramp added with a grin. "No stealing!"

"And what exactly is the moral of that story?" Lady asked.

Tramp laughed. "Why, good things come to those who wait, of course!"

# The Search for Hamm

Woody the cowboy doll opened his eyes. The sun was up and Andy had left for school. The house was quiet. Too quiet. Woody realized that something was wrong. Hamm was nowhere in sight!

Woody asked the other toys, but no one had seen the piggy bank since the night before. The toys decided to form a search party.

The Aliens found the first sign of Hamm on Andy's desk—a pile of coins. Had Hamm lost his coins? Woody wondered. What if Andy had decided that he didn't need a piggy bank anymore?

The toys set off to search the rest of the house. Suddenly, Rex cried out from the hallway. Buzz and Woody rushed out. There was another pile of coins on the floor, and they were wet!

"Do you think it's dog slobber?" Buzz asked.

"What?" Rex cried. "You mean Buster took Hamm? Oh, no! I always knew that dog was out to get one of us!"

Woody, Buzz, and Rex walked into the living room. Sarge was on the sofa.

"The troops have found a trace of the missing-in-action toy up here," Sarge said. On the cushion was a cluster of coins.

Just then, one of the Green Army Men sounded the alarm. Andy and his mom had arrived in the driveway! The toys raced back to Andy's room.

Seconds later, Andy dashed into the room. He threw his backpack on the floor, and then ran back out of the room.

Suddenly, the toys heard a noise. *Clink, clink, clank, clink.*

"What was that?" Rex asked. The noise was coming from Andy's backpack. It sounded like . . . coins!

Woody rushed over and unzipped the backpack. Out tumbled Hamm!

"Hamm!" Woody said. "What were you doing in there?"

"Andy took me to school to collect money," Hamm said.

"We thought you were in trouble," Buzz said. "There were piles of coins all over the house."

"Oh, that was just Andy playing," Hamm replied. "He was tossing me in the air like a baseball when we left this morning. And Buster was following us, drooling everywhere."

"Well, it's sure good to have you back," Woody said, and he gave Hamm a big hug!

# Albatross Taxi Service

Orville sighed and leaned against a lamppost at the busy intersection of 45th and Broadway. He liked to watch the cars zoom back and forth. Just then there was a tap on his wing. He looked down to see an elderly mouse couple.

"Excuse me, sonny," said the grandpa mouse. "Would it be possible for you to help us cross this busy street?"

Orville looked confused. "You want me to go in the middle of the street and stop traffic?"

"Perhaps you could give us a lift *over* the traffic," the grandma mouse suggested. "We'll buy you a hot dog as payment."

Mmmmm! Orville couldn't say no to the promise of a tasty hot dog with mustard and sauerkraut, so he readily agreed.

Just then, the grandma mouse whistled to a group of mice standing nearby. "Harvey, Mildred, Polly, Carl—let's go. We have a ride!"

"Wait!" Orville said. "I can't give *all* of you a ride. Just how strong do you think I am?"

"Think about it this way," said the grandpa mouse. "The more mice, the more hot dogs."

Well, that was certainly true. With that in mind, Orville agreed to help all the mice across the street. Orville's landings left something to be desired, that was for sure, but soon everyone was across the street, safe and sound.

"Here are your hot dogs!" the mice said.

Orville was disappointed to see that they were offering him hot dogs from the mouse vendor, which were considerably smaller than the human kind. Still, a deal was a deal, and Orville was not one to look a gift horse—er, make that a gift *mouse*—in the mouth.

Not long after, Orville found a discarded sardine tin to use for seats and began the Albatross Taxi Service for Mice. Word spread, and soon Orville couldn't keep up with the demand! He was quite a successful businessbird.

One day it hit him—he was selling himself short! Forget about Albatross Taxi Service—it was time to think bigger. He'd get himself a scarf and goggles and start Albatross Airlines! He sold his city taxi business to an entrepreneurial pigeon and set up shop at the airport.

Now, if he could only learn how to land, everything would be perfect!

# The Scare Games

Mike Wazowski had dreamed of being a Scarer his whole life, but he had failed out of the Scare Program. Now he only had one hope left: he had to win the Scare Games and prove that he had what it took to be a world-class Scarer.

There was just one problem. In order to compete, he had to join a team.

Looking around, Mike found only one option: Oozma Kappa. OK was a fraternity full of students who had also failed out of the Scare Program. But the team still needed one more member.

"The star player has just arrived," said James Sullivan, joining the rest of the Oozma Kappas.

Sulley had done nothing but cause Mike trouble. In fact, he was the reason Mike had been kicked out of the Scare Program. But without Sulley, they wouldn't be able to compete, so Mike had to agree.

Now that he had a full team, Mike proposed a deal to Dean Hardscrabble, the head of the Scaring program. If his team won the Scare Games, she would have to let them all into the Scare Program.

Dean Hardscrabble agreed, but on one condition. If they lost, Mike and Sulley would leave Monsters University for good.

Mike and Sulley moved into OK's fraternity house with the other OKs—Don, Squishy, Terri and Terry, and Art. Soon an invitation to the first Scare Games event arrived. It was called the Toxicity Challenge, and it was to take place that night in the sewers.

When the teams arrived for the first event, they learned that the object of the challenge was to make it through a pitch-black tunnel filled with stinging glow urchins as quickly as possible. The last team through would be eliminated.

The teams took off! Mike and Sulley charged ahead while the other OKs struggled through the urchins. The Roar Omega Roar team stormed through to win, with Mike and Sulley finishing closely behind them. But the rest of the OKs finished last. OK was eliminated.

Just then, the judges discovered that the Jaws Theta Chis had cheated.

They were disqualified. Mike sighed with relief. The OKs were back in the Games!

# Patch and the Panther

One dark night, fifteen Dalmatian puppies sat huddled around a black-and-white television set. They watched as Thunderbolt, the canine hero of the show, crept through a deep, dark jungle. Suddenly, Thunderbolt pricked up his ears. The puppies held their breath. Two yellow eyes peered out of the bushes. It was a panther!

"How will Thunderbolt escape the hungry panther?" the TV announcer asked. "Don't miss next week's exciting episode!"

"Aww!" the puppies groaned, disappointed that their favorite show was over.

"All right, kids. Time for bed," Pongo said, shutting off the television with his nose. He watched as the puppies padded upstairs and settled down in their baskets. Then he switched off the light. Moments later, the sound of soft snores filled the room. The puppies were fast asleep.

All except for one. Patch was wide awake. He was still thinking about Thunderbolt and the panther.

"I wish some ol' panther would come around here," Patch said to himself. "I'd

teach him a thing or two."

Outside his room, a floorboard creaked. Patch pricked up his ears. Then he crawled out of his basket to investigate.

The floorboard creaked again. What if it's a panther? Patch thought with a shiver. But I'm not scared of any ol' panther, he reminded himself.

A shadow flickered across the doorway. The shadow had a long tail. Panthers have long tails, thought Patch. Then two yellow eyes peered out of the darkness.

"Aroooo!" Patch yelped. He turned to run, but he tripped on the rug. In a flash, the panther was on top of him. Patch could feel its hot breath on his neck. He shut his eyes . . .

"Patch, what are you doing out of bed?" the panther asked.

Patch opened his eyes. It was Dad!

"I—I was just keeping an eye out for panthers," Patch explained.

Pongo smiled. "Why don't you get some sleep now?" he suggested. "I can keep an eye out for panthers for a while."

"Okay, Dad," Patch said with a yawn.

Pongo carried Patch back to his basket. In no time at all, the puppy was fast asleep.

# A Roaring Field Trip

Andy was excited. He was going on a field trip to the science museum! His mother was even going to give him some money to spend at the gift shop.

Andy's toys were worried that Andy might find some new toys at the gift shop, so Woody, Buzz, and Rex decided they should go along.

The next morning, the toys climbed inside Andy's backpack for their big trip. When Andy's class arrived at the museum, they excitedly followed their teacher inside.

Much to the toys' dismay, Andy left his backpack in the coatroom!

"I didn't come all this way to sit in a closet," Buzz said. "Let's go!"

And so the toys set off to explore on their own. They found a map and hid beneath it as they made their way across the museum floor. Rex led them to the dinosaur exhibit and had fun mimicking the other dinosaurs. Then Buzz spotted an outer space exhibit!

"Buzz, we don't have time for this!" scolded Woody.

Suddenly, the ceiling lit up. Planets, moons, and stars moved in the sky above them.

"That, my friends, is our solar system," said Buzz. "The planet closest to the sun is Mercury. Then comes Venus, Earth, Mars, Jupiter, Saturn, Uranus, and Neptune."

"All this is extremely informative," said Woody. "But isn't anyone else worried that Andy might get back to the coatroom before we do?"

Suddenly the toys heard, "Your attention, please. The museum will be closing in five minutes."

"We'll never make it back there in time!" cried Woody. "Andy's going to leave without us!"

"No, he's not," replied Buzz. He pointed to a spaceship hanging from the ceiling.

"Everybody, lean forward!" Buzz commanded as they climbed aboard. Below them, Andy walked out of the coatroom. The spaceship picked up speed, zipping along the cable that attached it to the ceiling. When the toys were above Andy's bag, they jumped.

Inside Andy's bag, Woody found a bag from the gift shop. Andy had bought a roll of stickers.

"Now that's a good choice!" Rex said.

"It's out of this world!" Buzz replied.

# A Job for the Incredibles

Mr. Incredible, his wife Elastigirl, and their children Violet and Dash had just defeated a deadly robot created by a villain named Syndrome.

Syndrome's real name was Buddy. As a boy he'd wanted to be Mr. Incredible's sidekick. When Mr. Incredible told him that Supers were born, not made, Buddy had vowed to prove him wrong.

Syndrome had created an Omnidroid robot that only he could defeat. He'd sent the robot to the city and turned up at the last moment to "save the day"—but his plan had gone wrong. The robot had turned against him, and the Incredibles had saved the city instead.

When the Incredibles got home from defeating the Omnidroid, they found that a new babysitter had come for their youngest child, Jack-Jack—it was Syndrome!

Syndrome blasted a hole in the roof and flew off toward his waiting jet with Jack-Jack. But Jack-Jack was upset. He began to transform using Super powers!

Suddenly Syndrome was no longer holding a sweet baby, but a flaming monster! Jack-Jack tore through Syndrome's rocket boots. Syndrome quickly dropped the baby and raced for his nearby jet.

Mr. Incredible and Elastigirl were shocked. Until now, they'd had no idea that Jack-Jack had any Super powers!

Mr. Incredible used his strength to throw Elastigirl into the air. She caught Jack-Jack and then stretched out into a parachute to bring him safely back to the ground.

"This isn't the end of it!" Syndrome raged. But he was wrong. Mr. Incredible picked up a car and threw it at the jet. Syndrome's cape got caught in one of the engines, and with one last yell, he was gone.

Their mission over, the Incredibles returned to their undercover life. But fitting in was a little bit easier now. Vi was more confident, and Dash was allowed to use a little of his Super speed—but just a little.

One day, as the Super family left school sports day, the ground began to rumble. A monstrous machine broke out of the earth, with a menacing figure riding on top of it. It was time for the family to put on their masks and change into their Super suits. This was a job for the Incredibles!

# Great Minds Think Alike

Tito the Chihuahua stopped suddenly in the alleyway and sniffed the air.

"Why'd you stop, shorty?" Einstein the Great Dane complained, shoving the smaller dog with his huge paw.

"For your information," Tito said, "I was locating our next meal."

Einstein looked confused. "You were what?"

Tito sniffed again. "Check it out, *amigo*." He pointed to an apartment window two stories above them. "Up there!"

Einstein lifted his nose and sniffed. "Meat loaf!" he exclaimed hungrily. "But how are we going to get it? It's way up there!"

"Leave it to me," Tito said.

Tito raced across the alley and climbed up a pile of crates. His plan was to reach a clothesline stretching between two buildings and use it as a tightrope to the windowsill

Meanwhile, Einstein noticed a Dumpster pushed up against the wall of the apartment building. If he climbed up there and stood on his hind legs, maybe he would be tall enough to reach the windowsill.

"Ha," Einstein said. "I'll show you that bigger is better, my little friend."

"Oh, yeah?" Tito glared at Einstein. He grabbed the clothesline and began to wriggle his way across.

Einstein clambered atop the Dumpster. He carefully stretched up, up, up. . . . Both dogs reached the windowsill at the same time.

"Hey!" Tito yelped. Someone had taken the meat loaf inside!

"Darn," said Tito. "But hey, Einstein, that was a good trick with the Dumpster. Do you think you could do it with me standing on your head? Because there are a lot of clotheslines that are too high for me to reach."

"Sure!" said Einstein. "I could lift you up to a clothesline, and— Hey! I smell chicken potpie!"

Sure enough, there, on another windowsill, was a steaming dish. And right under that window was a clothesline—a clothesline that would normally be too high for Tito to reach by himself. But with a little help . . .

Tito looked at Einstein. "Are you thinking what I'm thinking?"

Einstein grinned. "Great minds think alike!"

# Explorers to the Rescue

Deep in South America, Carl Fredricksen was sitting inside his house. He had flown there using thousands of balloons tied to his roof. Carl had brought a stowaway along with him, a little boy named Russell. Carl felt sad because he had allowed a mean old explorer to steal Russell's friend, a bird called Kevin.

Suddenly, Carl heard a noise up on the roof. He rushed outside. Russell was rising into the air with a bunch of balloons!

"I'm gonna help Kevin, even if you won't!" Russell called.

"No, Russell!" Carl cried. He tried to follow him, but the house was too heavy and the balloons had lost too much air.

Carl made a decision. He'd kept his promise to Ellie—now he had to keep his promise to Russell, too. He pushed everything he owned out of the house until it rose into the sky.

Together, Dug—a talking dog they had befriended—and Carl set out to find Russell. Dug's master, an explorer named Muntz, was holding the boy prisoner aboard his ship, the *Spirit of Adventure*.

At last, Carl reached the airship.

Russell and Kevin climbed into the house. Suddenly, *BANG!* Balloons popped, and the house fell on top of the airship. Carl toppled out of the house onto the airship, and Muntz raced into the house to get the bird. Thinking quickly, Carl pulled out a chocolate bar from his pocket.

"Russell! Hang on to Kevin!" he yelled. When Kevin saw the chocolate, she leaped through the window, taking Russell and Dug with her. They landed safely on the airship.

Muntz wasn't so lucky. His foot caught on a bunch of balloons, and he drifted away in the sky.

After returning Kevin to her children, Carl, Russell, and Dug flew home in the *Spirit of Adventure*. Not long after they arrived home, Carl proudly stood by Russell's side as the boy became a Senior Wilderness Explorer!

Carl had something special to give him, too. He pinned a grape-soda cap pin on Russell's sash—the badge that his wife, Ellie, had given to him when they were young. "The Ellie Badge," he said.

Carl smiled. He knew that he and his friend had many new and exciting adventures ahead.

# Avoid the Parent

It was the day after the first event of the Scare Games at Monsters University, and Mike Wazowski was very upset. His future at the university was dependent on his team winning—and his team members were useless! OK had almost been eliminated in the first event! The only one who had any scaring skills was Sulley, and he was the one who had gotten Mike into this mess in the first place!

Dean Hardscrabble, the head of the Scare Program, had thrown Mike and Sulley out. The Scare Games were their only way back in. If the Oozma Kappas didn't win, Mike had promised to leave the school!

Sulley wanted to ditch the OKs and find another team, but the rules didn't allow it. So Mike insisted that the team do things his way from then on.

The next event was "Avoid the Parent." The competitors had to make their way through the library and capture their team's flag without getting caught by the librarian. If the librarian caught them, she would grab them with her giant tentacles and launch them out of the library.

Mike told his team to move slowly and quietly. He even made them practice tiptoeing.

But Sulley thought he knew better. He climbed a sliding ladder and zipped sideways toward the flag. Suddenly, there was a loud *CRACK!* The ladder broke and Sulley crashed to the floor with a loud crash!

The librarian turned to Sulley, but Don distracted her by making noises with his tentacles. Then Terri and Terry created a distraction to save Don, and Art created a distraction to save Terri and Terry.

Mike didn't know what was going on! The librarian chased the OKs, who escaped through the back door.

"Woo-hoo! We did it!" yelled Art.

"No, we didn't. We forgot the flag!" said Mike.

Just then, Squishy appeared with the flag. The Oozma Kappa team took fourth place.

As the triumphant team walked back home, another team drove up in their car. They asked if the OKs were going to the party with the other teams that night.

The OKs were thrilled. They'd never been invited to a party before! Had their luck finally changed?

# A Super Summer Barbecue

One hot summer afternoon, Helen Parr stood in the kitchen frosting a cake. It was almost time to leave for the neighborhood barbecue.

"Hey, Mom," said Helen's elder son, Dash, running into the room at Super speed. "Why do we have to go to some silly barbecue?"

"Dashiell Robert Parr," said Helen. "We're lucky to have been invited. You know we're doing our best to fit in here. And remember: no Super powers outside the house."

A little while later, the Parrs walked around the block to their first neighborhood party. Dash watched some children compete in a sack race, but he couldn't join in because it might reveal his Super speed.

"Are you too chicken to play?" a boy teased.

Dash scowled. When the mean boy hopped by the young Super, he mysteriously tripped and fell. Dash smiled to himself and brushed off his sneaker. His speed had come in handy, after all!

Meanwhile, out of the corner of her eye, Helen saw Jack-Jack atop a high brick wall. He was about to topple off! In a flash, she shot her arm all the way across the yard and caught him. She sighed with relief and cuddled Jack-Jack. The other women just rubbed their eyes and mumbled something about not sleeping much the night before.

As the day wore on, Helen saw the neighbors enjoying her cake. She looked around the yard and spotted Dash telling a story to some other kids. Violet was eating an ice-cream cone with a girl her age. Wow, it looks like we really fit in here, Helen thought. But then she overheard the neighbors.

"There's something strange about those Parrs," he said.

Had someone discovered them? Were their Super powers about to be revealed?

"All that may be true," someone else added, "but that Helen sure makes a terrific cake!" Everyone agreed, and the conversation ended.

Helen Parr chuckled to herself. Their cover wasn't blown after all! Maybe they were a little strange compared to the average family, but they were doing their best to act normal.

# Secret Agent Mater

British secret agent Finn McMissile had received a distress call from a fellow agent. Finn traveled to the agent's location, He was on an oil rig in the middle of the Pacific Ocean. Using his grappling hooks and magnetic wheel armor, Finn drove up the side of the rig. Inside, he saw a wanted criminal named Professor Z. Beside the Professor was a special TV camera. But where was the secret agent? Finally Finn found him. He had been crushed into scrap metal!

Meanwhile, in the town of Radiator Springs, Mater had called all his friends together to welcome home his best friend, Lightning McQueen. The race car had just won the Hudson Hornet Memorial Piston Cup!

Mater wanted to hang out with his best buddy, but Lightning was exhausted. He went off to spend a quiet evening with his girlfriend, Sally.

Later that night at the Wheel Well restaurant, Mater called in to a TV show. He defended Lightning against an Italian race car named Francesco Bernoulli. Francesco swore that he was faster than Lightning. Soon, Lightning was on the phone, too. He reluctantly agreed to race in the World Grand Prix—a three-event race hosted by former oil tycoon, Sir Miles Axlerod.

Soon "Team Lightning McQueen" was on a plane heading to the first race in Japan! When they arrived, they went to a fancy welcome party. Finn McMissile and another British agent, Holley Shiftwell, were also there. They were looking for an American agent who had some top secret information.

When Mater embarrassed Lightning by leaking oil on the floor right in front of Miles Axlerod, Lightning sent the tow truck to the bathroom to clean up. Outside Mater's stall, Professor Z's goons, Grem and Acer, had cornered the American agent. When Mater came out, the agent secretly stuck the top secret information on Mater.

Holley met Mater outside the bathroom and thought he was the American Agent. Little did Mater know, but this was just the beginning of his secret agent adventures.

# Catching Gold

One cool autumn day, Woody the cowboy sat in front of the TV with his horse, Bullseye. They were watching *Woody's Roundup*.

On the shore, the Prospector grabbed his gold-mining pan and went down to the water's edge. "I've got a hunch there's some gold in this riverbed!" he exclaimed.

Jessie went for a walk to look for some wildflowers, while Woody stayed in his favorite fishing spot. He hadn't had a single bite yet, but he was hopeful.

Meanwhile, the Prospector came to a shallow pool. He held out his gold-mining pan and began to sift through the sand from the riverbed. When the water had all sloshed out, he looked at the empty pan. There was no gold. He headed back up the river to where Woody was fishing.

"Any fish yet?" the Prospector asked.

"Nope," replied Woody. "What about you? Any gold?"

Just as the Prospector was about to answer, he saw something shiny in the water. He stepped closer to take another look. "Eureka!" he cried. "I see gold!"

He jumped into the river. *Splash!* He tried catching the gold with his pan, but it kept sliding back into the water.

"Come help me, Sheriff," the Prospector shouted. "This is the slip-slidin'est gold I ever saw!"

Woody set down his pole and leaped into the water. Together they dove after the gold. But each time, they came up empty-handed. Then, Woody had an idea. "We can use our hats!"

"Good thinking," said the Prospector.

The two used their hats to try to scoop up the swirling bits of gold. Just then, Jessie appeared. "What are you two doing?" she asked.

"Catching gold!" said Woody.

Jessie took a closer look inside their hats and began to laugh.

"What's so funny?" the Prospector asked

Jessie smiled. "Take a look at your catch!"

Woody and the Prospector looked at their hats. They were surprised to see goldfish swimming around!

"I can't believe it!" Woody laughed. "The Prospector was looking for gold, and I was looking for fish."

Jessie giggled. "I guess you both found what you were looking for!"

# Orator Owl

On their way home from a leaf-collecting excursion on a cold, blustery autumn afternoon, Pooh, Rabbit, Piglet, and Eeyore made their way past Owl's house. They could not help but notice the cheerful light glowing in all the windows—a light so warm and so inviting that the chilly group seemed to thaw just looking at it. And so it happened that they soon found themselves warm and cozy in Owl's living room.

"Owl, thank you for having us in to warm up," said Pooh. "It's awfully windy and cold outside."

"Well, it is getting on toward winter," Owl replied. "Naturally that means it will only get colder before it gets warmer."

Owl was just beginning to expound upon the particular subject of frostbite when Rabbit interrupted, hoping to give someone else a chance to talk.

"Yes, Owl," he said. "I know that Piglet was very glad to have his scarf on today, weren't you, Piglet?"

"Oh yes," Piglet said. "Kanga knitted it for me."

Owl cleared his throat. "Ah yes, knitting," he said. "An admirable hobby. Did you know that knitting is done with knitting needles? But they aren't sharp, as one might assume. They are not, for example, as sharp as sewing needles. Or cactus needles, or . . ."

Owl continued with a comparison of many, many different types of needles. An hour later, when Owl seemed ready to jump into a discussion of pins, Rabbit again tried to change the subject.

"Speaking of pins," Rabbit began, "how is your tail today, Eeyore? I hope it is suitably secure and well-attached?"

"Seems secure," Eeyore replied with a shrug, "but it always falls off when I least expect it."

Rabbit saw Owl sit up in his chair and take a deep breath—a sure sign that he was preparing another speech about tails, or expectations, or Rabbit knew not what—so Rabbit decided it was time to go.

Good-byes and thank-yous were said, and soon the four visitors were outside, making their way home through swirling leaves. And all the way home, Rabbit tried to decide who was windier—the great autumn wind or long-winded Owl!

# Stitch Upon a Time

Lilo was telling Stitch a story. But as she started, he scampered away. He wanted a snack.

"You'd better not let Nani hear you," warned Lilo. "She thinks we went to bed."

Stitch crept into the hall, lifted his big ears, and listened. "No Nani," he whispered. Then he dashed downstairs and into the kitchen.

"Soda, pineapple, pickles, coleslaw," recited Stitch, peering into the fridge. "Hmm . . . pineapple-pickle-coleslaw sandwich . . ."

Lilo tiptoed up behind him. "You can't put all that in a sandwich," she whispered into his ear.

"*Yaaaaaahhhhh!*" shouted Stitch, jumping. Lilo had scared him!

"What is going on in here?" demanded Nani, storming into the kitchen.

"Stitch wants a snack," Lilo explained.

"It's not time for snacks," Nani said. She shut the refrigerator and marched them both back up the stairs. "It's time for bed."

"*Story,*" said Stitch as he climbed into bed and held up the book. "Time for story."

Nani sighed and said, "Oh, all right.

But it had better be a short one."

"Goody!" cried Stitch as Nani climbed into bed, too.

After Nani settled in between Lilo and Stitch, Lilo opened the book and began to read: "Once upon a time, there was a sad little puppy named—"

"Stitch!" cried Stitch.

Lilo continued, "There was a sad little puppy named . . . *Stitch*. He was sad because he was lost."

Lilo passed the book to Nani and said, "Your turn."

Then Nani began to read, "But one day, he met a little girl named—"

"Lilo," whispered Lilo.

Nani smiled. "He met a little girl named . . . Lilo."

Then Nani continued reading the story, until she reached the very end. ". . . and they lived happily ever after." Nani shut the book.

"Ever after," murmured Stitch, closing his eyes.

"Ever after," echoed Lilo.

Nani waited till they were both sound asleep, then headed downstairs for a snack. Maybe she'd have a pineapple-pickle-coleslaw sandwich!

# Superspeedy Spiral Slide-tacular

'Whee!" Kuzco the mighty emperor ran, jumped, and landed the most royal belly flop of all time in the gigantic pool at Kuzcotopia, his own personal water park. Then he climbed to the top of Kuzco's Superspeedy Spiral Slide-tacular. "Here I go!" he yelled. He slipped and slid, descending in circles faster and faster, until at last he splashed down into the grand pool. *Thonk!*

"Whoa. Hey. Hang on a second. Did I just get hit in the head with a hoof?"

Kuzco looked around. Something was wrong. Very wrong. The majestic pool was gone. Kuzcotopia was nowhere to be seen. Kuzco was wading in not-so-majestic grass, and instead of hands, his arms ended in hooves!

He had been dreaming! And worst of all, he had woken to this nightmare: he was still a llama! His royal adviser had given him a potion that changed him into the four-legged creature, because she wanted to take over his kingdom.

Kuzco pursed his llama lips in exasperation.

"What's for breakfast?" he asked Pacha, nosing the peasant's bowl.

"Just a few nuts and berries I found," Pacha said. "You can go get yourself some."

"Why don't you give me yours?" Kuzco asked as he narrowed his eyes.

Pacha pulled his bowl closer. "Why don't you go get your own?"

"Emperors do not forage for their own food," Kuzco said regally.

"Fine." Pacha turned his back and kept eating. "But you'll be sorry later. We have a long way to go."

The sun grew hot as the pair headed out of camp.

Kuzco was so busy sulking, he wasn't watching where he was going. He slipped. Frantically, he tried to grab something—anything! What he grabbed was a long, thick, spiraling vine. Kuzco zoomed toward the bottom of the ravine. *Thonk!*

"Ouch." The mighty llama emperor landed roughly in a patch of prickly bushes. But luckily, they were berry bushes! Kuzco began eating the ripe berries. Farther up the ravine, he could hear Pacha laughing.

"Go ahead, laugh," Kuzco said. "But you have just seen a preview of Kuzcotopia's Superspeedy Spiral Slide-tacular!"

**SEPTEMBER**
**8**

# Follow Your Star

Jiminy Cricket was a wanderer. He loved the independence, the excitement, and the simplicity of his way of life.

But lately, Jiminy had noticed that there was one thing missing from his vagabond lifestyle: a purpose. Camping one night by the side of the road, he sat on his sleeping bag and gazed into his campfire.

"I wonder what it would feel like to be really helpful to someone," he said.

Jiminy tried to get comfortable on the hard ground as he looked up into the starry night sky. As his eyes scanned the many tiny points of light, one star to the south jumped out at him. It seemed to shine brighter than all the rest.

"Say, is that a Wishing Star?" he wondered aloud. Since he couldn't know for certain, he decided it would be best to make a wish on it, just in case.

"Wishing Star," he said, "I wish to find a place where I can make a difference and do a bit of good."

His wish made, Jiminy Cricket suddenly felt a strange impulse: an urge to get up, gather his things, and follow that star—the Wishing Star.

Jiminy put out the campfire. Then he gathered his things and he took to the road.

The little cricket followed that star all through the night. In fact, he walked until the sun came up and he could no longer see the star to follow it. Then he made camp and he slept.

After many nights of walking in this manner, at last Jiminy came to a village.

It was very late as Jiminy Cricket walked into the village and looked around. Every window of every house was dark—except for one window in a shop at the end of a street. So Jiminy hopped over to the window.

Peering inside, he saw that it was a wood-carver's workshop, dimly lit by the embers of a fire dying in the fireplace. It seemed a warm and pleasant place to stop for the night.

Little did Jiminy Cricket know that it was the home of Geppetto, a kind old wood-carver who had just finished work on a puppet he called Pinocchio.

Jiminy did not know it, but he had found a place where he would do more than just a bit of good.

# Packing for College

Woody, Buzz, and the rest of Andy's toys were sad. Andy hadn't played with them in ages.

"Andy's going to college any day now," Woody said. "We all knew this day was coming. Every toy goes through this."

Just then, Buzz noticed Sarge and his men climbing up to the windowsill. "What are you doing?" he asked.

"We've done our duty," Sarge replied.

"When the trash bags come out, we Army guys are the first to go," added another soldier.

With a final good-bye, the Green Army Men parachuted out of the window.

"We're getting thrown away?" cried Rex. The toys started squeaking and shouting. No one wanted to get thrown away!

"Whoa! Hold on!" shouted Woody. "Through every yard sale, every spring cleaning, Andy held on to us. He must care about us, or we wouldn't still be here. You wait—Andy's going to tuck us in the attic. . . ."

"And we'll all be together," added Buzz. "Let's get our parts together, get ready, and go out on a high note."

Just then, the toys heard footsteps in the hall. They scrambled back into the toy box as Andy came into his room. His mom was right behind him, carrying trash bags.

"Okay, let's get to work here," she said. "Anything you're not taking to college either goes in the attic, or it's trash."

Andy's mom suggested Andy donate his old toys to the day care center. But Andy shook his head. "No one's going to want those," he told her. "They're junk."

"Fine," Andy's mom replied. "You have till Friday. Anything that's not packed for college or in the attic is getting thrown out."

Andy opened the toy box. He scooped up Rex, Hamm, Slinky, and Mr. and Mrs. Potato Head—and dumped them into a rubbish bag! But when Andy came to Woody and Buzz, he paused. They had always been his two favorite toys. He looked at each, then made his decision: Buzz went into the trash bag, and Woody went in the box bound for college.

Buzz lay on top of the other toys, shocked. Had he really been dumped? What were they going to do now?

# Special Delivery

Roger and Anita had a lot of puppies, and that meant they needed a lot of food. Every Thursday, a truck pulled up full of dog food. And every Thursday Rolly waited by the window for the truck.

One Thursday, Rolly and Pepper noticed that the back of the truck had been left open. "Are you thinking what I'm thinking?" Pepper asked Rolly.

Rolly nodded. "Snack time!" Rolly and Pepper made a dash for the truck and leaped into the back. Pepper clambered up onto the pile of bags and sniffed around. There had to be some loose food somewhere. . . .

"Bingo!" Pepper cried. "Rolly, up here!"

Rolly was there in an instant. *Slurp, slurp, crunch!* The two puppies were so busy eating that they didn't see the truck driver come out of the house.

*Slam!* He closed up the back of the truck. A second later, it was rumbling down the road.

"Uh-oh," Rolly whispered.

After what seemed like a very long time, the vehicle lurched to a halt. The back door opened, and the driver began unloading bags of food.

Pepper and Rolly jumped out of the van while he wasn't looking. They ran and hid behind the house.

"What do you two think you're doing?" a gruff voice asked.

The puppies spun around. A big bulldog was looking down at them.

"This is my property," the dog said. "It's time for you to scram."

"You don't scare me," Pepper said boldly. "You're not half as bad as Cruella."

The bulldog's mouth fell open. "Do you mean Cruella De Vil?" he asked. "You must be Pongo and Perdita's puppies! I heard about your adventures over the Twilight Bark! Your parents must be worried about you. I'd better get you home!"

Luckily, Pongo and Perdita were out that day and didn't realize what a pickle Rolly and Pepper had gotten themselves into. But there were ninety-seven puppies waiting in the front yard as Rolly and Pepper arrived with their escort.

"Wow," said Lucky, after he'd heard their tale. "Were you scared of that big mean bulldog?"

"No way!" Pepper said. "That bulldog was all bark and no bite!"

# A Growing Boy

**H**ercules's mortal parents, Amphitryon and Alcmene, had known Hercules was a special child from the moment they had found him, alone and crying in the wilderness, wearing a medal that bore the symbol of the gods. But as the baby grew, they were surprised to see Hercules's superhuman strength grow stronger and stronger with each passing day. He could tie poisonous snakes into knots and lift grown-ups high into the air.

"Ma," said Hercules one day when he was five years old, "I'm bored."

So Alcmene gave Hercules some marbles to play with. She showed him how to use his thumb to shoot one marble at another.

Hercules shot tentatively at first. But soon he grew more confident. Lining up a shot, he flicked his thumb as hard as he could. The marble flew out of his hand, sending the target marble rocketing toward the horizon.

Luckily, the nearest neighbors lived several miles away. But one by one, all of Hercules's marbles were lost this way.

"Amphitryon, I simply don't know

what to do with Hercules," Alcmene said to her husband the next day. "He's too strong for ordinary toys. And if he plays with the other children, I worry he may hurt them without meaning to."

"Hmm," Amphitryon replied. "Yes, the boy is stronger than he realizes. Why, I do believe he's gotten to be as strong as an ox!"

That gave Amphitryon an idea. That afternoon, he walked to the marketplace. When he returned to the farm, he was leading an ox by a rope.

"Hercules," he said, leading the ox over to his son, "come meet your new playmate."

Amphitryon took the rope lead from around the ox's neck. He handed one end of the rope to Hercules. He offered the other end to the ox, who took it between his teeth.

Within seconds, Hercules and the ox had fallen into a friendly game of tug-of-war.

Hercules laughed. The ox twitched his tail playfully. Hercules's parents looked on and smiled.

"That's our boy," Alcmene said proudly.

# The Journey Begins

Bernard couldn't believe this was really happening. Even though he was just a janitor, he had been selected by the Rescue Aid Society to come to the aid of a little girl named Penny, who appeared to be in grave danger. And what's more, he, Bernard, had been selected over all the other mice to be partners with the very beautiful and clever Miss Bianca.

Bernard was very proud to have been chosen. It was Bernard's first rescue mission ever, and even though he was very nervous, he was excited to get started. He had gotten himself packed and ready to go in minutes, and now he had arrived to pick up Miss Bianca. But she was running late.

"Uh, Miss Bianca?" called Bernard after a while. "We really ought to be going, I think. We don't want to miss our flight!"

"All right, darling!" said Miss Bianca. "Come give me a hand with this suitcase, please!"

Bernard found Miss Bianca trying to close her overstuffed suitcase. She had already packed several boxes, as well.

"Are you quite sure you'll be needing all those evening gowns, Miss Bianca?"

Bernard panted as he sat on the bag and tried to zip it up. "And that tea set? And . . ." He paused to count. "Fourteen pairs of shoes?"

"A lady must be prepared for anything, darling," she crooned. "Now, I'll just put on my hat and we'll be off."

After what seemed like hours, Miss Bianca appeared at last in a dizzying cloud of perfume.

"I'll take that!" said Bernard as Miss Bianca reached for the suitcase. It felt as though it were full of bricks, but Bernard managed to maneuver it out the door, where he grabbed his much lighter bag in his other hand.

"Darling," Miss Bianca said sweetly as they headed to the airport, "please don't fret. Everyone knows that flights are always delayed!"

*Even when the plane is an albatross?* Bernard wondered to himself.

Yes, Miss Bianca and Bernard certainly made an unusual team. But Bernard was sure that they would get the rescue job done.

Just as long as he didn't drop her suitcase on his toe!

# Monkey Trouble

Mowgli was being carried off through the treetops by a band of wild monkeys! The monkeys laughed and chattered as they swung Mowgli from one tree to another.

Soon Mowgli was out of breath and confused. "Hey!" he yelled. "Quit it! I want to go back to Baloo! Let me go!"

The monkeys laughed. "Sorry, Man-cub!" one shouted. "We can't let you go. You might as well forget about that bear!"

"Yeah!" another monkey said, catching Mowgli by the arm. "You're with us monkeys now. We're better than any old bear!"

The monkey tossed Mowgli straight up in the air. Mowgli felt himself flipping head over heels. A second later, a pair of monkeys caught him by the legs. "See, Man-cub?" one of them said. "Monkeys know how to have fun!"

Mowgli laughed, feeling dizzy. "That was kind of fun!" he cried. "Do it again!"

The monkeys howled with laughter. They tossed Mowgli in the air over and over again. Mowgli somersaulted through the treetops until he couldn't tell up from down anymore. Then the monkeys taught him how to swing from branch to branch and vine to vine. They even showed him how to shake the trees to make bananas fall into his hands.

"Being a monkey is fun!" Mowgli exclaimed through a mouthful of banana.

Maybe it was good that the monkeys had found him, Mowgli thought. Being a monkey might even be more fun than being a wolf or a bear. And it was definitely more fun than going to the Man-village.

Mowgli swallowed the banana and looked around at his new friends. "What are we going to do next?"

A monkey giggled. "We're going to see King Louie."

"Yeah!" another monkey said gleefully, clapping his hands. "He's the most fun of all!"

"King Louie?" Mowgli said suspiciously. He didn't like the way the monkeys were grinning at him. "Who's that?"

"You'll see, Man-cub!" the monkeys cried, swinging through the treetops.

Mowgli shrugged. How bad could this King Louie be?

# Turner Goes to the Library

Manny was reading the tools a story when the phone rang. It was Marion the librarian.

"Marion needs us to fix the turnstile at the *biblioteca*," Manny said as he hung up the phone.

"We're here to check out the turnstile, Marion!" Felipe hollered when Manny and the tools entered the library.

"Thanks for coming!" Marion called. "I'll be right there."

Manny put some oil on the turnstile. Then Squeeze grabbed a handle and spun the turnstile around. The turnstile broke off and fell to the floor! Squeeze felt awful, but Manny told him not to worry.

When Turner realized he wasn't needed, he hopped away.

"Why aren't you helping the others, Turner?" asked Marion.

"Why bother?" Turner scowled. "They're not interested in hearing any good ideas."

"Well, there are always plenty of great ideas in a library," Marion said with a smile. "There's something for everyone here: storybooks, picture books, even repair manuals—almost anything you can think of!"

Turner perked up. "Repairs? Now that's an exciting subject!"

Marion smiled. "You know, I bet this is a book you might enjoy!"she said, pulling a book off the shelf.

Turner jumped up and down. "Hey, guys, come over here! I've got a book to show you. It's a real page-turner!"

Felipe was puzzled. "What's Turner doing with a book?"

"It's a repair manual with instructions for fixing a turnstile!" said Manny.

With the help of the manual, the team fixed the turnstile.

"Wow, you finished just in time," Marion said, looking at her watch. "Okay, the library is officially open for business! The readers of Sheet Rock Hills are waiting outside!"

Back at the shop, Manny and the tools settled into his armchair, ready for story time.

"Uh, I have a book I'd like to share with everyone," Turner said. "Would you please read it to us, Manny?"

"*¡Naturalmente!* Of course," Manny said, looking at the book. "*How to Fix Broken Stuff*! It's one of my favorites, Turner."

Turner smiled. "Mine, too!"

# Secret Agent Mater

British secret agents Finn McMissile and Holley Shiftwell were on the trail of a wanted criminal named Professor Z. They were in Tokyo, where Lightning McQueen was competing in the first race of the World Grand Prix.

On the day of the race, Professor Z's goons, Grem and Acer, aimed a special TV camera at one of the race cars. The camera emitted a beam of radiation that made the fuel in the car boil and explode! Then Acer headed down to the pits to grab Mater. Professor Z and Holley both thought Mater was an American secret agent!

Suddenly Mater heard Holley's voice in his headset. She knew Grem and Acer were after him and guided him to safety. Mater happily followed Holley's instructions. He thought he was going to meet her for a date!

Suddenly, Grem and Acer started to close in on Mater. Finn arrived just in time and rescued the tow truck.

Mater thought he was watching a karate demonstration. It was the coolest thing he'd ever seen!

Back at the race, Lightning had lost to Francesco Bernoulli. Lightning was upset. Mater had been repeating Holley's directions aloud, and the race car thought Mater was giving him driving tips.

On the racetrack, reporters surrounded Miles Axlerod and asked him if his fuel, Allinol, was to blame for the engine blowouts.

Meanwhile, Mater had returned to the pit garage and was trying to explain to Lightning what had just happened. But Lightning didn't believe him. He was angry with Mater for making him lose the race. Mater felt terrible. He left a good-bye note for Lightning and went to the airport to fly home. But Finn, disguised as an airport security guard, was waiting for him. Finn still thought Mater was a secret agent!

Soon Grem and Acer showed up and tried to capture Mater again. Holley saved Mater and Finn from the attack by whisking them off on a spy plane named Siddeley.

At his hotel, Lightning read Mater's note. Lightning hadn't wanted him to leave, but at least now he wouldn't have to worry about Mater getting into trouble.

# Flik Wings It

Flik knew that Hopper and his gang of hungry grasshoppers would soon come to steal all the food from the peaceful ants of Ant Island. So Flik headed off to the big city to find warrior bugs to help fight the grasshoppers.

On his way, Flik saw a shiny dragonfly flitter across the sky.

"Wow, I wish I could fly like that!" he exclaimed.

Suddenly, Flik had an idea. "I wonder if I could invent a flying machine?"

After a lot of hard work, Flik took a step backward and studied his invention.

"Well, it certainly *looks* like it could fly," Flik said finally.

Flik decided it was time for a test flight. He put his feet on the little pedals and started to pump.

The green wings began to flap. Flik pushed them faster and faster. Soon, the flier began to rock from side to side; then it leaped into the sky!

"It's working!" Flik cried. He was flying! With the air racing between his antennae, Flik watched the world flash under his feet.

"Flying is so much safer than walking," said Flik.

But he spoke too soon, for high in the sky above Flik, a mama bird was teaching her three little hatchlings how to fly.

The bird spied Flik's strange-looking contraption and thought one thing—dinner!

Flik looked up and saw the mama bird and her babies coming down on him like dive-bombers.

"Test flight over!" Flik cried.

Pedaling faster, Flik steered his flier through the limbs of a tall tree. The mama bird and two of her babies were blocked by the branches. But the third baby bird raced between the leaves and caught up with Flik.

Pecking wildly, the little bird ripped a wing from Flik's flier. The machine crashed to the ground.

Luckily for Flik, he had also made a parachute out of a spider's web, and he made a soft landing in the middle of a daisy.

"Another failed invention," Flik said with a sigh. "Maybe someday I'll have a chance to make a flying machine that really works!"

# Super Annoying

**D**ashiell Robert Parr was bored. It was Saturday afternoon, and he had run out of things to do.

"You know, you could do your math homework," his mother, Helen, said.

Homework, now? Dash thought. I'll do that tomorrow. Right now I want to do something fun.

*Brrrng!* The telephone rang, and Dash's sister, Violet, raced out of her bedroom to answer it. Dash had spotted his target.

Five minutes later, Violet returned to her bedroom and stopped in her tracks. Things were not as she had left them. The bedspread was upside down, and the pictures that hung around her mirror were rearranged.

Only one person could have done it.

"Mom!" Violet yelled. "Dash messed up my room!"

As Helen walked down the hall, a breeze whipped through Violet's room. Helen looked inside. "It looks fine to me, honey. Dinner's almost ready," she said.

Violet looked at her room again and saw that everything was back in place. Then her eyes fell on the closet door, which was slightly ajar.

"Dash!" Violet exclaimed. "Get out of here, you little insect!"

Dash zoomed around Violet's bedroom—up onto the bed and down to the floor, all at such Super speed that Violet couldn't tell where he was. Dash only came to a halt when he spotted Violet's diary, which had fallen open on her bed.

"Ooooh," Dash said, picking up the diary. "What have we here?"

That was it. Violet had had enough of Dash. "Give that back!" she yelled. Dash tried to race out of the room, but Violet threw a force field in front of the door. Then she turned invisible and lunged at her brother.

Dash and Violet continued to chase each other around Violet's room in a blur of Super powers until they heard their mom calling.

Dash froze. Then, in the blink of an eye, he zipped out through the bedroom door and down the hall to the kitchen table.

"Dash," Helen asked, "did you finish your homework?"

Then Violet appeared at the table. Her hair was all mussed.

"Nah," Dash replied with a smile. "I found something much better to do."

# School Days

**R**obin Hood was looking forward to a jolly day of giving to the poor (and maybe stealing from the rich) when he ran into a troop of happy children.

"Cheerio, kids!" he called.

"Come play with us!" shouted Skippy, Sis, and their friends.

"Ah, I wish I could," said Robin. "But, alas, my work is never done. Enjoy yourselves, though. That's what childhood is all . . . Hey, now! Just a minute. Shouldn't you scalawags be in school?"

"School!" exclaimed Skippy. "We haven't been to school in ages!"

"And why not?" asked Robin.

"No teacher will come to Sherwood Forest. They fear Prince John will jail them for not paying taxes!" said Sis.

"Will *you* teach us?" asked Skippy.

"Ah . . . well . . . I think not," said Robin. For while Robin Hood knew his sums and spellings backward and forward, his sciences and histories had grown a little rusty.

"Then who will?" asked Sis.

"Never fear," said Robin. "A teacher I will find." But where? he silently wondered.

Robin Hood went back to the forest to seek out his Merry Men. "Little John!" he called. "The children need a teacher, and I think you're just the man!"

"Why, thank you, Robin," said Little John. "But I don't think I can do it. I've already promised my help to the baker and the blacksmith."

In fact, not one of his Merry Men could help Robin Hood. They were all too busy.

Robin sighed. "Is there no one with time to help the children?"

He walked around a bend, and there was Friar Tuck, dozing, as usual, in a mossy glade.

"Wake up, Friar!" said Robin, giving him a shake. "Do I have a job for you!"

Robin explained the situation, and Friar Tuck accepted happily. Then Robin headed off the other way. There was one more thing he had to do.

Later that day, just as Friar Tuck was finishing up his alphabet lesson, Robin Hood appeared, toting a heavy sack.

"What's that?" inquired the children.

"Books!" Robin replied. "Courtesy of Prince John's library! Although," he said with a wink, "he doesn't know it yet."

# A Trash Mistake

**A**ndy was a teenager. He would be leaving for college soon. Andy had decided to take Woody to college with him, but he had put Buzz and the rest of his toys into a trash bag!

Woody was shocked. When Andy carried the bag out of his room, the cowboy sprang to the door.

Woody watched as Andy pulled down the attic ladder. Andy wasn't throwing his toys away. He was putting them in storage!

Suddenly, Andy' sister called him. She needed his help. Andy left the trash bag in the hall. While he was gone, the ladder started to go back up into the ceiling! When Andy's mom walked by, she noticed the trash bag on the floor. Assuming it was garbage, she picked it up and brought it outside.

"We're on the curb!" Jessie cried.

"Pull, everyone! Pull!" Buzz said, desperately trying to rip open the bag.

"Andy doesn't want us!" Mrs. Potato Head wailed. "What's the point?"

That gave Buzz an idea. He told everyone to push Rex's pointy tail into the side of the bag. The friends shoved the dinosaur against the plastic!

Meanwhile, Woody climbed out the window and slid down the drainpipe. He pulled out a pair of scissors he had tucked into his holster. Frantic, he sliced open one bag, then another—but his friends weren't inside any of them. When the garbage truck arrived, Woody hid. He watched as the man hurled the bags into the back of the truck.

Seconds later, the truck rumbled off to the next house. Woody watched in horror as the truck's compactor activated, crunching its load! Then Woody noticed an upside-down recycling bin moving across Andy's driveway. His friends were alive!

In the garage, the toys came out from underneath the bin.

"Andy threw us out!" exclaimed Slinky.

Jessie had an idea. By the time Woody arrived, she had convinced everyone to climb into a box that was being donated to the day care center. The toys thought the nursery would be the ideal place for them to go. They had no idea what awaited them there. . . .

# Spring Cleaning

Mickey Mouse hummed as he straightened up his messy house. He swept up some leaves that had blown in through the front door. Then he shook the mud off his doormat. He was picking up some old magazines when one of them caught his eye.

"'Make a Fresh Start with Spring Cleaning,'" Mickey read aloud. "Hmm. Spring cleaning, eh?" He looked out the window. It wasn't spring—it was fall! What was he doing cleaning his house?

"Whew!" he exclaimed as he dropped his broom and flopped onto the sofa. "Looks like I have a whole day free now. I think I'll see if Minnie wants to come over!"

A short while later, Minnie Mouse rang the doorbell. "Hi, Mickey!" she said cheerfully. "What do you want to do to—"

She gasped. Mickey's house was a mess!

"What's wrong?" Mickey asked.

"Mickey," Minnie said, "um, when was the last time you cleaned your house?"

Mickey laughed. "Don't be silly, Minnie!" he said. "I don't need to clean this place for months."

"M-m-months?" Minnie gasped.

"Sure!" Mickey shrugged. "Haven't you ever heard of spring cleaning?"

Minnie wasn't sure what to do. She didn't want to be rude, but she had to convince Mickey to clean his house—and that it couldn't wait until spring!

"You know, Mickey," she said casually, "I just read something about a fun new trend."

"Really?" Mickey smiled. "What's that, Minnie? Maybe it's something we could do today, since we have the whole day free!"

"Oh!" Minnie pretended to be surprised at the idea. "Why, I suppose we could! I hadn't thought of that."

"So, what's the trend?" Mickey asked eagerly. "Waterskiing? Rock climbing? Fondue parties?"

"No," Minnie said cheerfully. "Fall cleaning! It's the newest rage."

"Fall cleaning?" Mickey said doubtfully. He blinked, then smiled. "You know, that's so crazy, it sounds like fun! Come on, let's try it!"

Minnie smiled and picked up the magazine with the spring cleaning article in it. "Good," she said. She stuffed the magazine into the trash. "I'll start right here!"

# Monster Moneymaker

Every morning as Mike and Sulley walked through the lobby of Monsters, Inc., to the Scare Floor, they passed the Scarer of the Month photos of Sulley hanging on the wall. One day, Mike turned turned to his big blue friend.

"Sulley," he said, "do you ever think that we deserve a little more?"

"More?" Sulley asked.

"Oh, you know," Mike continued. "You're the top Scarer month after month. All you get is a lousy picture in the hallway, and I get nothin'. We should be famous!"

Then Mike had another idea. "We should set up a gift shop right here in the building featuring 'Sulley the Super Scarer' memorabilia."

"Why would we want to bother with all that?" Sulley asked.

"Money!" Mike exclaimed, rolling his eye.

"I don't know, Mike," Sulley said. "It just doesn't seem right, us making money off these things. But what if we . . . That's it!" Sulley jumped up, nearly knocking Mike over. "We'll donate the money to charity!"

"Who said anything about donations?" Mike asked.

"That's a great idea!" Sulley said, ignoring Mike.

"How will we bask in any glory if we give the money away?" Mike asked.

"Well, we will, sort of," Sulley explained. "We'll make the donation on behalf of Monsters, Inc."

"I don't know about that," Mike said.

"This will work, Mike," Sulley said. "It's a wonderful idea. And when we help the company make a generous donation, Mr. Waternoose will be very proud of us!"

Mike was suddenly warming to the idea. "And we'll get lots of press!" he added.

"Sure, why not?" Sulley said with a shrug.

"It's a great idea!" Mike cheered.

"I agree!" Sulley said.

"I'm glad I thought of it!" Mike gave his best friend a huge smile.

"You always have such good ideas," Sulley agreed with a grin.

"It's like I always say," Mike added. "Scaring's important, but it's the brains behind the monster that matter most. Right, buddy?"

# First Day of School

It was the first day of a brand-new school year for Nemo and his friends.

"Hey, Tad! Hey, Pearl!" called Nemo as he swam into the playground. "Isn't it great to be back at school?"

"Well," said Tad, "I wouldn't go *that* far."

"What do you mean?" asked Nemo. "It's gonna be awesome! I heard this year we get to learn how to subtract and speak Prawn."

"Sure," said Tad, "but did you also hear who's gonna be teaching us all that?"

"No," said Nemo. "Who?"

Just then, up swam Sheldon, Jimmy, and Jib.

"Hey, Sheldon," Tad called out. "Why don't you tell Nemo here about our new teacher, Mrs. Lobster?"

"Mrs. Lobster?" said Nemo.

"Yeah," said Sheldon. "Ooooh, they say she's the worst!"

"Who says she's the worst?" asked Nemo.

"Well, Sandy Plankton, for one. He says his cousin Krill had her last year—and that she was so mean, he'll never go to school again!"

"And you know what I heard from Sandy?" said Tad. "I heard she has these great big claws, and that she uses them to grab students real hard when they give the wrong answer!"

Nemo shuddered. All summer long he'd been looking forward to this day. And now school hadn't even started yet and already he wished it would end!

"Don't look now," Sheldon whispered, "but I think she's coming!"

"I'm gonna ink!" whimpered Pearl.

Nemo shut his eyes and wished with all his might for his dad to come and take him back home. . . .

"Hello there," said a warm voice. "You must be my new pupils!"

Huh? thought Nemo. Surely this wasn't the Mrs. Lobster the kids had been talking about. And yet, when he opened his eyes, there she was, taking attendance.

"Jib, Jimmy, Nemo, Pearl, Sheldon, Tad . . . my, what a smart looking class. I do hope you kids are ready to have fun."

Nemo sighed. That silly Sandy Plankton! They should know by now not to believe anything he said. Nemo was pretty sure this was going to be a great year, after all!

# Leaping Llamas!

Things had not been going very well for Kuzko. First, he had been turned into a llama! Then he had learned that his trusted adviser, Yzma, had been plotting to get rid of him so she could take over the kingdom.

No, Yzma was no friend of his. Kuzco paused to scratch his ear with a hind hoof. And now he was all alone, without a friend in the world—not even that grubby peasant, Pacha.

Actually, Pacha had probably been the closest thing Kuzco *had* to a friend. But now he was gone, too.

Kuzco sighed. "Why me?" the llama whined to himself as he wove in and out of vines and bushes. He was pretty sure he was headed in the right direction, but the forest was so dark. Why, there could be *anything* hiding in that tree . . . under that fern . . . behind that rock. . . .

Behind that rock! Kuzco quickly leaped back as a panther lunged at him from behind a large boulder. The panther's hungry jaws clicked shut just inches from Kuzco's snout.

"Heeeelp!" the llama bleated. Kuzco ran as fast as he could, but the panther was still gaining on him.

Up ahead of him, Kuzco spotted a deep ravine. It was only about ten feet wide.

"Okay," Kuzco said to himself. "Here's your chance. Llamas are nimble. Llamas are quick. Llamas can jump . . . really . . . faaaaaar!"

*Thump.*

Kuzco shook his head and looked around him. He had leaped across the ravine!

Kuzco stuck his tongue out at the panther and trotted on his way. He had done it! He had escaped a panther all by himself! "But I know," he said thoughtfully, "that I could do even better with a friend at my side. I wonder where Pacha in now."

Just then, the forest opened up into a broad, sunny field. Kuzco heard a faint bleat. Llamas!

There were llamas here, and Pacha was a llama herder. A broad smile appeared on Kuzco's furry face. He headed toward the herd, and, sure enough, there was Pacha. For the first time since the day he had woken up as a llama, far from home, Kuzco began to feel like he might really stand a chance. It was good to have friends.

# Welcome to Sunnyside

Andy would soon be leaving home for college. He had meant to store his toys safely in his attic, but his mom had mistaken the bag of toys for trash and thrown them out! Luckily, the toys had escaped.

Woody knew what had really happened, but the other toys didn't believe him. Jessie had convinced them that they should go to Sunnyside Daycare—the nursery that Andy's mom was donating some old toys to. They were in the trunk of the car, in the box marked SUNNYSIDE DAYCARE, when Andy's mom got into the car and pulled out of the driveway.

Woody instantly began planning their return to Andy's house. "We'll hide under the seats. . . ." he began.

But the others didn't think it was a good idea. "He left us on the curb!" Jessie pointed out.

Woody knew the toys would be sorry. "Daycare is a sad, lonely place for washed-up old toys who have no owners," he said.

But when they arrived, Sunnyside Daycare didn't look sad or lonely at all. It looked cheerful and colorful! Inside,

Andy's mom greeted the receptionist and the woman's young daughter, Bonnie. The receptionist took the box of toys right to the Butterfly Room.

Andy's toys couldn't contain their excitement. The room looked wonderful. And the other toys were so friendly.

The friendliest of all was a big, pink bear who smelled like strawberries.

"Welcome to Sunnyside!" he called warmly. "I'm Lots-o'-Huggin' Bear! But, please, call me Lotso!"

Lotso's smile was comforting. "You've been through a lot today, haven't you?" he asked. "Just you wait—you'll find being donated was the best thing that ever happened to ya."

"Mr. Lotso," asked Rex. "Do toys here get played with every day?"

"All day long. Five days a week," Lotso answered.

"But what happens when the kids grow up?" Jessie asked.

"When the kids get old, new ones come in," Lotso replied. "You'll never be outgrown or neglected. Never abandoned or forgotten. No owner means no heartbreak."

Day care was sounding better and better!

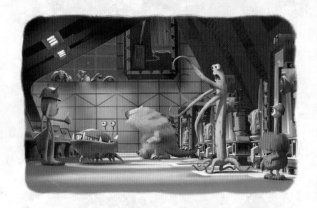

# All Shapes and Sizes

It was a great day for the Oozma Kappas. Mike, Sulley and the rest of the team had taken fourth place in the second event of the Scare Games. It was the first time anything had gone right for Mike since arriving at school. It meant that Dean Hardscrabble couldn't kick Mike out of Monsters University—yet!

Mike had been kicked out of the Scare Program, but he'd made a deal with Dean Hardscrabble. She would let Mike and the rest of the Oozma Kappas back in the Scare Program if they won the Scare Games. But if they lost, Mike had to leave school forever.

That night, the OKs went to a party at the Roar Omega Roar house. The OKs were nervous. They had never been to a party before, but everyone gave them a warm welcome. It felt great— and a little strange. Their classmates weren't usually this nice to them.

The OKs started to relax and have fun. Suddenly, paint showered down on them, followed by confetti, flowers and stuffed animals. The entire room burst into laughter. The OKs looked ridiculous.

The next day, photos of the humiliated Oozma Kappas were everywhere. They were even in the school newspaper.

"Real Scarers look like us, not like you," Johnny told Mike. "But if you really want to work at Monsters, Inc., they're always hiring in the mailroom."

That gave Mike an idea. He ran after his teammates. "Guys, I've been doing this all wrong," he called. "We're going on a field trip!"

Squishy's mom drove them all to Monsters, Inc. Mike led the others onto the roof, where they had a perfect view of the Scare Floor.

"Take a good look, fellas," Mike said. "See what they all have in common?"

"No, not really," Squishy replied.

"Exactly," said Mike. "The best Scarers use their differences to their advantage."

Just then the security guards spotted them. The OKs started to run, but they weren't fast enough. Sulley picked them all up and carried them back to the car!

The OKs drove home feeling inspired. They knew now that monsters of all shapes and sizes could be Scarers. It was their differences that made them great at what they did!

# A Silo Scare

Flik took a step back and gazed up at the giant silo he and a troop of ants had just finished building. Now that the colony was using his harvester, they had a surplus of wheat.

"Nice job, Flik," Queen Atta said.

Flik blushed. A compliment from Atta always made his face feel warm. Atta was the smartest and prettiest ant in the colony. She was also its new queen.

"Thanks, Atta," Flik said, trying to sound casual. "It should keep our wheat dry all winter."

Suddenly, a voice called down from the top of the silo. "Hellooooo," it said.

Flik and Atta looked up. It was Dot, Atta's little sister. She and her Blueberry friends were sitting on top of the silo.

"The view up here is amazing!" Dot called.

"Dot! Be careful!" Atta said worriedly.

"Don't worry," said Flik. "I built in several safety—"

Atta interrupted him. "I have a meeting," she told Flik. And with that, she was gone.

"Come on up, Flik," Dot called as Atta hurried away. "You just have to see the view!"

"Coming!" Flik replied.

But just as Flik got to the top, one of the Blueberries leaped into the silo.

"Wheeeeee!" she cried as she zoomed down toward the pile of wheat.

"The silo is not a playground," Flik told the other girls. "It's for storing wheat, and I built in all these extra safety devices—"

"Come on, Flik," Dot interrupted. "We don't need any safety devices!"

Grinning, she jumped into the silo and the pile of wheat at the bottom. Two other Blueberries followed. But one accidentally pushed down a lever. A big pile of wheat tumbled into the silo, heading straight for the Blueberries below!

Panicked, Flik hit a switch. The falling wheat was caught halfway down by a handy dandy wheat stopper—one of the safety devices he'd built into the silo. The Blueberries stared at Flik.

Just then, Atta walked by. "Dot, what are you doing?" she asked.

"Uh, Flik was just showing us his great safety devices," Dot said, looking sheepishly at the silo.

"And they really work," said Flik, sighing with relief.

# A Nose for Trouble

School was out for the day, and Pinocchio was ready to have some fun.

"Wait for me!" Jiminy Cricket called. He caught up with Pinocchio in front of the small shop where he lived with Geppetto, his father.

"Father, I'm home!" Pinocchio called. "What are you making?"

"A cuckoo clock," Geppetto replied. "I even brought home a live bird for a model." He pointed to a birdcage.

"May I take the bird out and play with him?" Pinocchio asked.

"I'm afraid not," said Geppetto. "You aren't the only one who's been watching him." Geppetto nodded toward Figaro the cat.

At the end of the day, Geppetto went out to the market. As soon as he left, Pinocchio hurried over to the birdcage.

"Pinocchio?" Jiminy said. "What are you doing?"

"Taking the bird out," the puppet replied.

As Pinocchio opened the cage door, Figaro jumped onto the table.

"Watch out!" Jiminy cried. The bird zipped out of the cage, spotted an open window, and flew outside.

Just then, Geppetto walked in. He glanced at the empty birdcage.

"Pinocchio!" he yelled. "I told you not to open the cage!"

Panicked, Pinocchio lied. "I didn't do it! It was Figaro! He opened the birdcage!"

At that moment, the puppet's nose began to grow. Pinocchio didn't want his father to know that he had lied. "Father," Pinocchio said, "I'm going to bed. I'm not well."

The next morning, Pinocchio got up early and spent the day looking for the cuckoo. But there was no sign of it anywhere. Finally he headed home, determined to tell the truth.

"Figaro didn't open the cage," Pinocchio told his father. "I opened it, and the cuckoo flew away. I'm sorry I disobeyed you, but most of all, I'm sorry I lied."

As Pinocchio spoke, his nose became shorter and shorter.

"I'm glad you finally told the truth," said Geppetto. "And the cuckoo came back. I was working on the clock today and he flew in through the window. I think he likes it here!"

"He should," Pinocchio said. "It's the best home anyone could ever want."

# A New Life

Andy would soon be leaving home for college. He had meant to store his toys safely in his attic, but his mom had mistaken the bag of toys for trash and thrown them out! Luckily, the toys had escaped. They jumped into a box that was being donated to the day care center.

A pink teddy bear named Lotso welcomed the new toys to Sunnyside Daycare.

"Now let's get you all settled in," Lotso said. "Ken! New toys!"

Ken emerged from the doorway of a dollhouse. "Folks, if you wanna to step right this way . . ." Then he spotted Barbie. It was love at first sight.

Lotso broke the romantic spell. "Recess don't last forever!" he reminded Ken. The children would soon be coming in from outside. Barbie linked her arm through Ken's, and the toys set off to see Sunnyside.

Lotso and a doll named Big Baby led the tour. "You got a lot to look forward to!" declared Lotso. "The little ones love new toys." Lotso nodded toward Big Baby and whispered sadly, "Poor Baby. We were thrown out together, me an' him."

Finally, Lotso and Ken ushered the group to their new home: the Caterpillar Room.

"Look at this place!" cried Jessie excitedly.

It was time for Lotso, Ken, and Big Baby to head back to the Butterfly Room, but Ken hesitated. "Barbie!" he blurted out. "Come with me. Live in my Dream House!" The toys smiled and nodded their approval, and Barbie joined Ken.

Andy's toys stood in the Caterpillar Room, counting the seconds until the children would arrive. They hadn't been played with in a long time, and they couldn't wait.

"We can have a whole new life here, Woody," Jessie said. "A chance to make kids happy again."

"What's important now is we stay together," said Buzz.

"We wouldn't even *be* together if it weren't for Andy," Woody shot back.

"Woody, wake up!" Jessie yelled. "It's over. Andy is all grown up!"

The cowboy shook his head sadly. "I gotta go."

Woody just couldn't abandon Andy. He had to get back to his oldest friend.

# Like Father, Like Son

Tramp had a whole new life. He had gone from being a stray to becoming a member of the Dear household. And now he and Lady were proud parents. But Tramp was finding it difficult to change some of his old ways.

"Tramp," Lady said gently, "you need to set an example for the puppies—especially Scamp."

Scamp had an adventurous side, just like his dad, so it wasn't surprising that father and son often got carried away when they played together. They couldn't resist the urge to roll in a puddle of mud—and then chase each other across the clean kitchen floor.

Aunt Sarah and her two troublesome cats were going to be visiting soon. Lady was worried about how Tramp and Scamp would behave.

"Don't worry. I promise to keep Scamp away from those troublemakers," Tramp said.

"And?" replied Lady.

"And I promise to stay away from them, too," Tramp added.

When the big day came, Lady and Tramp herded their pups into a bedroom and told them to stay put. But Scamp was curious. He slipped out of the room and hid behind the living room sofa. Then he sneaked up behind the cats and swiped at their tails as they flicked back and forth. The cats turned and chased Scamp into a cupboard.

Seconds later, Scamp emerged. When no one was looking, he and his father shared a victory wink.

Father and son were banished to the garden for their antics. When Lady came out that evening, she found that they had dug up the entire garden looking for bones. The two saw the look on Lady's face and knew that they were about to get a lecture.

Tramp looked at Lady innocently. "You want him to get exercise, don't you?" he asked.

"What am I going to do with you two?" Lady said, laughing.

Tramp and Scamp dragged a huge bone out from behind the doghouse.

"Join us for dinner?" Tramp replied.

"Well, all right," Lady said. "But as soon as we're done, we're cleaning up this yard."

"Yes, ma'am!" chorused Tramp and Scamp, looking very pleased with themselves.

# We're the Vultures!

"Nothing exciting ever happens around here," Buzzie complained to his vulture singing buddies.

"That's not true," said Flaps. "What about that fight we had with the tiger Shere Khan last week?"

"Blimey, you're right," said Ziggy. "That was pretty exciting."

"But what are we gonna do now?" asked Buzzie.

"Let's sing," suggested Ziggy.

"Only one problem," said Dizzy. "We need a tenor."

"So, what are we gonna do?" asked Buzzie.

"How 'bout we hold an audition?" suggested Ziggy.

"Good thinking," said Flaps.

So the vultures put the word out in the jungle, and a week later there was a line of animals ready to try out for the group. First up was a monkey.

"Name?" Buzzie asked the first applicant.

"Coconut," the monkey replied.

"All right, Coconut, let's hear ya sing," said Flaps.

Coconut shrieked for a few minutes, and the four vultures huddled together.

"He's not very good," said Buzzie.

"And he's a monkey," added Flaps.

"Next!" said Dizzy.

The vultures auditioned a lemur, two sloths, a wolf, a hippo, a toad, and an elephant. None seemed like the right fit. Finally, another vulture stepped up.

"Name's Lucky," said the vulture. "Hey, aren't you the four fellows that helped that little Man-cub scare away that tiger, Shere Khan?"

"Yeah," said Buzzie. "We are."

"Then I guess you four might be called 'lucky' yourselves!" cried Lucky.

"Go ahead and sing," said Ziggy, rolling his eyes.

Lucky sang for a few minutes, and then the four vultures huddled together.

"He's not bad," said Dizzy.

"Plus, he's a vulture," said Ziggy.

"And he's the last auditioner left," pointed out Flaps.

That settled it.

"You're hired!" the vultures sang.

"See? Told you you I was Lucky!" cried the vulture.

"But only with auditions," said Dizzy.

"Yeah," said Buzzie. "When we meet Shere Khan again, we'll see how lucky you really are!"

# The Lost Boys Get Lost

The Lost Boys were walking single file through the woods of Never Land, on their way home after an afternoon of adventure seeking, when Slightly, who led the way, stopped in his tracks on the bank of Mermaid Lagoon. The others—Rabbit, the Raccoon Twins, Cubby, and Tootles—came to an abrupt halt behind him.

"Wait a minute," said Slightly. "We already passed Mermaid Lagoon. What are we doing here again?"

Behind a bush, Tinker Bell giggled as she watched the Lost Boys looking around in confusion.

Tink had spotted them on their march and had not been able to resist playing a joke. She had flown ahead of them and used her fairy magic to make various landmarks on their route home look different than normal.

Now, here they were, walking past Mermaid Lagoon, when Slightly remembered passing the same spot a good while back.

"I think we're walking in circles!" Slightly proclaimed. "Lost Boys, I think we're . . . lost!"

Tinker Bell overheard and tried desperately to stifle her laughter. But before she could contain it, one giggle exploded into a full-fledged laugh, and—

"Hey!" said Cubby. "Did you hear that?" He darted over to a bush growing alongside the path and moved a branch to one side. There was Tinker Bell, hovering in midair, holding her stomach and shaking with laughter.

"Tinker Bell!" cried Tootles.

It didn't take them long to work out that Tinker Bell was laughing at *them*—and that she was the cause of their confusion.

Still laughing, Tinker Bell flitted away, taking her normal route home to the fairy glade: left at the Weeping Willow Tree, right just before Sparrow Bird Grove, right again at Spiky Rock, and on toward the Sparkling Stream, which led to Moon Falls and the fairy glade entrance.

But—wait a minute! After turning right at Spiky Rock, Tinker Bell saw no sign of the Sparkling Stream anywhere. Where was she? She had gotten completely lost.

# The Greatest Gift

Pinocchio was the luckiest boy in the world—and he knew it. No longer a wooden puppet, at last he was a real live boy! Pinocchio knew he owed it all to Geppetto for believing in him.

"I wish I could give Father something in return," Pinocchio said to himself one day. He didn't have any money, so he decided that he would make a gift for Geppetto instead.

"Perhaps I should use Father's tools and carve a present for him out of wood!" said Pinocchio.

So, one day while Geppetto was out, Pinocchio sat down at the woodworking bench. The problem was, Pinocchio didn't know how to woodwork.

"That looks dangerous," said Pinocchio, eyeing a chisel. "I don't think Father would want me to use that on my own." He decided he needed another gift idea.

Pinocchio looked around the little house and spotted Geppetto's accordion sitting on the table.

"Of course!" cried Pinocchio. "Father loves music. I could write him a song as a gift and then perform it for him!"

So Pinocchio picked up the accordion and began to play. But it sounded . . . well, awful!

"Hmph," Pinocchio said in frustration. "I don't know how to play the accordion *or* write a song."

He put the accordion down and stood in the middle of the room. Tears were welling up in poor little Pinocchio's eyes when Geppetto came in through the front door.

"My boy," Geppetto said, "what's the matter?"

Through his tears, Pinocchio explained that he had wanted to make a gift to show Geppetto how much he appreciated everything he had done for him.

As Geppetto listened, his look of worry softened into a smile, and then *his* eyes welled up with tears. "My son," he said, "don't you know that you, and you alone, are the greatest gift a father could ever want?"

"I am?" Pinocchio asked.

"You are," replied Geppetto.

"Well, in that case," said Pinocchio with a sly grin as he hugged his father, "you're welcome!"

Then Geppetto picked up the accordion and they sang and danced all evening!

# Destructo-Boy

"**H**ercules!" Amphitryon called. "This hay pile is about to fall over. Could you hold it up while I go get the cart?"

"Sure, Pop!" Hercules told his father. Hercules was the strongest boy in his village. He easily held the enormous stack of hay bales up with one hand.

Soon, another farmer approached, struggling to hold on to a team of six disobedient mules.

"Need any help?" Hercules asked.

"Hercules!" the farmer gasped. "If you'll hold these mules, I can go get my sons to help me get them home."

"Be glad to!" Hercules took the mules' ropes with his free hand.

Just then, a woman came by dragging a cart filled with pottery. She was panting.

"Good day, ma'am," Hercules said politely. "Could I give you a hand with that?"

"Why, thank you," the woman replied. "But it looks like you have your hands full!"

"Oh, I'll be finished here in a second," Hercules said. "Then I can . . ."

His voice trailed off. He'd just noticed some kids his own age running down the road, laughing and shouting as they tossed a discus.

"Hey, guys!" he called as the discus sailed toward him. "I've got it!"

He lunged toward the discus. The mules' ropes went flying. The hay pile teetered.

"Uh-oh," Hercules said. He tried to grab the hay and the mules at the same time, but he accidentally tripped one of the mules, which crashed into the hay pile, which fell right onto the woman's pottery cart and all over the boys.

"My pottery!" the woman wailed.

"What's the big idea?" one of the kids demanded, standing and brushing himself off.

"Yeah." Another boy grabbed the discus from Hercules. "Stay out of our way from now on . . . Destructo-Boy!"

Hercules's shoulders slumped. Why did this sort of thing always happen to him? Whenever he tried to help, he only made things worse. But he knew that someday, his strength would help him be a hero. He just hoped that day would come soon. There was only so much unbroken pottery left in Greece!

# The Caterpillar Room

Andy was leaving for college soon. He had planned to store his toys in the attic, but there had been a mistake, and the toys thought Andy was going to throw them away! They had escaped the trash and gone to Sunnyside Daycare instead. Woody knew the truth, but the toys wouldn't listen to him. And so he left them in the Caterpillar Room at the day care center and set out to find a way home.

Woody climbed through the bathroom window and onto the roof. Beside him was an old kite. Grabbing it, he leaped off the building. The kite soared wildly through the air. Then, suddenly—SNAP!—the kite broke, sending Woody hurtling into a tree outside the day care center. Luckily, his pull-string caught on a branch, saving him from a crash.

A little girl named Bonnie was playing outside. She ran over to see the dangling toy. Just then, her mom honked the car horn. It was time to go home.

The little girl grabbed Woody, shoved him into her bag, and ran to the car.

Woody couldn't believe his bad luck. He just wanted to get back to Andy!

Back at Sunnyside, playtime was about to begin! Andy's other toys waited as footsteps thundered toward them and a crowd of excited toddlers burst into the room. Shrieking with delight, the children grabbed the new toys.

But this playtime was not what the toys expected. The toddlers tangled Slinky's coil, dipped Jessie's hair in paint, and covered Hamm with glitter and glue. They hammered with Buzz's head and stuck the Potato Heads' parts in their mouths. The toys couldn't believe it! Andy had never treated them like this!

Suddenly, a toddler tossed Buzz into the air. Buzz flipped himself onto the windowsill and lay still, looking out of the window . . . into the other day care room, the Butterfly Room. Inside, Buzz could see a group of older children playing gently with Lotso and the other toys. Buzz wondered why he and his friends been put into a room where they were handled so roughly. There must have been a mistake. Buzz knew he'd have to ask Lotso—if he survived the afternoon!

# Abu's Blues

Abu couldn't believe it. One second he was a monkey. The next—*POOF!*—he was an elephant! Worst of all, nobody seemed to notice that Abu wasn't thrilled about his new shape. Aladdin was too busy with the Genie and the Magic Carpet.

Abu watched as the Genie waved his arms and—*POOF!*—dozens of exotic white monkeys appeared. Then the Genie conjured up a group of snake charmers.

Abu wandered off, looking for space. He almost tripped over his new trunk a few times as he headed to a quiet spot. He sat down, wishing he had a nice juicy melon or a banana. Would he and Aladdin ever wander through the marketplace again, searching for a free meal?

Abu scowled. Princess Jasmine. Talk about trouble—that was where this had all started. Ever since Aladdin had met her, it was as if Abu didn't matter anymore. . . .

"Abu! Abu!"

Suddenly, Abu realized that someone was calling him. It was Aladdin!

"There you are, Abu!" Aladdin cried.

"We were looking all over for you."

Abu glared at him suspiciously. What did he want? Was the Genie going to turn him into something else—maybe a big, ugly cobra for Prince Ali's new snake charmers?

"Come on," Aladdin said. "It's almost time!"

Abu had no idea what Aladdin was talking about. He trumpeted at him angrily, complaining about how Aladdin didn't seem to want him around anymore.

"Don't be silly, Abu!" Aladdin exclaimed. "You're the most important one in this whole parade! Now come over here. . . ."

"Ready, Monkey-boy?" the Genie said. "Er, I mean, Elephant-dude?" He waved his arms, and a luxurious litter suddenly appeared on Abu's back. The Genie lifted Aladdin into it. Suddenly, Abu understood—he and Aladdin were at the head of the parade! Aladdin wasn't going to forget him just because he'd met other friends!

Lifting his trunk proudly, he let out a loud trumpet and led the way toward the Sultan's palace. There was a princess waiting for them!

# The Un-Fun House

Manny had just finished the blueprints for the fun house at Sheet Rock Hills' carnival. He told his tools that the blueprints would be their guide for cutting and putting together all the pieces of wood they would need.

"It doesn't look like the house will be much fun," said Turner.

Manny smiled at the tools. "Well, Turner, blueprints give you a basic idea of how the building will be made. They don't show all the colors and decorations we'll be adding."

Just then, the phone rang. "*Hola,* this is Manny. Hi, Principal Chu. The supplies have arrived at the school? *Excelente!* We'll be right there!"

Manny and the tools arrived at the school and unloaded the truck.

"I think we're ready to get started," Squeeze said. Manny's smile faded.

"Wait a minute, guys. We can't start work yet. I forgot to bring the blueprints. I'll be right back, tools."

With Manny gone, the tools started fighting. They were nervous that the job wouldn't be finished in time for the carnival, but they couldn't agree on what to do about it. They were so busy arguing, they didn't see Dusty cutting up the wood!

"Dusty, what did you do?" shrieked Felipe. "This isn't the way the blueprints said to cut the wood."

"Gosh, I just wanted to help, but I've ruined everything!" cried Dusty.

At that moment, Manny's truck and Kelly's car pulled up. "Hey, tools," Manny called. "I brought some friends along! They've all offered to help build the fun house."

"Uh," Turner groaned. "I think we can officially rename this project the un-fun house!"

"Oh, Manny, I'm so sorry!" Dusty said with a sob. "I should have waited for the blueprints!"

"Dusty, now do you see why you can't start any job without being fully prepared?" Manny asked.

"Why don't we pick up each piece and think about how we can use it in a new design?" suggested Kelly. "For example, this big triangle looks like the roof of a tower."

Working together, Manny and his friends made a fun-castle!

"Ta-da!" shouted Felipe, admiring the castle. "It's a fun house fit for a king!"

# Gas-Guzzling Engine

Lightning, Mater, and their friends from Radiator Springs had been in Tokyo for the first event of the World Grand Prix—a three-city race hosted by oil tycoon Miles Axlerod. During the race, some cars working for a known criminal, Professor Z, had used a special TV camera to blow up several race cars. The press had asked Axlerod if his new alternative fuel, Allinol, was to blame, but he said it wasn't.

Two British secret agents named Finn and Holley were on the trail of Professor Z. In Tokyo, an American spy had placed a secret device on Mater. Now Finn and Holley thought *Mater* was the American spy!

Finn met Mater at the airport and brought him to a private jet. Onboard, Holley showed Mater a holographic photo that was on the device that the real American spy had given Mater. Mater realized that the photo was of a poorly made, gas-guzzling engine with some expensive new parts. But he didn't know who the engine belonged to.

Finn, Holley, and Mater flew to Paris. Finn was hoping a parts dealer named Tomber could tell them who the mysterious engine in the photo belonged to.

Mater explained that the engine must belong to a Lemon—a car that didn't work right. Gremlins and Pacers were both types of Lemons. Tomber agreed and told the agents that there was going to be a big meeting of Lemons in Porto Corsa, which was also the location of the next World Grand Prix race!

Lightning and his crew had just arrived in Italy for the next race. Their first stop was Luigi and Guido's hometown.

Lightning told Luigi's Uncle Topolino about his fight with Mater. The wise old car told Lightning that even good friends fight sometimes. The important thing was to make up fast.

Meanwhile, Holley was disguising Mater as one of the Lemons' tow trucks so that he could sneak into the meeting. She gave Mater lots of cool spy gadgets, too!

Lightning was starting to really miss his best friend, Mater. He didn't realize that Mater was actually nearby —and had been caught up in a secret agent adventure!

# The Hottest Thrill Ride Ever

Scout Leader Kronk wanted to reward his pupils for learning to speak Squirrel. He decided to fix the roller coaster hidden inside Kuzco's castle. Kronk headed into the entrance chamber.

He jumped when a small shadow slid across the floor in front of him. It was Yzma, who had been turned into a cat by one of her own potions.

"Do you know where you are standing?" Yzma asked with a smug purr.

"Over the trapdoor that leads to the roller coaster," replied Kronk.

"Isn't that dangerous?" said Yzma, curling her tail around his leg.

"It's safe as long as no one pulls the lever," Kronk replied.

"What lever?" Yzma asked slyly. She was planning to pull the lever and drop Kronk through the trapdoor!

"This one," said Kronk. He put his hand on the lever to show her, but— "Oops!" He pulled it by mistake!

Down they went, right through the trapdoor.

"Ouch!" Kronk cried when he landed in the roller coaster car. To Yzma's surprise, she landed right next to him. She hadn't planned to fall down here, too!

The out-of-control coaster car headed into a dark tunnel.

"Hold on. It's going to be a bumpy ride," said Kronk.

"You don't know the half of it, you dolt!" Yzma cried. "The brakes don't work and the tracks are broken!"

Kronk grabbed Yzma, and down they plunged.

"AAAAAHHHH!" screamed Kronk.

"MEEOOOWWW!" howled Yzma.

"In Squirrel that's pronounced 'chit-chit-chitter-chit,'" said Kronk.

"Who cares?" yelled Yzma.

"*Yikes!*" yelled Kronk as they raced around a corner. Then they saw the broken track. Kronk jumped out of his seat and landed in front of the roller coaster car. Bracing himself against the car, he used his feet as brakes. The car slowed and finally stopped, just inches away from a giant hole in the track.

"Ouch, ouch, ouch!" Kronk cried, dancing up and down on his smoking feet.

"Serves you right for pulling that lever," said Yzma.

"Yeah," said Kronk with a goofy smile. "But when I fix the brakes and the track, this'll be the hottest thrill ride ever!"

# Scare Tactics

It was still a few weeks until Halloween, but Jack the Pumpkin King and his crew were already busily planning for the big day.

"We've got to come up with something positively terrifying," Jack said. "The kids are getting harder and harder to scare every year."

He was right. Last year, the kids had loved Jack's screeching pumpkins—but they hadn't been afraid of them.

"So let's all put our heads together," Jack said. "I'm counting on you!"

The citizens of Halloweentown removed their heads and put them in a large pile.

"Oh, brother!" Jack said with a sigh. "This is going to be harder than I thought!"

A week later, the creepy creatures assembled once again and offered up their suggestions. First, a gaggle of witches stepped forward, cackling with excitement. "We've cooked up a horrible concoction to feed the children. It's made of worms and dirt. It's terrifying!"

"Nice try," said Jack, "but I believe there is a Halloween treat made of cookie crumbs and gummy worms that is quite similar. And the kids love it."

"What if we stuck their hands in a bowl full of eyeballs?" asked a witch.

"They'll just think they're peeled grapes," Jack said with a sigh.

"We know! We know!" Lock, Shock, and Barrel said in unison. "We'll steal all the candy in the trick-or-treaters' bags and replace it with math homework. Now *that's* scary!"

Jack rubbed his skull. "Interesting . . . but not exactly what I had in mind," he said.

As Jack continued to think, Sally sneaked up behind him. She put her finger to her lips and crept closer. When she was right behind him, she screeched, "BOO!"

"Ahhhh!" Jack yelled, jumping in the air.

"Sometimes the simplest things can be the most effective, don't you think?" Sally asked.

A smile spread across the Pumpkin King's face. "Sally, that's brilliant! A well-timed 'BOO!' never fails to scare the living daylights out of people, day or night."

Jack looked at Sally with admiration. She may have been a rag doll, but her head was full of a lot more than stuffing!

# The Best Fisherman of All

Simba and his friends Timon and Pumbaa were hungry. They wandered through the forest until they came to an old, rotten tree. Timon knocked on the trunk.

"What's it sound like, Timon?" Pumbaa asked.

"Like our breakfast!" Timon replied.

He yanked at the bark, and hundreds of grubs slithered out. Timon tossed Simba a grub.

"No, thanks." Simba sighed. "I'm tired of grubs."

"Well, the ants are tasty," said Timon. "They come in two flavors: red and black."

Simba shook his head. "Don't you eat anything but bugs?"

"Fish!" Pumbaa declared.

"I love fish!" Simba exclaimed.

"Why didn't you say so?" said Timon. "There's a pond at the end of this trail." The three friends started off toward the water.

"What now?" asked Simba when they arrived at the pond.

"That's the problem!" said Timon. "We're not the best fishermen in the world."

"I'll teach you!" Simba said.

The lion climbed up a tree and crawled onto a branch that hung over the water. Then he snatched a fish out of the water with his sharp claws. "See?" Simba said, jumping to the ground nimbly. "Not a problem. Fishing's easy."

"Not for me!" Timon cried. He dangled from the branch, but his arms weren't long enough to reach the fish.

Simba laughed. "Better let Pumbaa try."

"What a joke!" cried Timon. "Pumbaa can't even climb this tree."

"Want to bet?" asked Pumbaa.

"Stay there," Timon warned. "I don't think this branch is strong enough for both of us."

With a hop, Pumbaa landed on the branch next to Timon.

"Yikes!" Timon cried as he leaped to another tree.

*Crack!* The branch broke under Pumbaa. With a squeal, he landed in the pond.

Simba started to laugh. So did Timon. Pumbaa was sitting in a pool of mud where the pond had been. He'd splashed so much of the water out that dozens of fish squirmed on the ground, just waiting to be gobbled up.

"Wow!" Timon cried. "I think Pumbaa is the very best fisherman of all!"

# Annie's Solo Mission

Leo was giving Annie flying lessons! "Today you'll learn the three most important tricks for flying Rocket," Leo said. "Are you ready?"

"Ready!" Annie said excitedly.

"Okay, here's the first lesson: the Up-and-Down Trick," said Leo. "If you want to make Rocket jump over something, you need to reach your arms up really high and then bring them down really fast."

"I think I've got it!" exclaimed Annie.

"Great job, Pilot Annie!" Leo said, beaming. "Next, you'll need to know the Squeeze Trick," explained Leo. "It comes in handy when you need to fly Rocket through a really tight space. Just cross your arms and pat your shoulders."

"This is fun!" Annie shouted.

"Okay, this next one is a bit difficult," cautioned Leo. "To make Rocket do big roller-coaster loops in the air, you need to clap your hands in a circle."

Annie made big clapping circles in the air.

After Annie's flying lesson, the team decided to blow some superbubbles.

The Little Einsteins blew their superbubbles into some pretty wild shapes! Annie ran to find her camera. She wanted to take pictures before they all popped. Just then, June, Quincy, and Leo blew a superbubble so big that it carried all three of them away! Annie raced back, but her friends were nowhere to be found.

"Hey, where did they go?" Annie wondered aloud. "I wanted to take a picture!"

"Up here, Annie!" shouted Quincy.

"We need you to rescue us," said June. "If you fly Rocket up here, you can catch our bubble in his Bubble Wand."

Annie was nervous. "Me? But I've never flown Rocket by myself before!"

"You can do it, Annie," Leo assured her.

Inside Rocket, Annie prepared for her solo mission. She was nervous, but she knew the others were counting on her. She took off and followed the flight plan perfectly.

"We're so proud of you, Pilot Annie!" exclaimed June.

"Way to go, sis!" Leo beamed. "I'm bubbling over with pride!"

# Dig Deep!

**M**ike and Sulley woke up early and leaped out of bed. They needed to get ready for the next event of the Scare Games. Mike and Sulley were part of Oozma Kappa. Their fraternity was full of students who had failed out of the Scare Program. But the two were sure they could win the Scare Games. Their team had survived the first two events. Now they had three more to go. Mike was determined to lead his team to victory. If they lost, he'd have to leave the university. His dream of becoming a Scarer would be over.

The third event was called Don't Scare the Teen. The OKs successfully worked their way through a maze by scaring all the cutouts of human children and hiding from the cutouts of the teens. Only their biggest rivals, the RORs, made it out of the maze before them. That meant there were only three teams left for the fourth event: ROR, HSS, and OK!

The Hide and Sneak event required all of the competitors to hide in a dark house while referees searched for them with flashlights.

The referees soon discovered HSS—but no one else. The OKs had made it to the final event. They would be competing against the RORs for the Scare Games trophy!

As Sulley headed home from the fourth event, he spotted Dean Hardscrabble, the head of the Scare Program. It had been her decision to kick Mike and Sulley out of the program.

"When we get back," Sulley said to her, "I hope there'll be no hard feelings."

But Dean Hardscrabble told Sulley that she doubted they would win. Mike just wasn't scary enough.

Sulley wondered if Dean Hardscrabble was right. He decided to teach Mike how to be scary.

Sulley told Mike to forget what he had read about scaring in books. He needed to stop *thinking* scary and start *feeling* it.

Mike tried a heartfelt roar.

"Let the animal out!" Sulley coached. "Dig deep!"

Mike gave it all he had. It was an improvement. Sulley just hoped it would be enough to win. He would find out soon.

The battle for the trophy was about to begin.

# Woody Meets Bonnie

Woody had escaped Sunnyside Daycare, but he had been picked up by a little girl named Bonnie!

"Look," Woody said when Bonnie left her room for a minute, "I just need to know how to get out of here."

Bonnie's toys were confused. Why would Woody want to leave?

Before Woody could answer, Bonnie returned and swept the toys up into a game of make-believe that ended with the toys being launched into the air! They landed on the bed. Bonnie laughed happily and hugged them all close. Woody hated to admit it, but he was having a great time.

Back at Sunnyside, Andy's toys were unhappy after being played with by some rough toddlers! The children had gone home for the day and the toys were putting themselves back together.

"Andy never played with us like that!" cried Rex as he freed his tail from a pegboard.

"We should be in the Butterfly Room with the big kids!" said Mrs. Potato Head.

Buzz offered to talk to Lotso about changing rooms. But when he tried to leave, he discovered that all the doors and windows were locked.

"We're trapped!" said Mrs. Potato Head.

Finally, Buzz spotted an open space above the door. Working together, the toys managed to get Buzz through the space and out of the room. Below him, Buzz heard two toys named Twitch and Chunk talking. The pair stopped by the Butterfly Room to pick up Ken, then continued to the teachers' lounge. When they had disappeared inside, Buzz jumped down and followed the group. He sneaked into the lounge just as the toys were climbing into a vending machine.

Buzz secretly followed Ken and the others.

"What do you guys think of the new recruits?" Ken asked the others. "Any keepers?"

"All them toys are disposable," replied Twitch. "We'll be lucky if they last us a week!"

Buzz was shocked! These toys knew how dangerous the Caterpillar Room was. They had sent Andy's toys there on purpose! He had to warn his friends!

But when Buzz turned to go, Big Baby was waiting for him. . . .

# A Bright Idea

One day, Geppetto told Pinocchio, "I am off to deliver these puppets. I will be gone for a few hours. Stay out of trouble!"

Geppetto had not been gone for fifteen minutes before Pinocchio became bored. "I have nothing to do," he said.

"You could clean the shop," said Jiminy Cricket.

"That's no fun," said Pinocchio. "I'll paint a picture instead."

"Where will you get the paint?" Jiminy asked.

"From the workbench," said Pinocchio.

"You know you're not supposed to go near Geppetto's workbench," warned Jiminy.

But the cricket's warning came too late. "Oops!" Pinocchio cried. He'd spilled red paint all over the workbench. Hurriedly, he grabbed a rag and tried to clean up the mess, but the paint just smeared. He'd made the mess even bigger!

Pinocchio looked around desperately. When he noticed Geppetto's kitten, Figaro, sleeping by the hearth, he had an idea.

"I'll say Figaro did it," Pinocchio said.

Jiminy shook his head. "That would be wrong," he told the puppet. "Why don't you paint it?"

"That's a very good idea!" said Pinocchio.

So he set to work. First, he painted the bench's top bright red. Then he painted the drawers green and yellow. Figaro woke up and investigated, getting paint all over his whiskers.

Soon, the job was done.

"It's a work of art!" Geppetto cried when he got home. "It's so colorful, it makes the whole shop cheerful."

Then Geppetto saw the paint on Figaro's whiskers. "Did Figaro knock over the paint again?" he asked. "Is that why you painted the workbench?"

"No," Pinocchio said. "*I* spilled the paint. I couldn't clean it up, so I painted the whole workbench. I'm sorry."

Geppetto was quiet for a moment, and then he said, "I'm proud of you, Pinocchio. You told the truth and apologized instead of telling a lie. That takes courage. Now, every day when I see my workbench, I'll remember you did the right thing, and that will make the colors seem even brighter!"

OCTOBER
15

# Stuck in the Mud

"**C**ome on, Robin!" Little John called as he stepped over a fallen log.

"Shhhh." Robin put a finger to his lips. "I think I hear something."

"Let's have a look-see," said Little John. A minute later, they stopped at the edge of the forest and peered out from behind a bush.

There, stuck in a muddy ditch, was a fancy coach.

"I'd know that coach anywhere," Robin whispered. "It belongs to Prince John."

"Get me out of the mud *now*!" a voice whined from inside the coach. It was Prince John, all right.

The driver's shoulders slumped. "But, sire, the coach is laden with gold. I'll never be able to push it out by myself. Perhaps Your Highness would consider stepping out of the coach so as to lighten the load?"

"Step out of the coach?" Prince John bellowed. "And stand in the rain? I most certainly will not!"

"I believe I have a plan that will help Prince John and his driver," Robin said. "Not to mention the poor."

Little John nodded with a grin. He knew exactly what sort of plan his friend had in mind. Robin reached into his satchel, pulled out a few items, and put them on. Little John did the same. Now they looked like two ordinary hunters on a walk.

Little John stepped onto the road. "Need some help there?" he asked the driver loudly. "I'd be glad to lend a hand."

Meanwhile, Robin sneaked around to the side of the coach. He was just opening the door when Prince John leaned out the window on the other side. "Hurry up, you fools!" he hollered.

Robin saw his chance. While the prince was distracted, he opened the other door and removed several bags of gold.

"Get pushing, then," Prince John snapped.

"I said I'd be glad to," Little John replied. He strolled to the back of the coach and, along with the driver, gave a single push. And while Robin slipped into the woods with the gold, Prince John and his muddy-wheeled coach rolled down the road to Nottingham, the load just a little bit lighter than before.

# Undercover Mater

Lightning was in Italy, competing in the second event of the World Grand Prix. He had lost the first race after Mater had confused him over the headset.

Meanwhile, Mater had been mistaken for an American secret agent and was now caught up in a mission with two British agents, Finn McMissile and Holley Shiftwell!

With a new disguise provided by the British agents, Mater had made it into a meeting of Lemons—bad cars that didn't work properly—at a casino.

A wanted criminal named Professor Z introduced the Lemons to their Big Boss. The Big Boss appeared on a TV screen, but only his engine was visible. The Big Boss said that once a new alternative fuel named Allinol was proven lethal, cars would be forced to use gasoline again. Then the Lemons, who owned the most of the world's gasoline, would be rich and powerful!

As the Big Boss spoke, Professor Z's goons, Grem and Acer, arrived at the next race. They aimed a special TV camera at Carla Veloso, the race car from Brazil. Finn and Holley watched from their lookout point as Carla's engine exploded on the racetrack! Finn raced to stop Grem and Acer, but he was captured by a helicopter with a giant magnet! As Finn was taken away, Grem and Acer aimed their camera at the racetrack again. Soon, there was a pileup on the track!

Meanwhile, Lightning zoomed across the finish line. He had won. By now, everyone thought Allinol was to blame for the crashes. But Lightning insisted he would still use Allinol in the final race. The Big Boss heard Lightning's statement and gave the order to destroy the race car. Mater had to warn his friend! As he tried to sneak out of the meeting, his disguise disappeared! Luckily, he escaped using his new spy gear.

When Mater finally arrived at the race track, he saw Lightning surrounded by a crowd. But before Mater could get to his friend, the Lemons captured him.

The next thing the tow truck knew, he, Finn, and Holley were tied up inside a giant clock called Big Bentley! They were in London, England, the location of the final race! How would Mater save Lightning now?

# Stuck at Sunnyside Daycare

Andy's toys were stuck at Sunnyside Daycare— all except Woody, who had been found by a little girl named Bonnie. The toys thought Andy wanted to throw them away, so they had jumped into a box going to the nursery instead.

The trouble was, the toys were trapped in the Caterpillar Room— where young toddlers played very roughly with them! Buzz had just learned that Lotso, the leader of the Sunnyside toys, had put Andy's toys in the Caterpillar Room on purpose. He *knew* the toddlers would play rough!

Back in the Caterpillar Room, the other toys gathered around Mrs. Potato Head. She had started to see strange images through the eye she'd lost at Andy's house.

"Andy's out in the hall," she said, holding a hand over her remaining eye. "He's looking in the attic. Why is he so upset?" She gasped. "Andy's looking for us! I think he *did* mean to put us in the attic!"

Meanwhile, Big Baby and the others day care toys had discovered Buzz. They tied him to a chair inside a cabinet. When Lotso arrived, he released Buzz and acted as if the space ranger's capture had been a mistake. Lotso even told Buzz that he could move to the Butterfly Room—as long as his friends stayed behind. But Buzz refused to accept.

Angry, Lotso called for the Bookworm to bring the Buzz Lightyear Instruction Manual. The gang held Buzz down. Using the booklet as a guide, they opened up Buzz's back panel and flipped a switch in his back.

A little while later, Lotso and his henchmen went to the Caterpillar Room. Andy's toys were relieved to see him.

"There's been a mistake," Mrs. Potato Head explained. "We have to go!"

But Lotso didn't care. "Here's the thing, Sweet Potato," he said, grinning nastily. "You ain't leaving Sunnyside."

Suddenly, Buzz appeared. He began knocking them over with kung-fu kicks!

Jessie and the others stared in shock, wondering what had happened to their friend. Why was Buzz acting so strangely?

# The Sky's the Limit

Captain Amelia and D— Delbert Doppl— smart couple. — young age, their quadrupl— nicknamed Matey, Jib, an— for "Tiller"), and a boy, Su— show evidence of having i— parents' intelligence. Unb— their parents, little by little, the Doppler quadruplets were using their talents to make changes to the house where they lived with their parents.

"Jib!" called Amelia, one windy afternoon. "Why are there large sails flying from the roof?"

"I thought they looked pretty up there," answered Jib.

"Tillie, what is that you're building in your room?" wondered Delbert.

"A rocket booster," she answered.

"Well, be careful!" her father warned. "Jet propulsion can be a tricky thing."

Amelia really became suspicious when she found Matey installing a giant steering wheel in front of the attic window. "And this would be . . . ?" she asked her daughter.

Matey looked innocently at her mother. "Something that's fun to spin?" she asked.

"Very curious," Amelia said to herself. —— Then one night, after the children —— went to bed, the house began to shake. —— ran to their children's —— and found it empty. A second —— house began to lift off! Amelia —— —rt looked at each other in

"We did it!" cried Sunny's triumphant voice. It was coming from the attic.

Amelia and Delbert rushed upstairs.

"What's going on here?" demanded Delbert.

"I'm steering," said Matey, from behind the giant wheel.

"I'm controlling the sails," said Jib, as she pulled some levers.

"I blasted us off," Tillie admitted.

"And I designed the whole thing," bragged Sunny.

"What thing?" asked Amelia.

"Mom and Dad, welcome to your new motor home!" Jib announced.

Amelia and Delbert stared at their children.

"Well, what do you think?" Matey asked eagerly. "Do you like it?"

Her parents both broke out in proud grins. "Aye, aye, Captain!" boomed Amelia.

It's your Mommy's Birthday!

**OCTOBER**
**19**

# Teamwork

Aladar smiled at his dinosaur baby. The little iguanodon was growing fast.

The little tyke jumped to his feet and took off toward a rocky hill.

"Be careful!" Aladar's mate, Neera, called out.

"I will, Mom!" the baby dinosaur called back. "I just want to see what's on the other side of this hill. I won't be long!"

"He'll be fine," Zini, their lemur friend, reassured Aladar and Neera. "He's been off on his own dozens of times."

Neera sighed. "I know," she agreed. "It's just that . . . he's my baby."

Aladar lay in the sun, waiting for the tiny iguanodon to reappear. He waited, and waited, and waited . . .

"Son?" Aladar called. "Where are you?"

Zini leaped up onto a nearby boulder and looked around. "I don't see him," he said.

"We have to go find him," Neera said.

The three friends were unusually quiet as they searched for the baby iguanodon.

"Shhhh," Zini said. His ears twitched. "I think I hear something."

They all listened. Zini was right. There was a noise coming from a nearby cliff.

Zini squinted.

"There's a cave up there," he said. "It looks like the entrance has been blocked off."

The lemur bounded easily up the steep hill and through a small opening at the mouth of the cave.

"I found him!" he cried from inside.

"I'm okay!" the young iguanodon added. But his voice sounded a little shaky.

Aladar and Neera were already climbing up the steep incline. The going was slow, and they tripped on several boulders before they got to the mouth of the cave. Then, working together, the iguanodons and Zini moved the rocks blocking the cave's entrance.

"Mommy! Daddy!" The baby dinosaur scampered forward and gave his parents a hug. Then the foursome made their way home.

"I'm never going exploring again!" declared the young dinosaur. "Well, almost never. Well, maybe just a little. Hey, look at that dry lake bed! Can we go explore it?"

Aladar and Neera smiled.

"Maybe tomorrow, son," Aladar said. "But I think one of us will be going with you!"

# A True Hero

"Hercules! Slow down!" Amphitryon yelled to his son, who was pulling their cart to the market. His son was headed straight for a marble archway that was under construction. Because Hercules didn't understand how strong he really was, his attempts to be helpful often turned into disasters.

Amphitryon and his wife, Alcmene, decided to tell their son Hercules the truth: they weren't his real parents. They'd discovered him when he was a baby and raised him as their own. Amphitryon handed Hercules a medallion. "This was around your neck when we found you," he said. It had a thunderbolt on it—the symbol of the gods.

Hercules wanted to know more, so the next morning, he journeyed to the temple of Zeus. As Hercules stood before the giant statue of the god, the great stone hand suddenly reached down. "My boy. My little Hercules," Zeus said.

Hercules's eyes widened. Zeus, the most powerful of all gods, was his father! Zeus explained that as a baby Hercules had been stolen and turned into a human. Hercules's superstrength was the only godlike quality he still had.

"If you can prove yourself a true hero on Earth, your godhood will be restored," Zeus told him. "Seek out Philoctetes, the trainer of heroes."

Zeus whistled, and a winged horse named Pegasus flew into the temple. Hercules and Pegasus had been best friends as infants. Happy to see each other again, the two picked up right where they'd left off!

Soon, Hercules felt he was ready to test his strength in the real world. Phil took him to Thebes, where Hercules heard that two boys were trapped in a rock slide. He and Pegasus flew to the boys. Hercules lifted a giant boulder and freed the trapped children.

There was no time to celebrate, though. A terrible monster called the Hydra was emerging from a nearby cave . . . and it was hungry. The Hydra trapped Hercules with one of its claws. Hercules slammed his arms against a cliff wall with all his might. Within seconds, the wall broke apart. Huge boulders tumbled down, killing the monster. Hercules was overjoyed. He was well on his way to becoming a true hero!

# The Final

It was the final event of the Scare Games. Mike, Sulley, and the rest of the Oozma Kappas were competing against their biggest rivals, the Roar Omega Roars, for the trophy. The RORs were the reigning champions. Could the OKs beat them?

The RORs and the OKs entered the packed stadium. The crowd roared for the OKs. No one had expected them to make it this far, and the crowd was rooting for them.

"It's time to see how terrifying you really are in the scare simulators," said Brock Pearson, the vice president of the Greek Council. "Be warned. Each simulated scare has been set to the highest difficulty level."

One member from each team took their places at the starting line. After four rounds, the RORs had a significant lead over the OKs. It was up to Mike and Sulley to win it for the team.

Sulley went up against Randy, Mike's old roommate. Sulley entered the simulator. He successfully dodged every obstacle in the room, crept up to the bed, and let out a thunderous roar. It was so loud that it shook Randy's simulator. Sulley easily won the challenge. Now the RORs and the OKs were tied!

The last two team members to compete were Mike and Johnny Worthington, president of ROR.

"Don't take the loss too hard," Johnny sneered at Mike. "You never belonged here, anyway."

Mike knew it was up to him. He couldn't let anything distract him from doing his best.

Johnny entered his scare simulator and got a huge scream. Next Mike entered his room.

Mike ruffled the scare simulator curtains and crept along the side of the bed. Then he closed his eye and concentrated. This was it. He took a deep breath, jumped, and let out his most explosive roar.

The robot-child sat bolt upright. Mike's scream can filled all the way to the top. The OKs had won the Scare Games.

The stadium cheered wildly as Mike walked out of the simulator. The RORs were stunned. They had never imagined that they would lose the Scare Games—especially to the Oozma Kappas!

But had the OKs won fairly?

# Rolly's Midnight Snack

"I'm hungry," Rolly complained as the puppies settled down for the night.

"You're always hungry," said Patch.

"And you always want to stay awake and have adventures," said Rolly.

Patch sighed. "Too bad we never get what we want."

Hours later, Rolly felt a tap on his shoulder. "Is it morning?" he asked with a yawn.

"No," said Patch. "It's midnight. Wanna explore? I'll get you a snack."

Rolly followed Patch to the kitchen. Patch nodded toward the table. "After dinner, I saw Nanny put some juicy bones up there. She's saving them for tomorrow's soup."

"Soup!" cried Rolly. "What a waste! Bones are for chewing on."

So Patch and Rolly came up with a plan. First, Patch climbed onto Rolly's shoulders to reach the table. Everything went fine until Patch threw down the first bone and it landed in the trash can. Rolly took off after it and leaped inside!

"Uh, Patch?" Rolly called. "I think I'm stuck in here." He tried to climb the walls of the can, but it was too slippery.

Patch tried hard not to panic. He thought and thought until he came up with another plan—a Rescue Rolly Plan!

Patch raced upstairs and woke Lucky and Pepper. The two puppies followed Patch into the kitchen. Then Patch found his father's long leash and tossed one end into the trash can.

"Take hold of the leash!" Patch told Rolly.

"Okay," said Rolly.

Patch turned to the other puppies and said, "Now, let's all pull on this end of the leash on the count of three."

The three puppies pulled. The trash can fell over, and Rolly tumbled out onto the kitchen floor.

"Thanks!" said Rolly as the four puppies ran back up to bed.

Before Rolly drifted off to sleep, he whispered to Patch, "Guess you finally got your adventure."

"Yeah," said Patch. "But I'm sorry you didn't get your snack."

"Sure, I did," said Rolly. "While I was waiting for you to rescue me, what do you think I was doing? I was eating that juicy bone. And, boy, was it good!"

# A Blustery Day

"Oh dear," said Pooh as the wind whipped around him. "It's very windy. Are you sure this is a good idea, Tigger?" He and Tigger were carrying Pooh's kite out into a clearing in the middle of the Hundred-Acre Wood.

"Don't be silly, Pooh Boy," Tigger responded. "Today is the perfect day to fly your kite. After all, what else is wind for?"

"Yes," Pooh replied. "I suppose you're right."

At last, struggling against the wind, Pooh and Tigger reached the middle of the clearing and got ready to launch the kite. Pooh unrolled some kite string while Tigger held the kite.

"Okay, Pooh," said Tigger. "Get ready! You hold on to the string, and I'll toss the kite up into the wind. One . . . two . . . THREE!"

With that, Tigger tossed the kite, and it was immediately seized by the strong wind and carried high into the air, where it danced and darted this way and that. Pooh struggled to hold on to the roll of kite string.

"Let out some more string, Pooh!"

Tigger suggested. "Let's see how high we can fly it!"

Pooh let out some more string. The kite sailed higher into the air and, blown around by stronger and stronger gusts, it tugged harder and harder on Pooh's end of the line.

"Fly it higher, Pooh!" exclaimed Tigger.

Pooh let out more and more string, until he had let it all out. Then, all of a sudden, a tremendous gust of wind blew through the clearing. At the end of the kite string, Pooh felt his feet leave the ground as the wind grabbed hold of the kite and carried it sharply upward.

"My goodness!" said Pooh, realizing that he was being lifted up. Then, before he could be carried too high, he let go of the kite string and tumbled gently to the ground.

But the kite sailed on—up and away, dancing on the breeze for what seemed like forever, until it came to rest at last in the high branches of a very tall tree at the edge of the clearing.

"Oh, well," said Tigger, patting his friend sympathetically on the back. "Guess you flew it just a little too high there, Pooh Boy."

# Woody Discovers the Truth

Buzz, Jessie, and most of Andy's other toys were at Sunnyside Daycare. They wanted to escape and get home, but Lotso, the doll in charge, wouldn't let them go.

Lotso and his helpers had found Buzz's reset button. The Space Ranger didn't remember his friends and was helping to hold them captive!

Lotso's gang put Andy's toys into wire crates. When Mr. Potato Head fought back, Big Baby put him in "the Box"—a covered sandbox in the playground.

Suddenly, Barbie walked in. "Ken? What are you doing to my friends?" she asked in surprise. When she realized what was happening, she insisted on staying with Andy's toys.

"We got a way of doing things here at Sunnyside," Lotso explained. "Life here can be a dream come true. But if you break our rules. . . ." He threw Woody's hat, which he had found outside, onto the floor.

The toys gasped. "What'd you do to him?" cried Jessie.

Lotso simply chuckled and left, leaving the prisoners under Buzz's guard.

Meanwhile, Woody had been found by a little girl named Bonnie, who brought him home with her. Woody was planning to escape to go home to Andy.

"If any of you guys ever get to Sunnyside Daycare," Woody told Bonnie's toys, "tell 'em Woody made it home."

"Sunnyside?" Bonnie's toys gasped. Quickly, they took Woody to Chuckles, an old clown toy who knew all about Sunnyside—and Lotso. Long ago, Chuckles explained, he, Lotso, and Big Baby had belonged to a little girl named Daisy. One day, the toys were accidentally left behind during a trip. Lotso led them on a long journey home, but when they arrived, Daisy had a new pink bear. Eventually, the three had ended up at Sunnyside. But Lotso had never stopped being angry. Now he controlled the nursery with cruelty.

Andy's toys were in danger. Woody was worried. He wanted to get back to Andy, but he couldn't leave his friends.

The next day, Woody hitched a ride back to Sunnyside in Bonnie's bag. He sneaked into the Caterpillar Room and looked for his friends. It was up to him to save them.

# Traveling at the Speed of Stitch

Stitch was bored. Everyone seemed to have somewhere to go and something to do during the day but him. Lilo went to school. Nani went to work. And Jumba and Pleakley headed off to serve beachgoers at their new snack stand, the Galactic Burger.

Stitch decided he needed a job. He and Lilo looked through the newspaper, searching for a job just right for a small, blue alien with a huge love of adventure. "Listen," said Lilo, pointing to an ad. "'Wanted: tour guide. Must have an outgoing personality and lots of energy.' That's you!"

The next morning, Stitch arrived at the tour agency wearing his best Hawaiian shirt and a big smile. Since no one else had applied, Stitch got the job!

"Aloha!" Stitch exclaimed when the vacationers arrived. He loaded them on a tour bus and pressed down on the gas pedal as far as it would go. "Palm trees!" he yelled as the scenery passed by in a blur. "Pineapples!" he shouted as they drove through a fruit stand.

Finally, the bus screeched to a stop at the beach. "Surfing!" Stitch announced, hurling his group onto surfboards and pushing them out to sea. After being battered by the waves, the tourists were eventually tossed back onto the beach.

Stitch herded them over to a barbecue pit. "Luau!" he explained.

But instead of food, Stitch returned with several flaming torches. Nani's friend, David, had taught Stitch how to juggle fire. The little alien was sure the vacationers would want to learn, too. Thank goodness Stitch just happened to bring along a fire extinguisher!

The last stop on Stitch's tour was the twenty-four-hour Hula Marathon. He gave his guests grass skirts and insisted they dance until they dropped as he played the ukulele. When they returned to the tour agency that night, the vacationers emerged from the bus exhausted, battered, bruised, and confused. The first thing they saw was the sign on the front of the tour agency: HAWAII: THE MOST RELAXING PLACE ON EARTH. Unless, of course, your tour guide happens to be from the planet Turo!

# A Rainy Night Out

"Yip!" Scamp barked at the squirrel nibbling on an acorn in the grass.

"Yip!" Scamp barked again, and the squirrel darted across the lawn. Scamp gave chase. The squirrel zipped over the fence and leaped onto a nearby tree branch. That was the problem with squirrels. They always got away too easily.

Disappointed, Scamp trotted along the pavement, stopping when he got to an open field. The grass here was tall, and butterflies flitted from wildflower to wildflower.

"Yip! Yip!" Scamp raced through the tall grass. He chased the butterflies to the end of the open field and back again.

It was getting dark. Scamp decided it was time to head home. He hadn't caught a single butterfly, but he'd had fun trying. He couldn't wait to tell his sisters about the new game he'd invented. They'd be so impressed!

Scamp trotted up to the front porch and tried to get through the doggie door. *Thunk!* His nose hit the wood, but it didn't move. The door was locked!

Scamp sat there for several minutes, barking. Nobody came to the door.

Suddenly—*boom!*—thunder echoed overhead. Lightning flashed, and rain began to fall.

Scamp bolted over to the big oak tree, sat down, and covered his eyes with his paws. Thunderstorms were scary!

"I'm not going to cry," he told himself as his eyes started to mist over. He shivered in the dark. He'd probably catch a cold by morning!

Scamp let out a little whimper and moved even closer to the tree trunk. He buried his wet nose in his wet paws and closed his eyes. He was just falling asleep when a sound made him start. Somebody was coming up the drive!

By the time Jim Dear and Darling were out of the taxi, Scamp was dashing across the lawn as fast as he could go. He bolted through the door just as it opened.

"Scamp, you're soaking wet!" Darling declared as the puppy found his sisters napping in front of the fire. As he lay down among them, Jim Dear came over with a warm towel to dry him off.

Home sweet home, Scamp thought happily as he drifted off to sleep.

# Mater Saves the Day

**B**ritish secret agents Finn McMissile and Holley Shiftwell had mistaken Mater for an American secret agent. Now he was helping them track the activities of a known criminal, Professor Z. The professor was blowing up race cars that used the new alternative fuel, Allinol.

Meanwhile, Lightning McQueen was taking part in the World Grand Prix—a three-city race sponsored by Allinol. Lightning thought Mater had gone back to Radiator Springs after the two of them had a fight. Little did he know that Professor Z had actually tied Mater, Holley, and Finn up inside a huge clock called Big Bentley in London!

Professor Z's goons, Grem and Acer, told Mater that they had planted a bomb inside Lightning's pit at the final race. After the pair left, Mater escaped and rushed to save his friend.

As Mater arrived at the pits, Finn radioed the tow truck. He had realized that the bomb was on *Mater*. Mater tried to leave the pits to save his friend, but Lightning was so happy to see Mater that he hooked himself on

to his buddy. Mater rocketed off before Professor Z could set off the bomb.

Holley flew off to help Mater, while Finn went after Professor Z.

Back on the streets of London, Grem and Acer were about to crash into Mater and Lightning. Holley rammed into the bad cars, who went flying into the air!

Just then, Finn arrived with Professor Z. He ordered him to deactivate the bomb on Mater, but Professor Z explained that only the car who activated the bomb could turn it off—and that was not him.

Suddenly, Mater figured out who the Lemons' Big Boss must be. He flew straight to Buckingham Palace with Lightning attached to his tow hook! Mater explained that Miles Axlerod had invented Allinol and made it look dangerous so everyone would go back to using gas. Then Axlerod and all the Lemons who owned the supply of oil would get rich! Axlerod was trapped. He had no choice but to deactivate the bomb. Mater had saved the day! As a thank you, the Queen made Mater a knight. No one was prouder of him than Lightning.

**OCTOBER**
**28**

# Kronk's Feast

"One more time!" Kronk cried. The Junior Chipmunks looked at their leader, took deep breaths, and launched into "We're Not Woodchucks" for the fourth time. Next to them, Bucky the squirrel and three of his friends sang along—in Squirrel. "Squeak sq-sq-squeak. Sq-sq-squeak squeak, squeaker, squeak."

While the kids and chipmunks began another verse, Kronk stood at the fire. He mixed, flipped, and seasoned in a frenzy. He had been cooking for hours, and the smells drifting toward the pooped troop were delicious.

"I'm . . . almost . . . ready." Kronk struggled to balance several platters on his arm before spinning around to present them to the kids in the troop. "Voilà!" The big man grinned. "Bon appétit!"

The kids leaned forward and smiled. The food looked as good as it smelled! They began to help themselves.

Everyone was pleased. Everyone, that is, except for Bucky and the squirrels. Where was *their* food? This was an outrage! The squirrels were Junior Chipmunks, too!

"Squeak! Squeaker, squeaker, squeak," Bucky mumbled behind his paw. He gave a quick nod, and all of them ran off toward Kronk's tent.

Bucky held open the tent flap, and the squirrels ducked inside. "Squeak," Bucky commanded as he pointed at Kronk's sleeping roll. The other squirrels nodded. They knew what they were supposed to do—chew holes in Kronk's bedding!

Just as the squirrels were about to get to work, they were interrupted.

"Oh, squeeeaak," Kronk's deep voice crooned from outside. "Squeaker squeeaak!"

The squirrels peeked outside the tent.

There was Kronk, holding a new platter. Balanced upon it were a golden-brown acorn soufflé and a bowl of steaming wild-berry sauce.

Bucky shrugged sheepishly at the leader.

"Thought I forgot you, huh? Would Kronk do that?" The leader set down the tray. "How about a hug?"

The four squirrels grasped the large man's legs and squeezed. All was forgiven. Together, all the Junior Chipmunks enjoyed their meals.

# The Great Escape

Buzz, Jessie, and most of Andy's other toys were trapped at Sunnyside Daycare. Woody had escaped, but he had come back after hearing that an evil bear named Lotso controlled the nursery. Woody crept inside the room where his friends were trapped and watched as a group of toddlers played roughly with them. He was shocked!

*RIIING!!! RIIING!!!* A toy telephone sidled up to Woody. The cowboy picked up the receiver and heard, "You and your friends ain't ever gettin' outta here now." The phone explained that Lotso kept tabs on everyone. The only time toys left was when they were thrown away.

When the kids went outside to play, Woody came out of hiding. The others told him about Lotso's cruelty, and Buzz's strange behavior. Lotso had reset Buzz, and he didn't recognize his own friends anymore.

"Oh, Woody," said Jessie, "we were wrong to leave Andy."

"It's my fault for leaving you guys," Woody replied. "From now on, we stick together."

But Jessie knew Woody needed to get home before Andy left for college.

Woody nodded. He had a plan. They would escape through the garbage chute.

That night, the toys put their escape plan into action. Some of the toys distracted Buzz, while Barbie forced Ken to confess that Buzz had been reset to "demo" mode. Then Mr. Potato Head distracted Big Baby, which gave the toys a chance to capture Buzz.

Jessie and the others found the keys to the playroom, and the toys slipped into the playground!

Meanwhile, Barbie had found Buzz's instruction manual. She, Woody, and Slinky held Buzz down while Hamm found the instructions to reset the space ranger. Suddenly, Buzz beeped— and began speaking Spanish! There was no time to figure out what had happened. They hustled Buzz out the door and into the playground. When Buzz saw Jessie, he dropped to his knees: "*¡Mi florecilla del desierto!*"

"Did you fix Buzz?" asked Jessie, confused.

"Sort of," Woody replied.

But could they ever *really* fix Buzz?

**OCTOBER**
**30**

# Handy Helpers

It was a special day at the Clubhouse. Everyone was coming over for dinner!

Suddenly, the doorbell rang. As the professor's Handy Helper went to open the door, it got stuck!

"None of the Handy Helpers are working," said Professor Von Drake. "Handy Helpers' springer-dingers aren't spring-a-dinging! The Handy Helpers are broken! Something must be wrong with the Handy Dandy machine that makes the Handy Helpers work!"

Mickey knew they needed some help. "Oh, Toodles!" he called.

Soon Toodles arrived with four Mouseketools: a bottle of shampoo, a net, shaped wrenches, and the Mystery Mouseketool.

Mickey, Minnie, and Goofy took the Silly Slide downstairs to where the Handy Dandy machine was.

"Hyuk. The bolts are loose!" said Goofy. "We need the shaped wrenches!"

Mickey quickly tightened the bolts. Then Minnie turned the crank. Slowly the gears started to turn. The machine was working.

Then, suddenly, the gears stopped working again. They were stuck—and so

was Goofy! He had gotten caught in the machine's gears!

"We need a Mouseketool to make the gears slippery so that Goofy can slip out of them," said Mickey. "Oh, Toodles!"

Mickey took the bottle of shampoo from Toodles and poured in on the gears. Soon Goofy had slipped free. But the Handy Dandy machine still wasn't working.

"Maybe some other parts need fixing, too," said Minnie.

Suddenly, Pluto started to bark. He had found something!

Mickey bent down to take a look. Pluto's squeaky ball was stuck under the gear.

"That must be what has stopped the machine from working," said Mickey. "But how can we get the ball out? Oh, Toodles!"

This time Mickey needed the Mystery Mouseketool. It was a giant pair of tweezers!

Mickey pulled Pluto's squeaky blue ball out of the Handy Dandy machine! Finally, the gears started to turn and the Handy Hands began working again.

"Phew, that was a lot of work," said Mickey. "I'm hungry!"

Fixed at last, the Handy Helpers helped Mickey and his friends make dinner.

# Happy Halloween

"**B**oo?" James P. Sullivan whispered, poking his head through the door. "Hey, Boo, are you here? I came to wish you a happy Halloween. Boo?"

There was no answer. The big, furry blue monster took one step into the quiet bedroom, then another. There was no sign of his little human friend.

Sulley sighed, his shoulders slumping. "Oh, well. Guess you're not here right now," he murmured. He couldn't help feeling disappointed. He'd been looking forward all day to visiting his favorite human child that evening.

There was no Halloween in Monstropolis, but Sulley knew that it was the one day of the year when human kids actually *liked* being scared. It seemed like a good day for a visit from a monster—especially a friendly monster.

Sulley yawned. "Guess I could just sit down here and wait," he murmured, sitting on the edge of Boo's bed. His eyes drooped. He leaned back on the bed and yawned again.

"Guess I could just rest my eyes for a little . . ." Sulley mumbled as he drifted off to sleep. "*Zzzzz.*"

The next thing Sulley knew, a cool breeze was tickling his fur. He felt someone poking him in the foot. "Not yet, Mike," he grunted. "It's too early to get up for work, I—AHHHHH!"

He had just opened his eyes. Instead of Mike's familiar round green body, he saw . . .

"A GHOST!" he shrieked. He leaped up and started to run out of the room to escape the horrifying, flapping white creature standing at the end of the bed. "Oh, nooooooo!"

The ghost giggled. "Kitty?" it said happily.

Sulley stopped in his tracks. "Er, what did you say?"

"Kitty!" the ghost cried again. It reached up, grabbed its ghostly white hood and pulled it back from its face.

When Sulley saw what was under the hood, he broke into a smile.

Suddenly Sulley felt very foolish. He'd completely forgotten that every Halloween, human children dressed up in costumes to try to scare each other. It sure had worked on him!

"Boo!" he exclaimed joyfully, reaching out to hug her. "It's you! Happy Halloween, you little monster!"

# Slugger

Pinocchio, as you know, was not always a real boy. First he was a puppet. And before that, he was a log. And before that, he was the trunk of a tall, shady tree. But that's of no great importance to our story; it's simply to remind you that Pinocchio was not always a boy—and that to him, being a real boy was indeed a dream come true.

One day, when Pinocchio was walking home from school, he spied a whole group of boys gathered in a field just down the road.

"What are you doing?" asked Pinocchio.

"Playing baseball," said a red-haired boy.

"Baseball?" Pinocchio hadn't heard of that game before. But it sounded like fun! "Can I play?" he asked.

The boys nodded. "You can play first base."

Pinocchio grinned. First base! That sounded important! This game was going to be fun. Now, if he could just work out which base was first . . .

Luckily, the other boys ran off to their bases, leaving just one empty. Pinocchio trotted out to the dusty square. Then he waited to see what came next.

"Batter up!"

*Whoosh!*

*Crack!*

It didn't take long. One fast pitch, and before Pinocchio knew it, a ball was sailing over his head and a tall boy was running full speed at him!

"*Ahhhhh!*" Pinocchio screamed, covering his face with his big glove.

The runner was safe. And Pinocchio was moved to right field. But on the very next pitch, where should the ball fly, but up . . . up . . . up . . . and down to right field. This time, Pinocchio tried to catch it—but it landed with a *plop* on the grass behind him.

But Pinocchio never gave up, and when it was finally his turn to bat, he stepped into the batter's box and held his head high. To Pinocchio's surprise, the bat felt strangely natural in his hands . . . almost like a part of his old wooden self.

He watched the pitcher carefully, and on the first pitch—*crack!*—he sent the ball high and away, into the sky.

"Hooray!" the boys cheered. A slugger had been born! And a real boy had learned a new game.

# We're Going on a Picnic

"Cap'n?" Mr. Smee knocked softly on Captain Hook's door. There was no answer. The chubby first mate pushed his way inside, carrying a breakfast tray. "I've got breakfast, Cap'n."

"I'm not hungry!" Captain Hook replied. "Go away!"

"But, Cap'n, you have to eat." Smee was getting worried. The captain hadn't eaten in days. In fact, he hadn't even gotten out of bed! "I know you feel bad about Pe—" Smee stopped himself from saying the dreaded name just in time. "—that flying boy. And the croc—I mean, that ticking reptile, too."

Captain Hook was really angry about being beaten by Peter again. Even worse, Peter had set the crocodile right back on Captain Hook's trail. "But we haven't seen hide nor scale of either of them for a week. I think the coast is clear."

There was no reply from Captain Hook.

Smee thought for a minute. "I know how to cheer you up!" he cried. "We'll have a nice old-fashioned picnic! Won't that be lovely?"

Again, silence from Captain Hook.

"Ah-ah-ah! No arguments!" Smee left the breakfast tray and hurried down to the galley. A picnic on Mermaid Island was just what the doctor ordered!

When the picnic basket was packed, Smee called down to Hook, "It's time to go, Cap'n!"

After a while, Captain Hook finally appeared on deck, blinking in the sunlight. "Fine," he said grumpily. "But I know I'm not going to have fun!"

Smee let the rowboat down into the water, and Hook began to climb down the rope ladder. Once he was safely in the boat, Smee picked up the picnic basket.

*Tick tock tick tock tick tock!*

"Smee!" cried Hook. "Help me!"

Smee peeked over the side of the ship. The crocodile was about to take a bite out of the rowboat! In a panic, he threw the only thing he had on hand— the picnic basket. It landed right in the crocodile's open mouth. The crocodile stared at Smee in surprise. Then, without a sound, it slipped back under the water.

"Next time you have any smart ideas about cheering me up," said the captain, glaring at his first mate, "keep them to yourself!"

# Bring a Friend

Hercules was training to be a hero, and boy, was it a lot of work. One day, Phil, his coach, set up a practice course for Hercules. Phil had put a doll in the course. He said it was a "practice damsel in distress" and Hercules was supposed to rescue it.

So the hero-in-training barreled into the first section of the course—a darkened cave. Herc plunged into darkness and fell headfirst into stagnant water.

"Yech!" Hercules spit out the putrid water and scowled.

Feeling his way through the dark water with his feet, Herc noticed something slithery slipping around his ankles. Snakes! He hurried toward the other end of the cave and dove into the daylight, shaking the last snake off his feet. Panting, Herc lay down on the grass to rest for a moment.

"Rest later!" Phil shouted.

Herc slowly rolled over. The doll had to be around here somewhere.

Then Hercules heard stamping hooves behind him and turned around. A huge ox was barreling down on him! Herc jumped to his feet and dodged the ox.

At last, he spotted it: The doll was sitting twenty feet above him on the edge of a steep cliff.

At least Phil had left him a rope. In fact, it looked as though Phil had left two. Gripping the first rope in his jaws, Herc inched steadily upward. He was about halfway up when Phil lit the end of the second rope, which was soaked with oil! The fire raced up the rope toward a stack of dry wood under Herc's damsel.

Hercules threw himself the last few feet. He tackled the damsel, rolling away from the stack of wood, which was now blazing merrily away.

Breathing hard, Hercules finally relaxed.

"And another thing . . ." Phil's gruff voice echoed up to him from the base of the cliff. Hercules held his breath, but not because he was waiting for Phil's next words. Herc was holding his breath because he had spotted a scorpion next to his foot. The insect was poised to sting!

*Crunch.* Hercules's winged horse, Pegasus, used his hoof to flatten the creature. Hercules smiled at Pegasus as Phil's final words of advice reached his ears. It was the best tip yet:

"Always bring a friend!"

# The Storm

One summer afternoon, Jenny invited Dodger and his gang to go on a picnic with her and Oliver in Central Park.

"Go play with your friends," Jenny told the kitten.

As Jenny, Fagin, and Winston the butler unpacked the picnic basket, they didn't notice that the animals were romping farther and farther away. Suddenly, thunder boomed and rain poured down. Then lightning struck a tree.

"I must get you home!" Winston insisted, rushing Jenny out of the park.

"Where's Oliver?" she cried.

"Don't worry," said Fagin. "Dodger will take care of him."

In the morning, Dodger woke up under a tree. Oliver had climbed it when the storm had started. The rest of the gang ran to find shelter, but Dodger had stayed with Oliver all night.

"Hey there, kid!" Dodger called. "You ready to go home now?"

"Yes!" said Oliver, climbing down. "And I've made a new friend. He says he's lost. Maybe Jenny will adopt him, too."

"Wow," said Dodger. "I didn't know cats could grow so big!"

"I'm a bear cub," the creature said.

"Where did you come from?" Dodger asked.

The bear started to cry. "I don't know!" he wailed. "I was scared of the storm, so I climbed a tree. Then a big wind blew me out of the tree. The next thing I knew I was out here on the lawn. So I climbed this tree and met Oliver. Can you help me find my mama?"

Oliver shook his head sadly. "I'm afraid I don't know where bears live in New York City."

"Wait!" Dodger said. "I think I do." He took Oliver and the cub to a fancy entrance with a big iron gate that read CENTRAL PARK ZOO. When the zookeeper saw the cub, he rushed over and led him back to his mother.

"Mama!" cried the bear cub. The mama bear hugged her cub close, and Dodger smiled down at Oliver.

"Time to get you home, too."

When Jenny saw that Oliver was safe and sound, she kissed and hugged him— and Dodger, too.

"Thank you, Dodger!" Jenny cried. "You're my hero!"

"Mine, too," said Oliver. "A friend like you makes even the scariest storm *bear*able!"

# My Heart Belongs to Daisy

Andy's toys were escaping from Sunnyside Daycare, and from the evil bear, Lotso. They wanted to get back home to Andy before he left for college.

The friends crept past Lotso's sidekick, Big Baby, and across the playground. Then the group headed over to the garbage chute.

Woody climbed inside and slid down the dark chute. When he stopped, he was outside. Beneath him was a big trash bin.

"Come on down!" he called to the other toys.

When all of the toys had arrived, Slinky formed a bridge between the chute and the lid of the huge bin. But before the toys could make their escape, Lotso appeared! He kicked Slinky's paws off the bin's lid.

As Andy's toys stared at Lotso and his toys, a garbage truck turned into the alley. The toys could hear it rumbling toward them.

"Why don't you come back and join our family again?" Lotso asked the toys.

"You're a liar and a bully and I'd rather rot in this dumpster than join any family of yours!" Jessie replied.

Lotso scowled. "I didn't throw you away," he replied. "Your kid did. There isn't one kid who ever loved a toy, really."

"What about Daisy?" Woody asked. "She lost you. By accident."

Woody had learned that Lotso had once belonged to a little girl named Daisy. He had been replaced when she'd accidentally lost him. Woody held up the old pendant a clown called Chuckles—who had also belonged to Daisy—had given him. It read: "My heart belongs to DAISY."

Lotso was stunned. "Where did you get that?" he demanded.

"She loved you, Lotso," declared Woody. "As much as any kid ever loved a toy!" He threw the pendant across the huge bin, where it landed at Lotso's feet.

"She never loved me!" Lotso exploded. "She left me! Love means being together forever or it isn't love!"

Lotso's gang stared at him in disbelief. They had never seen Lotso so angry and upset. Would he remember how much Daisy had loved him and let Andy's toys go home?

# Friends Forever

Experiment 626 was a blue creature from a distant planet who was punished for being very naughty and destroying everything around him. One day, he escaped his planet in a police cruiser and headed straight for Earth!

On the tiny island of Kauai was a little girl named Lilo. She found it hard to make friends and was very lonely.

One night, Lilo had a fight with her sister, Nani. Lilo went to her room and slammed the door shut. Out of her window, Lilo saw a falling star and made a wish: "I wish for someone to be my friend," she whispered.

The falling star that Lilo had seen was actually Experiment 626's ship crashing on the island! A truck driver found him and took him to an animal shelter. All the other animals were scared of 626, but he didn't care. He scrunched two of his four arms in toward his torso so he would look more like a dog. That way, he'd be adopted and have a place to hide from the aliens who were chasing him.

The next day, Nani decided to take Lilo to the shelter to pick a new pet.

"Hi!" Lilo said when she saw 626.

"Hi," the creature replied, and then he gave her a hug. Lilo walked back to the front room and told Nani she'd found the dog she wanted.

"He's good," she said. "I can tell. His name is . . . Stitch."

They took Stitch home even though Nani thought he looked strange. Nani was glad Lilo finally had a friend.

At home, however, Stitch began to tear things apart and cause trouble for Nani.

"We have to take him back," Nani said.

"We adopted him!" Lilo cried. "What about *ohana*? Dad said *ohana* means *family*! And family means—"

"Nobody gets left behind," Nani finished. "I know."

She remembered how welcoming her parents had been and how important family was to them. She changed her mind. She would give Stitch another chance—for Lilo's sake.

From then on, Lilo and Stitch stuck together through anything that came their way. Lilo helped Stitch learn how to behave, and Stitch became the friend that Lilo had wished for on a falling star.

# The Best Repairman

Manny ran to answer the phone. "Handy Manny's Repair Shop. You break it, we fix it!"

"Manny? It's Jasmine Chung from the *Sheet Rock Hills Herald*. I'm calling to let you know you've been picked as the county's best repairman!"

Manny couldn't believe it. Jasmine wanted to interview Manny at his next repair job. He was going to fix Sparrow Fountain at the park.

"A reporter is coming to interview me at the park!" Manny told the tools.

At the park, Manny inspected the damage to the fountain. All the pipes inside were broken and the fountain was empty. The park's birds had nothing to drink

Just then, a woman raced over. "Manny! Jasmine Chung here," she said quickly. "Ready for the interview? Yes? Okay, then. Take a seat!"

Manny was unsure. He thought he should fix the fountain first. But Jasmine was talking so fast. Maybe she was in a rush.

"So, did you always want to be a repairman?"

"Oh, yes." Manny grinned. "My parents tell me that 'fix' was my very first word!"

"That's a great quote," Jasmine said. "I may even put that under your picture!"

"Picture?!" shouted Dusty, as she and the other tools gathered around. Manny decided it was time to start fixing the fountain. Jasmine got her camera ready. Not wanting to miss out, the tools began practicing their best poses. Soon they were all hopping around Jasmine.

"Tools—STOP!" Manny ordered. "I know you want your pictures in the paper, but you're forgetting why Jasmine wants our picture to begin with—because we help others by fixing things. But we can't help anyone if you're all too busy posing. So, let's think about why we're really here."

"To help others!" cheered Dusty. "Let's get going and fix it right!"

So Manny and the tools worked together to fix the fountain.

"Wow, Manny, you really *are* the county's best repairman!" raved Jasmine.

The following week, all of the tools appeared in the paper. "I may be the county's best repairman," Manny said. "But you're the county's best tools!"

# Mater in Paris

One lazy afternoon, Mater was listening to music. Suddenly the music stopped and a voice spoke to Mater through the radio. It was British secret agent Holley Shiftwell!

"Hello, Mater!" she said. "Sorry to startle you. I'm contacting you because Finn and I need your help. We're in Paris tracking several Lemons who escaped from the World Grand Prix. Will you help?"

"Sure thing!" Mater said. "Love to!"

Suddenly, Siddeley the spy plane landed in the middle of Main Street! Mater's best friend, Lightning McQueen, drove up.

"Mater, what's going on?" he asked.

"I'm going on a secret mission to Paris," whispered Mater. "You wanna come, too?"

Lightning agreed, and the two set off to meet Holley and Finn.

"We've been tailing these Lemons for a while, but they keep getting away," Finn said.

"Them Lemons are tricky," said Mater. "You just gotta learn how to think like them. If I was a Lemon, I'd make sure I had plenty of spare parts."

"Brilliant," said Finn. "You and Lightning can visit the spare parts dealer at the marketplace. Holley and I will head to the markets on the west side of Paris."

But Lightning and Mater were too late. The spare parts dealer had been robbed!

"Them Lemons was here already," said Mater. Then he spotted a trail of spare parts on the ground. The pair followed the trail all the way to a nearby café where Mater noticed two strange-looking cars. One of them backfired and his grille fell off. It was a disguise!

"Lemons!" cried Mater. "Their old exhausts make 'em backfire!"

The Lemons quickly fled the café. Lightning and Mater followed them through the city. Suddenly, there were not one, not two, but six Lemons surrounding them!

Mater quickly spun his tow hook. He caught one of the Lemons and knocked it out. Soon more Lemons arrived. Mater had an idea. . . .

Lightning and Mater led the Lemons on a chase, all the way to the top of the Eiffel Tower. By the time they stopped, the Lemons were so exhausted, they tipped over. It was another great mission completed by secret agent Mater!

# Late for Supper

Widow Tweed filled the large baking pan with meat and vegetables, then rolled out a flaky crust and set it on top. After crimping the pie's edges, she slipped the pan into the oven.

"Chicken potpie," she said. "Tod's favorite!"

Widow Tweed looked out the window and noticed that the sun was setting.

"I wonder where that clever little devil has got to," she said.

She watched the sun sink behind the rolling forest hills, then sat down and picked up her knitting. She had a project to finish. Besides, the potpie should be ready soon, and Tod was never late for supper.

"Knit one, purl two, knit one, purl two," the widow said quietly as she put the finishing touches on a soft blanket she was knitting for Tod's bed.

The smell of chicken potpie drifted past her nose, and the widow got up to take it out of the oven. Suddenly she heard a scratching at the door.

"Right on time, as usual," she said as she opened the door. "Dinner's ready, Tod."

But Tod wasn't there. The scratching had just been a small twig blown against the door by the wind.

"Tod?" Widow Tweed called, peering into the darkness. "No playing tricks, now." But the little red fox did not appear.

"Oh, Tod," she said. "Where are you?"

Stepping back into the house, she pulled on her shoes and a sweater. She'd just have to go out to look for him. After lighting an old kerosene lantern, she opened the door for a second time—and nearly tripped over the red fox on her front porch. He sat there quietly, a colorful bouquet of wildflowers at his feet.

"Oh, Tod!" Widow Tweed cried. She picked up the bouquet and scooped him into her arms. "You sweetie pie."

Tod nuzzled the widow's neck as she carried him into the house and deposited him on his chair at the kitchen table. Soon, the two were sharing a delicious feast of chicken potpie. And after supper, the widow admired her bouquet above the mantel while Tod curled up in his bed with his cozy new blanket.

# Crack the Whip!

Mickey woke up and looked outside. It had snowed last night! "It's a perfect day for ice skating!" he cried. "I'll invite all my friends."

When Mickey and his friends got to the pond, everyone laced up their skates and made their way onto the ice.

"Hey, I have an idea!" shouted Mickey. "Let's play crack the whip!"

Nobody else knew how to play, so Mickey explained the game. "I'll start out as the leader," he said. "We all join hands and form a line. Then we all skate around and around in a big circle. Once we get going, the skater at the end of the line lets go!"

"That sounds like fun!" said Goofy.

They all joined hands and began skating in a circle.

"Okay, Donald, let go!" Mickey said.

Donald let go and went sailing away. Around and around and around the rest of the gang went.

"Now, you go, Daisy!" cried Mickey. Daisy let go and went flying away across the ice.

Next went Huey, then Dewey, and finally Louie. Goofy followed them.

Now just Mickey and Minnie were left. Around and around they skated. Then Mickey shouted, "Let go, Minnie!"

Minnie let go and zoomed off with a squeal.

Mickey continued to skate. When he finally came to a stop, it took quite some time for his head to stop spinning.

"Wasn't that fun, guys?" he said. "Want to do it again? Guys? Where is everyone?"

Mickey looked around. Where had everyone gone?

And then he saw them: seven pairs of ice skates at the ends of seven pairs of legs were sticking out of seven different snowbanks, kicking away!

"Uh-oh," said Mickey. He dashed over to the side of the pond and, one by one, he pulled all of his friends out of the snow.

Goofy shook his head, and snow flew everywhere. "That was fun!" he said cheerfully. "But I sure could use a cup of—"

"Yoo-hoo!" came a cheerful cry. It was Grandma Duck, standing at the edge of the pond. She was carrying a thermos filled with hot chocolate!

"Hooray!" cried all the friends. It was the perfect way to warm up.

# Big Baby Gets Revenge

Andy's toys were escaping from Sunnyside Daycare. They wanted to get back home to Andy before he left for college.

But an evil pink bear named Lotso didn't want Andy's toys to leave the day care center.

Standing on the edge of a huge garbage bin, Woody mentioned Lotso and Big Baby's owner, a girl named Daisy. Daisy had loved them very much, but she had lost them.

Listening to Woody talk about Daisy upset Big Baby. Furious, Lotso shoved Big Baby. "What? You want your mommy back? She never loved you!"

But Big Baby wasn't taking Lotso's orders anymore. He hoisted Lotso into the air and threw him into the huge bin! Then Big Baby slammed the lid shut. He'd had enough of Lotso's cruelty. He was ready for a better life.

"C'mon! Hurry!" cried Woody, running across the closed lid toward safety. A garbage truck was on its way to collect the trash. If they were still on the lid, it would take them, too.

The toys followed Woody and climbed to safety on a wall. Suddenly,

Woody heard a squeak. He turned and saw an Alien caught between the bin lids!

Woody rushed back to free his little friend. He wasn't leaving anyone behind.

Just then, Lotso's paw reached up from the bin and grabbed Woody's leg! Horrified, the toys watched as Woody was yanked down—just as the garbage truck arrived!

Jessie, Buzz, and the rest of Andy's toys fearlessly jumped onto the huge lid and tried to force it open. But the garbage truck was lifting the entire container and tilting it toward the back of the truck.

The lid swung open, with Woody desperately holding on.

"Woody!" Jessie shouted, grabbing the cowboy doll's hand just as Lotso tumbled past.

But as the huge bin tilted upside down and trash rained down on them, Woody and Jessie lost their grip.

Woody and the rest of the toys fell into the back of the garbage truck. They were heading for the landfill! How were they going to get home to Andy now?

# Jake and the Spyglass

Captain Hook and Smee were searching for treasure on Pirate Island. "Blast it, Smee! There's nothing but seashells on this seashore," said Hook. "Where is all the treasure?"

Just then, Captain Hook noticed something shiny in the water. "There's treasure out there on the water!" he said. "Give me my spyglass."

"Oh, dear," said Smee. "I'm afraid I . . . I don't have your spyglass, Cap'n."

Hook and Smee decided to row out and fetch the treasure in their dinghy. But they needed the spyglass to find the dinghy!

On another part of the beach, Jake and his pirate crew were splashing about and having fun in the sea. Suddenly, Hook spotted their belongings on the beach.

"Do you see what I see, Smee?" asked Hook. "It's Jake's spyglass on that towel!" And using his fishing hook, he nabbed Jake's spyglass!

"Crackers!" cried Skully. "That not-so-sneaky snook just ran off with our spyglass!"

"Hurry, mateys, into the rowboat," said Jake. "We'll catch them in the water!"

"Well, hello, Captain," Jake said. "I think you have something that belongs to us!" He took his spyglass.

Hook was upset, but then he remembered the shiny thing in the water. "Who needs the spyglass when there is treasure here!"

"Look, Cap'n, it's your spyglass!" said Smee pointing at the shiny thing.

"At least something has gone my way today!" said Hook.

Hook looked through his spyglass and saw . . . a giant eye! It was Tick-Tock Croc!

"Smee, what are you waiting for? Row!" yelled Hook, dropping his spyglass back in the water.

Jake and his crew were watching from afar. "Whoa!" said Izzy. "It looks like Hook might never see his spyglass again!"

"That's too bad," said Jake. "If Hook had just asked us if he could borrow our spyglass, we could've helped him."

"It's like you always say, Jake," said Cubby. "You should ask permission before you borrow something that isn't yours."

"I hope that sneaky snook learns his lesson," said Skully.

"Let's head back to Pirate Island," said Jake.

# Just Like Everyone Else

There was wild cheering in the stadium at Monsters University.

The Oozma Kappas had won the Scare Games!

The OKs hoisted Mike Wazowski, their team leader, up into the air. He had gotten the loudest scream of any of the competitors in the scare simulator.

Mike was delighted, but he was also relieved. It meant he could rejoin the university's Scare Program. Dean Hardscrabble had kicked Mike and Sulley out after they had accidentally broken her famous scare canister. But she had agreed to let the whole team join if they won the Scare Games.

For Mike, this was a special moment. He had proven to everyone that he had what it took to become a top Scarer.

Alone a few minutes later, he went back into the simulator to relive the moment. He turned to the robot-child and said, "Boo!"

Once again, the robot screamed.

"I knew I was scary. I didn't know I was that scary," Mike told Sulley, who was watching from the doorway.

Mike bent down to look at the settings on the simulator. Someone had changed them from "hard" to "easy." It was Sulley!

Mike was hurt and angry.

"You said you believed in me, but you're just like everyone else!" he yelled and stormed away.

As Sulley wandered across campus, students congratulated him on his win. Even the RORs, the best fraternity on campus, asked him to join them. Sulley felt awful. He knew he didn't deserve their praise.

Meanwhile, Mike snuck over to the Door Tech department and stole a key to the lab where students tested doors to the human world. He was going to prove to everyone once and for all that he was scary.

Back on campus, Sulley confessed everything to Dean Hardscrabble.

"You did what?" she exclaimed. "I expect you off campus by tomorrow!"

Suddenly, the alarm sounded in the Door Tech Lab. Dean Hardscrabble flew off to investigate.

Sulley's heart sank. He was sure it was Mike who had set off the alarm, and that meant he was in serious trouble.

Sulley had to help his friend!

# Bring on the Scare!

"No, no, no!" Jack Skellington cried, swooping down on a small ghoul carving a grisly face into a pumpkin. "That's much too scary! Didn't I tell you that Santa Claus is coming today?"

"Sorry, Jack." She started to carve a fuzzy kitten face into a fresh pumpkin.

"That's better." Jack beamed at her, then moved on. He walked through Halloweentown, overseeing the preparations.

"This year will be even better than last year," Jack said to himself. "We've learned so much from dear Santa Claus!"

The year before, Jack and the rest of Halloweentown had tried to take over Santa's holiday, Christmas. But they had learned that it was better to stick to what they knew best.

Jack peered into the graveyard and gasped. Several citizens were dressing up the ghosts in chains and tattered rags.

"Oh, this won't do at all!" he exclaimed.

"Sorry, Jack." The Halloweentown citizens quickly traded the chains for garlands of flowers.

Finally Santa arrived.

"Welcome, Santa!" the Mayor cried.

"Welcome to Halloweentown!"

"Thank you," Santa said. "I'd love to see what you have prepared."

"Of course!" Jack clapped his hands, and the townspeople paraded past Santa. They showed off their pretty pumpkins, flowery ghosts, and all the rest of their work.

Santa looked a little disappointed.

"What's the matter?" Jack asked anxiously. "Was that too scary? We tried to make sure you wouldn't be frightened."

"Is that what's wrong?" Santa cried. "Don't be silly! You can't de-fright Halloween."

"But we thought you didn't like what we did to Christmas last year," Jack said.

"I didn't," Santa explained. "But that's because it was Christmas—the children were expecting sugar plums and teddy bears, not ghouls and goblins. But at Halloween, it's just the opposite!"

"You're right," Jack mused. "Okay, let's get back to work!"

Instantly, the townspeople produced an array of horrifying tricks and treats, scary jack-o'-lanterns, moaning ghosts, and more.

"Ho, ho, ho!" Santa cried as a gang of shrieking banshees chased him out of Halloweentown. "That's more like it!"

# For Old Time's Sake

Prince John had taken advantage of the people of the kingdom while his brother, King Richard, was away at war. He had taxed them until no one had any money—and he had it all! But at last, good King Richard had returned to Nottingham and sentenced greedy Prince John and his cronies, the Sheriff of Nottingham and Sir Hiss, to hard time in the rock mines.

The king summoned Robin to the castle one day soon after his return. "Brave Robin Hood," he said, "in recognition of all you have done to defend and protect them while I was gone, I ask if you would do the honor of returning this money to the citizens of Nottingham, to whom it rightfully belongs."

Robin Hood beamed. "Your Majesty," he replied, "it would be my honor."

The next day, at the appointed time, Robin Hood arrived at the castle, ready to perform his duty. He found King Richard waiting for them just inside the main gate. Next to the king was a wagon overloaded with bags of gold coins.

Robin Hood smiled and looked at the wagon. He looked at Little John. He looked at the king. He looked back at the wagon. Then his smile faded.

"Something doesn't feel right," Robin Hood said, turning to face Little John. "Something is . . . *missing*."

"Missing?" Little John said, surprised.

"Of course!" Robin Hood cried. For all those years under Prince John's rule, he had *robbed* from the rich to give to the poor. That was his thing. Giving to the poor without the robbing from the rich part felt somehow . . . incomplete. Now that generous King Richard was back, there would be no need to rob from the rich.

Naturally, thought Robin, that was a good thing. And yet . . . it *was* the end of an era.

"Your Majesty," Robin Hood said to the king, "I don't suppose you could make this handing over of the money a bit more . . . oh, I don't know . . . *challenging*?"

King Richard wrinkled his brow. "Challenging?" he replied, puzzled.

Robin Hood turned to Little John, who also looked confused. "What do you say? One last heist . . . for old times' sake?"

# Pooh Welcomes Winter

Pooh had heard that Winter was coming soon, and he was very excited about having a visitor. Pooh and Piglet decided to throw a party to welcome Winter to the Hundred-Acre Wood. The two friends set off to tell everyone.

Outside, it was snowing. They met Tigger along the way, and they walked to Kanga and Roo's house together. They all decided to go by sled to the party. Owl landed on a branch overhead.

"Winter has arrived!" he declared. "I heard Christopher Robin say so."

Pooh told Owl about the party, and then they all jumped on the sled and slid down the hill toward Christopher Robin's house together.

"There's Winter!" Tigger cried. "Tiggers always know Winter when they see him. That big white face—that carroty nose. Who else could he be?" said Tigger.

"Well," said Pooh, "he looks shy. We should be extra friendly." He walked right up to Winter. "How do you do? We are giving a party in your honor."

But Winter did not say anything.

"Oh d-d-dear," said Piglet. "He's frozen!"

"Quick!" cried Tigger. "We'd better get him to the party and warm him up."

They hoisted Winter onto the sled. When they slid up to Pooh's house, the others were already there. Owl had hung a big friendly sign over Pooh's door. It said WELCOME WINTER. Pooh and Tigger wrestled Winter off the sled.

Just then, Christopher Robin tramped up to the door in his big boots. "Has anyone seen my snowman?" he asked.

"No," said Pooh glumly, "but we brought Winter here for a special party. He doesn't seem to like it."

Christopher Robin laughed. "Silly old bear!" He explained to Pooh that Winter was not a person, it was a season. A time of year for cold snow, hot chocolate, warm fires, and good friends.

Pooh scratched his nose thoughtfully. "Yes, I see now," he said. "Of course, I am a bear of very little brain."

With Christopher Robin's help, Pooh put the snowman back where it belonged. He and his friends decided to have the party anyway to celebrate Winter. So everyone sang songs and danced around the snowman until they couldn't dance anymore. What a party!

# All in this Together

Andy's toys we[re] in trouble. [Recentl]y [a]s they toddled off toward
They had bee[n] [... ] [the crane.]
to escape Sun[ny ... ] [... Woody] [t]ried to go after them, but
Daycare and had ended up [... ] [a huge b]u[l]ldozer roared across his
a garbage truck. The truck [... ] [path. The A]liens were gone. Suddenly
forward, then lurched to a [... ] [Woody ... ] [... ]er turned toward Woody
could hear its forklift picki[ng] [... up ... ] [frie]nds. Soon, the toys were
another huge bin. "Agains[t] [the wall ... ] a tumbling pile of trash!
Quick!" he yelled.

*It's your Daddy's Birthday!*

Jessie was stuck! Buzz raced over
and freed her just as the bin began
emptying above them. He threw her
out of the path of falling trash. But he
wasn't fast enough to get away. A TV
crashed down right on top of him!

Buzz's friends desperately dug him
out. When they found him, they were
thrilled to discover that Buzz was back
to his old self! He had been reset to
"demo" mode by Lotso, and had ended
up speaking Spanish when the others
had tried to fix him.

Soon the truck arrived at the Tri-
County Landfill. It dumped its whole
load out onto the ground. The dirty,
frightened toys struggled out from
under the debris and saw a giant trash
heap. In the distance, they could see a
huge crane.

"The claaaaw!" shouted the Aliens

The toys fell down and down until
they landed on a conveyor belt. Buzz
got his head stuck in a can, which
flew up and stuck to another conveyor
belt above them. It was magnetic!
Slinky got pulled up, too—and saw
that the lower belt led right into a
shredder! The rest of the toys tried to
save themselves by grabbing onto any
metal they could find.

Suddenly, a pink paw reached out
from beneath a bag. "Help!" begged
Lotso.

Woody and Buzz dropped down and
used a golf club to pry the bag off the
trapped bear. The shredder was just
inches away!

As Lotso scrambled free, Woody
grabbed his paw. They pointed the golf
club toward the magnet and all three
were lifted to safety.

But could they get free?

It's your Antie grace's Birthday!

Disney·PIXAR
MONSTERS, INC.

**NOVEMBER**
**18**

# Monster Day Care

Mike always arrived at Monsters, Inc. at half past eight, stowed his lunch box in his locker, and promptly reported to his station on the Laugh Floor. But one morning, as he came out of the locker room, Celia was waiting for him.

"We have a little problem, Mike," she said. "The day care teacher is sick today, so we need a sub. And seeing as how you've already met your laugh quota for the month, I thought maybe *you*—"

"Day care!" cried Mike. "Wait just a—"

Just then, Sulley stepped in. "Happy to do it, Celia," he interrupted. "Day care, here we come."

"Are you crazy?" Mike grumbled.

"What's the big deal?" Sulley shrugged. "We handled Boo, didn't we? What's a few more kids? We'll eat a few snacks. Watch a few videos. Play a little peekaboo. It's like having a paid vacation, Mike, my man!"

But the minute they opened the day care room door, they both knew Sulley was wrong.

There were monster children everywhere! Swinging from the ceiling. Slithering up the walls. Bouncing from corner to corner. Mike's and Sulley's jaws dropped open. What were they going to do?

Sulley took a deep breath. "We just have to let them know who's in charge, that's all," he told Mike.

"I think they know who's in charge," Mike said as an oversized, six-handed monster kid scooped him up and tossed him to his twin. "*Help!*"

Sulley quickly intercepted Mike and set him back down on his feet.

"All we need to do," said Sulley calmly, "is get their attention. Let's see . . . a video?" But the TV was too covered with monster slime and finger paint for anyone to watch it. A snack? Nope. Every graham cracker and fright roll-up had been gobbled up already.

"How about a song?" said Mike finally, out of desperation.

"Great idea!" said Sulley.

And do you know what? It was! They sang "The Huge Gigantic Spider" and "The Wheels on the Monster Bus."

"What did I say, Sulley? I said it'd be like paid vacation, and it is! I don't understand why you were so reluctant," Mike said.

Sulley rolled his eyes. "Whatever you say, Mike."

# Runaway Hippo

"Mmm, crispy, crunchy bugs," said Timon. He was eating breakfast with Simba and Pumbaa.

Suddenly, a sad cry came from the jungle.

"The sound is coming from over here," said Pumbaa.

He led them to a muddy pond full of thick vines. In the middle of the swamp was a baby hippo. He was tangled up in vines and half buried in mud.

"Help!" the hippo cried.

When the little hippo saw Simba, he became very frightened. "Oh, no, a lion! He's going to eat me!" he cried.

"Take it easy," Simba replied. "These guys have got me on an all-bug diet."

Timon grabbed a vine and swung over to the hippo. He began digging the little hippo out of the mud. Meanwhile, Simba jumped onto the hippo's back and began tearing at the thick vines with his teeth. That made the hippo even more afraid!

"You *are* trying to eat me!" he cried.

Finally, Simba and Timon got the hippo unstuck.

Free at last, the muddy creature started to cry. "P-p-please don't eat me," he said to Simba.

"I'm not going to eat you, I promise," said Simba. "How did you get stuck in the mud?"

"I was angry at my little brother and I bit his tail and made him cry. I was afraid my parents would be upset, so I ran away from home," said the little hippo.

"I'll bet your parents *are* upset," said Simba, "because you're gone and they're worried about you."

"They won't care," the hippo said.

"Come on," said Simba. He led the little hippo to the edge of the river. When they got there, they could hear the other hippos calling: "Oyo! Oyo! Oyo!"

"Listen!" said the hippo. "Oyo's my name. They're calling me! They miss me!"

"Sure," said Simba. "You can't just run away without being missed. When you're part of a family, no matter what you do, you'll always belong."

"What about *your* family, Simba?" Timon asked as they watched the little hippo rejoin his family. "Do you think they miss you?"

"I didn't used to think so," Simba replied thoughtfully, "but now I wonder . . ."

# El Materdor

**M**ater and Lightning were out for a drive when Mater stopped to look at some grazing bulldozers. "I was a famous bulldozer fighter in Spain," he began. "They called me 'El Materdor'. . ."

El Materdor stood in the center of a packed arena. With a nod of his head, he signaled that he was ready. A door at the side of the ring opened and an angry looking bulldozer rolled out. El Materdor raised his tow hook. One glimpse of the red cape dangling from it and the bulldozer charged toward the cape. El Materdor stood his ground.

Again and again, the bulldozer charged. Each time, El Materdor dodged him with a last-second move. Finally the bulldozer surprised him. He came up behind El Materdor and pushed him across the ring, driving him right into the ground!

El Materdor dusted himself off and bravely faced the huge bulldozer again. Suddenly, the bulldozer smacked his front blade on the ground. Two doors at the side of the ring opened and two more bulldozers drove out. Now it was three against one! The bulldozers charged! For a time, El Materdor

fought off all of them. But then the three bulldozers circled him and began to close in. There was nowhere for El Materdor to go. Nowhere but up, that is. El Materdor waited until the last moment. Then, with a mighty leap, he jumped out of the path of the charging bulldozers, who collided and collapsed in a heap.

"Olé!" El Materdor cried, landing on top of the wrecked bulldozers.

Back in Radiator Springs, Lightning interrupted Mater's story. "Mater," he said, "that did not happen."

"Well, try telling that to them there bulldozers," Mater replied, pointing behind Lightning. The bulldozers that had been grazing were now surrounding Mater, and they looked angry!

"Huh?" Lightning noticed the bulldozers eyeing his shiny red paint job. "AAAAAAhhh!" He took off down the dirt road, the bulldozers speeding after him.

Just then, two fans rolled up alongside Mater.

"Señor Mater," they said together.

"Señoriters," Mater replied with a smile. He tossed on a matador hat. "Olé!"

**NOVEMBER**
**21**

# Fish Food

Figaro the cat was scared. He, Geppetto, and Cleo the goldfish had just been swallowed by a whale!

"Don't worry, Figaro," Geppetto said, seeing the cat's worried look. "We'll get out of here somehow—and when we do, we'll keep searching for Pinocchio."

Pinocchio! Figaro growled. After all that Geppetto and the Blue Fairy had done for Pinocchio, he had run away from home without a care in the world. That was how they'd ended up inside the whale! They had been searching for Pinocchio when the whale swallowed their whole boat.

Figaro decided then and there that if they ever found Pinocchio, he would use both of the wooden boy's legs as scratching posts. It would serve him right.

Meanwhile, Geppetto was peering into the puddle of water at the bottom of the whale's stomach. Figaro watched curiously.

"Let's see," Geppetto murmured, bending over and poking at the water. "There must be something in here . . . Aha!" he cried happily. He was clutching a small, soggy clump of seaweed.

Seaweed was *fish* food, Figaro thought with a scowl. Surely Geppetto didn't expect *him* to eat that for dinner.

But as he watched, Geppetto carefully divided the seaweed into three portions. He placed one portion in Cleo's bowl. He set one portion in front of Figaro. The third he kept for himself.

"Let's eat!" Geppetto said, smiling bravely.

Figaro sniffed his seaweed. He stirred it around with his paw. But he just couldn't eat the soggy green stuff. With a twitch of his tail, Figaro turned away.

Geppetto watched the little cat with sad eyes. Figaro sighed. He couldn't help but feel ungrateful.

Reluctantly, Figaro turned back to his dinner. He nibbled at the seaweed. It was cold. It was slimy. But it tasted like . . . *fish*!

Figaro gobbled down the rest of his meal. With his belly full, the little cat felt better. He decided that if they found Pinocchio, he would only use *one* of the puppet boy's legs to sharpen his claws on.

Probably.

# A Circle of Friends

After escaping the Sunnyside Daycare nursery, Andy's toys had ended up at a landfill. The toys had saved themselves from being shredded, but now they were holding on to a magnetic conveyor belt.

Suddenly, the conveyor belt angled upward toward a bright light. At first, the toys thought they were heading for daylight. But then they realized it was an incinerator! The toys ran as fast as they could! Lotso, who had ended up at the landfill with them, managed to reach an Emergency Stop Button.

Lotso was about to push the button and save everyone. Then he stopped. He looked back at the other toys and, with a cruel smirk, he ran off.

The toys tumbled toward the fiery blaze. A terrifying roar filled the air. They struggled to climb and claw their way back out, but the trash that poured off the belt kept pushing them closer to their doom.

Finally, the toys grabbed hold of one another. They were determined to face their fate the best way they knew how—together.

A large shadow passed over the toys. A giant crane lowered down, down, down over them. The jaws opened, scooping up Woody and the other toys! The toys were lifted up and away from the fire. As they soared through the air, the toys saw into the cab of the crane—the Aliens were controlling it!

"The clawwww!" The Aliens steered their friends over the pile of trash and dropped them gently to the ground.

"Come on, Woody," said Jessie. "We gotta get you home."

"What about you guys?" Woody asked. "Maybe the attic's not such a great idea."

"We're Andy's toys," said Jessie.

"We'll be there for him," said Buzz.

Woody was supposed to go to college with Andy, while the other toys went into storage. The toys wondered if they could make it before Andy left.

Luckily, they spotted their local trash collector nearby. The toys hurried toward the truck to hitch a ride home.

Lotso found his way onto a truck, too. But he wouldn't be hopping off anytime soon! He was strapped to the front!

Andy's toys smiled. They were on their way home.

**NOVEMBER**

**23**

# You Look Funny

M ike Wazowski was a
monster on a mission.
He was trying to prove
that he deserved a place in the Scare
Program at Monsters University. Mike's
fraternity, Oozma Kappa, had just won
the Scare Games. But Mike had learned
that his teammate, Sulley, had cheated.
He had changed the settings on the scare
simulator to easy for Mike's turn. He
didn't think Mike was scary enough to
win on his own! Mike was determined to
prove him wrong.

Mike broke into the Door Tech Lab
at the university. He grabbed a door
and placed it in the docking station—
the portal to the human world. All he
had to do now was walk through it and
perform a real Scare on a human child.

Mike quietly entered the room. He
rolled across the floor and ruffled the
curtains. Then he crept closer to the
child's bed. He could hear her stirring.
Mike leaped up.

"*ROAR!*" he cried as ferociously as
he could.

The child just looked at Mike and
smiled. "You look funny," she said.

Mike couldn't believe it. His Scare
hadn't worked. Everyone was right. He

really *wasn't* scary after all.

Suddenly Mike realized that he
wasn't in a child's bedroom at all. He
was in a big room . . . and it was full
of kids . . . and they were all looking at
him. Mike had walked into a cabin full
of campers!

Back in the Door Tech Lab, Dean
Hardscrabble and her guards were
holding back a crowd. "No one goes
through that door until the authorities
arrive," she announced.

Sulley arrived at the lab and told the
OKs that it was Mike who had entered
the human world without authority.

"But he could die out there!" cried
Squishy.

Sulley wasn't going to let that
happen. He would rescue Mike—but he
needed the OKs' help to lure the guards
away from the door.

Mike's friend Don quickly created
a distraction. While the guards were
dealing with him, Sulley charged
toward the door. Hardscrabble spotted
him at the last minute.

"Sullivan, don't go in there! It's
extremely dangerous!" she cried.

Sulley knew the dangers, but he had
to save his friend.

# You Always Look Twice

"**A**re you ready for today's training exercise, Oso?" Dottie asked.

Special Agent Oso grinned. "Dodging paintballs? You bet!"

"Great! Now remember, the paintballs will be coming at you from the left and from the right," explained Dottie, "so you need to first look left, then right, and then left again before moving forward," Dottie said.

Oso took his position in the hallway. He tried to dodge the paintballs, but he forgot what Dottie had told him. *SPLAT!* A yellow splash of paint landed on his left shoulder. "Oops!" Oso said.

"No worries," said Dottie. "It's all part of the plan . . . more or less."

Meanwhile, a little girl was in need of Oso's help. Her name was Josie. Her neighbor was away and she needed to collect a package that had been left outside their house. But she wasn't quite sure how to cross the street.

Special Agent Oso was there in no time! Josie was thrilled to see him. "I'm so glad you're here! What should we do first?"

"Step one: Look to the left and then to the right to make sure there's no traffic in either direction," said Paw Pilot.

"Step two: Now look to the left again, just to be sure the coast is clear," advised Paw Pilot.

"Aha!" cried Oso. "No wonder I got hit by the paintball. After I looked to my left, I forgot to look to my right and then look left again!"

"No traffic in either direction," said Josie.

"Good! That means it's safe for us to cross the road and collect your neighbor's package," said Oso.

"Come on!" Josie picked up the package.

Oso cheered. "Now let's take it home."

"Ready to cross the street again?" asked Paw Pilot. "Just follow the three special steps."

First, Josie and Oso needed to look to the left and then to the right for traffic. Next, they need to look left again. Finally, when they saw it was all clear, then it was safe to cross the road!

"Assignment complete!" shouted Oso.

"Thanks, Special Agent Oso," Josie said. "I couldn't have done it without your help!"

# The Secret Adventure

Early one morning, Thumper hopped over to a thicket and woke up Bambi.

"Come on! It's time for an adventure. But where we're going is a secret," he said.

On the way, Bambi and Thumper spotted their skunk friend, Flower.

"We're going on a secret adventure," Bambi said. "Do you want to come?"

"Oh, gosh! I do," Flower said shyly.

Above them, a bird named Red sat unnoticed. They are heading out all by themselves, Red thought. I'd better tell their mothers.

Meanwhile, Bambi, Thumper, and Flower reached a meadow.

"Shhh!" Thumper whispered. "We are close to where all the bunnies graze—including my mama."

But Thumper's sisters had seen them. They wanted to know what their big brother was up to, so they followed him.

Soon the three friends came to a stream. A beaver walked up to them.

"My name is Slap," the beaver said. "Where are you going?"

"I wanted to show my friends what you build in the river," Thumper explained.

"We call it a dam," said Slap.

Carefully, Slap and the three friends stepped out onto the logs. There were other beavers there working on the dam.

"Why do they call you Slap?" Flower asked their new friend.

Slap slapped the logs with his flat tail. The dam shook so much that a log broke loose and started drifting downriver.

"Help, Thumper!" four little voices cried. It was Thumper's younger sisters! The log they were sitting on was floating away!

The beavers jumped into the water and quickly swam toward the log. High above, Red saw the whole thing and went to get help.

Thumper's sisters held on, but they were getting close to a waterfall! The beavers eventually reached the log. They slapped their tails with all their might and got the log to the riverbank. Thumper pulled his sisters to safety and thanked the beavers.

Just then, Bambi's, Thumper's, and Flower's mothers arrived!

"Oh, I'm so glad you are safe!" cried Bambi's mother. "Luckily, Red was keeping an eye on you."

"I'm very happy to see you, too, Mother," Bambi said, glad that the adventure was over.

# A Not-So-Relaxing Vacation

No doubt about it: Hercules needed a vacation—badly!

"But what about your training?" argued Phil. "You can't stop now! If you're ever gonna be a god, you've got to train like one!"

"If I don't take a break," said Hercules, "I'm never going to become a god because I'll be so burned out."

And with that, he put away his dumbbells and his javelins and rounded up Pegasus.

"We're off to the Greek islands, my friend," he told the winged horse. "Sand castles, beach blankets, umbrella drinks, here we come!"

And before you could say *Mount Olympus*, there they were, at the finest resort in the ancient world, soaking up the sun and doing absolutely nothing.

"A hero could get used to this," said Hercules as he bobbed in the water, sipping a smoothie.

Suddenly, a cry rang out from the beach.

"Shark! Shark!"

"Shark?" said Hercules. "In the Aegean Sea?"

Sure enough, a big gray dorsal fin was speeding toward the crowded shore!

"Help!" cried the people in the water.

"Help!" cried Hercules . . . until he realized he was the one who could save them.

He swam up to the shark, grabbed it by the tail, and tossed it up into the sky, all the way to the Atlantic.

"Whew," said Hercules as the people clapped and cheered.

But not five minutes later, another frightened scream rang out—this time from the hills.

"Volcano!"

Hercules knew what he had to do. He raced around the island until he found the biggest boulder. He rolled it all the way to the top of the mountain and then, with one great push, he tipped it over the edge and into the bubbling mouth of the volcano. The volcano was stopped.

Before any more natural disasters could occur, Hercules decided it was time to pack up and head back home.

"Back so soon, Herc?" asked Phil, pleasantly surprised.

Hercules shrugged. "Let's just say that for a hero, work can sometimes be easier than vacation!"

# A New Home

Andy's toys had run away from home because they thought Andy wanted to get rid of them. But they had realized they were wrong and come back. The toys arrived home just as Andy was loading up the car to leave for college. They snuck into Andy's room and into the box labeled ATTIC. Woody headed for the box marked COLLEGE.

"This isn't good-bye," Woody said, shaking Buzz's hand.

"You know where to find us, Cowboy," Buzz said, then climbed into the box with the other toys.

Woody waited in the box as Andy and his mom entered the bedroom. "I wish I could always be with you," Andy's mom said sadly.

"You will be, Mom," Andy told her.

Woody looked over at a photo of Andy surrounded by his toys. He knew they would remember their special time together, forever. Suddenly, he knew what to do. He snuck across the room, wrote a note, and stuck it on the attic box. When Andy returned, he opened the box and got a wonderful surprise. The toys he thought had been thrown away were inside! Then he looked at the note.

"Hey, Mom," he called. "So you really think I should donate these?"

"It's up to you, honey," she called back.

A little while later, Andy pulled up in front of a house. A little girl was playing on the front lawn. Her name was Bonnie.

"Someone told me you're really good with toys," Andy told Bonnie. "These are mine, but I'm going away now, so I need someone really special to play with them."

Andy took each toy from the box and introduced them to Bonnie. When he got to the bottom, he was surprised to see Woody! But Bonnie recognized Woody. She'd played with him before. Though it was hard for him, Andy decided to let Woody stay with Bonnie, too. He could see that she already loved him.

Back in the car, Andy took one last look back at his toys. "Thanks, guys," he said pulling away.

As Bonnie went inside, the toys watched Andy disappear down the street. "So long, partner," said Woody. The others gathered around him. Their life with Andy was ending, but their adventures with Bonnie had just begun.

**NOVEMBER**
# 28

# Wild Life

Tod the fox had just arrived at the game preserve, a vast, beautiful forest where wild animals were protected from hunters. His kind owner, Widow Tweed, had brought him there to keep him safe.

At first, Tod didn't understand why Widow Tweed had abandoned him in the middle of this strange forest, alone and afraid. But she had seemed to be as sad about leaving him as he was about being left.

The first night was dreadful. It had poured rain, and though he tried to find shelter in different hollows and caves, they were always inhabited by other animals. There was no room for the poor, wet little fox.

But the next morning, things began to look up. Tod met a pretty young fox named Vixey. She showed him around the forest, which had many beautiful waterfalls and streams full of fish.

"I think I'm going to like it here, Vixey," said Tod.

Having lived his whole life with Widow Tweed, he had never met another fox before, least of all one as lovely as Vixey. But Vixey had lived the life of a wild fox, and she knew more about the world than Tod.

"You must be very careful, Tod," she warned him. "Remember, we're foxes, and we have many enemies. You must always be on the alert for danger!"

"Come on, Vixey," scoffed Tod. "We're in a game preserve! What could possibly happen to us here?"

Suddenly, a huge shadow fell over the two foxes. A look of great fear crossed Vixey's face.

Turning around slowly, Tod saw why. A huge bear was standing up on its hind legs. And it was staring straight at them!

"Run!" yelled Vixey.

Tod didn't need to be told twice. The two foxes dashed away from the bear, scampering over hills, racing through a hollow tree, and jumping over a narrow stream. When they were well away from the bear, they stopped and leaned against a rock, panting hard.

"Okay," Tod said when he had caught his breath a bit. "I see what you mean about the dangers, Vixey. I promise to be careful."

"Mmm-hmm," she replied. Then she smiled. "Come on," she said to Tod. "Let's go fishing!"

# Berry Blunder

Madame Medusa thrust a pail into Penny's hand. "I only want the plumpest, juiciest berries!" she screeched. "And don't come back until the pail is full!"

"Yes, Medusa," Penny replied.

Carrying Teddy in one hand and the pail in the other, the little girl started off into the swamp.

Penny looked around. It wasn't easy to find her way through the swamp because everything sort of grew together. Luckily she knew where to go. A few minutes later, Penny stood before a bush heavy with plump berries. She set Teddy down in a tangle of branches. "You'll be comfy here while I pick," she explained.

She was plucking the first berry off the bush when Brutus, one of Medusa's alligators, lumbered forward and opened his massive jaws. He grabbed Teddy and tossed him into the murky water.

"Teddy!" Penny cried. She snatched her friend up, hugged him to her chest, and glared at Brutus, who was munching on the berries.

"You creep!" she said. "You could have hurt Teddy. And those berries are for Medusa!"

Brutus responded by snatching another several dozen berries off the bush. Then Nero, Medusa's other alligator, joined him, chomping away. Soon, half of the branches were empty.

Scowling and holding her dripping Teddy, Penny looked around. When she spied a patch of bright red fruit growing several yards away, she smiled to herself.

"Nero, Brutus!" she called cheerfully. "There's another berry patch over there! Take a look!"

Lifting their massive heads, the two gators looked where Penny was pointing. A second later, they had crossed the swamp and were scarfing down the plump red fruit.

Penny began to giggle. With their eyes wide and their nostrils flaring, Nero and Brutus began to desperately gulp down gallons of swamp water. The nearby "berries" looked like berries, but they were actually hot peppers!

"You shouldn't eat so fast, boys," she said sweetly as they squirmed in the water.

Penny picked until her pail was full. Then, taking Teddy by the arm, she headed back to the ship. How *berry* sorry I am! she thought.

# Doggone It, Stitch

Stitch was sitting and waiting for Lilo to come home from school. At last, Lilo burst into the house—but she was carrying a puppy.

"Hi, Stitch!" Lilo said excitedly. "My neighbor Leilani asked me to take care of her puppy, Rover."

"Stitch wants to listen to music," Stitch said.

"Not now," Lilo said. "I have to take care of Rover."

Stitch watched Lilo make a bed for Rover. "Can we listen to music now?" he asked.

"I want to teach Rover some new tricks," Lilo said. Lilo taught Rover tricks all afternoon while Stitch watched.

That evening, Lilo gave Rover a bath. Stitch wanted to play, too, so he jumped into the water.

"You need a time-out," Lilo told Stitch. "Go to our room while I take Rover for a walk."

Stitch waited until Lilo and Rover were gone. Then he hurried outside and ran toward town.

When Lilo got home, she wondered why Stitch wasn't there. Suddenly Cobra Bubbles called. He was a social worker that Lilo and Nani knew.

"You need to hide Stitch," Cobra told Lilo and Nani. "Two scientists are looking for him."

"But I don't know where Stitch is!" Lilo said.

"Well, I suggest you find him before the scientists do," Cobra said.

Lilo and Nani looked for Stitch. "Stitch has been acting weird all day," Lilo told Nani. "His badness level was way up. He acted just like Rover!"

Suddenly, Lilo knew where Stitch had gone.

"I bet Stitch went to the animal shelter to watch the puppies!"

When Lilo and Nani arrived, Stitch was there. "Stitch learning to be cute like puppy," he explained.

"Stitch, I like you just the way you are," Lilo answered. "Now, let's go home!"

But when they started to leave, they saw the scientists. Lilo put a leash on Stitch, and they walked out past the scientists.

Just then, Cobra Bubbles drove up. "Hey!" he called to the scientists. "I just saw an alien heading out to sea."

The scientists jumped into the car, and sped off. Stitch was safe!

# Showtime

Andy's toys had just moved into their new home in Bonnie's room. Dolly had a plan to help everyone get to know one another better. "Let's have a talent show!" she said.

All the toys were excited. But as they started practicing, Buzz stood by himself. His friends all seemed to know what to do, but he wasn't sure. He wanted to do something truly spectacular—something that would impress Jessie.

Buzz noticed Hamm and Buttercup working on their comedy routine. Buzz knew Jessie loved a good joke. Grabbing Woody's hat, he shouted, "Howdy partners, I'm Sheriff Woody. Did you know there's a snake in my boot?"

"I don't know about sounding like Woody," said Hamm with a smirk, "but you definitely sound wooden."

Buzz wasn't listening, though. He'd noticed that Mr. Pricklepants and the Aliens were doing a play. Jessie loves to watch plays, Buzz thought to himself. The Aliens were very excited about their show. Mr. Pricklepants was the director.

"There are plenty of parts," Mr. Pricklepants said. "We're doing Romeo and Juliet!"

Buzz wanted to change the play so it was set in space! But Mr. Pricklepants didn't think that was such a good idea.

"Hey, guys! Time to start the talent show!" shouted Dolly.

Up on the stage, Bullseye turned on the music. A lively tune filled the room. Suddenly, Buzz's whole body shook. It was as if the music was taking over his body! Unable to control himself, Buzz started dancing. He couldn't stop! He danced straight to Jessie. Jessie grinned.

She knew exactly what had happened—the music had switched Buzz into his Spanish Mode! "It's okay, Buzz," she whispered. "Just go with it!"

Buzz smiled shyly back at Jessie. "Um, well then," he said. "May I have this dance?"

Jessie nodded and the two danced across the stage and smiled at each other. All their friends cheered. When the music ended, Buzz and Jessie took a bow together. Buzz was beaming. He'd finally impressed Jessie, and discovered a talent he never knew he had!

# The Winter Trail

One winter morning, Bambi was dozing in the wood when Thumper came over to play.

Bambi followed Thumper through the forest. The sky was blue, and the ground was covered in a blanket of new snow.

"Look at these tracks!" Thumper said excitedly. He pointed to a line of footprints in the snow. "Who do you suppose they belong to?" Bambi didn't know, so they decided to follow the trail. They soon came to a tree.

"Wake up, Friend Owl!" called Thumper.

"Have you been out walking?" Bambi asked.

"Now why would I do that?" Friend Owl replied. "My wings take me where I need to go."

Bambi and Thumper continued on. Next, they spotted a raccoon sitting next to a tree, his mouth full of red berries. "Hello, Mr. Raccoon," Bambi said shyly. "Did you happen to see who made these tracks in the snow?"

The raccoon shook his head and began tapping the tree.

"I know!" Thumper cried. "He thinks we should ask the woodpeckers."

Soon, Bambi and Thumper found the woodpecker family. "Did you make the tracks in the snow?" Thumper called up to the birds.

"No, we've been here all day," the mother bird answered.

"Who can these tracks belong to?" Bambi asked.

"I don't know," Thumper replied.

They soon reached the end of the trail, and the tracks led all the way to a snowy bush, where a family of quail was resting.

"Did you make these tracks?" Thumper asked.

"Why, yes," Mrs. Quail answered. "Friend Owl told me about this wonderful bush. So this morning, my babies and I walked all the way over here."

Satisfied that they had solved the mystery, Thumper and Bambi turned to go home. Behind them, they found a surprise—their mothers!

"How'd ya find us?" Thumper asked.

Thumper's mother looked down at the tracks in the snow.

"You followed our trail!" Bambi cried. His mother nodded.

"Now, let's follow it back home," Bambi's mother said. So that's just what they did.

# Family Reunion

**M**eg paced up and down the room.

"What's wrong?" Hercules asked his girlfriend.

"We're going to visit your parents," Meg told him. "I want to make a good first impression."

"You're smart and kind and intelligent," Hercules said, smiling. "How could you make anything other than a great first impression?"

Meanwhile, Hercules's parents, Amphitryon and Alcmene, were getting ready for their son's visit. Amphitryon was pacing, too.

"Is everything all right?" Alcmene asked.

"Yes, of course," Amphitryon answered. "Why wouldn't it be?"

"Maybe you're nervous because your son is coming home and you haven't seen him in quite a while," Alcmene said.

Before Amphitryon could answer, they heard a sound.

"Look!" Amphitryon cried. "It's Hercules!"

And sure enough, Hercules came barreling up to the door. He leaped off Pegasus and gave a hearty hug to each of his parents. Then he introduced Phil.

"Mighty fine to meet you," Phil said as he slipped them his business card. "Fine boy you raised! Feel free to contact me if you find any more like him."

"This is my friend Meg," Hercules continued, blushing.

Just then, Pegasus snorted. "Oh, and how could I forget my pal Pegasus?" Hercules cried.

"All right, all right, enough with the niceties," Phil interrupted. "It's been a long trip. I'm hungry. Where's the grub?"

"Wait!" Hercules said. "I know you have prepared a wonderful meal, but first, I want to tell you what has happened since I left." He took a deep breath. "I've learned that I'm the son of Zeus and Hera. That's where I've gotten all my physical strength. But without everything I learned from you, my adoptive parents," Hercules continued, "all that would mean nothing."

Amphitryon and Alcmene beamed with pride. Then they all sat down for a feast worthy of the gods. Amphitryon and Alcmene were glad to have Hercules home; Hercules was happy to be home; Meg and Pegasus were honored to be their guests; and Phil was thrilled to finally get to dig into some home-cooked grub!

# Elliot Minds the Store

One morning, Manny and the tools headed to Kelly's hardware store to buy some supplies. When they arrived, Kelly was teaching a nervous Elliot how to serve customers.

"We need a strong hook for our bulletin board," Manny said.

"No problem!" said Kelly. "I'm sure Elliot could help you with that."

"Me? Oh, I d-d-don't know," Elliot sputtered.

Kelly assured Elliot that he would do fine, and then he left to run an errand. Elliot tried to help Manny, but he made a lot of mistakes. Elliot dropped the parts catalog on his foot. He forgot to ring up the purchase on the cash register, and then he caught his sleeve in the till.

"I'm so totally bad at this!" he cried.

"*Está bien*! It's all right, Elliot," assured Manny. "Everybody makes mistakes when they're learning something new. The important thing is to learn from your mistakes . . . so you can be ready the next time."

Stretch had an idea. "You know, I always heard that if you do something that you're good at, confidence is sure to follow. I have a great idea. Why don't you go get your skateboard?" he suggested.

Manny looked nervous. "Um, I don't think skateboarding in Kelly's shop is such a good—"

Manny was interrupted by a huge *CRASH!* Elliot had collided with the shop's new display! "Oh, no!" he cried.

"Hang on, Elliot," said Manny. "You know, the balance you use on your skateboard might come in handy for piecing that display back together! And that drumming of yours is perfect for using a hammer."

"Really?" Elliot was shocked. "Are you saying that I could actually fix the shelf before Kelly gets back?"

"Well, with a little help, I don't see why not," said Manny. "You just have to believe in yourself."

So, using a shelf like a skateboard, Elliot rounded up all of the spray paints. Then he put his drumming skills to work and hammered the shelves back into place.

"*Muy bien*, Elliot," said Manny. "Very good! See? You have more talents than you thought you did!"

"You're right. I should have believed in myself all along," said Elliot. "Thanks, Manny. Thanks, tools."

# Win Some, Lose Some

Sulley and his assistant, Mike, were in a race to become the Top Scare Team. Randall and Fungus were right behind them, so it was lucky that Sulley and Mike were racking up the scares!

"We'll beat Randall easily," said Mike, giving Sulley a high five.

Suddenly, the Scare Floor exploded in panic. George Sanderson had returned from his closet with a ball stuck to his foot with chewing gum. Now, special teams from the CDA, the Child Detection Agency, swarmed into the factory to decontaminate George.

During the excitement, Randall crept over to Sulley and Mike's workstation. He stole Mike's paperwork and tossed it into a shredder. After George had been cleaned—and shaved!—the Scare Teams got back to work.

"My paperwork is gone!" Mike cried, his eye blinking in confusion.

"Oh, no!" cried Sulley. "Without that paperwork, none of today's work will count."

"Too bad," said Randall, chuckling. "That makes me today's Top Scarer."

Mike felt terrible. He knew Sulley should have won. He also knew that Randall had something to do with the missing paperwork. So Mike decided to teach him a lesson.

A few days later, Randall was ahead of everyone else in scares.

"This is my best day ever!" Randall crowed to the other Scarers. "Pretty soon I'll be Scarer of the Month!"

Then the alarm went off. George had come back with a lollipop stuck to his ear! Poor George.

As the teams rushed to decontaminate George, Mike sprang into action. When no one was looking, he hurried over to Randall and Fungus's workstation and grabbed all their paperwork.

"This is contaminated, too!" Mike cried as he tossed the papers to the floor.

With a *whoosh*, a flamethrower burned all of the papers to ashes.

"Where's the paperwork?" Randall cried when he returned to the scare floor.

"Yikes!" Fungus yelped. "Where did it go? It was right here!"

"Well, this is just great," Randall said. "Now my points don't count."

"Looks like you're cooked. Just like your paperwork," Mike said with a chuckle.

# Mango Hunting

Once upon a time, long before Mowgli came to the jungle, Bagheera the panther met Baloo the bear for the first time. This is how it happened.

Bagheera was younger then, but no less serious. One day, Bagheera was edging along the branch of a mango tree leaning out over a river. There was one perfectly ripe mango right at the end of the branch, and Bagheera loved mangoes. The only problem was that the branch was slender, and when Bagheera moved toward the end of it, it began to creak and bend alarmingly.

Bagheera, crouched on the middle of the branch, was just coming up with a clever plan when he heard a noise. He looked down and saw a great big gray bear. "It looks like you could use a hand," said the bear.

"No, thank you," said Bagheera politely. "I prefer to work on my own."

But the bear paid him no heed and began climbing up the tree. "I'll tell you what," huffed the bear. "I'll just sit at the base of that branch and grab your tail. You can climb out and grab the mango, and I'll keep a hold of you in case the end of the branch breaks off."

"No, I don't think that's a very good idea," said Bagheera impatiently. "I doubt this branch can hold both of us any—"

*Snap!*

The bear had, of course, ignored Bagheera and climbed out onto the branch. And the branch had, of course, snapped under their combined weight. And now a very wet, very unhappy panther sat in the river next to a very wet, very amused bear.

"Oh, ha-ha-ha-ha!" hooted Baloo (for it was Baloo, of course).

"Oh, come now," he said, seeing how angry Bagheera was, "it's not a total loss, you know." Baloo held up the broken branch with that perfect mango still hanging from the end of it.

"I'll tell you what," said the bear, "let's go climb onto that rock and dry off in the sun while we eat this mango. I'm Baloo. What's your name?"

"Bagheera," said the panther as they climbed up onto the warm, flat rock. And then, almost despite himself, he smiled. And then, very much despite himself, he laughed. And Baloo laughed right along with him.

# Don't Mock Jock

**A**unt Sarah was visiting, and she had brought her Siamese cats, Si and Am with her. Before long, Si and Am had found the doggy door that led out to the garden.

"What works for doggies works for kitties, too," hissed Si.

They slunk out into the garden and found a small hole in the garden fence. They poked their heads through the hole and spied Jock snoozing by his doghouse.

"Time for a wake-up call?" asked Am. Si smiled and nodded. They squirmed through the hole and stole silently across the yard until they were sitting on either side of the sleeping Jock. Then, at the same moment, they let loose a shrill, earsplitting yowl.

Jock awoke with a start. By the time he had identified the culprits, Si and Am were halfway across the lawn, heading for the fence. Jock tore after them, but the cats squirmed through the small hole and out of Jock's reach. The opening was too small for Jock. He had to be content with sticking his head through and barking at the cats

as they strolled casually up the back steps of Lady's house and through the doggy door. Then they collapsed in a laughing fit on the kitchen floor.

"Dogs are so dim-witted," Si cackled.

They waited a while, then crept out through the doggy door again, itching to try their trick a second time.

Peeking through the hole in the fence, Am and Si spied Jock sleeping in front of his doghouse again.

But this time Jock was ready for them. When the cats got within five feet of him, the feisty Scottie leaped to his feet and growled. The cats gave a start, wheeled around, and raced for the fence, only to find the way blocked by Jock's friend, Trusty the bloodhound, who stood, growling, between the cats and the hole.

Jock and Trusty chased Si and Am around Jock's garden until Jock was confident they had learned their lesson. Then they allowed the cats to retreat through the hole in the fence.

This time, Si and Am didn't stop running until they were through the doggy door and safely inside.

And inside is where they stayed!

# Around the World

"**I** can't believe it!" the Genie shouted as he sped away from Agrabah. "I'm *freeeeeeee!*"

Now that the Genie didn't have to hang around in his lamp anymore, he couldn't wait to see the world. First he transported himself to the Great Wall of China. "Ah!" he exclaimed as he looked over the view of the Chinese countryside. "Now, *this* is what I call a wall! Eh, Al?"

The Genie looked around, and then laughed at himself. Aladdin couldn't answer. He was back in Agrabah.

"Oh, well." The Genie scratched his head. "Now what? I know . . ."

A second later, he was in India, staring at a magnificent palace. It was big. It was white. It was an awful lot like the Sultan's palace back in Agrabah.

The Genie shrugged. Not every place could be totally new and different. But for his next destination, he wanted a real change of pace.

The Genie went to the Amazon rain forest, the Sahara desert, and the Mount Olympus. But as he leaned against a column of the Parthenon at the Acropolis, he couldn't help thinking that his travels weren't quite all he had expected them to be.

"It's like there's something missing, you know?" he commented to a passing eagle.

The eagle soared up into the sky, not seeming to have any answers. The Genie sighed. What was wrong with him? Why wasn't he having more fun?

"Al would probably know," he muttered. "He has a knack for figuring things out. He and that crazy little monkey, Abu. And, of course, Princess Jasmine—now she's a smart cookie. . . ."

The Genie gasped, realizing the answer had been right there in front of him all along.

"That's it!" he cried. "That's what's missing—friends!"

Being free and traveling was fun. But all the interesting and exotic sights in the world couldn't offer the one thing that Agrabah had—the Genie's best friends.

He laughed out loud. Now that he was free to do anything he wished, he knew exactly what he wanted to do next. Gathering his suitcase, he sped toward the horizon.

"Next stop, Agrabah!" he cried.

# Sunnyside Boot Camp

Early one morning, Buzz and Rex arrived at Sunnyside Daycare. As soon as it was safe, they popped out of Bonnie's backpack. Even though they lived with Bonnie now, Buzz and Rex liked to come and visit the toys at Sunnyside.

Buzz greeted Sarge and asked how things were going. Sarge told Buzz he wished his ranks weren't so thin.

"There are recruits all around you," Buzz said. "Let's have a boot camp."

"I have lots of boots in my closet!" Ken cried. He ran off to get them before anyone could explain what a boot camp really was!

During the children's naptime, the toys snuck outside and started training. Sarge ordered everyone onto the bouncy trucks in the playground. Rex hopped on one and started rocking it slowly. Big Baby joined Rex and rocked it faster!

"Too fast!" cried Rex. "Stop!"

But when Big Baby stopped rocking, Rex went flying! He landed on top of the climbing frame! Sarge and Buzz had a new mission: to rescue Rex.

"We're going to have to work together," Buzz said.

All the toys agreed to help—except Ken. "These are vintage," he said, pointing to his boots.

The other toys made themselves into a tower, but it was too short to reach Rex! They needed Ken's help.

Ken thought for a moment, then nodded.

"Fashion has never held me back before!"

He quickly removed his boots and climbed to the top of the tower. But he still couldn't reach Rex!

Then Ken had an idea. "Stretch," he called, "hand me my 1972 cherry-red striped platform boots!" He put them on and reached out to Rex. "Gotcha!" said Ken.

"We did it!" cheered the toys.

"Good work, troops," said Sarge. "Mission accomplished."

It was time for Buzz and Rex to go. They said good-bye to the other toys, but Buzz couldn't find Ken. Finally he spotted him. "Thanks for your help today," Buzz said. "You're a great soldier!"

"Thanks, Buzz. But great doesn't cut it," said Ken. "Once I finish designing our new army boots—we'll be fabulous!"

# Royal Help Wanted

Prince John and Sir Hiss had just finished repaying their debt to society in the rock mines. They discovered that Robin Hood had given back the citizens' hard-earned money. And that meant that Prince John had not a penny to his name and no one to boss around anymore—except Sir Hiss, of course!

"Well, it's quite obvious that you will need to get a job," the prince told Hiss.

"Me, ssssssire?" hissed the snake.

"Of course!" John replied. "You can't very well expect *me* to get a job."

And so Hiss set out into the town.

First, he stopped by Friar Tuck's church.

"Everyone deserves a second chance," Friar Tuck told him. "And I just happen to need a bell ringer." He pointed up to the huge bell that hung in a tower of the church.

And so, every hour, Hiss grabbed hold of the rope and pulled with all his might. The sound of the bell was deafening! It wasn't so bad at one o'clock, when he had to ring the bell once. But around six o'clock, the clanging started to give him a colossal headache. At twelve o'clock, he quit and went looking elsewhere for a job.

Hiss tried the bakery, but they told him he needed hands (or at least paws) to knead dough. Then he went to the blacksmith and asked him for a job putting horseshoes on horses. But the horses were terrified of snakes.

Finally, Hiss gave up and returned home.

Prince John was not pleased. "Now what are we supposed to do for money?" he demanded. "I refuse to beg! Those wretched commoners would give anything to see me humiliated."

"You're absolutely right, sire—they would!" exclaimed Hiss. "That's it! Follow me!"

Before Prince John could protest, Hiss had the lion locked in the stocks in the middle of the village square. "Pay a farthing and pelt the prince with a tomato!" called Sir Hiss. In minutes, a line of adults and children stretched into the distance. Most of them had pretty good aim.

"Wah!" cried Prince John, his face dripping with tomato juice.

"But, sire," Sir Hiss said, "look at all these coins!"

# Space Adventure, Part 1

Mickey and the gang had a treasure map from Professor Von Drake, and they were going to outer space to find the treasure!

"Let's go, space adventurers!" said Space Captain Mickey.

"Not so fast," said the professor. He explained that Mickey and the gang must first find ten Treasure Stars. These stars would lead them to a mystery planet, and to the treasure!

Everyone was on board. But the gang didn't know that Space Pirate Pete was spying on them. . . .

Pete had found a new helper named Quoodles, who looked a lot like Toodles. Pete asked Quoodles for a tool to stop Mickey's ship, and Quoodles brought him milk cartons. All the milk cartons blocked Mickey's spaceship.

Space Pirate Pete said, "You're surrounded by milk. Give up the treasure map!"

"No way!" said Mickey. "We need a Mouseketool. Oh, Toodles!"

Toodles had seen Quoodles outside the ship. Toodles had never seen anyone else who looked like him! They smiled at each other.

"Oh, TOODLES!" called Mickey.

Toodles heard Mickey. He waved good-bye to Quoodles. Toodles brought a Mouseketool—a giant cookie! The cookie floated away, and the milk cartons followed it!

Minnie giggled. "Everyone knows milk goes with cookies."

On the moon, Mickey met Moon-Man Chip and Moon-Man Dale. Mickey asked if they had seen any Treasure Stars.

Moon-Men Chip and Dale led them to their locker. Goofy opened it. There were Treasure Stars one, two, and three!

On Mars, Mickey met Martian Mickey and Pluto from Pluto! Mickey asked Martian Mickey if he knew where to find any Treasure Stars.

Martian Mickey said, "They may be in the Star Tree Forest!"

Martian Mickey took the gang to the Star Tree Forest. Stars four, five, and six were on a tree! But Space Pirate Pete had another trick up his sleeve. He pretended to be a little old lady who was lost in space. The little old lady asked Goofy for a map.

"Goofy, nooooo!" cried Donald.

But it was too late. Goofy had given Pete the treasure map!

# Starry Night

Bonnie was camping out. She gathered her toys and brought them to the garden. Then she carefully set up her tent and arranged the toys inside.

Just then, her mom called to her. "Bonnie! Dinnertime!"

"I've got to go and eat my dinner. But I'll be back," Bonnie told the toys.

Left alone in the tent, the toys began to explore.

"This is a right comfortable spot," Jessie said, admiring Bonnie's sleeping bag.

"Yes, the accommodations are quite satisfactory," Mr. Pricklepants agreed with a nod.

"Well, shine my spurs!" Woody cried, noticing a camping lantern. He turned it on, and a warm glow lit up the tent. "How about a sing-along," Woody suggested.

Soon all the toys were singing. Then they decided to head outside. They all wanted to explore.

"Look!" Buttercup said.

"The stars are coming out!" Buzz smiled.

"That is the Big Dipper—seven stars that form a ladle shape," said Dolly.

Jessie hopped on Bullseye. "I'm gonna look around the yard!" she shouted.

"Follow me!" called Buttercup. "I'll show you the rose bed."

Trixie turned to the other toys. "Who wants to play freeze tag?" Before anyone could answer, she tapped Rex with her horn. The rest of the toys began running away as Trixie chased after them.

"I'm wiped out," Hamm said a little later.

"How about a shadow-puppet show?" said Mr. Pricklepants.

"Good idea," Woody said, leading all the toys inside the tent.

The toys used Bonnie's flashlight to create shadow puppets on the wall.

"A sleepover wouldn't be complete without a scary story," Mr. Potato Head said. He clicked off the flashlight. "Once there was a toy in a forest. The forest was dark. Very dark."

Suddenly, the toys heard the sound of someone running.

"Ahhh!" Rex shrieked as a huge shadow loomed over the tent. The toys all flopped over and went still. The tent flap opened up. . . .

"I'm back!" Bonnie said, smiling at her toys. "Did you miss me?"

# Holiday Shopping

**J**ack Skellington, the Pumpkin King, came upon four doors— one decorated with a shamrock, another with a heart, a third with a turkey, and the last with an egg. He walked from door to door, staring at each of them, searching for some meaning. All the while, Jack's ghost dog, Zero, was right beside him. Finally, Jack turned to Zero.

"What is a door," Jack said, "but a chance for something more?"

Zero nodded, so Jack swung open the first door with the shamrock. There was a noisy crowd of people inside—all wearing green. They were busy cutting shamrocks out of green construction paper. Zero was ready to dive right in, but Jack pulled him back by the collar.

"How bizarre!" Jack exclaimed. "It's not shaped like a diamond or a star."

Next Jack opened the door with the heart on it. Inside things were very red. There were lots of boxes of chocolates and tons of roses being arranged in vases of all shapes and sizes.

As Zero was about to sink his teeth into a chocolaty caramel, Jack pulled him back.

"Oh, no!" Jack began to blush. "All this romance is a no-go!"

Zero slunk away with his tail between his legs. Still, there was hope. Jack was already standing in front of door number three—the door with the turkey. He opened the door with a flourish. You wouldn't believe what he found inside! There were people roasting turkeys, mashing potatoes, and whipping cream for pumpkin pies. It smelled delicious, but all that cooking had made the room as hot as the inside of one of the ovens. Jack quickly closed the door again. This time, even Zero was relieved.

They stood in front of the last remaining door. The egg painted on it was staring back at them in all its colorful glory. Jack looked to Zero, who nodded reassuringly. Then Jack opened the door. There were people painting eggs and filling baskets with bright green grass, multicolored jelly beans, and chocolate bunnies. Zero barked gleefully. He was about to take off after the white rabbit hopping past him when Jack caught hold of his tail.

"I'm not sure about that bunny," Jack warned. "To me, he seems sort of funny."

Zero looked up. They had tried all the doors. What would they do now? Jack looked at him knowingly.

"I think we'll have to stick to Halloween!"

# Rescue Squad Mater

Red the fire truck was watering some flowers in front of the fire station. "I used to be a fire truck," Mater said, out of the blue.

Rescue Squad Mater was lounging at the fire station when an emergency call came in. "Fire in progress at one-two-zero-niner Car Michael Way."

"That's the old gasoline and match factory!" he exclaimed. He zoomed out of the station and roared down the street. Moments later, Rescue Squad Mater sped up to the burning building. Rescue Squad Mater aimed a water hose and started spraying. Ignoring the danger, he bravely battled the flames.

"Mater," Lightning said, stopping the story. "I can't believe that you were a fire truck."

"You remember," Mater replied. "You were there, too!" Then he went on telling his tale. The fire had spread through the entire factory, but Rescue Squad Mater continued to fight it. Suddenly, a frightened voice called out. "Help! Help!" Lightning was stuck on the top floor of the burning building!

The rescue truck raised his ladder. Soon the ladder was right beneath Lightning. The crowd watched, waiting on the edges of their tire treads. *KA-BLAM!* The factory blew up in a huge explosion! Luckily, Lightning escaped just in time. Mater used his ladder to lift him into an ambulance. Finally, Mater turned toward the crowd and smiled.

When Lightning arrived at the hospital, he was rushed into the operating room. There was a whole team of nurses, but where was the doctor? Then Lightning heard a nurse's voice over the loudspeaker. "Paging Dr. Mater."

Lightning blinked. Had he heard that right? Seconds later, the doctor rolled in. Lightning could hardly believe his eyes. It was Mater!

"Mater, you're a doctor, too?!"

"That's right, buddy," Dr. Mater replied. Lightning spotted Dr. Mater's diplomas on the wall. "Clear!" Dr. Mater called out as he swung the arm of a scary-looking medical instrument toward Lightning. Then Mater stopped telling his story.

"What happened?" Lightning asked.

"I saved your life," Mater said.

# Start Being You!

**M**ike was in big trouble. He had snuck into the human world to prove that he was scary. But instead of scaring a human child, he had found himself in a cabin full of campers who thought he was cute!

Meanwhile, back in the Door Tech Lab at Monsters University, Sulley had snuck past the guards protecting the door Mike had used. He had to save his friend!

Sulley slipped through the door into the human world and found himself in an empty cabin. Where had Mike gone?

Looking out the window, Sulley saw a group of rangers gathered in the dark outside. Realizing that Mike must have fled to the nearby forest, Sulley made a break from the cabin. The rangers shined their flashlights on him as he disappeared into the trees. They thought they'd seen a bear.

Sulley found Mike sitting by a lake.

"You were right," Mike said sadly. "The children weren't scared of me. I thought I could show everybody I was something special . . . but I'm just not."

Sulley told Mike that he had messed things up his entire life, too. "You're not the only 'failure' here," he said.

Together, the two made it back to the cabin. But when they opened the door back to Monsters University, they found that it was an empty closet. Dean Hardscrabble had shut it down from the other side.

Meanwhile, the rangers were getting closer. Mike had a plan.

As the rangers entered the cabin, Mike and Sulley turned on a fan, shook the shutters, and fluttered the curtains. This unnerved the rangers. Then Mike slammed the door, which made them jump. Next they clawed on the walls and toppled the bunk beds over like dominoes.

The rangers screamed.

Finally, Mike gave Sulley the signal. The big blue monster rose up menacingly and let out a deafening roar.

The petrified rangers screamed . . . and screamed . . . and screamed.

At the Door Tech Lab at the university, the humans' screams filled the scream can to the brim. In fact, they filled all the scream cans in the room!

Suddenly the light above the door turned red. The door burst open and Mike and Sulley flew through it.

# Hanukkah Fun

"Happy Hanukkah, Pooh Bear!" Roo exclaimed as he opened the door for his first guest. It was the first night of Hanukkah, and Roo and Kanga were having all of their friends over to participate in some Hanukkah fun.

"Happy Hanukkah, Roo!" Pooh replied. Just then a delicious smell wafted by his nose.

"Something smells yummy!" Pooh cried.

Kanga was making little potato pancakes called latkes, a special Hanukkah treat. "Try to be patient, Pooh," Kanga said with a smile. "We'll have these latkes a little bit later."

Before long, Piglet, Eeyore, Rabbit, Tigger, and Owl had also arrived and it was time to light the menorah.

"First," Kanga explained, "we light this center candle, called the *shammosh*. Then we use the shammosh to light one other candle for the first night of Hanukkah."

Tigger noticed that there weren't any candles in the other seven candleholders of the menorah. "When do we light the other candles?" he asked Kanga.

"Well, Tigger," Kanga said, "Hanukkah lasts for eight nights. So tomorrow, on the second night, we will light two candles with the shammosh. On the third night, we will light three candles, and so on . . . until, on the eighth night, we will light all the candles!"

Just then Pooh said, "Um, Kanga? Is it a little bit later . . . now?"

Kanga understood: Pooh was hungry for a latke! Kanga brought the potato pancakes to the table, and everyone enjoyed the delicious treats.

When they were all eaten, Roo said, "Now let's spin the dreidel!" He got out a four-sided clay top. Roo explained the rules, then each player took turns spinning the dreidel. Depending on what side the dreidel landed on, the player might win or lose treats.

"This is fun!" Piglet exclaimed. "And to think, there are seven *more* nights of Hanukkah!"

"Hey, Mama," said Roo, "there are eight of us and eight nights of Hanukkah. Can our friends come over every night of Hanukkah and take turns lighting the menorah?"

Everyone, including Kanga, thought that was a wonderful idea. So that was exactly what they did.

# The New Neigh-bor

Pegasus grazed peacefully outside his home. Hercules and Meg had gone to greet their new neighbors, and had left Pegasus behind.

Suddenly, Pegasus heard a soft whinnying. He turned to discover a beautiful mare approaching him. His heart soared. But then Pegasus remembered the time he had been kidnapped by bad guys pretending to be a filly. He was determined not to fall for their trick a second time. He spread his wings and charged, shooing the horse down the hill.

The mare raced past Meg and Herc as they returned home. "Pegasus, what are you doing?" asked Meg. "That's no way to make our neighbors' horse feel welcome."

Pegasus gulped. The beautiful horse who had tried to meet him really *was* a beautiful horse!

"If I were you, I'd get over there and try to make it up to her," said Hercules.

Within minutes, Pegasus pranced across the neighbors' field, stopped in front of the mare, and struck a noble pose. But the lovely horse was unimpressed. She turned so that her tail swished right in Pegasus's face! Herc's horse knew he would have to do something amazing to impress this beauty. He flapped his wings and rose into the air. Then he dipped and swooped and somersaulted across the sky. When the filly started to walk away, he flew alongside her—and crashed right into a tree!

Hercules was watching from the hillside. "Pegasus sure does need some help," he said.

Meg had an idea. "The right gift might convince that mare to forgive him," she said.

She piled a basket high with apples and oats and tied a huge red ribbon around it. But when Pegasus went over to deliver the gift, holding the basket handle in his teeth, the female horse kicked it over.

Finally, Pegasus realized what he had to do. He sheepishly walked over to the filly with his head bowed. Then he gently nudged her with his muzzle.

The filly neighed and nuzzled him back. All she had wanted was for Pegasus to say he was sorry. Now she understood that her new friend had a good heart.

**DECEMBER**
**18**

# Buzz's Space Adventure

**B**onnie was away and the Peas-in-a-Pod were bored. Buzz knew just what to do. He decided to tell them a story about space!

"Once upon a time," Buzz began, "the evil Emperor Zurg stole a top-secret Space Ranger Turbo Suit. Star Command knew I was the only one who could get it back!"

"Wow," said Woody. "I wonder how it feels to be a space hero."

"Me, too," said Rex. "Hey, Buzz! Can I be in your story?"

"Sure, why not?" Buzz said, continuing his story.

"I was heading into dangerous space. I knew I needed backup, so I called on First Lieutenant Woody and Second Lieutenant Rex!

"As we touched down on Planet Zurg, we heard a loud humming noise. Suddenly, we spotted an army. Hundreds of Emperor Zurg's loyal Zurgbots were grouped together, humming. I knew that Woody and Rex could take care of the Zurgbots, so I went off to find Zurg's headquarters . . . and the Turbo Suit!

"I hadn't gone far when I saw a lone Zurgbot. I knew that something strange was happening. Zurgbots rarely traveled alone. His humming sounded odd, almost like a melody.

"'Hold your fire!' the Zurgbot cried. 'My name is Zenny. I'm not like the others!'

"Apparently this Zurgbot also opposed Zurg! But with the entire galaxy at stake, how could I trust him?

"'I will take you to the Turbo Suit,' Zenny promised.

"True to his word, Zenny led me into the heart of Zurg's lair—and to the Turbo Suit. But as I reached for the suit, a band of Zurgbots captured me. They had my lieutenants, too!

"Suddenly, Zurg appeared. Our doom seemed near.

"'Not so fast, Zurg,' a voice called out. It was Zenny!

"Before Zurg could say a word, Zenny began to sing. As his voice grew louder, stalactites fell from the cave's ceiling. They dropped to the floor, trapping Zurg. Zenny freed us and I climbed into the Turbo Suit. With the help of Zenny and my lieutenants, I defeated the Zurgbot army!

"As we headed home, we could see Zenny below, teaching the other Zurgbots to sing. We knew that Planet Zurg would be a happier place from then on. The end."

# Mater Saves Christmas

One morning, Mater arrived at Flo's V8 Café with his letter to Santa Car! All the townsfolk had written one. Just as Mater was dropping his letter in the mailbox, Chick Hicks, one of Lightning's rivals, showed up. He began to tease Mater, saying that Santa Car didn't exist.

Just then, Sheriff raced up to them with some bad news. All the fuel from the area had been stolen!

The townsfolk were shocked. Without fuel, the mail trucks couldn't deliver letters to Santa Car! But Mater wouldn't give up. He decided to deliver the letters to the North Pole himself.

Lightning was worried about his friend. He couldn't let him go by himself! "Mater, I'm coming with you," he said. Luigi and Guido gave Mater and Lightning new snow tires and the two set off.

Finally, Lightning and Mater arrived at the North Pole. Lightning stared in wonder. "Santa Car is real!" he said.

But Santa Car had some bad news. His reindeer snowmobiles had been stolen!

Just then, Mater remembered how strangely Chick had been acting. He realized that Chick wanted the top secret flying fuel the reindeer used. "Chick Hicks took your reindeer!" he cried.

Santa Car filled Mater's tank with the top-secret fuel and the three cars set out for Radiator Springs.

Back in town, Luigi and Guido had been cornered by Chick and his gang.

"Ha! You're too late, boys!" Chick shouted. "I'll fly around the track and never lose to Lightning McQueen again! And you know the best part? No more Christmas! If I can't have presents, no one can!"

Suddenly, the air filled with the sound of jingling bells. Mater soared over the hill, towing Lightning and Santa Car. Chick raced away, flying just above the ground. Lightning flew after him. Santa Car had filled his tank with the magic fuel, too!

Chick was no match for Lightning McQueen. The thief soon spun out of control.

"Tow him straight to jail," said Doc.

Later, the Radiator Springs gang celebrated with Santa Car and his reindeer snowmobiles. Everyone cheered. Mater had saved Christmas!

# Tod's Homecoming

Tod the fox wanted to show his fox friend Vixey where he had grown up. He took her to the top of a hill where they could look down on a beautiful valley.

"I grew up on Widow Tweed's farm," said Tod, pointing with his paw at a farm nestled in the valley. "She took care of me when I was just a cub. And that's my best friend, Copper," Tod said, pointing to a handsome hound on a nearby farm. "Copper lives at Amos Slade's farm. His house is right next door to Mrs. Tweed's." He sighed. "Let's go visit him."

"Not me!" Vixey declared. "I'm a fox, and I'm not fond of hounds. I'll catch some fish for our dinner. See you later."

Alone, Tod scampered down the hill, excited about seeing his old pal. But when he got there, he spotted a strange man sneaking into Amos Slade's henhouse.

"Wake up, Copper!" yelled Tod. "A chicken thief is raiding the henhouse!"

Copper woke with a start and leaped into action. But the rope around his neck held him back. "You'll have to stop that chicken thief yourself!" cried Copper.

"But I can't stop him alone!" Tod replied.

"We'll help," someone chirped. Tod looked up and saw Dinky the sparrow and Boomer the woodpecker sitting on the fence.

"Let's go!" said Tod.

Tod burst into the henhouse first. The thief was there, holding squawking chickens in both hands.

Tod bit the man's ankle.

"Ouch!" howled the thief.

Boomer flew through the window and pecked at the chicken snatcher's head. The thief dropped the chickens and covered his head with his arms.

Meanwhile, Dinky had untied the knot that held Copper. Now, Copper was free—and angry, too! Barking, he charged at the burglar.

Eggs flying, the chicken snatcher screamed and ran. As he raced down the road, Dinky and Boomer flitted around his head, pecking him until he was out of sight. The fox and the hound trotted back to the farm.

"Good to see you, Tod," said Copper, wagging his tail. "What brings you here?"

"I just stopped by for a quiet visit," Tod replied.

"It was real quiet, all right!" said Copper.

# Jim Hawkins: Space Cadet

On the first day of his second semester at the Interstellar Academy, Jim Hawkins stepped aboard a solar sloop. For a second, he felt like he was back on board the *Legacy*—the vessel where he had become a real spacer. But the feeling vanished as his classmates pushed past him, eager to begin the fun part of training.

Jim allowed the more confident students to crowd in front of him. Just a few days ago he couldn't wait to get back to the Academy and resume studying to be a captain—especially since the second semester was when pilot training began. But now he felt as if he'd lost his space legs.

"Tie up." A multilegged purple kid beside Jim handed him a lifeline. "We're out of here."

As Jim secured his rope, the instructor showed one of the more daring students how to navigate away from the port. Several other students anxiously waited their turn at the helm. One by one, the instructor let them take the wheel.

The instructor looked up, spotted Jim, and waved him over with a catlike paw. Her almond eyes reminded Jim of Captain Amelia. So did her way of barking orders.

"You there! Stop skulking. Come take the wheel." Jim shuffled over and flipped his hair out of his eyes. Grasping the wheel, Jim pulled to the right. He wanted to try something tricky. The craft lurched. The awkward ship was not at all what Jim was used to.

"Look out!" an insectoid alien shrieked.

"Turn!" someone else yelled.

Silver's voice echoed in Jim's head. *Take the helm and chart your own course.* "Trim the sails!" Jim yelled loudly. He must have sounded commanding because three students sprang into action. Jim held the wheel steady. He did not turn, and as the sloop picked up speed, he maneuvered between two space whales, smoothly emerging on the other side.

"Unconventional," the instructor said sternly, "and well beyond your years, Hawkins. But one thing—never, ever do that again."

Jim smiled. He knew a challenge when he heard one.

# Space Adventure, Part 2

Goofy had sure goofed! He and the other space adventurers had come to outer space with Professor Von Drake's treasure map. But Goofy had accidentally given the map to Space Pirate Pete! Mickey, Goofy, and Donald chased Pete around the rings of Saturn. On the way, they found the last four Treasure Stars: seven, eight, nine, and ten!

Back on Saturn, Toodles brought a Mouseketool—a big birdcage—to trap Pete. Donald grabbed the map back. But then Quoodles brought a Space Chicken to help Pete get away!

Now Mickey and his crew had the map and all ten Treasure Stars. The stars lit the way to the mystery planet. "Let's call it Planet Mickey!" said Goofy. The stars shone on the X that marked the spot. They were off to Planet Mickey to find the treasure!

Uh-oh—Space Pirate Pete got to Planet Mickey first and found the X that marked the treasure spot. Pete had one last trick. He threw out a sticky web. "Now when those little space adventurers try to pass through here and get the treasure, they'll get stuck!" said Pete.

But it was Quoodles who got stuck!

"Poor Quoodles," said Pete. "I gotta rescue you! But I can't do it alone. Help!" he yelled. "Somebody HELP!"

Mickey heard him and came right away. Toodles came, too, and spied his friend caught in the web. He tried to rescue her, but then he got stuck in the sticky web, too!

"I'm going to use a Mouseketool!" Mickey said.

"That's a great idea," said Pete. "And I'll use a Quoodles tool!"

Toodles sent Mickey a Mouseketool. It was . . . Space Pirate Pete! And Quoodles's tool was Space Captain Mickey Mouse!

"It means we can save Toodles and Quoodles if we work together as friends!" said Mickey.

Working together, the two rescued Toodles and Quoodles.

Later, Pluto pointed to the map. He knew where to dig.

Pluto dug up the treasure chest. Inside was Professor Von Drake's remote control. Mickey pushed the button. The ground shook and up came . . . the Mickey Mouse Space House!

What a terrific treasure!

# Oliver Plays Piano

"I've got to get rid of that kitten," Georgette the poodle muttered.

Georgette was used to being the only pet in Jenny's house. But now there was also a little lost kitten named Oliver.

Georgette waited until everyone had gone to bed. Then she tiptoed over to Oliver, grabbed the sleeping kitten, tossed him inside the big piano, and shut the lid. *Bang!*

Inside the piano, Oliver yawned and looked around. He was surprised to find himself in the dark wooden box. He began to move around, trying to find a way out, but every time he moved, his paws hit the piano strings. *Plink! Plunk!*

Oliver started moving faster, hitting note after note and chord after chord. "This is fun!" he exclaimed. *Plunk! Bing! Plink!* "I'm playing piano, just like Jenny!"

Soon, the terrible racket woke everyone in the house!

"What is that horrid noise?" cried Winston the butler. He hopped out of bed and hurried into the living room.

Georgette was standing nearby, doing her very best to look innocent.

"It's that cat!" Winston huffed. "That creature is just too noisy. It's got to go!"

"Success!" Georgette said to herself— until Jenny appeared in her nightgown.

The little girl rushed past the butler and opened the lid of the piano. When she saw Oliver inside, she squealed, "How cute!"

The butler scratched his head. "Cute?"

"Oliver is trying to play a song on the piano," said Jenny, "just like he saw me do earlier today. What a wonderful kitty you are!"

Jenny hugged Oliver, and he began to purr. When the butler saw how much Jenny loved Oliver, his heart melted. "Oh, well," he said. "I guess a little noise isn't the end of the world. Off to bed with you now, Jenny."

"Good night," Jenny said. Then she kissed Oliver's head and told him, "You must go to bed now, too. Let me tuck you in."

Before she left, Jenny patted her poodle's head and said, "Oh, Georgette, aren't we lucky to have a new friend like Oliver in the house!"

"Drat!" Georgette said to herself. "I'd say it's that little fur ball who's the lucky one!"

# Under the Tree

**W**oody and the other toys gathered around the baby monitor. Downstairs, Andy was unwrapping his Christmas presents. Christmas morning was always difficult for Andy's toys. They all lived in fear of being replaced by something bigger and better.

Rex wrung his tiny hands. "Let it be a new video game!" he cried.

"As long as it's not another spaceman," Buzz said.

"It's a . . ." The toys leaned closer. But before Sarge could finish his report, Woody shut off the monitor.

"What are you doing?" Hamm cried.

"Woody, we need to be debriefed in order to face the enemy!" Buzz sounded alarmed.

"Now hold on a minute, guys." Woody put his hand up to silence the toys. "Let's just think a minute. I want each of you to remember what it was like when you were unwrapped. Remember when you first met Andy."

"He chose me from the shelf himself," Rocky Gibraltar boasted.

"And it was a great day, right?" Woody asked, looking around at everyone.

"I was a birthday present," Rex said.

The other toys all chimed in, smiling and laughing as they told each other about their arrival.

"And we're a team, right?" Woody interrupted.

"Sure we are." Buzz nodded. "We can fight the new enemies together."

Woody shook his head. "No, Buzz. That's what I'm talking about. These new toys aren't our new enemies. They're our new friends!"

Slowly, Woody's words began to sink in. "You mean, they come in peace," Buzz said.

"Exactly!" Woody cried. "So instead of sitting around here moping, we should be planning a welcome party!"

"Oh, Woody," Bo Peep said. "I love it when you show your soft side."

Woody blushed. Then he turned the monitor back on. "Sarge, I want you to stand down. I have new orders. I repeat, new orders."

"Yes, sir. What can we do for you, sir?" the sergeant barked.

"Gather your troops and come upstairs. Andy's toys are throwing a hoedown for the new toys. It'll be our first annual Christmas Welcome Party! Let's get started!"

# Merry Christmas, Pooh!

Pooh was sitting at home thinking when there was a knock at the door. When he opened it, he found himself face-to-face with a snowman!

The snowman's voice seemed strangely familiar to Pooh. He invited the creature inside. As it stood in front of the fire and began to melt. Pooh discovered with surprise that the snowman was his friend Piglet! He had been covered in snow on his walk to Pooh's house.

Suddenly Pooh realized he had forgotten to get Christmas presents for his friends! Piglet seemed a little disappointed, and he went back home to wrap his own Christmas presents. Pooh watched him heading off in the snow. Though Pooh didn't know how to sort out his mistake, he knew someone who would.

Pooh arrived with frozen paws at the house of his friend Christopher Robin. The little boy happily invited him in. Pooh saw the stockings hanging on the fireplace and, intrigued, asked him, "Are you drying them?"

"No, Pooh. Santa Claus will leave presents in there," the little boy explained.

"Oh, my! Presents, that's right. *That's* what I forgot!" exclaimed Pooh. "And I don't have any stockings, either!"

Christopher Robin was a good friend, and he gave Pooh a stocking for each of his friends in the Hundred-Acre Wood. Pooh hurried off to put the stockings outside of his friends' homes with a little note saying FROM POOH.

When the bear arrived home, he was exhausted. He settled down in his armchair in front of the fire. He was pleased his friends now had stockings, but he still didn't know what he could give them for Christmas. He closed his eyes and fell asleep.

The next morning, Pooh was woken by his friends knocking on his door. Pooh invited his friends inside and was preparing to apologize to them when they all started thanking him!

Each of them had found a special use for the stocking Pooh had left at their house: a vegetable holder for Rabbit, a stone pouch for Gopher, a warm layer for Eeyore, and a hat for Piglet. Pooh was happy—he had realized that Christmas really was magical! Merry Christmas, Pooh!

# Rematch!

Lightning McQueen and Francesco Bernoulli had challenged each other to a race in Monza, Italy—Francesco's hometown.

As they left the airport, the cars were surrounded by photographers. "Everyone loves Francesco. He has too many fans," said Francesco.

"Nobody has more fans than Lightning!" Mater piped up. He showed Francesco some bags overflowing with fan letters.

"Francesco has much, much more fan mail!" said Francesco.

Lightning cruised over to Francesco. "How about a warm-up before the big race—just you and me?" he asked.

Francesco nodded. "Ah, good idea, Lightning! Try to keep up, if you . . ."

Before Francesco could finish, Lightning was gone.

Francesco had almost caught up when he nearly spun out on a left turn. "How do you make those left turns so well?" Francesco asked Lightning.

"Get equipped with some treaded tires," said Lightning. "Then turn right to go left. A very good friend taught me that once."

Finally the two stopped. Francesco sighed. "Ahh, Italia is beautiful, no? Just like Francesco!"

Lightning chuckled. "Do you always think about yourself?" he asked.

"Of course," said Francesco. "On the racetrack, Francesco only thinks about himself and doing his best. This is why he always wins!"

The next day was the big race. Francesco came out of the first left turn ahead. He showed off his new treaded tires. "Perhaps Lightning has taught Francesco too well!"

As Lightning zoomed out of the pits, he got distracted by the camera flashes and the screaming fans. Suddenly Lightning remembered what Francesco had said about focusing on himself and doing his best. Lightning looked straight ahead and took the lead!

As the two cars crossed the finish line, the crowd gasped. The two race cars had tied!

The cars tried to figure out what to do. Then Francesco shouted, "No more talk! Talk is slow. What do we do? We race!"

And so the two fastest cars in the world zoomed away together!

# Scary Claus

Sally and Dr. Finklestein were working in the lab when a package arrived. The label read: A SPECIAL GIFT FOR A SPECIAL PERSON.

"The most special person in Halloweentown is Jack Skellington," said Sally. "This must be for him!"

When Jack arrived, Sally and Dr. Finklestein showed him the package.

"Why, it's a gift!" cried Jack. "Let's open it together."

"It's a shame to rip the pretty bloodred paper," cooed Sally.

But they opened it anyway.

"What is this?" said Jack, holding up a string of twinkling lights.

"It's a necklace," said Sally.

"And this?" said Jack. He held up a glass ball. Painted on it was a picture of a chubby ghost with a long white beard. When Jack touched the glass ball, it said, "*Ho, ho, ho!*"

"Eek!" cried Sally. "That's the scariest ghost I've ever seen! It gives me the chills."

"Well," said Jack, "since this is a gift, I guess I should wear it."

He put on the necklace, then hung the ball from it. With every step, the ghost cried its horrid call. "*Ho, ho, ho!*"

On his way home, Jack met the Mayor.

"Eek!" the Mayor screamed.

"This will be perfect for Halloween," Jack mused.

As Jack walked home, everyone was frightened by the image of the scary ghost.

Later that week, Sally visited Jack. "I'm here to tell you that your gift is just too scary, even for Halloweentown," Sally said. "The children are having nightmares about a man with a long beard and red cheeks coming down their chimneys and eating their Halloween cookies!"

"That's terrible," said Jack. He decided to return the package to Dr. Finklestein.

"I'll put this gift in a safe place where it won't frighten anyone," said the doctor.

Later that day, there came a knock at the castle door. Dr. Finklestein answered. "It's the scary ghost!" he screamed.

"I'm not a ghost," said the visitor.

"Yes, you are!" cried Dr. Finklestein. "I recognize those chubby red cheeks, that long white beard, and the bloodred suit!"

Dr. Finklestein ran into his castle to hide.

"But my name is Santa Claus," the stranger insisted. "I'm looking for a Christmas package that was delivered here by mistake!"

# Team Wazowski and Sullivan

Mike and Sulley had entered the human world without permission and found themselves stuck. Now they needed to think fast!

Dean Hardscrabble, the head of the Scare Program at Monsters University, had turned off the power to the door they had used. Now there was only one thing to do. Mike and Sulley needed to generate enough scream power to activate the door from the human side.

With Mike's brains and Sulley's fearsome roar, the two monsters made the humans around them scream and scream and scream!

Suddenly, the light above the door in the Door Tech Lab at the university went on. The humans' screams filled the scream can to the brim. In fact, they filled all the scream cans in the room!

"Impossible!" Dean Hardscrabble said just as Mike and Sulley exploded through the door.

"How did you do this?" Dean Hardscrabble asked in disbelief. But Mike and Sulley didn't have a chance to answer. CDA (Child Detection Agency) agents burst in and led the two away.

Mike and Sulley and were expelled from the university. But it wasn't all bad news. Their friends in Oozma Kappa were being allowed to join the Scare Program, just as Dean Hardscrabble had promised if they won the Scare Games.

"You're the scariest bunch of monsters I've ever met," Mike told them. "Don't let anyone tell you different."

Everyone hugged. Then Mike and Sulley were on their way.

"So what now?" Sulley asked Mike.

Mike thought for a moment. "For the first time in my life, I don't really have a plan," he said.

Just then Dean Hardscrabble appeared with a copy of the school newspaper. They were on the front page. "You surprised me," she admitted. It was clear that she admired their epic Scare.

Mike looked at the newspaper. Next to their photo was an ad for mailroom workers at Monsters, Inc. Suddenly Mike had a new plan!

The friends got jobs working in the mailroom at Monsters, Inc.

Team Wazowski and Sullivan were on their way!

# Buzz Off

The toys were excited. Bonnie was going to the park with Woody, Jessie, and Dolly. The others were looking forward to a day of fun, too. But Jessie was worried. "Keep an eye on Buzz," she told her friends. "I think he may have a loose wire."

Bonnie rushed in and grabbed her bag. "Buzz, you're in charge now," she said as she left.

The peas started bouncing excitely on their shelf. "Wait! This looks dangerous," said Buzz.

Just then, Slinky slipped from the shelf, causing the Aliens and peas to fall, too! They tumbled down on top of Buzz.

Buzz stood up and looked around. "*¿Donde está mi nave?*"

"Oh great," Hamm sighed. "He's switched into Spanish mode again."

The toys tried to catch him, but Buzz grabbed a curtain from the doll's house and held it up like a bullfighter's cape. Hamm ran to tackle his friend, but he slid right into the bookshelf. A book fell onto Buzz's head! After a moment, Buzz pushed the book away.

"Buzz, are you okay?" Rex cried.

"Buzz, are you okay?" Buzz repeated.

"He must have gotten knocked into Repeat Mode!" Hamm whispered to Buttercup. "We're gonna have to jiggle his wires," Hamm sighed.

Just then, the toys heard the car pull into the driveway.

"Hurry!" Hamm cried. Rex undid Buzz's back panel and stared at the wires. He didn't know which one to fix! There was a noise outside and the toys went limp just as Bonnie's mother walked in. She put down Bonnie's bag and left again.

Jessie climbed out. "Buzz, are you okay?" she asked.

"Oh, he's fine." Trixie propped Buzz into a sitting position. But he fell over with a thunk.

"It's not my fault!" Rex wailed. "There are too many wires!"

Jessie laughed, then she whacked Buzz on the back. Buzz blinked and looked at his friends.

"Do I have something on my face?" he asked.

The other toys sighed with relief—Buzz was back to normal!

A minute later, Bonnie arrived. Everything was the way she had left it.

"Thanks for looking after everyone, Buzz. I knew this place would be okay with you in charge!"

# Timon and Pumbaa Tell All

It was a very hot day on the savannah. Simba, Timon, and Pumbaa were lying in the shade, barely moving. Pumbaa had just finished telling a story about the biggest insect he had ever eaten. A silence fell over the little group.

"I know," said Simba. "Hey, Timon, why don't you tell me the story of how you and Pumbaa met each other?"

Timon looked at Pumbaa. "Do you think he's ready for it?" he asked his friend.

"Knock him dead," said Pumbaa.

"It all started in a little meerkat village far, far away . . ." began Timon. "In that little meerkat village there was one meerkat who didn't fit in with the rest. All the others were content to dig, dig, dig, all day long," said Timon.

"I was that isolated meerkat. How I hated to dig! I knew I needed to go elsewhere, to find a home of my own, a place where I fit in.

So I left. Along the way I ran into a wise old baboon who told me what I was seeking—*hakuna matata*—and pointed me in the direction of Pride Rock. So I boldly set off toward this rock of which he spoke. And on my way there, I—"

"Met me!" Pumbaa interrupted.

Timon gave him a dirty look and continued. "I heard a strange rustling in the bushes. I was scared. What could it be? A hyena? A lion? And then I found myself face-to-face with a big, ugly warthog!"

"Hey!" said Pumbaa, insulted.

"We soon realized we had a lot in common—our love for bugs, our search for a home to call our own. So we set out for Pride Rock together. A lot of bad things happened along the way— hyenas, stampedes, you name it. But before long we managed to find the perfect place to live. And then we met you, Simba!"

"That's a nice story," Simba said with a yawn. "Now I think I'm going to take a nap."

Pumbaa cleared his throat. "It all started near a little warthog watering hole far, far away," he began. "Back then, I—"

"You always have to get the last word, don't you?" said Timon.

"Not always," said Pumbaa. And then he continued telling Simba his side of the story.

# An Out-of-this-World Party

**E**very year, on December 31, one of Lilo's classmates had a party. This year, Lilo begged Nani to let her have the party at their house.

Lilo wanted to show off her new friends Jumba and Pleakley to her classmates—and to prove to them that even though Stitch wasn't a very good dog, he was a great alien!

Lilo gave invitations to all her classmates—even Myrtle, but only because Nani said Lilo had to invite her.

Myrtle didn't want to go to the party any more than Lilo wanted to have her there, but she didn't want to be left out, either.

On the night of the party, Lilo ushered all the kids over to a stage in the backyard. Then she pulled back the curtains to reveal Stitch in a fancy rock-and-roll costume.

Stitch crooned into a microphone while swiveling his hips and strumming his guitar. All the kids thought he was cool—except Myrtle. When Stitch tried to give her a kiss on the cheek during a love song, she shrieked, "Ooooh! Yuck! Dog germs!"

and ran away as fast as she could.

Jumba turned to Lilo and gave her a wink. "Who wants to play Pin the Smile on the Man in the Moon?" he asked.

"I do! I do!" shouted Myrtle.

Jumba hustled Myrtle into a small spaceship with no windows. Then he handed her a large paper smile.

"When you pass by the moon in a few hours," said Jumba, "try to pin the smile in the correct position. Remember that you will be traveling at several thousand miles per hour, so act quickly!" Then he shut the cockpit door.

"But the spaceship is fake," Lilo said to Jumba. "It's not moving or anything."

"Ah, but Myrtle doesn't know that," Jumba replied. "Inside the ship, it looks like she's heading to the moon. This should keep her busy for a few hours while we enjoy ourselves." He smiled. "Now, who's up for cake?"

The kids cheered, and everyone moved over to a picnic table, leaving the spaceship behind. "This is the best party ever!" Lilo heard one of her friends shout happily.